continued on next page . . .

THE STORE

"Bentley Little has solidified his place at the very top of the horror genre."
—BarnesandNoble.com

THE MAILMAN

"A thinking person's horror novel. *The Mailman* delivers. Very scary."
—*Los Angeles Times*

UNIVERSITY

"Bentley Little keeps the high-tension jolts coming. By the time I finished, my nerves were pretty well fried, and I have a pretty high shock level. *University* is unlike anything else in popular horror fiction."
—Stephen King

DOMINION

"Bentley Little is a master of the macabre!"
—Stephen King

The
HOUSE

Bentley Little

A SIGNET BOOK

SIGNET
Published by the New American Library, a division of
Penguin Putnam Inc., 375 Hudson Street,
New York, New York 10014, U.S.A.
Penguin Books Ltd, 80 Strand,
London WC2R ORL, England
Penguin Books Australia Ltd, 250 Camberwell Road,
Camberwell, Victoria 3124, Australia
Penguin Books Canada Ltd, 10 Alcorn Avenue,
Toronto, Ontario, Canada M4V 3B2
Penguin Books (N.Z.) Ltd, 182–190 Wairau Road,
Auckland 10, New Zealand

Penguin Books Ltd, Registered Offices:
Harmondsworth, Middlesex, England

First published by Signet, an imprint of New American Library,
a division of Penguin Putnam Inc.

First Printing, April 1999
21 20 19 18 17 16 15 14 13 12

REGISTERED TRADEMARK—MARCA REGISTRADA

Printed in the United States of America

PUBLISHER'S NOTE
This is a work of fiction. Names, characters, places, and incidents either are
the product of the author's imagination or are used fictitiously, and any resemblance to actual persons, living or dead, business establishments, events, or
locales is entirely coincidental.

BOOKS ARE AVAILABLE AT QUANTITY DISCOUNTS WHEN USED TO PROMOTE
PRODUCTS OR SERVICES. FOR INFORMATION PLEASE WRITE TO PREMIUM MAR-
KETING DIVISION, PENGUIN PUTNAM INC., 375 HUDSON STREET, NEW YORK, NEW
YORK 10014.

Thanks to my parents, Larry and Roseanne,
for the house I grew up in,
and thanks to my wife, Wai Sau,
for the house I live in.

Thanks also to my agent,
Dominick Abel.
It's been a long, strange decade . . .
but we're still here.

Prologue

California

Teddy had lived in the airport for the past eight years.

He knew it was a problem, knew it was a serious phobia, but he had not been able to venture outside the terminal in all that time. He could not remember exactly what had compelled him to seek refuge here, but it no longer mattered. This was his home, this was his world, and he was happy with it. He found money on the floor, in the coin returns of vending machines and pay phones; he begged for spare change when necessary; he bought his food in the snack bars and mini Pizza Huts and junior Burger Kings that made up the terminal's restaurant row. He purchased or shoplifted shorts and T-shirts from the gift shop. He read the magazines and newspapers that people left on chairs, the printed material they bought in order to waste time while waiting for their flights.

The airport terminal was heated and air-conditioned, open twenty-four hours, and it was constantly filled with people, a broad cross section of society. He was never bored here. There was always someone to talk with, a lonely traveler or waiting relative, and he would strike up a conversation, absorb the distilled story of a person's life, make up some impressive lies about his own, and move on, a little richer for the encounter.

He was a "people person," as they liked to say, and there was nothing he enjoyed more than meeting new people, making new friends, talking and listening, experiencing vicariously the life he had renounced.

He kept himself well groomed, storing his clothes in

a locker and changing each day, washing his laundry in a bathroom sink at night, drying everything with the wall-mounted hand-dryers, giving himself sponge baths, washing and combing his hair with travelpak toiletries from the gift shop. Save for the times when he was compelled to ask for money, no one would ever mistake him for a homeless person, and while he had been here so long that he knew work schedules and shift changes, knew when security guards patrolled the airport and the routes they took, was able to easily avoid detection by airport personnel, he had still been seen often enough around the terminal that many of the store clerks, janitors, and other airport workers knew him, believed him to be a frequent flyer, and treated him with the utmost respect.

But lately, he'd had the suspicion that he was not alone.

Something was living in the airport with him.

The idea chilled him to the bone. There was nothing concrete, no real proof, only a vague feeling that his living space was being invaded by another permanent resident, but that was enough to put him on edge.

Something else was living here.

Not someone.

Some*thing*.

He didn't know why he thought that, but he did, and it frightened him. He knew that he could, if necessary, leave the terminal, leave the airport, disappear into the chaotic bustle of Los Angeles, but he did not even consider that an option. Logically, intellectually, it made sense, but emotionally it was another story. Whether superstition or psychosis, he knew that he could never leave the terminal, and any plan that considered that a possibility was strictly off-limits.

Which meant that he was stuck here.

With whatever else lived in the airport.

In the daytime, the idea didn't bother him. But at night, like now, when the crowds faded, when the lights were switched to half power, when the world outside turned black . . .

He shivered.

Last week, he had returned from the bathroom after

a quick shampoo to his seat near the windowed east wall
of the Delta wing, and his magazines had been moved.
Not just moved. *Tampered* with. The page he'd marked
in *Newsweek* had been ripped out, the *Playboy* he'd kept
hidden between the other periodicals had been placed
on top and opened to the centerfold, and his *People*
magazine had been thrown on the floor. There'd been
no one else in this wing of the terminal for the past hour
and he'd seen no one on his way to or from the bathroom, but the proof was there, and he'd quickly gathered
up his stuff and hurried back to a more populated section of the terminal.

The next night, he'd had no magazines or newspapers
with him and was about to settle down to a little nap
when he saw, on the section of seats he'd chosen, an
array of magazines spread out: *Guns and Ammo, Hunting, American Hunter, Hunter and Prey.* On the carpeted
floor in front of the seats, drawn with spilled cherry Icee,
was the outline of a bloody claw and, next to that, a
toothy smile.

It was hunting him.

It had been a warning, Teddy thought. Or a game
being played with him. Either way, he didn't like it, and
he quickly gathered together today's belongings as he
suddenly noticed that this area of the terminal was emp-
tying out and that outside night had already fallen. He
saw himself reflected in the huge window that faced the
runway, a ghost against the blackness, and the insubstan-
tiality of his form made him nervous, made him feel as
though he'd already died.

He quickly headed back toward the shops. Ever since
the warning, he'd stayed near people, stayed near the
light. Security guards had looked at him suspiciously several times, and he realized that he was in danger of
giving himself away, of breaking cover, but he could not
help it. He was afraid to be alone.

Afraid of what might find him.

Afraid of what it might do to him.

He looked behind him as he walked. At the far end
of the darkened wing, by the empty lounge and boarding
area that had once been occupied by Pan Am, he saw a

jet-black shadow, a shifting amorphous shape that flut-
tered from an unused flight desk down the corridor to
the seat where he'd been sitting.

He started running. Sweat was pouring down his face
and his heart was pounding crazily. He was gripped by
the absurd but unshakable notion that the shadow, the
creature, the monster, the whatever-it-was, had seen him
and was chasing after him and was going to down him
and devour him in front of the snack bar.

But he reached the snack bar with no problem, saw a
security guard and a cashier, a businessman reading a
newspaper at a small table, a young couple trying to
soothe a crying baby, and when he looked back toward
the darkened wing he saw nothing out of the ordinary.

Breathing heavily, still shaking, he walked into the
snack bar. He was aware of how he looked and when
he walked up to the cashier, asked for a cup of water,
wiped the sweat from his forehead, and saw the look
she shot the security guard, he immediately dug through
his pocket for spare change and amended his order to a
small coffee.

He didn't really want coffee, but he wanted to sit
down and get his equilibrium back, wanted to be near
other people, and he thanked the cashier and grabbed a
seat near the pile of luncheon trays at the back of the
small eating area.

What the hell was going on? Was he going crazy?
Possibly. He knew he wasn't the most normal person in
the world to begin with. But he didn't think he was
hallucinating here, didn't think he was suffering from
delusions. Something *had* tampered with his magazines,
something *had* drawn that Icee picture.

And he *had* seen that black shadow shape.

He glanced up from the Formica table. The security
guard was still looking at him, and he thought that he
should check himself out in a mirror to make sure his
appearance was presentable. He couldn't afford to destroy
his entire life, to blow almost a decade's worth of clean
responsible living simply because he was frightened.

Because something was hunting him.

There were rest rooms adjacent to the snack bar, and

he left his newspaper, briefcase, and coffee on the table as he walked over to the men's room.

"Could you watch my stuff?" he called to the cashier. He put on his best Important Traveler voice, and she smiled at him and nodded. "Sure."

"Thanks."

He felt a little better. His disguise was in place and he was safely ensconced here with other people. He walked into the bathroom, looked at himself in the mirror. He hadn't shaved yet today and was starting to look a little raggedy, but his sweat-clumped hair was the main problem, and he took out a comb, held it under the faucet and ran it through his hair.

Much better.

He realized suddenly that he had to take a whiz, and he walked over to the closest urinal, unzipping his pants—

—and saw out of the corner of his eye a fluttering black shape.

It was there for only a second, in one of the mirrors, and he whirled around, already zipping up, his mouth suddenly dry, his heart once again pounding.

A cold hand touched his shoulder.

"No!" he screamed, jerking around.

But there was nothing there.

He ran out of the rest room as fast as he could.

Wyoming

It was an omen, her mother would have said, and Patty was not so sure she disagreed. Hube would laugh at her if she told him that, would make fun of her and her mother and her entire family, would tell her to move into the twentieth century, but Hube didn't know as much as he thought he did. There were a lot of things science could explain, but there were a lot of things it couldn't, and Patty wasn't so close-minded that she automatically dismissed anything that didn't agree with her preconceived notions.

She stared at the crow sitting atop the garbage can. The crow stared back at her, blinked.

It had been there when she'd come out to hang the wash on the line, the biggest crow she'd ever seen, and it had not flown away as she walked past it but had sat and watched her as she hung up the underwear and the socks and the towels. She'd told it to shoo, had stomped her foot and made threatening movements, but the crow had not been afraid. It seemed to know that she wouldn't hurt it, and it seemed to have its own agenda. It wasn't going to leave until it did what it had come here to do.

Just what that was, Patty didn't know, but she couldn't help thinking that the black bird was trying to warn her, that it had been sent here for a purpose, in order to tell her something, and it was up to her to figure out exactly what that was.

She wished her mother were here.

Patty stared at the crow for a few moments longer, then walked past it, into the house. She'd call her mother. That's what she'd do. She'd describe the crow, spell out the precise chain of events, and see if her mother could figure it out.

The crow cawed once as she entered the house. Twice more at the precise second she picked up the kitchen phone to dial.

She wished Hube were here as well. He might have some smart answer for why the crow's cries were timed so specifically to her movements, but she doubted that even he could fail to notice the correlation.

The line was busy, and she heard one more quick caw as she hung up the receiver. She opened the back door to check on the crow once again, but it was gone. She walked outside, hurried around the house, but it was nowhere to be seen. Not on the roof, not on the porch, not on the ground or any of the trees. She didn't even see any birds in the sky. It was as if it had just disappeared.

She walked up the front steps of the house and turned for a moment to look at the view. She could see the Tetons, rising grandly up, the permanent snowcaps blending in with today's white ceiling of autumn sky. Directly before her, on the other side of the pasture, the overgrown meadow, its grass brown and dry, sloped up and away from their ranch, the end of the meadow indistinguishable from the beginning of the foothills.

She looked to her right, past the garage at the side of the house, but saw no dust trail clouding up the road.

She wished Hube would hurry up and get back. He was supposed to have gone into town for coffee and bread flour, but it seemed like he'd been away for far too long. She hoped the truck hadn't had engine trouble again. The last thing they needed was another mechanic's bill. They were still paying off the water pump from July. They couldn't afford to have anything else go wrong. Not with winter coming on.

Patty walked into the house, automatically stomping her feet on the outside of the doorsill though she hadn't walked through any mud. She reached for the living-room phone on the small oak table next to the couch and was about to dial her mother's number once again when out of the corner of her eye, through the mesh of the screen, she saw movement outside. She stopped, slowly put the receiver back in its cradle, and walked back over to the doorway.

She could see them coming from the mountains. Dozens of them. It looked like a small army, speeding down the side of the hill toward the sloping meadow.

A *small* army.

For the runners were all the size of children. She could see that even from here. Only they weren't children. Something about the build of their bodies, the way they moved, indicated to her that they were older than that.

Much older.

They reached the high grass and leaped into it, and then she could see only the movement of the grass stalks, what looked like a narrow band of wind whipping through the center of the meadow.

What were they? Leprechauns? Elves? Something supernatural. Not dwarves or midgets or children. Even from this far away, their strangeness, their otherness, was apparent. They were not human.

She watched the grass whip back and forth, the narrow stream of movement heading straight toward the ranch. She stood her ground, not moving, and she realized that she was not as afraid as she should have been.

But that changed.

The grass in front of the pasture began to thrash wildly and then they emerged into the open, clutching weapons made of baseball bats and animal skulls, horseshoes and bones. They were made up like clowns: red noses, white faces, colored lips, and rainbow hair.

Only she wasn't sure it was makeup.

They kept streaming into the pasture from the tall grass. Five of them. Ten. Fifteen. Twenty. Nothing slowed them down, and their stubby legs pumped for all they were worth, carrying them around the clump of boulders in the center of the pasture, jumping over the small fence Hube had built for the cows. They were accompanied by what looked like a swarm of insects. Bees, maybe. Or beetles.

Patty closed the front door, locked it. But she knew, even as she did so, that she would not be safe in the house. Her only hope was to run, to get out before they overran her home and hope that it slowed them down enough to let her escape. She had no idea what they were or what they wanted, but she knew it was not good, and she could not believe she'd been so stupid as to just stand there and watch them approach when she could have been fleeing.

This was what the crow's appearance had foretold, she knew. The crow had been an omen, a warning, and she probably would have known that if she'd paid a little more attention to her mother growing up and a little less attention to boys.

A judgmental review of her entire life passed through her mind as she ran through the house and out the back door, locking it behind her. A critique of her faults and shortcomings, an analysis in hindsight of her mistakes and misjudgments. The thrust of it all seemed to be that she could have avoided finding herself in this predicament if she'd done things differently, but she did not really believe that to be the case.

She could not hope to outrun them. She knew that.

So she ran toward the barn, thinking that if she could get to the old root cellar and lock it from the inside, she might be able to survive. The house was between her and the creatures and she was counting on it to hide her movements, to shield her whereabouts, at least until she could get into the cellar, but even before she reached the barn she heard the rattle of bones behind her. Grunts and the sharp exhalation of breath. She looked over her shoulder as she ran and they were upon her, moving faster than humanly possible, streaming around the house, over the dirt. Tiny hands grabbed her upper thighs, reached between her legs to pull at her crotch. They were already swarming past her, around her, and even as the hands on her legs yanked her down, she was tripping over the ones in front. One, the leader apparently, stood on the stump to the right of the clothesline, jumping up and down and shaking what looked like a maraca made from the skull of a rat.

The creatures were even smaller than she'd originally thought, two feet high at the most, but they were powerfully built and they all had weapons and there were far too many of them. They rolled her over, onto her back, and one held each side of her head. Two took her left arm, two her right, two more each foot, spreading her limbs.

One continued to grab between her legs.

She was crying hysterically, but even through her tears she could see that she'd been wrong at first. It was not just bees or beetles that accompanied the creatures but a whole host of bugs. And they were all strangely wrong, profoundly changed and disturbingly incorrect versions of ordinary insects.

Onto her face alighted a butterfly with the screaming head of a baby. It spit on her nose and flew away.

She was going to die and she knew it, and she was crying out for all she was worth, hoping someone—the returning Hube, a passing hiker, a visiting rancher—might hear her, but the clownish monsters did not seem to care and made no effort to gag her mouth or stifle her. They let her scream, and more than anything else, it was their lack of concern, their certainty that no one would come to her rescue, that impressed upon her the dire hopelessness of her predicament.

The creature holding the left side of her head looked down on her, opened its mouth, and the sound of a piano emerged from between its green lips.

The one with the rat-skull maraca jumped up and down on the stump, pointed at her, yelled, and the sound that came out of its mouth was that of a string quartet.

She was no longer screaming, but was crying, sobbing, tears and snot pooling in the various indentations of her face.

The skull of a possum was placed on her chest.

As if in a dream, she heard the sound of Hube's truck in the drive and then in front of the house, heard him slam the pickup's door and call out her name. For a very brief fraction of a second, she considered yelling at the top of her lungs, telling him to get out of here, save himself. But her love was not that altruistic and she did not want to die alone here with these monsters. She wanted her husband to save her, and she screamed out his name: "Hube!"

"Patty?" he called.

"Hube!"

She wanted to say more, wanted to be able to impart additional information, wanted to tell him that he should bring his shotgun from the truck so he could blow these monsters to Kingdom Come, but her brain and her mouth could not seem to get it together and she just kept screaming out his name.

"Hube!"

She was raised up, tilted forward, and was able to see her husband dash around the corner of the house and run into a wall of the clown creatures. They leaped onto his head, onto his chest, onto his arms, dragging him down. Weapons were lifted, bones and baseball bats, skulls and horseshoes.

The one on the stump jumped up and down, ordered Hube's murder in the voice of a string quartet.

They beat him to death with the sound of a symphony.

Michigan

This was the life.

Jennings followed the guide through the brush, bow extended. Last year, he'd taken Gloria to Palm Springs, and the year before that to Hawaii, but this year, by God, he'd put his foot down, and they'd booked their time share in northern Michigan. He was going to do something *he* wanted for once, and if that meant that Gloria had to either watch videos in the condo or shop at The Store in this little podunk town, then so be it.

He'd arranged for several short hunting trips during their two-week stay. One daylong duck-hunting expedition. One overnight bear hunt.

And this one.

A three-day bow hunting trip.

Of the three, this was the best, the one he was enjoying the most. He'd never used bow and arrow before, and though it had taken him a while to get used to both the physicality and limitations of this sport, the guide, Tom, told him that he was a natural. He felt that himself, and he found that he liked the added handicaps bow hunting placed on him. It made him feel more in tune with nature, like he was a part of this forest rather than just a dilettantish intruder, and that resulted in his increased enjoyment of the hunt. It gave everything a slight edge, and while they hadn't bagged any game yet, even his misses were more exciting and more fulfilling than some of his rifle scores.

There were four of them on this trip: Tom; himself; Jud Weiss, a retired deputy sheriff from Arizona; and Webb Deboyar, an air-traffic controller from Orlando, Florida. Jud and Webb were still at the campsite, and Tom was taking him out on his solo, an elk tracking that would hopefully lead to a kill and mounted antlers over the fireplace back home.

The two of them had been tracking this elk, a big bull, since before noon, and by Jennings' watch it was already pushing three. The time had flown, though. It was exhilarating being out here like this, taking part in nature's

cycle, and he could not remember ever having felt
more alive.

Tom suddenly held up a hand, motioned for him to
halt.

Jennings stood in place and followed the guide's gaze.
It was the bull elk.

Unmoving, the animal was standing in a copse of
bushes on the other side of a dying fir tree. Jennings
probably would have missed it on his own, would have
blundered ahead and scared the beast away, realizing
what it was too late to shoot, but Tom knew these woods
like the proverbial back of his hand, and he'd spotted
the animal instantly.

Jennings' blood was rushing, the adrenaline pumping.
He was psyched, and as silently as he could, he repositioned his bow, notched the arrow, and drew back the
line. The plan was simple: he would shoot the elk, and
if it wasn't a clean kill, if the beast was injured and not
killed, Tom would finish it off.

The details of *that* had been a little too gruesome even
for Jennings back in the trading post where they'd
started, but now the idea of leaping onto the animal with
a big buck knife, subduing it in hand-to-hoof combat,
and cutting out its heart seemed like the pinnacle of raw
experience, and he wished Tom had taught him how to
do it.

The elk moved, looked up, looked at them.

"Now!" Tom yelled.

Jennings aimed the arrow, let it fly.

He brought the elk down with one shot.

Tom immediately ran forward, through the under-
brush, through the bushes, knife extended. Jennings followed the guide stumblingly, saw the other man leap on
the animal, cut it open.

The hairy skin split and the stomach contents spilled
out.

His father's body emerged from the open wound.

Jennings dropped his bow, backed away, all of the
saliva suddenly drained from his mouth. Tom was scrambling away from the dead animal as well, an expression
of shock and uninhibited fear on his face. The knife in

his hand was dripping blood, and he gripped it tightly, pointed outward.

Jennings felt a warm wetness spread from his crotch down his leg as he pissed in his pants. He wanted to scream but could not, and neither he nor Tom said a word, made a sound.

His father rose to his feet. He was wearing a suit, but both the suit and his skin were covered with blood and a clear sort of viscous goo. He was smaller than he used to be, almost dwarfish, but he hadn't aged at all or at least the age had not registered on his face. Jennings' initial dumb thought was that his father hadn't died, they'd buried the wrong man, but he remembered seeing his father's body and knew that he *had* died and that this was some sort of . . . monster.

His father bounded instantly away from the gutted elk and toward Tom. The guide started stabbing outward, but his reactions were slow and the knife cut only air.

Tom's neck was broken with one quick snap, and then his father changed directions and loped across the small open space toward him, grinning crazily.

There was elk blood on his teeth.

Jennings tried to get away, clawed his way through the brush, through the bushes, started heading back through the trees toward camp, but his father caught him before he'd gone more than a few feet. He was knocked to the ground, and he felt the weight of his father's compacted body on his back. Strong hands slipped around his neck, fingers digging into his flesh.

Dad! he wanted to scream.

But the air in his lungs could not escape to form words, and the world around him faded, and he saw only blackness.

New York

Shelly emerged from the bathroom and glanced over at Sam on the bed. He looked up from his magazine, smiled warmly at her, and she turned away. He was getting maudlin as he grew older and it was something that had begun to irritate her. He cried now in movies—

formulaic, simplistic, emotionally manipulative movies
that were transparent in their sentimentality even to
her—and it was annoying to hear his light occasional
sniffles next to her, to see his finger wipe wetness from
the corners of his eyes. He had not cried when David
died, nor when his own parents had passed on, yet he
was now shedding tears for not particularly well-drawn
fictional characters artificially embroiled in embarrass-
ingly contrived plots.

She wondered sometimes why she had married him.

Shaking her head, Shelly walked over to the dresser,
picked up her brush and—

There was another face in the mirror.

She blinked, closed her eyes. Looked away, looked
back. But the face was still there, an ancient hag with
impossibly wrinkled parchment skin, dark eyes narrowed
into an evil slit, a hard cruel smile on a nearly lipless
mouth.

Mary Worth.

Shelly backed up, all of the saliva in her mouth suddenly gone, but she could not look away. She could see
a reversed image of the bedroom in the mirror, Sam
sitting up, leaning against the headboard, reading his
magazine. In the foreground was the face, just on the
other side of the mirrored dresser, staring back at her
with malevolent intensity. She'd thought at first that it
was unattached to a body, but the longer she looked the
more she saw, and she could now make out hunched
shoulders beneath a black robe, although she could not
say whether the body had been there all along or had
materialized before her eyes.

Mary Worth.

It was exactly the face she had expected to see all
those years ago, when she and her sisters and her friends
had had sleepovers and had played those nighttime party
games indulged in by every schoolgirl in America. "Mary
Worth" had been their favorite, and they had dutifully
taken turns standing before the mirror with their eyes
closed repeating "Mary Worth, Mary Worth, Mary
Worth . . ." The story was that if you said her name a
hundred times, she would appear. None of them had

ever been brave enough to make it to a hundred, chickening out and running squealing back to their beds and sleeping bags somewhere around forty or forty-five, and she knew that she herself had always purposely kept it under fifty, no matter what she told her sisters and her friends, because that, too, seemed a magical number and she'd been afraid that Mary Worth might have been partially present by that point and she did not want to see her at all.

Shelly could not remember who had initially taught her the ritual or where she had first learned of it, and she could not recall ever having seen a picture of Mary Worth or ever having the hag described to her. All she'd known was that Mary Worth was ancient and utterly terrifying.

But she realized now that the face in the mirror was exactly how she'd pictured Mary Worth in her mind.

Shelly stared into the mirror, blinked.

Where was *her* reflection?

She had not realized it until this second, but although everything else in the bedroom was reflected exactly, she herself was not in the mirror.

Mary Worth had taken her place.

If before she had been frightened, now she was utterly terrified, and she watched with growing horror as the old crone withdrew from her robe a long silver knife, wrinkled bony fingers clutching the blackened hilt. Shelly quickly looked around the room to make sure there was no real Mary Worth present, then glanced down at her own body to make sure there was no superimposition upon her frame, to make sure she was not wearing a black robe and withdrawing a knife of which she was unaware.

No.

But in the mirror she was still not visible and Mary Worth, her twisted smile growing broader, turned around, gripping the knife tightly, and walked over toward where Sam lay on the bed reading.

Shelly was staring into the mirror as the old crone began to stab, and she whirled around when Sam started screaming behind her.

There was still no Mary Worth, but Sam was thrashing around on the bed, sudden slices opening up the skin of his chest and thigh, blood both welling and spurting, depending on the location of the slash, covering his skin and his fallen magazine, the pink sheets and pillowcases, the headboard and the nightstand and the Indian rug on the hardwood floor.

There was no noise save for Sam's ear-piercing screams, and that was perhaps the most frightening thing of all. In the mirror, Mary Worth was laughing, cackling, but there was no accompanying sound. Her voice, if she had one, was trapped behind the glass, audible only in that world, and while her actions were manifest in the real bedroom, her form and voice were not.

How had Mary Worth come? No one had invoked her name.

There was a missing piece here. Shelly could buy the concept of summoning up an evil spirit, but she did not quite believe that Mary Worth was able to show up on her own, without being called. That wasn't the way it was supposed to work, and while the story she'd been told might be part of a children's game, there was a kernel of truth to all legends.

Sam had stopped screaming. He was dead, but Mary Worth continued to stab, and his lifeless body jerked on the mattress with the force of her knife blows.

Shelly was not screaming either. She was not panicking, not afraid, and while she was probably just in shock, Sam's murder was not the horrifyingly cataclysmic event that it should have been. Indeed, she felt detached from it, the scene next to her in the room as distant, flat, and removed as something on television, the reflection in the mirror only slightly more immediate because of the frightening visage of Mary Worth.

Mary Worth.

Even the monster was not as terrifying as she had been. Shelly was getting used to the crone, and she thought that perhaps she *had* summoned the hag, had subconsciously wanted her to do just what she was doing.

No.

She and Sam might have drifted apart. Maybe she didn't even love him anymore. But never in her most vicious fantasies had she ever wished him dead. This was all Mary Worth's doing, not hers.

But she would be blamed for it.

The knowledge hit her all of a sudden. She once again faced the bed, saw her husband's bloody body, his chest cavity hacked open so wide that portions of organs were visible through the rent skin and muscle.

She turned back toward the mirror.

In the glass, Mary Worth was once again standing in her place on the other side of the dresser, looking back at her.

And she was smiling.

PART I

Outside

ONE

Daniel

"Wake up."

Daniel heard his wife's voice, felt her hands gently shaking him awake, but it had been a long time since he'd gotten up this early and his body resisted. He moaned, turned over, dug deeper into the blankets.

"Your interview's at ten," she said, and there was a no-nonsense undercurrent to the surface pleasantry of her voice that made him suck in a deep breath, throw off the blankets, and sit up.

Margot was already dressed, ready for work, and she stood next to the bed, looking down at him. "I'm sorry," she said, "but I'm leaving and I'm dropping off Tony, and I want to make sure you're up before I go. Otherwise, you'll never make it."

"I'm up," he said, standing. He tried to kiss her, but she wrinkled her nose and pulled away.

"Scope," she said.

"That's romantic."

"Tell me about it." She gave him a quick kiss on the cheek. "Give me a call at the office after your interview. I want to know how it goes."

He picked up his pants from the floor next to the bed. "I can take Tony, you know."

"It's out of your way. Besides, I have a little extra time." She started down the hall. "I'm serious about that Scope. Nothing'll lose you a job faster than B.O. or bad breath."

He followed her out to the living room, where Tony was waiting by the front door, backpack in hand. All of the drapes were open, and outside four or five identically dressed adolescents were leaning against the low brick

wall that separated their weed patch of a yard from the
sidewalk. One kid with a shaved head ground out the butt
of the cigarette he'd been smoking on top of the wall
and flicked it into their yard.

Margot must have seen the look on Daniel's face because she frowned at him, pointing her finger. "Don't
you say anything to those boys. We have to live here
and Tony has to go to their school. Anything you do to
them, they'll take out on him."

Tony said nothing, but the pleading in his son's eyes
told him that he agreed with his mother one hundred
percent, and Daniel nodded. "Fine," he said.

He watched them walk outside, waved good-bye, and
shut and locked the door behind them before heading
back to the bathroom to take a shower.

The hot water felt good on his skin, and he stayed in
the shower longer than he needed to, enjoying the warm
steam that fogged up the room and the comforting sensation of the pulsing water against his sleep-sore back.

It had been over a year since corporate downsizing
had caused him to be laid off from his last job at Thomp-
son Industries, and though the nightly news told him
continuously that leading economic indicators were up
and the stock market was at an all-time high, he had no
immediate prospects of finding a job and saw no change
on the horizon. He'd gone to every employment agency
in the Philadelphia metropolitan area during the past
thirteen months, but nothing had turned up in all that
time and the market was oversaturated with similarly
displaced middle-management workers all competing for
the same positions.

More than once he'd wanted to move, but Margot was
still employed, still bringing home a paycheck, and the
truth was that the house was the only tangible asset they
had. It was their anchor, bought and paid for, left to
them fair and square by her parents, and if Pennsylvania
wasn't his favorite state, that was just too damn bad
because if worst came to worst, if Margot lost her job
and their phone and gas and electricity were cut off,
they could always huddle in the living room in their

sleeping bags and eat crackers stolen from restaurant salad bars.

He smiled to himself as he shut off the shower, amused at his own train of thought. As Margot always said, he shouldn't be so melodramatic.

He'd always been melodramatic, though.

It kept life interesting.

Daniel dried, shaved, brushed his teeth, combed his hair, dressed. In his suit, he looked conservative, presentable, respectable. He straightened his tie, looked at himself in the mirror, practiced smiling. He didn't hold out a whole lot of hope for today. The fact that he was being interviewed instead of just rejected outright was of course a good sign, but he'd been to dozens of similar interviews since he'd been unemployed and none of them had amounted to anything.

Still, it had been quite a while since he'd had any interview at all, and at the very least, this would enable him to keep in practice.

He drove into downtown Philly and paid five bucks to park in an underground lot beneath the Bronson Building. Cutting Edge Software, the firm with the job opening, owned the top three floors, and he took an elevator up, quickly putting Chapstick on his too-dry lips before the metal doors slid open.

He was ushered immediately into the personnel office, where a young efficient-looking woman who could not have been more than a year out of college introduced herself as the personnel director. She bade him sit in one of the padded chairs opposite her desk, and the two of them talked for the next half hour or so. It was an interview, but it felt more like a conversation, and Daniel found that he liked this relaxed informal approach. They hadn't discussed the job specifically, had instead talked mostly about him, his life, his interests, but he knew she'd probably gotten a good read on him from the discussion, and he was gratified when she stood and said, "I think you'd work well here. You're self-motivated, intelligent, and I think you could do a good job. I'd like you to meet the president of our firm and talk to him for a few minutes."

He followed her out of the office, down a carpeted hallway to a bigger office. She rapped on the sill of the open doorway, then motioned for Daniel to walk in.

The president of the company was one of those men who tried too hard to be jovial and just-one-of-the-guys, and who referred to himself in company literature as "W. L. (Bud) Williams." Daniel hated men with nicknames. And he hated men who used only their initials even more. Together they were a lethal combination. "Never trust a man who doesn't use the name his parents gave him," his father had always said, and it was advice that Daniel had taken to heart.

Still, he needed the job and he couldn't afford to pick and choose, and he sat across the desk from W. L. (Bud) Williams and smiled.

The president looked over the résumé in his hand. "I see here that you've worked as a tech writer before."

Daniel nodded. "Yes. For the City of Tyler."

"Did you like the job?"

"No," he answered truthfully, realizing his mistake even as he said it. He scrambled quickly for damage control. "I mean, I liked the work, but I didn't like . . . a few of the people I worked with."

"Is that why you quit?"

"Yes, sir."

"We like team players here at Cutting Edge."

"No problem there," Daniel lied. "I'm a team player. That was just a fluke."

The president smiled. "Yes." He stood. "Well, thank you for coming."

Daniel stood as well, offering his hand. "Thank you for seeing me."

"We'll call you," W. L. (Bud) Williams said as he shook Daniel's hand.

But they wouldn't, Daniel knew. He'd put his foot in his mouth and flunked the test, and he left the building dejected and resentful, ticked off even more when he took the elevator down to the garage and realized that he'd wasted five dollars on parking.

In for a penny, in for a pound, he thought. He was in the city and had already wasted five bucks, what were a few dollars more? He drove to McDonald's and bought himself a value meal, consoling himself with junk food, taking the sting off his disappointment.

He was back home by noon, just in time to catch an old John Ford western on AMC. He sat in his recliner in front of the television, but he couldn't concentrate on the film and instead brooded about his dismal efforts to secure employment. On the screen, John Wayne rode through the desert sand in front of majestic red peaks that rose dramatically out of the earth behind him, and Daniel wondered what it would be like to live in Arizona. The West was supposed to have a booming job market these days, and once again he found himself thinking that it might be better to just pull up stakes and follow the sun rather than sit here in this crummy row house and wait for something to turn up.

At least he wasn't such a macho jerk that he resented Margot for bringing home a paycheck. He was grateful that she had a job, and he had no hangups about having to be the primary breadwinner of the household. He and Margot weren't in competition, they were a team, one for all and all for one, and he was proud of her success. Still, for his own sake, he wanted to work. He wasn't creative, was not an artist or a writer or a musician, and he had nothing productive to do with his free time. More than the money, it was the desire to dispel this feeling of uselessness that he wanted.

The phone rang. Margot. He'd forgotten that he was supposed to call her, and he quickly apologized before giving her a thumbnail sketch of his morning.

She sighed sympathetically. "Doesn't look good, huh?"

"I'm not holding my breath."

"Don't worry," she said. "Something'll turn up."

"Yeah."

"Are you busy this afternoon?"

He snorted. "Yeah. Right."

"I need you to go to the store and pick up some hamburger buns and ground beef. I forgot my ATM card and have no cash."

"I don't have any cash either."

"My card's either on the dresser or the bathroom sink."

"The sink?"

"I don't want a lecture."

"Sorry."

"I'll pick up Tony on my way home."

"I can do it."

"You can do it tomorrow. We'll switch cars."

Daniel understood. "He's embarrassed by the Buick?"

"He didn't say anything, but yeah. You know how kids are at that age. Embarrassed by everything."

"Especially parents."

Margot laughed. "Especially parents." There was noise in the background, talking. "Wait a sec," she said. There was a pause, the sound of muffled voices as she conversed with another woman. "Gotta go," she said, coming back on the line, "We have a crisis here. Make sure you stop by the store."

"I will. Love you."

"Me too. Bye."

He hung up the phone and switched off the TV, walking through the kitchen and down the hall. The house seemed silent with the television off, too silent, uncomfortably silent, and Daniel immediately began whistling a mindless tune in order to generate some noise.

He was filled with a vague sense of unease as he entered the bedroom, a feeling that intensified as he passed the dresser and approached the narrow doorway that led to the bathroom. It was a strange sensation, one he didn't immediately recognize, and it took him a few moments to realize that it was fear. Not the rational fear of physical danger he'd sometimes experienced as an adult, but a baseless, groundless, superstitious dread he associated with childhood. A fear of the boogeyman was what it was, a fear of ghosts, an emotion he hadn't experienced in decades, and though he felt stupid, he turned around, expecting to see a shape or figure behind him, unable to shake the feeling that he was being watched even after he saw that the room was empty.

Where the hell had this come from? A moment ago he had been on the phone to Margot, having a normal conversation, talking about buying food for dinner, now he was getting the shit spooked out of him walking through his own bedroom.

It was irrational, he knew, and made no sense, but the feeling did not go away, not even when he found Margot's ATM card next to her hairbrush on the tiled counter next to the sink, not even when he hurried out of the bedroom and back down the hall.

It was only when he was finally outside, on the stoop, locking the front door of the house, that the panic left him, that he finally felt as though he could breathe.

Stress.

Maybe he'd been counting on getting that Cutting Edge job more than he thought.

Either that or his house had suddenly become haunted within the past five minutes.

Maybe Margot had died.

Or Tony.

He pushed the thoughts out of his mind. This way lay compulsion. Obsession. There were no ghosts, nothing weird, only his overactive imagination which, after lying in a coma for the past two decades, had suddenly decided to announce its existence.

Stress.

It had to be stress.

Nevertheless, he breathed a little easier when he was in the car and on the road to the grocery store and the house was safely behind him.

After dinner, Daniel sat with Tony at the kitchen table, helping his son with homework while Margot did the dishes.

Tony finally finished his assignment and asked if he could watch TV.

"Only until eight-thirty," Daniel told him. "Then it's time for bed. This is a school night."

"But, Dad—"

"No buts."

Tony slumped out of the kitchen and through the swinging door out to the living room.

"Next year, we'll let him stay up until nine," Margot said.

"If he keeps his grades up."

She smiled. "Never thought you'd turn into your father, did you?"

Daniel pushed back his chair, walked over to the sink, and put his hands on her shoulders, giving her right ear a quick kiss. "I love you, Mrs. Anderson."

"I know."

"Aren't you supposed to say, 'I love you too'?"

"Actions speak louder than words." She dropped her voice. "I thought I'd show you later."

He grinned. "*That's* why I love you."

From outside, there was the sound of an unmuffled Charger engine, an earthquake rumble that roared to a crescendo before dying.

"Your brother's here." Daniel returned to his seat.

"Be nice to him."

"Always am."

"Brian looks up to you."

"How much you want to bet that he brings up the fact that I'm still unemployed?"

She looked out the kitchen window, quickly went back to washing, pretending as though she didn't know anyone was here. "Shut up."

Brian knocked once, walked in. He nodded to his sister, sat down at the kitchen table. "Hey, buddy, you found a job yet?"

"No."

"I got a lead on something. It might not pan out, but this guy at the site has a brother who deejays. You know, parties and dances and shit like that? He's looking for someone to help him haul equipment. It's a part-time gig, nights mostly, but, hey, it's something. Might even pick up a few tips."

Daniel shook his head. "I don't think so."

"Why not, man? Haul in a few speakers, hang, listen to some tunes, get paid for it? Can't get much breezier than that."

"Dance music depresses me."

"You really want to depress yourself, listen to *Pet*

Sounds. You know, by The Beach Boys? Most depressing goddamn album ever put to vinyl. I bum out every time I hear that thing."

The employment opportunity was forgotten as Brian began riffing on music, chronicling his likes and dislikes over the past twenty years. Just as well. He wasn't a bad guy, but he was a flake and a half, and he only brought up these so-called "job opportunities" to lord over Daniel the fact that he was working and Daniel wasn't. Brian was six years older than Margot, five years older than Daniel, and though he'd always been loving and supportive in his way, he'd also been slightly resentful that they both had better paying, more respectable jobs than he did, and ever since Daniel had been out of work, he'd been in hog heaven.

It was after eleven before Brian finally left, grabbing his sister around the waist and spinning her once around the kitchen floor. They stood in the doorway, waving, as he woke up half the neighborhood with his car and drove off.

Daniel closed the door, locked it, and Margot kissed him. "Thanks."

Daniel smiled wryly. "Hey, he's family."

"You went above and beyond. Ready for your reward?"

"I've been ready all night."

"Let me go check on Tony."

Margot went down the hall to Tony's room, and Daniel double-checked the doors to make sure they were locked before turning off the lights and heading back to their bedroom. Margot was already standing before the dresser, loosening her hair, and he closed and locked the door behind him as he stepped into the room. He glanced toward the narrow bathroom doorway, saw darkness, shadow. There was a vague feeling of unease, a sense once again that something was wrong, and he walked quickly over to the bathroom and turned on the light, gratified to see that there was nothing out of the ordinary.

This afternoon, taking out the trash, he'd seen a shadow down the alley behind their house, a shadow he couldn't identify but that looked vaguely familiar: small, almost dwarfish, wearing a tattered gown or smock that billowed in the breeze. It had been around two o'clock, probably the least scary time of day, but the blocky shadows cast by east-facing garages had covered the narrow alley and, along with the slightly overcast sky, had contributed to an uncharacteristically solemn scene. He'd tossed the Hefty bag into the garbage can, turned back toward his yard, and seen, out of the corner of his eye, movement. He looked down the alley and saw, several houses away, on a protruding section of white fence, the shadow of a small figure with longish hair and a raggedy knee-length gown that blew in the breeze. The figure did not move, was perfectly still, only its hair and tattered clothing waving in the wind, and the sight had instantly rung some mental bell. He knew he'd seen it before, but he could not remember where or when. He scanned both sides of the alley, looking for the figure that was creating the shadow, but saw nothing.

The shadow raised a hand. Beckoned.

A wave of cold washed immediately over him. He'd been afraid, instinctively frightened, though he had not known why, and he'd hurried quickly out of the alley, through the yard, into the house, locking the back door and closing the drapes so he wouldn't be able to see.

Daniel took off his shoes and pants, sat heavily down on the bed. The thought of the shadow had stayed with him all evening, haunting him, taunting him with its almost-recognizable familiarity, and though he had wanted to say something to Margot about it, he had not. He was aware how stupid it all sounded, and he did not want her to think that he was sitting here alone each day, inventing fantasies to frighten himself, letting his imagination work overtime because he had nothing better to do.

He unbuttoned his shirt, threw it on the floor, leaned back on the bed.

Margot had finished with her hair and had taken off her clothes. She started toward the bathroom. "I'm going to take a quick shower."

He sat up on one elbow. "Don't."

She stopped, looked at him, eyebrows raised.

"I like it dirty."

Smiling, she walked over to him, crawled into bed. "I like it that you like it dirty."

Afterward, they lay there, spent and sweating. Daniel reached for the remote, turned on the TV, started flipping through channels. Margot snuggled next to him. "Have you noticed," she said finally, "that Tony's been acting a little . . . strange lately?"

He looked at her. "Strange how?"

"I don't know. Secretive. Suspicious. He seems to be spending a lot of time alone in his room."

"A boy? In his room? Alone? Secretive? Suspicious?" Daniel smiled. "Hmmm I wonder what he could be doing."

She hit his shoulder. "Knock it off."

"You might check the stiffness of his sheets."

"You can be a real jerk sometimes."

"I'm sorry, but it's perfectly normal—"

"It's not normal. That's what I'm trying to tell you. I know about *that*. I do wash his underwear, you know. But this is . . . different."

"What? Drugs? Shoplifting? Gangs?"

"Nothing like that."

"What then?"

"I don't know. But it's kind of . . . spooky."

Spooky.

He didn't say anything, pretended to watch TV. She went off to take her shower, returned and climbed into bed next to him, and soon afterward, he felt her body relax, felt the pattern of her breath change as the even rhythm of sleep overtook her.

He waited for a few moments, then carefully extricated himself from her arms, moved closer to the edge of the bed. He stared at her while she slept, gently touched her hair. She was so beautiful and he was so happy with her, but the chilling thought that it would not last forced itself into his mind and would not be dislodged. It was the same feeling he'd had this morning an anxious, maddening sense that something was going to happen to her and Tony, and he found himself thinking again of the shadow.

Spooky.

He rolled over, onto his back, and closed his eyes, forcing himself to think of nothing, forcing himself to fall asleep. It took a long time. On the television, he heard a talk show give way to an infomercial, heard the infomercial end and a movie begin.

It was halfway through the movie before he finally drifted off.

He dreamed, and in his dream, the small shadow was in his house, and he sat in a chair, paralyzed, in the living room, as it roamed down the hall looking for his wife, looking for his son.

TWO

Laurie

Laurie Mitchell looked across the boardroom at the other department heads dutifully making notes on their legal pads.

Boardroom.

Bored room was more like it.

She glanced surreptitiously at her watch. Hoffman was still droning on about maximizing the division's profits, some generic claptrap he'd picked up at an executive seminar, and it didn't appear that he would be concluding his filibuster anytime soon.

God, she hated these meetings.

Outside the windows, the sky was clear, cloudless, and she could see all the way to the bay, the small dark shape of Alcatraz Island visible in the sea of blue space between two adjoining buildings. She found herself wondering what would happen if a major earthquake hit while they were up here. Would the building stand or would it collapse? If it collapsed, would they ride it down, squashing the floors beneath them, or would the structure topple over, sending them flying into space? More than likely, there'd be a random pattern of destruction, different areas on different floors that crumbled or remained intact, arbitrarily killing those who happened to have the misfortune of being in the wrong place at the wrong time.

Morbid, perhaps, but at least it made the time go by.

She glanced once more around the room, at her coworkers and peers, and thought, not for the first time, that she didn't belong here. She'd been hired by Automated Interface just out of college, had worked her way up the corporate ladder and had held her current position for the past five years, but she still sometimes felt

like an imposter, a child playing dress-up who had somehow successfully fooled adults into believing that she was
one of them.

Did she have anything in common with these people
at all?

No. It was a fake plastic yuppie world she lived in, and
it was one of the cruel tricks of fate that she happened to
have an aptitude for this business, that she happened to
be good at this job.

She'd grown up far differently, in a rural town south
of the Bay Area, at the tail end of the hippie movement,
and her parents had raised both her and Josh nontradi-
tionally, teaching them a reverence for nature, emphasiz-
ing individuality, all the counterculture clichés. The
obsession with appearances, the focus on finances and
materialism that were so much a part of the lives of her
peers were completely forcign to her. At the same time,
she recognized the need to fit in, and she had no problem putting on the mask of conformity, buying the right
clothes, ordering the right food, doing everything necessary to facilitate her created persona of successful businesswoman. It was why she was where she was today.

It was funny how life turned out. Her parents had
been killed in a freak auto accident her senior year in
high school, and amid the devastating grief and bottom-
less sense of loss, she'd been surprised to learn that her
parents had actually written a will, and that they'd specifically earmarked funds for her and Josh's college education. She never would have suspected such a straight
request from either her mother or her father, but it was
there in black and white, and the lawyer said that the
money could only be used for books and tuition. Anything else, and the money would be donated to Green-
peace.

So, in a way, her hippie parents were responsible for
her becoming the business executive she was today.

She had the feeling they'd be proud of her, though.

A half hour later, Hoffman finally finished talking, the
meeting finally ended, and the various department heads
went back to their offices. Tom Jenson, the division development coordinator, asked her if she wanted to go

out for drinks after work, but she begged off, saying that she wanted to get a head start on the weekend.

"I don't blame you," he said. "It's been a crappy week."

Laurie smiled. "See you Monday."

She left work an hour early, walking downtown. A cable car filled with Japanese tourists clattered past her, and she waved at one man who snapped her picture.

As she did each Friday, she stopped off to see her brother at The Shire. He'd been managing the bookstore for three years now, and it was nice to see him finally find a job that he liked, but recently he'd been delving a little too deeply into Eastern religion and philosophy books.

An interest he'd inherited from their mom.

It was one of the reasons she liked to check up on him.

Josh was helping a customer when she walked into the shop, and she waved at him and busied herself with the magazines while he talked with the customer about the works of Carlos Casteneda.

The customer finally bought a book and left, and Laurie walked over to the counter. "How goes it?" she asked.

He looked at her. "I was about to ask you the same question."

"That bad, huh?"

He nodded.

She placed her purse down on the counter and sighed. "It's been a long week."

"Tell me about it."

She described the petty infighting and office politics that had been indulged in since the division's recent restructuring, moved on to the boring meetings and endless memos, and finished with a lawsuit being filed against the company by an ex-clerk whom she had hired.

"Sounds like a party."

"Yeah. Right."

"How are things with you and Matt?"

"Fine. No problems there."

"You could always get another job."

"No. It's not the work, it's . . . it's the position. Ever since I took that promotion, I've had to spend all my time dealing with human resources rather than what's important."

He smiled. " 'Human resources'?"

"I admit it. I've been corrupted. I'm a corporate shill."

"Like I said, you could find another job."

She shook her head.

"You're under a lot of stress. That's your main problem. I have this book—"

"Josh."

"I'm serious. It's about spiritual awareness and energy management. There's a lack of spirituality in your life. That's at the root of your problems. It's what's at the root of most of the world's problems."

"I really don't want to hear it right now."

"Laurie—"

"Look, I'm glad you have a hobby, and it's really interesting and everything, but I just don't believe that I can walk into your store and buy a five-dollar vanity press book and find out answers to questions that the greatest minds in the history of the world couldn't solve."

"You don't have to be hostile."

"Yes, Josh, I do. I do because every time I come in here, you're trying to shove some new religion down my throat. I just want you to be my brother and give me a shoulder to cry on and not try to convert me all the time."

"You're just too closed-minded."

"If Albert Einstein didn't know the meaning of life, then neither do you."

He turned away, and she reached out and grabbed his arm, sighing. "I'm sorry. It's been a boring day and a long week, and I didn't mean to take it out on you."

He turned, smiled wryly. "What are brothers for?"

She hugged him. "I just need to go home, take a hot bath, relax with Matt, and watch a crummy movie." She picked up her purse from the counter. "I'll call you later, okay?"

He nodded.

"And next time we'll discuss your wacky religions."

He laughed. "Deal."

She waved good-bye and walked outside onto the crowded sidewalk. She'd taken BART to work this morning but decided to walk home. It wasn't that far, and she needed the exercise. She also wanted some time to think.

At the corner, at the stoplight, a convertible pulled next to her, its driver idly flipping through stations on a radio loud enough to be heard halfway down the block: rap, dance, metal, alternative. The light changed, the convertible took off, and as she walked across the street she heard the fading drone of a currently hot rock band.

She missed the music of the seventies. To the mainstream public, it was the decade of disco, but she'd been into fusion and progressive rock, movements on the edge of the mainstream that took chances, expanded boundaries, celebrated artistic ambition and musical ability. Everyone now had been ground down into mediocrity, afraid to shoot too high, afraid of being ridiculed as pretentious, and the result was a music scene that was terminally banal.

Art.

That's what she respected.

Which was why she was so happy with Matt.

They'd been going together for a year, living together for the past four months, and while the situation at work had been up and down, she'd never been happier at home.

Matt, she thought, was a true artist. He created his work not for money, not for fame, not for recognition by his peers.

He did it because he had to.

He didn't look or dress the part either, and that's what had sold her on his integrity. There were two looks for artists in San Francisco: designer duds and an up-to-the-minute coif, or thrift-store clothes and uncombed hair. Matt looked more like a sales clerk or a civil servant—average—and the fact that he didn't feel obligated to play into the media's conception of an artiste made her think he was the real thing.

In actuality, he did work as a sales clerk. At Mont-

gomery Ward's. Cameras and Luggage. He used the
money he earned at his nine-to-five to fund his art: films
he shot in and around Golden Gate Park with "found"
actors—people he picked off the street to read his
scripts. When he completed a film, he copied it onto
videotape, passed the tapes out to friends and coworkers, and told them to copy the film and pass it on as
well. Most of the people who watched his work, she
knew, were not even aware that he was the filmmaker.
He always acted as though this were just some low-budget movie he'd discovered and wanted to share with
them.

She found that charming.

Matt's Mustang was in the driveway when she arrived
home, and her spirits lifted as she hurried across the
small yard and up the porch steps. The front door was
unlocked—as usual—and she opened the door and
went inside. She was about to pull her Ricky Ricardo
routine and yell "Honey, I'm home!" but instead she
decided to surprise him, and she moved quietly through
the living room.

There was the sound of someone peeing in the bathroom, and she walked over to the open door—

—where a nude blond woman was sitting on the toilet,
legs spread.

Matt, her artist, was kneeling before the toilet, his
head in the woman's lap.

There was no silent second of shock, no delay of any
kind. She ran instantly into the bathroom and yanked
Matt up by his hair. "Get out!" she screamed. "Get the
hell out of my house!"

His erect penis was bouncing around comically and
the woman was frantically trying to recover her clothes,
but Laurie did not let up. She dug her fingers into Matt's
upper arm and shoved him as hard as she could into the
hall, picking his clothes up from the floor next to the
tub and throwing them after him. She did not touch
the woman but continued screaming all the while, anguished, angry invectives that included both of them.
The woman, pants and T-shirt now on, ran past her out
of the bathroom clutching panties, bra, nylons, shoes.

Laurie was crying. She didn't want to, wanted to wait until after they were gone, wanted to appear only mad, not hurt, but she couldn't help it and she was sobbing as she screamed, "Fuck you, Matt! Fuck you, you pervert! Fuck you!"

Still only half-dressed, the two of them ran down the hallway, through the living room, out the front door. They did not bother to close the door behind them, and Laurie caught a glimpse of Matt scrambling into his car, fumbling with his keys, before she slammed the door shut and dead-bolted it.

She slumped to the floor, leaning against the hard cold wood. It had all happened so fast. One minute she'd been happy, excited, ready to relax with Matt and begin her weekend; the next, her entire life had been turned upside down and it felt as though her guts had been scooped out as she realized that the man she loved had betrayed her. She hadn't had time to think, to absorb the shock, she'd simply been thrown in the water and forced to swim.

She sat there, crying, and after a while the tears stopped. The hurt had not lessened, but it had stabilized. It was no longer an intruder but a part of her, and she could deal with it. She stood, wiped her eyes, wiped her face, and went back down the hall to the bathroom. Walking over to the toilet, she grimaced with distaste and flushed, almost gagging.

She washed her hands in the sink, scrubbing hard, then walked into the bedroom, slumping onto the bed. She was still shaking with anger, but beneath the anger she felt hollow, empty. Her thoughts were rushing a mile a minute, scenes from the past months with Matt running through her head as she tried to determine whether she should have seen this coming.

She sometimes thought it would be easier if she were a lesbian. At least she understood the female mindset. And she wouldn't have to put up with asshole men who tried to tell her what to think and how to act and then betrayed her.

She leaned back onto the mattress.

Lesbian.

She remembered when she was little, promising to marry a girl who lived . . . where? Next door? Down the street? She couldn't remember. She couldn't recall the girl's name either, but she remembered the way she'd looked, dirty and thin, pretty in a natural, unaware, unself-conscious way. Even now, the memory stirred her, and Laurie sat up again, shaking her head.

What was wrong with her?

Maybe she *was* attracted to women. Maybe she'd been repressing her true feelings all these years and that was why she'd consistently picked losers, why she'd failed in her relationships with men each and every time.

No. She thought of Matt's blond bimbo, naked, frantically putting on her clothes, and there was no interest whatsoever, not even a subliminal attraction, only a white-hot anger and a burning core of hate. She'd always considered herself a nonviolent person, a pacifist, but she understood now how people could kill.

If there'd been a gun in the house, she probably would've shot both of them.

She sighed, thought for a moment, then stood and began rummaging through the closet and the drawers of the dresser, taking everything of Matt's and tossing it onto the floor. She gathered it all up, took it out to the living room, threw it on the couch, then went systematically through the rest of the house until she'd found everything he owned.

She threw it all out into the yard, everything, even his art, heaving his camera as hard as she could on the ground, stomping on his precious videotapes before tossing the shattered cassettes onto the grass. The driveway, the yard, the sidewalk were all covered with clothes and books, electronic equipment and CD's, and a group of kids playing baseball in the street had stopped to stare at her, but she didn't care, and she slammed the door again and locked it, already feeling better.

She'd leave it overnight, give him a chance to come back for it. But if his shit was still there in the morning, she'd call the Children's Hospital or some other charity and have them haul it away.

*   *   *

It was a morning without fog, a morning without clouds, and Laurie stood on the stoop staring up at the sky. It was rare in San Francisco that the sun shone this early in the day, that blue showed through before noon, and despite everything that had happened recently, the uncharacteristically good weather brightened her spirits, made her feel, for the first time in over a week, slightly hopeful.

Tia Guiterrez, the young woman next door, waved from her porch. "Beautiful day, huh?"

Laurie nodded. "For once."

"You should call in sick, take the day off."

"You should, too."

Tia smiled. "I am."

Laurie smiled back. It *had* been a long time since she'd taken a day off. And she had accumulated plenty of vacation hours. But, no, she couldn't. There was too much work to do. There was the Mieger account to go over: the customized software that the manufacturer had ordered had apparently not been satisfactory, and now Mieger was pushing for upgrades that he wanted for free and done yesterday. And she was supposed to chair a meeting on flexible benefits packages at three o'clock.

She couldn't take off today.

But she could walk to work. She went back inside, checked her hair in the mirror, popped a few vitamin C's, and picked up her purse and briefcase. Stepping out of the house and locking the door behind her, she waved to Tia, still on the porch, and started off. The day was indeed beautiful, and the sun felt good on her skin, warm and fresh and invigorating. People seemed friendlier on a day like this, and she said more hellos to strangers in the next hour than she had in the past six months.

She was twenty minutes late by the time she reached the office, but no one noticed and no one cared, and she told Mara to hold all of her calls for the next hour while she reviewed the Mieger file.

She didn't review the file, though. She seemed to be having difficulty concentrating, and after reading and rereading the same memo four or five times, Laurie finally gave it up and walked over to the window, looking between the buildings at the bay.

What was she doing here?

It was a question she asked herself periodically but for which she could not seem to find a satisfactory answer.

There comes a point, she thought, when what you do as a temporary stopgap until you "find" yourself hardens into your actual personality. The person you pretended to be, while waiting to discover who you are, becomes the real you.

Was that what had happened to her?

Yes.

She'd been the responsible one, and she'd tried to take care of Josh after their parents had died, to provide for him, to give him as stable a life as she could under the circumstances. She'd always intended to move on at some point, to abandon this job and this lifestyle once her brother settled down and got himself established, but Josh never had settled down, never had gotten himself established, and she'd been promoted onward and upward and at some point it had just not made sense to think about quitting and doing something else.

So here she was.

To top it off, she was now all alone. The foundation of the stable loving relationship in which she'd thought she'd been involved had turned out to be built on quicksand, and she was going to have to start over from scratch—although, after all this time, she was not sure that she still knew how.

Laurie sighed, stared once again out the window, looking down at the street and its tiny toy cars below. Her period was two days late. That's what she was really concerned about, that's what was really on her mind. And while a baby would certainly force a change in her life, she did not want to be carrying Matt's child. She wanted nothing more to do with that sick loser, and despite the fact that her biological clock was winding down, she was not sure that she wanted to be a mother at all. She didn't have any burning desire to reproduce, no deep-seated need to cuddle with something small and cute and fetchingly defenseless, no inclination toward spending the next eighteen years of her life catering to the material needs and overseeing the intellectual and emotional development of another human being.

She wasn't sure she was ready for the responsibilities of taking care of a kitten, let alone a baby.

What if she *was* pregnant? Would she abort it? She wasn't sure. She didn't think so, but she couldn't rule it out. At this point, she had no feelings for whatever might be growing inside her, no protective maternal urges, no bond of any sort. But how could she tell? She might keep it and it might turn out to be a good thing. It might force her to make just the changes she needed in order to slough off this midlife malaise or whatever it was that seemed to be afflicting her.

Or maybe not.

Laurie looked once more out the window, once more toward the bay, then walked back over to her desk and tried once again to get through the Mieger file.

Before heading home, she stopped by the bookstore. Josh was busy, discussing Taoism with an obviously like-minded customer. She wasn't in the mood to hang around for an hour or however long it took for him to wind down, so after browsing politely, waiting a respectable ten minutes, she smiled at him, blew him a kiss good-bye, and started out the door.

"Wait!" he called after her, holding up a hand.

She mimed dialing a phone. "I'll call you," she said in the exaggeratedly simplistic tone she'd use on a deaf person attempting to read her lips.

Her brother nodded from across the store, circled his thumb and forefinger in an "OK" gesture, and turned back toward the customer.

It was late afternoon, the sun already hidden behind two of the taller buildings, and in the shadows of the city this morning's cheerful warmth had disappeared. Above, the sky was still blue and cloudless, but the hidden sinking sun had robbed it of its attraction and Laurie felt cold, lonely, and curiously uneasy as she walked down the littered sidewalk toward her neighborhood. There were a lot of cars on the street but very few pedestrians, and something about it all didn't seem right to her.

Maybe she *was* pregnant. Maybe her hormones were all out of whack and affecting her emotions.

Twenty minutes later, she was out of the downtown business district and passing through an interim area of old buildings and Victorian homes that had been converted into boutiques and coffeehouses when she saw up ahead, parked by the curb in front of Starbuck's, Matt's Mustang.

Her heart started racing. Maybe it wasn't Matt's. Maybe it was someone else's, someone who had the same car in the same color and a similar bumper sticker on the back window. She took a few steps forward, then stopped, looking at the license plate.

It *was* Matt's.

What was he doing here? He didn't even like coffee.

He was probably here on a date.

But why was he staying this close to her neighborhood? She'd expected him to keep as far away from her as possible, had assumed that out of common decency he'd relocate to another area of the city. The last thing she figured he'd do was hang around here. Didn't he have any shame?

Maybe the bitch he was with lived in this area.

That would make sense. He'd probably met the slut when he'd been off one day, cruising around the neighborhood, pretending to work on his art, while she really *had* been at work at Automated Interface.

She thought of waiting for him by his car, embarrassing him, causing a scene, informing him loudly in front of a group of strangers that she was pregnant, but she knew that was just a fantasy. Even now, looking at his car, her heart was pounding so hard it was interfering with her breathing, and there was no way she could get up enough nerve to face him. Not now. Not yet.

She considered continuing down the sidewalk, pretending as though she hadn't noticed, ignoring him if he happened to walk out to his car at the exact moment she passed by, but she decided against it and opted for

crossing the street and cutting down the alley that led
to Union.

The alley was dark, the flanking buildings blocking out
what was left of the late afternoon light. Her uneasiness
returned. The shadows here made her nervous, and she
hurried over the pitted, eroded asphalt toward the opposite end, not running, not wanting to make that concession to fear, but striding quickly, hoping that her anxiety
did not show. She pretended as though it was only the
normal physical dangers of the city that worried her, that
she was afraid of gangs and muggers and derelicts and
drug addicts, but that was not the case. She could spin
it that way, rationalize it, but her nervousness was based
on something less concrete, something ephemeral that
she could not even put her finger on, and whether it was
stress or hormones or another entirely unrelated cause,
all she wanted was to get out of this alley and off the
streets and back home.

The girl was waiting for her at the alley's end.

Laurie was almost to Union, about to step off the
rough asphalt onto the sidewalk, when she saw movement in the shadowed darkness to her right, a flash of
white that startled her and made her suck in her breath.

It was a girl of about ten or eleven, a thin waiflike
child with dirty hair and face and even dirtier clothing:
a white party dress covered with smudges and handprints
and mud-edged rips. Her physical appearance resembled
that of someone who'd been beaten or abused, but there
was no sense of victimization about her, no fear or hesitancy or the sort of emotional withdrawal that would be
expected after such an attack. Indeed, the child seemed
remarkably self-possessed, and she stepped in front of
Laurie, looking up at her. "Hello."

"Hi," Laurie said, and she wasn't aware of it until
she'd spoken the word, but there was something old-
fashioned about the girl, an anachronistic formality evi-
denced by her "Hello," by her purposeful walk and
self-assured bearing, that under other circumstances
would probably be cute and charming but here, in the
alley, seemed unnatural and more than a little
disconcerting.

There was also something vaguely erotic about the child, something sensual in the way her hair fell over the left side of her face, the way she stood, hips out, bare legs slightly spread beneath her dirty dress.

What kinds of thoughts were these?

Laurie looked into the girl's face, saw raw beauty beneath the dirt and grime, saw a knowing, adult expression on those child's features, and she felt a strange and unfamiliar stirring within her, a feeling that was almost . . . sexual.

Sexual?

What the hell was wrong with her?

The girl smiled up at her slyly. "Do you want to see my underwear?"

Laurie shook her head, backed away, but the girl was already lifting up her dirty dress, exposing clean white underpants beneath, and Laurie was looking. She didn't know what was going on here, but the tight cotton and clearly outlined private parts were somehow arousing, and she was unable to turn away.

The girl laughed, a high child's giggle that segued halfway through into a woman's throaty chuckle. She turned around in a circle, still holding up her dress, exposing her pantied buttocks.

Laurie was frightened more than anything else. She did not know what was happening, but she had the sense that she should, that she was supposed to know who this child was and why she was doing this.

The girl was once again facing her, and she smiled knowingly. "Do you want to see my pussy?"

Laurie turned and ran.

She was almost to Union and could've walked around the girl and out to the street, but even the idea of running back through the shadowed alley and perhaps meeting up with Matt seemed preferable to moving any closer to the child and risking accidental contact.

She was out of breath when she reached the sidewalk, but she turned left and kept running, past Matt's unmoved car on the other side of the street, past businesses and houses, up the hill, not stopping until she was home.

She locked the doors, drew the drapes.

She dreamed that night of the girl, and in her dream

the child was naked and in bed with her. She was kissing the girl on the lips, and those lips were soft and knowing, the girl's smooth body warm and deliciously sensual, the feel of her budding breasts achingly erotic. Laurie had never been this aroused before, and though she became aware at some point that this was not real, that she was dreaming, she did not want it to end and she purposely tried to prolong the dream, to manipulate its specifics in order to draw it out. She was rubbing herself against the girl, feeling soft femininity between her legs, and she was wet, wetter than she had ever been in her life, her lubricating juices dripping down her thighs, smearing the skin between them. There was no penetration, but she was already reaching orgasm, and she bit her lip to keep from crying out, involuntary spasms wracking her body as wave after wave of pleasure coursed through her, spreading outward from between her legs.

When she awoke, her period had come.

THREE

Norton

Fall had arrived early this year. It was the end of August and school had just started, but already the trees outside the classroom window were a red and yellow rainbow against the flat gray of the Iowa sky.

Norton Johnson hated to be inside on a day like today. It ran counter to every impulse in his body, and it was on days like this that he seriously considered taking the Board up on their offer and retiring.

There was no way he could retire, though. He turned back toward his class, stared out at the blank bored teenage faces before him. These kids needed him. They didn't know it, but they did. The other teachers in school might think of him as a dinosaur, a relic from an earlier age, but he knew that the only way these students would ever learn anything, the only way they would ever overcome the lax parenting and media overstimulation that was their world, was through someone who cared enough to hold their noses to the grindstone. Straight teaching. That's what they needed. Lectures, notetaking, reading, essays, tests. Not this "cooperative learning," not the current fads of the current educational "experts."

He'd been here before. In the late sixties, early seventies. When teachers had "rapped" to their students. When one of the English classrooms had had beanbag chairs and pillows instead of desks. When students had been allowed to design their own course curriculum and grade their own papers, giving themselves the scores they thought they deserved. He alone had resisted that foolishness, had insisted that there was nothing wrong with the tried and true methods of teaching to which he'd been subjected and that he'd been successfully using for years.

He'd been laughed at then, too. But those days had come. And they'd gone.

And he was still here.

The current educational fallacy was that facts and dates weren't important, that students were better off learning "concepts" rather than information, and he was determined to wait out this trend as well, to remain at the school, to continue on as department chairman until this too had passed.

Still . . .

He looked wistfully out the window. The air probably smelled like fireplace smoke. The slight breeze rattling the trees was probably brisk and cold.

He forced himself to continue on with his lecture.

The fact was, as much as he hated to admit it, his mind wandered more often these days than it had in the past. He was not senile or unfocused or unable to concentrate. It was not that. It was simply that his priorities now were different. Intellectually, his work remained paramount, but emotionally his needs were shifting. He no longer received the same satisfaction from teaching as he had before. He sometimes found himself wanting to gratify simpler, more basic desires.

The verities of old age.

Norton glanced up at the clock above the blackboard. The period was winding down, so he gave a short talk on Mengele and Nazi experimentation and, as always, there was an appreciable increase in the level of attention paid by the class.

He attempted, as usual, to place the information in historical perspective, to give it some context, to impress on the kids why this subject was important. To make them think.

"We're facing the fallout even now," he said. "The Nazi experiments on human beings, onerous as they were, yielded valuable scientific information that could now be put to good use. Therein lies the dilemma. Is that knowledge tainted because of the way in which it was obtained? A lot of people believe that no good can come

of evil and that recognition of the worth of this information would indirectly validate what the Nazis did. There
are other people who believe that knowledge is knowledge, it is neither good nor evil in and of itself, and the
method by which it was obtained should have no bearing
on its validity. Still others believe that if any good can
come of this evil, all of those people would not have died
in vain. It's a complex question with no easy answer."

The bell rang.

"Think about it over the weekend. You may have to
write an essay." He smiled as the students picked up
their books and papers, groaning. "And enjoy your
days off."

"We always do!" Greg Wass yelled as he sped out
the door.

The weather was still gorgeous after school, and Norton cut across the football field to Fifth Street. At the
edge of the field, in the dirt border adjoining the chain-
link fence that separated school property from the sidewalk, he saw a line of huge red ants marching from a
hole in the ground to a discarded lunch sack, and he
stopped for a moment to watch them. It had always
seemed ironic to him that the ant, the Nazi of the insect
kingdom, was the bug most frequently subjected to geno-
cide. Flies and gnats, spiders and beetles, were usually
killed individually. But ants were squashed or sprayed
with poison, killed a hundred, two hundred at a time,
entire colonies wiped out in one stroke.

He frowned, recalling a memory from his childhood,
when he and a neighbor girl had set fire to an anthill,
dousing the small mound of dirt and the surrounding
grassy ground with kerosene before dropping a match
and watching the little insect bodies shrivel and blacken.
They'd thrown other bugs into the fire as well, beetles
and spiders, whatever they could catch, and they'd almost tossed in a kitten but the flames had sputtered out
before they could capture the animal.

He closed his eyes. Where had *that* memory come
from?

He felt suddenly ill at ease, slightly queasy, and he

took a deep breath and walked through the open gate onto the sidewalk. The day no longer seemed so perfect, and instead of strolling slowly, enjoying the cool weather and the premature season, he hurried down Fifth Street toward home.

Carole was cooking dinner in the kitchen when he arrived, but he wasn't in the mood to talk to her, so he called out a cursory greeting, threw his briefcase on the hall tree, grabbed a *Newsweek* from the magazine rack, and locked himself in the bathroom. He stayed in there for almost a half hour, until Carole knocked on the door and asked if he was going to spend the night on the toilet or come out and eat. He yelled that he'd be out in a minute, and when he walked into the dining room, the table was set and the good china was out. In the center of the table was a full salad bowl, a plate of mashed potatoes, and a small basket of rolls.

Uh-oh, he thought.

Carole emerged from the kitchen carrying a silver tray upon which sat a delicious-smelling roast.

"What is it?" he asked as she placed the tray on the table.

"What is what?"

"This." He gestured around the table. "What's up?"

"Nothing," she said. "I'm in a good mood and I wanted to have a nice dinner. Is that a crime?"

"No, it's not a crime. But you don't usually go to all this trouble unless you want something. Or . . ." He looked at her. "Did you have an accident? Is the car dented?"

She glared at him. "That's insulting. I told you, I was just in a good mood." She paused. *"Was."*

They stared at each other for a moment, then Carole turned and strode back into the kitchen. Norton sat down to eat. The food looked delicious, and he piled his plate high with generous helpings of everything. Carole returned, placing a glass of milk before him.

They ate for a while in silence, a welcome change and a state of affairs he thoroughly enjoyed, but Carole was obviously discomfited by the lack of conversation, and she finally broke down.

"Don't you even want to know why I'm in a good mood? Why I'm happy?"

He sighed. "Why are you happy?"

"Because we had our first CLO meeting of the season."

"So what are you doing this year? *Annie* again? The world always needs more amateur productions of *Annie.*"

She slammed her fork down on the table. "You pompous ass."

"What are you talking about?"

"Why do you always have to belittle everything that I do?"

"I don't belittle everything you do."

"What do you call it, then?"

"I'm not—"

"Not what? Criticizing? You sure the hell are. And for your information, we're doing Sondheim's *Company* this year." She glared at him. "And don't you dare say we don't have the talent for it."

"I wasn't going to," he said.

But he was. That was exactly what he'd been about to say. And he was only able to claim the high road now because she talked faster than he did and hadn't allowed him to put his foot in his mouth.

Why did he do this? he wondered. What compelled him to attack her, to disparage her abilities, to mock her accomplishments, to denigrate everything she did? It wasn't that he thought himself superior, as she often suggested. It wasn't that he felt inferior and belittled others in an attempt to make up for it, either. No, it was simpler than that. Simpler, and at the same time, more complex.

He liked to hurt people.

The ants.

He took a deep breath, stared down at his mashed potatoes. It was a hard admission to make, a clear-eyed yet withering self-assessment, an understanding of himself that he'd rather not possess. Not many people could recognize or acknowledge such a base and reprehensible motive—

Jesus, he thought. He was even using this as fodder for self-congratulation, complimenting himself for recognizing that he was a bastard.

What the hell was wrong with him?

It had all started with those damn ants.

He looked across the table at Carole. "I'm sorry," he said. "I'm . . . I've just had a bad day."

"It's not only today," she told him.

"I know, I know—"

"No. You don't know."

"What do you want me to do, Carole? I said I'm sorry."

"You're an arrogant, self-centered jerk sometimes."

"I—"

"I don't want to talk to you right now, Nort. Just shut up and eat your dinner."

They finished the rest of the meal in silence, and afterward he went out into the living room to watch a documentary on the Civil War on A&E while she retreated into the kitchen.

He finished grading the last test paper and put it on the pile, shaking his head. He hadn't had high expectations to begin with, but the scores were even worse than he thought they'd be.

Kids seemed to be getting dumber and dumber each year.

He sighed, grabbed his cup, finished off the last lukewarm swallow of coffee. They weren't really stupid, these students, but they weren't educated and had no desire to be so. They had no intellectual guidance, no one to tell them what they should know and why they should know it. "The post-literate generation," he'd heard them called, and that was as good a description as any. They did not read, were not conversant with the essential facts and ideas at the core of Western culture, were not even up on current events, but they had an encyclopedic knowledge of twenty-year-old television shows and bad popular music. Even his best students were smart in the wrong way: media-savvy kids who dealt in trivia, the intellectual currency of their time.

It was a sad state of affairs.

Norton rubbed his tired eyes, looked up at the clock over the bookcase. Midnight. Carole had gone to sleep several hours ago, and he should have too, but there'd been that Civil War show and then these tests to grade, and now it was already Thursday. He stood, stretched. He could've done what most of his colleagues did and postponed the grading for another day. Or he could have given a scantron test instead of an essay test and let the machine grade them.

But he wasn't about to sacrifice his principles, to change his teaching habits for the sake of expediency, and though he was bone-tired and would only be able to catch a few hours of sleep, at least he could face himself in the morning.

He walked into the kitchen, put his cup in the dishwasher, then walked down the hallway to the bathroom to take out his bridge.

Carole was dead asleep and snoring when he went into the bedroom, and she did not wake up even when he turned on the light. He took off his clothes, carefully folded them, and placed them on the cedar chest at the foot of the bed, then once again turned off the light. He felt his way through the darkness over to the bed, lifted the covers, and got in.

Carole moaned, stirred, rolled over.

Her body felt warm next to his, almost hot. She often called him a "corpse" because of their difference in body temperatures, and he had to smile when she said that because it wasn't too far off the mark. He was getting on in years, and a lifetime of soft self-indulgence had probably made his body even more decrepit than it ordinarily would be. He was old and he knew it, and he wouldn't be surprised when his heart or his liver or one of his other organs started to give out.

Carole was quite a bit younger than he was, forty-five to his sixty-two, and there was something comforting about knowing that he would die first. It was selfish, of course, but he'd always been selfish to a certain extent and the charge didn't bother him. He wouldn't have to carry on without her, wouldn't have to make another seismic shift in his life. It would be hard on her, of course, but she was stronger than he was, she could handle it. Hell, she'd probably remarry.

So why was he such a prick to her?

He wasn't a prick all the time. Even she had to admit that. He'd been head over heels for her when they'd first married, and while the passion may have cooled, he did still love her. Only these days, he seemed to be annoyed by her more often than entranced, easily irritated by her behavior, what she said and what she did consistently rubbing him the wrong way. He didn't know why. It was probably his fault. He didn't think she had changed over the years. But he had. Something in his life had shifted, some nascent gene of solitary bachelorhood kicking in as he got older, making him prefer to remain alone rather than in the company of others. There'd been a settling in his ways, a hardening of his attitudes, and though he still loved Carole, still cared about her, still needed her, it had become increasingly hard to like her, to be with her.

He glanced next to him. She remained very attractive, though. Even in sleep, even with her mouth open, her hair wild, face cream clumped on her cheeks, chin and forehead, she was an extremely pretty woman. And he could not imagine going to bed without her stretched out beside him. He still enjoyed being with her when she was awake as well—it was *talking* to her that was becoming increasingly difficult. When they sat alone in a room, he reading, she sewing, one or both of them watching TV, each performing separate activities, it was nice. Only talk brought out their differences, only conversation brought out his annoyance and hostility, made him feel that perhaps he should have remained a single man.

If they were both mute, they could have a happy life.

He settled into sleep beside her, and she turned onto her side. He stretched one arm over her shoulder, resting his hand on her breast, and she pressed her buttocks against his groin, automatically finding, even in sleep, the position they'd discovered to be most comfortable.

Despite his tiredness and the lateness of the hour, he

did not fall asleep instantly but drifted slowly off, his mind focusing on nothing and everything, his thoughts moving from Carole to school to old friends to his 1953 trip to Italy to the president's recent trip to Japan, floating gradually away in ever-widening circles, his brain making connections of logic that were at first tenuous, then not there at all but seemed perfectly natural as sleep overtook him.

He was awakened by violent shaking.

Norton sat up immediately, his panicked heart thumping as though it were about to burst through his chest. He thought at first it was an earthquake but realized almost instantly that only the bed was shaking, that the hanging plant next to the curtained window was still, that the rest of the room was not in motion.

A foot kicked his leg. A hand lashed out at his midsection.

It was Carole.

She was having convulsions.

He had no idea what to do, and even as he kicked off the covers and twisted around, grabbing her shoulders, trying to hold her down and stop her from shaking, he was cursing himself for not attending the CPR seminar the last time they'd had a teacher's in-service day. He hadn't thought there'd ever be a practical use for it. Carole was in better health than he was, and he couldn't see himself doing anything to help a stranger except dial 911, so he'd chosen to stay in his classroom and rearrange his bulletin boards instead of attend the emergency medical training.

Now he felt lost and frightened and completely out of his depth. Carole's eyes were wide open and jiggling crazily in their sockets as her entire head shook in staccato spasms. Her mouth was open, tongue hanging out, looking twice as long as he knew it to be, and saliva was flying out in all directions, strings of it stretched over her cheeks and chin, independent spray hitting the pillow and the blanket and his arm. Beneath his hands, the muscles of her chest and shoulders were knotted and tight, much stronger than any muscles he'd ever felt before, and they were jerking nonstop in a frighteningly unnatural way.

He didn't know what was happening. He was pretty sure this wasn't a heart attack, but whether it was an epileptic fit or a stroke or the result of some sort of brain tumor, he had no clue. It was like something out of a movie, like a possession, and he had no idea if he was supposed to be holding her still or leaving her alone or giving her some kind of medicine. He'd heard somewhere that if someone was having a fit you were supposed to put a wallet in their mouth to keep them from swallowing their tongue, but Carole's tongue was flopping around outside her mouth, and she appeared in no danger of swallowing it.

The fit wasn't letting up.

He didn't know how much time had passed since she'd started convulsing, since the shaking had awakened him, but even adjusting for his skewed perceptions, it had to have been several minutes.

Shouldn't it have stopped by now?

If anything, the muscles beneath his grip were becoming more rigid, their vibrating spasms stronger and more violent. How long could a body continue undergoing something like this without sustaining permanent damage? Wasn't her brain being smacked around in that jerking head? Weren't her organs being knocked about inside her chest cavity?

There'd been no sound coming out of her mouth, only the unnaturally silent, almost sibilant noises of her convulsing body, overpowered by the loud wood-on-wood sound of the headboard hitting the wall, but now there was a low humming coming from somewhere deep within her throat, a humming broken by vibrato as the sound escaped her wildly shaking head.

He let go, got off her, leaped from the bed. This had gone too far. It wasn't slowing or abating, and it was obvious that his attempt to hold her still, to force her body to stop shaking, to *will* her convulsions to end, was not working at all.

He ran out of the bedroom, ran for the phone, picked it up from the alcove in the hall, dialing 911 at the same time he tried to lift the receiver to his head. He told the robotically calm woman at the other end of the line who he was, where he was, and what was happening, and though the entire conversation probably took no more than one minute, it felt like fifteen. The woman promised to immediately dispatch paramedics and an ambulance, and he dropped the phone without bothering to hang up and ran back down the hallway to the bedroom.

By the time he returned, the attack was all over. Carole had stopped convulsing.

She was dead.

FOUR

Stormy

Stormy Salinger drove back from Taos along the series of interconnected roads that led through the Sangre de Cristo Mountains. The highway was faster, but he preferred the back way, and he hauled ass on the stretches between villages to make up the time.

Through the windshield, the huge sky was light blue, the ever-present white clouds retreating to infinity like a Georgia O'Keeffe painting.

He loved this drive. The meadows, the streams, the trees, the ranches. This was why he had moved here, why he had left Los Angeles. He shut off the air-conditioning, rolled down the car window, felt the wind in his face, smelled pine and hay, dust and water.

In L.A., he'd been afraid to roll down his windows as he drove. Not just because of the potential for carjackings and robberies, not just because he'd be hit up for money by the homeless vets who staked out intersections and on-ramps, but because the air itself was poisonous. The dirtiest air in the country, year in and year out. Hell, even on days that had what southern California's TV weathermen called "good air quality," it was still rare to see the San Gabriel Mountains until you were almost on top of them.

That was not a way to live.

He'd grown tired of Los Angeles: the place, the people, the lifestyle. He'd grown tired of his friends as well, their smugness, their self-absorption, their condescending attitude toward anyone outside their clique, the mandatory elitism that afflicted what passed for their culture. He'd fallen in with a group of film snobs—hip writers for entertainment publications, young academics from

prestigious film schools, wannabe indie figures—people
with little in common save their interest in cinema. As
a successful video distributor, a lifelong movie fan who
had made millions working on the fringes of filmdom,
he himself was an inspiration to his friends, proof that
the wall could be breached, yet he knew that while they
pretended to be supportive of him and had no qualms
about taking advantage of his generosity, they were, at
the same time, jealous, and when a serious discussion of
film came about—as it often did—his opinions were
treated with slightly less respect, just to let him know
that he was not really in their intellectual league.

That had always irritated the hell out of him.

He was the only member of the group who exhibited
even the least bit of independence, who did not automatically fall in with the prevailing opinion and conform to
preexisting tastes with lockstep homogeneity. They were
nobodies, really, but they always acted as though they
were society's arbiters of filmic quality, and it was a
given that any film of which they approved was a work
of art. They'd sit around and summarily dismiss contemporary comedies, yet rhapsodize about a Laurel and
Hardy pie fight. It wasn't that the pie fight was intrinsi-
cally better than, say, the slapstick antics in a Jim Carrey
movie, it was just that *they* considered it "classic," and
that was automatically supposed to elevate its level of
quality.

He'd grown increasingly tired of this intellectual inces-
tuousness over the years, weary of the monotonic interests and attitudes. It was partly his fault. They were his
friends and he had chosen them. He'd made his bed and
had to lie in it.

So he'd simply pulled up stakes one day, sold off his
Brentwood estate, and relocated to Santa Fe.

Now he conducted his business from here.

Stormy sped through Truchas, the small village where
Robert Redford had filmed *The Milagro Beanfield War*.

He'd first visited New Mexico as a teenager, on a trip
with his family, and he had never forgotten the place.
They'd done the tourist loop—White Sands, Carlsbad
Caverns, Santa Fe, Taos Pueblo—and it had made a big

impression on him. He was a city kid, born and bred in Chicago, and the dry heat, the open space, and the spectacular sky had all spoken to him in a way that nothing else had. He'd realized even then that this was where he wanted to live when he grew up, where he wanted to spend his life.

But the movie and video business was centered in southern California, and by the time he'd made enough money to move here, he'd gotten sucked into that L.A. lifestyle, and it was not until several years later that he finally made the break.

It was a decision he'd never regretted.

He passed through Chimayo and could not help glancing down the small one-lane road that led to El Santuario. The small adobe church had always creeped him out. All those crutches and braces hanging in the small dark room with the miracle dirt. Legend had it that the church was built on dirt that had healing powers, and each year, hordes of believers flocked to the spot to have their diseases and deformities cured, the ones who claimed to find relief from infirmity leaving their walking aides behind. He wasn't a religious man himself, he neither believed nor disbelieved, but there seemed something paganistic and primitive, something pre-Christian about this sort of Christianity. Maybe he'd just been watching too many of the movies he distributed, but the whole thing made him uneasy.

Ten minutes later, he hit the highway and was speeding toward downtown Santa Fe.

He arrived back at his office before three.

"How'd it go?" Joan asked as he walked through the door.

"Who knows? That bastard's impossible to read." He sat down in the oversized chair behind his desk, opened the jar of candy next to his computer, and popped a handful of M&Ms into his mouth. He'd been in Taos talking to the organizer of the film festival, trying to get one of his properties shown in competition this year. He had what he thought was a legitimate find, a retelling of *Macbeth* on an Indian reservation, made by an untrained twenty-five-year-old Hopi kid who'd financed the film by working as a park ranger at Betatakin and saving his money over several summers.

It was one of those success stories that the entertainment media seemed to love so much these days, and he knew he could get a lot of hype out of it. The movie was part of a package deal he'd made with Four Corners, a local distributor that'd gone belly-up, and while most of the titles were routine action flicks, this was an honest-to-God *film,* and for the first time in his life, Stormy saw the opportunity to present to the viewing public a legitimate work by an undiscovered talent.

Maybe he'd try to take it to Sundance.

That would certainly up his cache in the business.

And, besides, the kid deserved it.

He tried to imagine the reaction of his old L.A. friends when they discovered that he was distributing a film that had been shown in competition at Sundance, and the pictures in his mind made him smile.

"You want me to call back tomorrow?" Joan asked. "Apply a little pressure?"

Stormy nodded. "Tell him to make sure he watches the tape. And tell him he has forty-eight hours. Sundance is interested."

Her eyes widened. "Really?"

Stormy grinned. "No." He paused dramatically. "At least not yet."

"We have a winner here, don't we?"

"I think we do," he said.

He worked late sorting through contracts. Joan had already left, so Stormy closed up the office and locked up. Roberta would be at her class by the time he got home, so on the way back, he pulled into the drive-thru lane at Burger King and ordered a Whopper, fries, and a chocolate shake. Roberta was constantly harping on him about his dietary habits, claiming that a person who ate the way he did didn't deserve to be wealthy, as though it were his moral obligation to eat gourmet meals all the time, but he failed to see how the fact that his taste in food was different from hers made him a deserving candidate for poverty. Like most overweight people, she put far too much emphasis on food, considered it a much too important part of life. If she considered sex as important as eating and put as much effort into their lovemaking as she did deciding what she ate, they might still have a marriage.

Sex.

It had been what? A month? Two months? He wasn't sure. They hadn't done it in a while, that he knew.

He tried to remember the first girl he'd ever had. What was her name? Dawn? Donna? Something like that. Strange that he couldn't recall. Weren't you always supposed to remember your first? She'd been poor and dirty. He remembered that much. And that had been part of the allure. She was not like the perfectly scrubbed examples of femininity that were invited over to the house; she was different, wild, and he had liked that. She'd made him do things to her that he hadn't even known about, and in that one summer he had learned everything about sex he had ever needed to know.

It had been all downhill from there.

He hadn't thought of that girl in a long time, and he tried to recall what had happened, why they had broken up. It had probably been after the fire, after they'd moved, but he couldn't remember for sure.

He sighed. It didn't matter. He pulled up in front of the house, parked next to the ocotillo on the edge of the driveway. He sat for a moment in the car, staring through the windshield at the darkened windows of the house, and not for the first time, he wished that he had never gotten married, that he had never met Roberta.

On Friday, as usual, he left the office early and went to The Hogan. It was a regular bar, not an artist's bar, and there were none of the phony Southwest accoutrements that supposedly lent ambience to Santa Fe's hipper hangouts and that he found so annoying and distracting.

Jimbo was working today, and Stormy asked for a Bud Lite and stood at the bar waiting for his order while the bartender moved to fill it. There were two guys halfway down the counter having a loud conversation, and Stormy tuned it in.

"Whatever happened to strongmen?" the guy closest to him was saying: "Remember how we always called leaders of countries we didn't like 'Strongmen'? There was Panamanian Strongman Manuel Noriega, Libyan Strongman Mohammar Khadafi. We never used 'General,' 'President,' or whatever the hell their official title was. It was always 'Strongman.' Why don't we do that anymore?"

"You're drunk," his companion said.

"Maybe so. But it's a legitimate question."

"We only do that if we want to provoke a confrontation with them," Stormy offered. "We do it to teach our people that these are bad guys. It gets the public ready for war."

The drunk looked up. "Who are you, you anti-American son of a bitch?"

His friend put a restraining hand on his arm.

Stormy smiled apologetically. "Sorry. Didn't mean to butt in."

The drunk pointed. "I know your mama. She was giving pony rides, handing out ass candy."

Jimbo arrived with his beer, and Stormy paid. "Thanks."

He headed over to a table next to the jukebox at the far end of the room.

"I'm talking to you!" the drunk yelled.

"Shut up!" his friend told him.

Stormy ignored the man, sipped his beer. It had been a good afternoon. Taos had taken the Hopi kid's film, and had not only put it in competition but had given it one of the coveted prime-time slots. To top it off, the straight-to-video *Fat Lady,* a horror sexploitation flick that he'd picked up after a minor studio had dropped it, had just gotten a rave review in *Fangoria,* the slice-and-dice bible. Which meant that sales and rentals would probably go through the roof.

Sometimes life was good.

He looked at his watch. Four-ten. Ken was supposed to meet him here at four-fifteen, but his friend was chronically late and he was prepared to wait until four-thirty, He took another sip of beer, a small one, trying to make it last.

To his surprise, Ken arrived on time for once. He flagged down Carlene, the waitress, ordered a Miller, and settled heavily into the chair opposite Stormy.

"Nice day at the office?"

"It's always a party when you work for a coroner. I told you, anytime you want you can come on down and I'll give you a tour, let you see what it's like."

"No thanks."

"We had a cancer death today."

"I take it that's worse than a regular death?"

"Looking at it's not that bad, but the smell . . ." Ken shook his head. "When you pop someone open with colon cancer, that's a smell you won't forget."

"This is really appetizing. Are we going to order some hors d'oeuvres?"

Ken grinned. "Sure. Liver pâté?"

"That's truly disgusting."

"You're a wussboy."

"And you're a senseless psycho who's completely inured to blood and guts."

Ken shrugged. "You get used to it. I mean, before AIDS, we used to buy our lunch at McDonald's and put the sacks on top of the open bodies and eat. Sometimes, if people came to visit, we'd intentionally gross them out and play catch with, like, a spleen. You know, just to freak them," He laughed. "But now everyone's pretty careful. AIDS and O.J., man. They've really put a damper on the body biz. Things just aren't as fun anymore."

Carlene arrived with Ken's beer, and Stormy asked for another for himself.

"I'm telling you," Ken said. "You oughta put shit like that in a movie. Show 'em what it's like in a real coroner's office. People'd love it."

"I don't make movies, I distribute them. And aside from the *Faces of Death* crowd, I don't think there's a big market for stuff like that. There aren't as many weirdos in the world as you might think there are."

"Speaking of weird, I was talking to Tom Utchaca

yesterday about what's happening out by the reservation."

"What is happening out by the reservation?"

"A lot of strange shit's been going down."

Stormy leaned forward. This was getting interesting.

"You know Tom, right? He's not stupid and he's not superstitious." Ken lowered his voice. "He says his father's come back to the reservation."

"I thought his father was dead."

"He is."

Stormy blinked, started to say something, closed his mouth.

"Said he saw him in back of his parents' old place. The house is abandoned, I guess, and he was driving by on his way somewhere and saw his father standing there in the empty field. He stopped the car because he wanted to make sure he was seeing what he thought he was seeing, and his father smiled and waved at him and started walking over.

"Tom took off.

"And he's not the only one. A lot of the people say their dead are coming back. Tom doesn't know what the hell to think, but he said the word going around the reservation is that the netherworld is full, that there's no more room for the dead and some of them are leaking out, coming back into our world."

Against his will, Stormy felt a slight tingle pass down his spine. "Are these supposed to be ghosts or actual resurrected bodies?"

"Bodies. Resurrected and restored. They're not rotting zombies, they're back and good as new. Tom said his father looked like he did in his prime."

"You don't actually believe this shit, do you?"

"I've known Tom a long time, and I haven't seen anything myself yet but, yeah, I believe him."

"You deal with dead bodies every day. How can you—?"

"How can I what?" He paused. "You know, the more I learn, the more I realize how little I know. It's a cliché, but I thought I knew everything when I got out of school, and when I first started this job I wouldn't have believed a story like that if Tom's father had walked into my bedroom and grabbed my dick. But I've learned over the years to listen to more than just the textbook facts in my head. I've learned to read people and situations. And as crazy as this sounds, I think it's legitimate. I think it's true."

Stormy wanted to laugh at his friend, wanted to berate him for falling for such superstitious crap, but the sincerity of Ken's belief lent it a verisimilitude that Stormy found disconcerting.

"The thing is, it's not just the dead. Seems that people on the reservation have seen dolls that are . . . animated. Those kachinas they make for the tourists. I gather the dollmakers won't even go near the workshop anymore. It's all closed up."

"Tom told you all this?"

"Oh, no. You know him. I only found out about his father because I asked him. I'd heard elsewhere that some strange stuff was happening, and I wanted to check on it."

Stormy stared down into the bottom of his empty glass. Something about all this sounded vaguely familiar, but he was not quite able to put his finger on it. Had it been in a movie? He didn't think so. The connection was more real, more personal, more immediate. The specifics of it eluded him, but he saw these strange occurrences as an extension of something that had happened before—although he did not know what that "something" was.

He cleared his throat. "The 'animated' dolls. They walk? At night?"

Ken nodded. "You got it."

He could have guessed that. It was logical. What else would *animated* dolls do? But he hadn't guessed. He had known. Or remembered. He wasn't sure which. In his mind was a picture of a ragged primitive doll rocking slowly on unbending legs, making its determined way down a long dark hallway.

A long dark hallway?

He didn't want to think about this, and he was grateful that Carlene brought his beer over to the table at just that moment. He paid her and tipped her, made some small talk to try and keep her there, but The Hogan was getting crowded as other people got off work and she had to hurry over to fill their orders.

Ken was about to tell him something else about the reservation, some other supernatural event that had happened, but Stormy cut him off before he got out the first word, changing the subject, asking if Ken had had a chance to look at any of the videotapes he'd lent him last week. He had, and he'd really hated one of them, and he started going off on it, telling Stormy how much he'd disliked the movie, and Stormy pretended to be offended, pretended to defend the film, but inside he breathed a sigh of relief, thankful they'd gotten off the subject of the reservation.

But it was still there, in his mind, and he thought about it through drinks, through dinner, on the way home, and by the time he went to bed that night, crawling next to an already sleeping Roberta, he was almost positive that he himself had once owned a doll that had been alive.

FIVE

Mark

Kristen is dead.

Mark was sitting alone in the large corner booth of Denny's in Indio when the knowledge came to him, and it took a moment for the information to register. He was holding the cup of cold coffee in his hand, pretending to drink so the waitress wouldn't come over and ask if he wanted a refill, staring out the window at the rusted boxcars sitting unattached on the train tracks across the highway. The sky was brightening, the high desert clouds now sunrise pink against the light blue background sky. Early morning traffic—cross-country trucks and occasional cars—was beginning to congest the formerly empty roadway outside.

Then the realization hit him.

Kristen is dead.

He nearly dropped the cup but managed through a sheer effort of will to force his trembling hands to replace it on the saucer. He had no idea how she had died or why, there were no specifics, but he knew with certainty that she was gone.

He was the only one left.

He had not seen his sister in over a decade. When he'd left home, she'd been a sixteen-year-old girl with braces, just emerging from that ugly duckling stage, the beautiful woman she would become visible in the arrangement of her features but still a year or so away. It had been harder to leave Kristen than his parents or friends or anyone else, and it was for her that he'd almost stayed. He'd tried all that summer to convince her to come with him, to convince her that she could only escape by uprooting herself and running like hell as far away from Dry River as she could, but she'd told him that she didn't want to escape, didn't need to escape, was happy where she was.

Now she was dead.

In the back of his mind, he'd known it would come to this, and he felt guilty for not making more of an effort to save her, for not going back to talk to her. Of course, he'd sent letters, but that was not the same, and his letters had always been about himself, not her, about where he was, what he was doing, where he was going.

He had not felt bad when his father died. The information had come to him, he'd registered it, then gone on with his life. It was then that he should have gone back for Kristen. He'd thought about it. He'd been living in Colorado Springs at the time, working in a frame shop, and had been on his afternoon break, sitting on the steps in back of the shop, smoking, looking up at the clouds, when the knowledge came to him that his father was gone. He knew he should feel sad, and part of him had *wanted* to feel sad, but too much had happened over too long a time, and all he could feel was a slight regret that the two of them had not been able to make a closer connection.

He'd finished smoking his cigarette, ground out the butt with his boot, and gone back into the shop to finish his afternoon shift.

That was when he should have returned home. That was when he should have gone back for Kristen.

He'd considered it, and that night in his apartment he'd gotten as far as dialing the number of the house. Strange how he hadn't forgotten the number after all those years. But he'd hung up after the first ring and had spent the rest of the evening staring at the phone. He'd half hoped that Kristen would call *him*, but of course she couldn't. Even if she had sensed something, she didn't know his current phone number.

The next day he'd quit his job at the frame shop, collected his last paycheck, and sent a postcard to Kristen as he headed toward Utah.

Kristen.

He'd failed her. More than anything else in the world,

he had wanted to protect her, save her, keep her from becoming trapped like all the rest of them, but in that he had failed utterly. He had not been there for her when she'd needed him, had been too afraid for himself to go back for her.

The smart thing now would be for him to keep moving, not look back, to grieve for Kristen on his own, in his own way, and to continue on with his life. He had not gone home in all this time; there was no reason for him to return now. Everything would be auctioned off and sold in an estate sale when he could not be located and then it would all be over.

But he could not do that. Not this time. He owed it to Kristen to tie things up, to go back.

And he had to know how she'd died.

Dawn was giving way to morning, and outside the window he could see date palms where before there had only been trees. He picked up his cup, drank the last dredges of the cold coffee. Denny's was starting to fill up. There were families of travelers in two of the booths to his right, casually clothed construction workers ordering breakfast at the counter.

Mark reached down for his backpack. Through the door walked an old woman and her teenage niece or granddaughter. The young girl was dark, with long black hair, and for some reason she reminded him of Kristen. All of a sudden he felt like crying.

He scooted out of the booth, left a dollar in the ashtray for the coffee and a tip, and walked quickly outside.

He stood in front of the restaurant, breathing deeply. The air was warm and dry and felt good in his lungs, each breath seeming to siphon away the tears threatening to well up in his eyes.

What had Kristen been like as an adult? he wondered. Or had she ever been an adult? She was twenty-six years old, but years meant nothing. In his mind, he still saw her the way she was when he'd left, obsessed with cute boys and popular music and schoolgirl gossip. He remembered how she'd cried when he left and how he'd promised to come back and visit, and he remembered the way her arms had felt around him as she'd hugged him good-bye.

He began to cry.

Angrily, he wiped away the tears. He took a deep breath, shouldered his backpack, started walking. Most people, he knew, would want someone to talk to, a shoulder to cry on, but he was glad he was alone. Grief, he believed, was a private experience, not meant to be shared. He did not want to think about other people's needs at this moment, whether he was soaking their good shirt with his tears, whether he was keeping them from an appointment or making them late for a meal, whether he was being too needy or too emotional or not emotional enough. He needed at this moment to be completely alone, completely selfish, so that he could feel what he had to feel for as long as he had to feel it without the influence of another person affecting his emotions.

A pickup sped past him, and a half-full McDonald's cup splattered on the ground at his feet, coffee splashing onto the cuffs of his jeans. He heard a harsh laugh as the driver drove away.

"Asshole," Mark mumbled.

Still, the encounter had brought him back into the real world, the practical world, and for that he was grateful.

He thought for a moment, then hurried across the highway to the opposite side. He faced the oncoming traffic, held out his thumb. He'd been heading for southern California, planning to look for construction work in Los Angeles, but now he was going to do something he should have done a long, long time ago.

He was going to go home.

The Land Rover drove down Highway 60, the driver silent, Mark still mulling over in his mind the fact that his sister was gone. He'd slept last night in the desert outside of Quartzite, and though he'd expected to spend the entire night unable to sleep, staring up at the stars, he had dozed off almost immediately after crawling into his sleeping bag and had not awakened until the sun had come up over the mountains.

The Power was fading. As long as Kristen had been alive, as long as there had been that blood connection, he had been able to tap into it, reference it, but now it was growing weaker by the hour, only a faint pulse remaining, and soon it would be gone. Already, he was having to use his own memory, to rely on his own thoughts and hunches. He was dismayed to realize how much he had relied on The Power, how much a part of him it was, and now that it was disappearing, he felt more isolated than he ever had in his life, as though one of his senses—his sight or his hearing—had been taken away.

He hadn't even been aware of how often he used it.

That was a little scary.

He probably wouldn't have gotten into this vehicle if he hadn't been able to take a reading of the driver.

It looked like his hitchhiking days were over.

Kristen was the real loss, though. Not having The Power was a mere inconvenience. Kristen's death was a tragedy.

They drove toward Phoenix, a series of dying desert towns bleeding into each other, empty cinder-block buildings in the open spaces between them making it difficult to determine where one town ended and the next began.

Through the side window, Mark saw a rock shop. Faded pink paint on a dirty window read: SALE!! AGATES! JASPER! GEODES! Tireless cars sat on blocks next to the store, their exposed axles rusted and sagging, wrecked corners of their bodies twisted into unrecognizability.

A white cross near a burned section of desert memorialized some driver's death, and Mark wondered who was taking care of Kristen's burial arrangements. Would Billings still be there? he wondered. Would the assistant have remained even after their parents' deaths? Would Kristen have kept him on or would she have let him go? Did Kristen have any friends? Maybe they were seeing to the arrangements.

He just hoped he didn't arrive too late. He wanted to be there for the funeral. And if there was no funeral, if the county or some social services agency simply provided her with a generic burial, he wanted to make sure that that was rectified, that she was put to rest with dignity.

Kristen deserved at least that much.

Mark closed his eyes, lulled by the heat and silence and the motion of the Land Rover. In his mind, he saw Kristen as she'd looked the last time he'd seen her: shorts and a tank top, hair long and straight and blond, sunlight glinting off her braces, tears in her eyes, the house behind her.

The house.

He did not think of the house too often, tried not to think of it at all. He remembered as a child watching *Giant* on television and being freaked out by how eerily similar the gothic ranch house was to that of his own family. Like the structure in the movie, their home sat alone on a flat desert plain, an island of darkness in an endless sea of tan. Two and a half stories with a wraparound porch, the house, with its deep gray-black wood and permanently shuttered windows, its gables and wrought-iron weathervanes, gave the impression of age, permanence, and old-fashioned authoritarian power. It was an intimidating building, and it had always frightened his friends from school, had always been the recipient of wide-eyed stares and hesitant approaches, treated with trepidation and barely concealed fear—unlike the house in the movie, which, despite its appearance, had been treated as though it was not unusual, not out of the ordinary, yet another average ranch building.

The movie had disturbed him. It was not traditionally scary, was a light epic drama with comedic overtones, but the specter of the ranch house, its dark prominence, had been more than a little unsettling. Halfway through the film, the interior of the house had changed, been remodeled, and that wasn't so bad. The lighter walls and furniture looked fake, setbound, and that had enabled him to disassociate the movie home from his own.

His father, he remembered, had loved that film.

He'd known early on that there was something different about his family. They hadn't socialized with the other people in the extended series of adjoining ranches known as the town of Dry River, his parents keeping to themselves, associating only with his father's assistant Billings and with the occasional old friends or relatives who visited from back east. Even when Mark had started going to school and making friends of his own, he had the impression that his parents disapproved, that they would rather he not bring any other kids home—which seemed to be fine with his friends since they were afraid of the house anyway. He'd ended up spending most of his childhood at other people's houses, inventing a family that did not exist in the stories he told, lying and exaggerating in order to make his parents seem more normal, expanding his personal mythology to include Kristen when she'd come along.

It had been the ritualization of their lives, he supposed, that had first caused him to start thinking about moving away, the fact that his father made them eat breakfast every morning at exactly six o'clock, made them eat dinner at six each evening, made them sit in exactly the same spots each time, made them all go to bed at precisely nine o'clock, made them sit in separate rooms for an hour each night reciting their Daily Words. Other parents didn't do that, he knew. People sometimes said prayers, ate together, but they didn't regiment their lives to the extent that his parents did.

And they did not beat their children when some slight mistake or miscalculation made them a second or two late for one of these ritualized practices.

As his parents did.

But, still, they were his family. And there was no way that he could leave Kristen. She needed him. He took the heat that would have otherwise fallen on her. And he kept her from buying into their parents' wackiness completely, kept her grounded as much as possible in the real world.

Then it had happened.

Even now, goose bumps popped up on his arms when he thought about it.

It had been a Saturday afternoon. Midsummer. Monsoon season. Kristen and his parents had gone into town, and he was alone. Billings was somewhere on the property, seeing to the chickens. Mark did not like being by himself in the house, even though he had lived there his entire life, and until now he had successfully avoided finding himself in this predicament, had not been alone in here since the time when he was five and had gotten lost in the maze of passageways and his father had rescued him, screaming, from a darkened hall that seemed to have no end.

He was older now, a high school graduate, but he still felt like a little kid, still felt that same sense of oppressive fear as he sat in his bedroom and realized that there was no one home but himself. He considered going outside, finding something to do in the barn or in the field or in the coops until his parents returned, but his room was upstairs and he didn't want to have to walk all the way down the hall, down the stairs, through the living room and through the sitting room in order to go outside. It was a long way to the front door, and he thought it would be better if he just sat in here and waited with the door closed until someone else came home.

He had a stereo by his bed, and he kept his tunes cranked up while he read a car magazine, trying not to think of the silent emptiness of the house surrounding him, but the afternoon storm hit an hour or so later and, as often happened, the electricity went out. His lights flicked off, his music fading into a slowing deep-bassed growl before disappearing completely.

The window in his room overlooked the drive and the front yard, but the clouds were dark today and very little light entered the room. It wasn't like night, but it wasn't like daytime either, and there was something about this in-between state that accentuated the ominous aspects of the house.

He grabbed his magazine, pretending as though he wasn't scared, as though there was nothing out of the ordinary here. He was hoping that Billings had come in through the back door and was doing something in the kitchen or the workroom, but when Mark walked out from his bedroom, the silence of the house was total, and he realized that the assistant was still outside some-where and he was all alone in the house.

The hallway before him was dark. No windows opened onto here save one small inset square of stained glass at the far end, above the staircase. All of the doors to the other rooms were closed. There were goose bumps on his arms, and Mark ran as quickly as he could down the corridor, taking the steps two at a time as he sped downstairs.

This stairwell opened onto another hallway and he was already sprinting down it when he noticed move-ment somewhere in front of him.

He stopped in his tracks, heart pounding.

There was a small figure standing alone at the dark-ened end of the hall, pale white against the deep red and brown of the walls, floor, and ceiling.

Billings' daughter.

The girl was supposed to have been retarded. She did not live with her father in the house but slept on a cot next to the incubation room because she liked to be near the baby chicks. Billings never talked about her, and their parents had warned him and Kristen many times that they were not to speak of her in front of the assis-tant. Mark had not seen her in some time, had, in fact, almost forgotten about her, and he did not think he had ever seen her inside the house, but the girl still looked the same. She was at least as old as Kristen—she'd been around ever since he could remember—but she looked younger. Ten or eleven at the most.

Something about that did not sit well with him.

He stood in place, staring down the hallway at her, wondering how she'd gotten inside.

"Mark."

He had never heard her speak before, and the sound of her voice chilled him. She did not sound retarded at all. Her voice instead was clear, soft, feminine. It was not loud, but it carried clearly in the silent hallway, and there seemed something unnatural about it. She was wearing only a thin white shift, and though there was no light behind her, he could tell that she wore nothing underneath it.

The girl beckoned to him, one pale arm motioning for him to approach, and his chill intensified. There was a cold breeze blowing through the hall, even though the air conditioner was off and all of the windows in the house were closed. The only sound was the slight flapping of the girl's shift against her bare legs and the overloud pumping of his heart.

"Mark." She spoke again, smiling slightly, beckoning, and he began walking toward her, not wanting to admit his fear, not wanting to acknowledge his apprehension. He prayed desperately that his parents would come home right now, that Billings would enter the house looking for his daughter. He did not know why, but he did not want to be alone with this girl, and while even an hour ago he would have laughed had someone suggested that he would be trembling nervously at the sight of the assistant's retarded daughter, he was not laughing now.

His hands were sweaty, and he wiped them on his pants, stopping maybe ten feet in front of the girl. Behind her was a chair, a dark mahogany chair that matched perfectly the adjacent wall but that he could not remember having ever seen before.

The breeze blew against his face, caressed his hair. He tried to pretend as though nothing was wrong. "Hey," he said, "where's your dad?"

"Mark," the girl repeated.

Maybe it was the only word she knew, he thought. Maybe it was the only word she could say.

But her voice still didn't sound retarded, and this time there'd seemed something . . . sensual in it.

She moved slightly to her left, repositioned the chair, and bent slowly over its seat, smiling at him, her shift hiking up to expose the creamy whiteness of bare buttocks. "Fuck me," she said softly. "Fuck me in the ass."

Shocked, he backed up, shaking his head. "No . . ."

"I like it hard. Fuck me hard."

There was something wrong here, something fundamentally awry, something that went far deeper than an overexperienced underage girl and her frighteningly unnatural nymphomania. He could feel it, sense it, a palpable presence in the hallway, a malevolence in the setting and the situation that included Billings' daughter but was not limited to her. Whatever he had feared in this house, whatever subliminal danger he had felt, it was here, now, and Mark knew that he had to get out and get away as quickly as possible before something horrible happened.

He continued backing up, keeping his eyes on the girl.

"I want it," she said. "I want it now."

"No."

"I want you to fuck my ass."

"No!" he said more firmly.

"Your father does it." She smiled at him over her shoulder and there was evil in that smile, a corruption that went far beyond mere sex, a deeply depraved immorality of which this was only the simplest and most obvious manifestation. "He makes it hurt."

Mark ran. He turned tail and ran back upstairs to his room, and he heard behind him the girl's mocking laughter, the soft sounds echoing and amplifying in the dark hall and stairwell.

He had not come out until his family had returned home and Kristen had knocked on his door to tell him that he had to help unload groceries from the car.

It was after that that he had been able to tap into The Power. It had always been there, he supposed, and he attributed the dread and apprehension he felt about the house to its low-level influence, but the encounter with Billings' daughter had somehow jump-started it, kicked it into gear. It truly was like a sixth sense to him, and he didn't have to think about it or concentrate on using it. Like seeing or hearing or smelling or touching or tasting, it was a physical response to people and places and things that he experienced, a natural part of him that provided sensory input which his brain accepted and sorted.

He could sense now the corruption in the house, in his parents, and he knew that sooner or later he would have to leave. He did not belong here, he did not fit in, and either he had to reject the house or the house would reject him.

He did not want to know what would happen if that occurred.

He received no such vibes from Billings—the assistant was a complete blank—and that frightened him. He and Billings had always gotten along famously, the assistant was like an uncle to him, but now every time he saw the man he thought of his daughter, and the traits that had made Billings seem so kind and caring before now made him seem false and secretive, and Mark stayed as far away from him as possible.

His parents seemed to realize that something had happened, they seemed to recognize his newfound Power, and their attitudes toward him shifted. Not profoundly but subtly. He was still required to follow his father's rules, to be in certain places and do certain things at certain times, but there was a wariness now, a slight emotional distancing, and while nothing changed in their behavior toward his sister, he got the feeling that they would not mind at all if *he* left the fold.

He'd begun staying out of the house as much as possible, staying at friends' homes, sleeping outside when he could, camping out on the porch, but he'd seen her again one night, in the door of the first chicken coop, white in the moonlight, beckoning to him, and he'd hurried back into the house, back up to his room, hearing once again the sound of her light laughter behind him.

He tried after that to convince Kristen to leave with him, to run away, but though she too was not happy with the house, though he sensed within her a secret unacknowledged fear of Billings' daughter, there was no way that she was willing to leave their parents. He told her that they could write or call, let their mother and father know where they were and why they had left, but she put her foot down. This was her home and she did not want to leave.

He worked on Kristen the rest of the summer, but his entreaties seemed to have the opposite effect of that intended. She became more resolute in her intention to stay, more devoted to her current life. She understood why he wanted to leave, and though, for selfish reasons, she wanted him to remain, Kristen told him that she would always love him and always support him in his choices, whatever they were.

And then one night the retarded girl came into his bedroom.

She looked retarded this time, and she did not speak, but the eroticism of her movements had not lessened, and the juxtaposition of her mental handicap and her obvious sensuality was truly disturbing.

He had locked the door to his room, had locked his window, and he quickly looked around to see which one had betrayed him. Both door and window were closed and locked, untouched.

The girl giggled.

He clutched the blanket tightly, pulling it to his chin, sliding back against the headboard, and pulling his feet under him as far as they would go. He was terrified and he wanted to scream, but his brain seemed to have lost all power over the actions of his body and only a dry exhalation of air escaped from between his lips.

The girl bent over, her shift sliding up, and grabbed her ankles. He could see once again her pale buttocks, and she looked between her legs at him and smiled.

He knew then and there that he had to leave. Whether Kristen went with him or not, he had to get out of this house.

He did scream then, and Kristen and his parents were at his door in a matter of seconds, and he rushed around the bent-over girl to unlock and open the door, but of course she was gone by the time they entered the room. Though his parents roughly insisted that he had had a nightmare and was acting like a child, and Kristen claimed to believe him, he used The Power and understood that his parents *did* believe it had happened and Kristen, bless her kind heart, did not.

He'd taken off the next morning, telling Kristen and no one else, pretending he was just going into town to meet some friends. Leaving, he'd seen the girl in the dormer window of the attic, white against the darkness, waving at him, and while he could not see the details of her face, he'd known that she was smiling.

"Hey! You okay?"

Mark opened his eyes to see the driver of the Land Rover looking at him. He shook his head, blinked. "Huh? Yeah."

"I thought you were having some sort of fit or something there. You were thrashing around, kicking the door."

"Sorry."

"Looked like you were having a seizure."

He surreptitiously pressed down on his erection.

"Nightmare," Mark said, shaking his head. "It was just a nightmare."

SIX

Daniel

Someone had thrown a dead cat into their yard, one of the punks who hung out on the street no doubt, and as Daniel gingerly picked up the stiff body with his shovel he vowed to kick the shit out of the little bastard who'd done this. It was probably random, not personal, but that didn't make it any less offensive, and he found himself thinking that whether they owned their house or not, maybe it was time for them to leave. The neighborhood was going downhill and they should probably get out while they could still get a decent price for their home, before the street segued completely into slum.

Margot wouldn't buy that, though. This was her neighborhood, this was the street on which she'd grown up, and in her mind it was the same now as it had been then. She seemed to see this area through rose-colored glasses, her mind filling in niceties that were no longer there. The houses to either side of them were falling into disrepair, their small lawns little more than dirt patches dotted with weeds, their tenants an endless succession of increasingly trashy renters, but to Margot's eyes they were simply the residences of her childhood friends with new owners.

Grimacing, Daniel held the shovel in front of him, walking through the backyard and out to the alley, where he deposited the cat in a garbage can. He was probably supposed to call the city and report this, have Animal Control come out and take care of the body, but he wanted to get rid of the cat as quickly and quietly as possible. He didn't want to draw attention to what had happened. He didn't want to give the perpetrators the satisfaction.

He glanced up and down the alley before walking back through the gate and was gratified to see nothing unusual, no strange shadows, nothing out of the ordinary. He returned the shovel to the garage and went inside the house, where Margot was finishing her orange juice and yelling for Tony to hurry up and brush his teeth, they had to go. He slipped a quick hand up her skirt, but she pulled away and shot him a look of annoyance.

"Why're you up so early today?" she asked. "You don't have an interview do you?"

"No." He thought of telling her the truth, that he'd had a nightmare and couldn't fall back asleep, that when he'd gone out to pick up the paper he'd found a dead cat in their front yard, but he didn't want to worry her before she went off to work, and he said, "I was going to clean the house today. I thought I'd get an early start."

She looked at him skeptically.

"It's true!"

He was trapped now, he'd painted himself in a corner, so after Margot and Tony left, he swept and mopped, dusted and vacuumed, and it was past lunchtime before he finally finished. He slept most of the afternoon, dozing off during the hottest part of the day, and only a chance call from a phone solicitor woke him before it was time to pick up Tony.

Waiting in the parking lot of Tony's school, the need to move struck him once again. School was not even out yet and there was a group of tough-looking boys smoking openly on the sidewalk in front of the administration building, all of them wearing white T-shirts and identically baggy pants. They were joined by two slutty-looking young girls dressed far too provocatively for their age.

Then the bell rang and the floodgates were turned loose. Hordes of students streamed out from doorways and hallways, walking, running, talking, screaming. Individuals separated from the crowd, moving toward their parents' cars. A large contingent headed over to the two waiting school buses. Others started walking home in pairs or small groups.

He looked for Tony, tried to spot his son's face amid the sea of similar looking students, and finally saw him walking alone toward the car. One skinhead near the administration building halfheartedly threw a Coke can, yelling, "Pussy! Going to ride home with your daddy and your mommy?" but Daniel pretended he didn't hear it for Tony's sake and smiled as his son got into the car. "How was school?" he asked.

"Great," Tony said sarcastically.

Daniel laughed at the boy's tone of voice. "Well, at least it's Friday."

"Yeah," he said. "At least it's Friday."

They did not talk on the way home. Daniel got into an old Joe Jackson song on the radio, listening to the lyrics, singing along in his head, remembering when that album had first come out, and it wasn't until they were pulling into the driveway that he realized he and Tony had not spoken since leaving the school. He glanced over at his son. "Is everything all right?"

Tony nodded.

"You sure? Nothing you want to talk about?"

"No." Tony grabbed his books, got out of the car.

Daniel followed the boy into the house. Margot wasn't home yet, but she'd be back from work within the next hour, and he decided to start making dinner. She had a series of stressful meetings today and though she'd told him she'd fix something when she got home, he thought it would be a nice surprise if he made dinner tonight, gave her a little treat.

He looked through Margot's cookbooks, looked through the refrigerator and cupboards to see what they had, and finally decided on a hamburger casserole from Julia Child. The instructions classified it as a "quick and easy" dish, estimated preparation time fifteen minutes, but he knew himself and he figured he'd be lucky if he finished within the hour.

Tony plopped his books down on the kitchen counter and grabbed a can of Dr Pepper from the refrigerator before heading off toward his bedroom.

"Homework!" Daniel called out.

"It's Friday!"

"Do it today and your weekend will be free."

"I'll do it Sunday."

Daniel thought of arguing with him, but decided to let the boy go. He picked up the books from the counter and carried them into the living room, where he placed them on the coffee table on top of the pile of today's newspapers.

It took over an hour to prepare the meal, and Margot came home before he was finished, but she was touched by his thoughtfulness and she gave him a big hug as he slid the casserole dish into the oven. "I love you, Mr. Mom."

He turned around, gave her a quick kiss. "I love you, too."

Dinner wasn't great, but it was better than he'd expected, and Margot praised the meal to high heaven, exaggerating its quality to such an embarrassing extent that Tony rolled his eyes and said, "Give it a rest, Mom."

Daniel laughed, looked over at his wife. "Is this your subtle way of telling me you want me to cook dinner more often?"

"No—" she began.

"No!" Tony repeated.

"—I'm just touched by your thoughtfulness and I wanted to let you know."

Tony pushed back his chair, stood. "This is getting too pukey for me. I'm out of here."

They watched him go, smiling.

"It really is pretty good," she said. "I'm proud of you."

"Thanks."

As always, he offered to do the dishes and, as always, she turned him down. So he went out to the living room and watched the last part of the local news, then the national news. There was nothing on after that except reruns, game shows, and syndicated entertainment news, so he shut off the television and walked back into the kitchen, where Margot was eating an orange over the sink.

"Where's Tony?" she asked.

He shrugged. "I don't know. His room, I guess."

"Hiding in there?" She looked at him significantly. "Why don't you go see what he's doing."

"He's all right.

"Why don't you check?"

He understood her concern, thought of his son walking alone through the crowds of students at school, thought of him sitting silently in the car, and nodded. "Okay."

The door to the boy's bedroom was closed, and Daniel walked quietly down the hallway and stood outside it for a moment, listening. He heard nothing, and he reached for the knob, turned it, pushed open the door.

Tony moved quickly, trying to hide something beneath the unmade covers of his bed.

A bolt of primal parental terror shot through Daniel. *Drugs,* was his first thought.

He walked toward the bed, desperately trying not to think the worst. *Let it be a* Playboy, he prayed. *Let it be a* Penthouse.

He forced himself to smile at his son. "What you got there, sport?" He reached for the covers, pulled them up.

It was not drugs. It was not porno magazines.

It was a figure, a doll, the body made from an old 7-Eleven Big Gulp cup, the arms straws, the hands and fingers toothpicks, the legs and feet bent toilet-paper tubes. The face was paper, topped by whisk-broom bristle hair, and it was the face that stopped him cold. A seemingly haphazard composite of eyes, nose, and mouth culled from disparate newspaper photos, the face nonetheless possessed a strange unity, an off-center cohesion that seemed natural in an unnatural way and awakened within him a dread déjà vu.

He had seen the face before.

In the House

When he was a child.

In the House

But he couldn't quite remember where.

"What is that?" he demanded.

Tony shrank back, shaking his head. "Nothing."

"What do you mean, 'nothing'?" He was aware that he was yelling, but he couldn't help it, and though he was addressing his son, his gaze remained fixed on the figure. It repulsed and frightened him at the same time. There was something abhorrent in its makeup, something repugnant about its form and shape and the way ordinary objects had been used in its construction. But it was the doll's familiarity that frightened him, the sense that he had seen it before and could not quite place it.

"What is it?" Margot ran up behind him, an edge of panic in her voice. "What's happening? What's wrong?"

Tony was still cowering on the bed before him. "Nothing!" he told his mom. "I was working on an art project and Dad went crazy!"

"Art project?" Daniel said. "For school?"

"No, I'm doing it on my own."

"Then why were you trying to hide it?"

"I didn't want you to see it!"

"What's going on?" Margot pushed past him, stood before the bed. She looked down at the doll. "Is this what all the commotion was about?"

"Yeah," Tony admitted.

Margot turned on Daniel. "Why are you screaming at him? Because of this? I thought you'd caught him using drugs or something."

"Mom!"

Daniel stood there, not sure what to say, not sure how to defend himself. Margot was acting as though there was nothing unusual here, nothing out of the ordinary, and it threw him. Couldn't she tell that there was something the matter with the doll? Couldn't she see?

Obviously not.

Maybe it was him. Maybe there really was nothing wrong. Maybe he was just overreacting.

Daniel looked once more at the doll, again felt repulsed, scared.

He tried to tell himself that he was having some sort of breakdown, that the stress from being out of work for so long had finally gotten to him, but he did not believe it.

Wasn't that the definition of mental illness, though? If you had it, you didn't know it?

He didn't believe that either.

What did he believe?

He believed that Tony's doll was evil. He believed that his son was doing something wrong in making it and that he knew it was wrong and that's why he had tried to hide it. He believed that, for whatever reason, Margot couldn't tell what was happening and didn't understand.

"It's not for school?" Daniel asked again.

Tony shook his head.

"Then throw it away. If you want art supplies, we'll get you art supplies."

"We can't afford—" Margot started to say.

"I don't want art supplies!" Tony said. "I just want you to leave me alone!"

Margot pulled at Daniel's sleeve, pulled him toward the door. "Come on."

Daniel stood his ground. "I don't want that thing in the house."

"What's the matter with you?" Margot frowned at him.

"I'll do it in the garage," Tony said.

Daniel didn't know what to say, didn't know what to do. He knew his attitude appeared irrational, but he could not seem to articulate his aversion to the figure, could not seem to explain and communicate his feelings toward the horrid object. The threads were there but he could not pull them together. He glanced from Tony to Margot. He did not want to get into a fight with them over this. He knew the truth, felt it in his gut, but he was aware that he was in the intellectually weaker position here and that in a fair fight he would lose.

It was best to back off, throw the thing away later, when they were both out of the house.

He allowed himself to be led by Margot out of the room, and she waited until Tony's door was closed and they were safely in the kitchen before confronting him. "What was that back there? What did you think you were doing?"

He didn't even try to explain. Out of the room, away from the figure, it almost seemed silly even to him, and he could think of no way to defend himself that would sound even remotely plausible.

"If that's all he's doing by himself in there, making 'art projects,' then we should consider ourselves lucky."

"Yeah," Daniel said. "You're right."

But he didn't think that at all.

He walked back into the living room, flipped on the television, found a movie.

The thing was, Tony didn't seem to really understand what the doll was either. He obviously knew enough to try to keep it hidden from his parents, obviously felt as though it was something he should not be doing, but there'd been no deception or dishonesty in his defense of his "art project." He'd seemed as naive as Margot in that way, sincere in his straightforward appeal. It was as if, on one level, he recognized the abnormal and abhorrent nature of the object, and on another level he saw it as merely an ordinary product of an ordinary hobby. He didn't seem to understand what he was doing or why. He was like . . . like a baby playing with fire.

What made him think of that analogy?

Daniel didn't know, but it was accurate nevertheless. There was a danger here. He sensed it. And he would not feel comfortable until that thing was out of his son's room and out of his house.

Margot finished the dishes and came out in the living room with him. She sat next to him on the couch, read the newspaper, snuggled into the crook of his arm, but there was tension between them, and though they tried, they could not regain the relaxed and happy atmosphere of dinner.

The doll.

The shadow in the alley.

Something was going on here that he couldn't quite grasp. It was like a word on the tip of his tongue that he knew but could not immediately articulate. He had the strong feeling that on some level he did understand what was happening, that somewhere inside him was the key that would unlock this puzzle, but he could not seem to find it.

They went to bed at eleven, made love quietly, perfunctorily, then rolled over, automatically moving to opposite sides of the mattress.

He lay awake long after Margot fell asleep, long after the timer shut off the TV, staring up at the ceiling through the silent darkness.

Silent?

No, not quite.

There was a rustling whisper of movement from down the hall.

From Tony's room.

Ordinarily, he would not have been able to hear the noise, so subtle was its intonation, but in this quiet the faint sibilance was clearly audible, its changing location pinpointed by slight increases and decreases in volume. He listened carefully. It was a sound he had heard before, a long time ago—

In the House

—and, soft as it was, it sent a powerful chill through him. He could not quite place it, but its origin was in his past and there was something about it that frightened him. Daniel closed his eyes, concentrated on listening. The noise faded, moving away from their bedroom door, then grew louder, returning.

It was the sound of . . . a doll patrolling the halls, hunting little boys who dared to leave their rooms.

What in God's name had made him think of that?

He didn't know, but it was the image that came to his mind, and it stayed there, refusing to budge. His first instinct was to get Tony and Margot out of the house. They might be in danger. But he could not act on that impulse. As concerned as he was for their safety, he was paralyzed, afraid to get out of bed, afraid to wake up Margot, afraid even to move.

It would not harm Tony, he told himself. Tony had made it.

And it wasn't after Margot.

It was after him.

Just as it had been—

In the House.

He heard it outside, shuffling by on toilet-paper-tube feet.

He held his breath, praying that it would not stop in front of their bedroom, praying that Margot had locked their door.

He waited until both Margot and Tony left.

Then he searched through Tony's room.

Daniel wasn't sure what he thought he'd find. Some clue, he supposed. Something that would jog his memory, something that would let him know what was going on.

Something.

But there was only the doll itself, at the bottom of his son's closet, in a plastic grocery sack sitting atop a jumbled pile of old worn-out sneakers. There were no notes, no diary, no hints as to why Tony was working on the disturbing figure, no reference of any kind to anything remotely connected to the object. There were only Tony's books and toys and tapes and clothes. His rock collection and bug collection and a pile of old homework.

And the doll.

Daniel carried the sack out of the closet and put it on the bed, taking out the nearly finished figure. He picked the doll up gingerly.

It was as repugnant as it had been before, and once again it seemed familiar to him. He thought of the noises in the night, in the hall, his certainty that the doll was on the prowl, looking for him, and though it was daytime and he could hear the sounds of the street outside, the television in the family room, he was acutely aware of the fact that he was alone in the house with this horrible figure.

Its expression was fixed, formed from the newspaper photos, but it seemed different from yesterday, more purposely hostile, its eyes narrowed, its teeth bared. Maybe he remembered it incorrectly, but he could have sworn the eyes had been more open, the mouth closed.

Maybe Tony had altered the face after their confrontation.

There was no indication that the doll could ever be mobile, much less animate, and its taped and stapled limbs hung limply down as he gripped the midsection, but Daniel had the impression that it was playing possum, pretending to be dead when it wasn't.

That was ridiculous.

Of course it was. This whole thing was ridiculous. It was ridiculous for him to be secretly searching through his son's room in the first place. But he felt no embarrassment, and no matter how much he tried to intellectually discount his feelings, they were still there.

He looked down at the doll and was suddenly afraid. What would happen when Tony finished his "project," when the doll was complete?

He didn't know and he didn't want to find out.

He knew what he had to do.

Daniel shoved the doll back in the bag and carried it outside. He dropped it on the grass next to the back porch and walked into the garage, wheeling out the barbecue. Opening the lid, he picked the sack up off the ground and unceremoniously dumped the doll into the ashes.

He walked back into the garage, emerged with lighter fluid and a book of matches. He knew this was going to extremes, but he could not be sure if he simply tore the doll up and threw it away that it wouldn't return, that it wouldn't drag its pieces out of the alley and over the fence and through the backyard to his bedroom. He couldn't afford to chance that.

He'd seen the Telly Savalas *Twilight Zone*. He knew how these things worked.

His feelings did not make any kind of rational sense—the fact that he was referencing a TV show as validation for his actions should have told him that—but as he doused the doll with lighter fluid and put a match to it, he felt an absurd sense of exhilaration. He saw the face go up in flames, the toilet-paper tubes blacken and crumble, the Big Gulp cup melt off its wax and burn, and for the first time since he'd seen Tony with the doll, he was able to breathe easily.

He would tell Tony that he had gotten rid of the doll when his son came home, and he would forbid him to make another one. He should have done that last night. It might seem irrational to Margot, but he was still the boy's father, and if he wanted to enforce an irrational rule or prohibition, well, he wouldn't be the first father to have done so.

The components of the doll had all burned themselves out, but he turned on the hose and soaked everything with water, just to make sure, before going back into the garage and getting a shovel. He scooped up the ashes from the barbecue, dumped them in the plastic sack, and tossed everything in one of the trash cans in the alley. He mashed down the sack with his foot, transferred garbage from one of the other cans to throw on top of it, then replaced the lid. Once again, he found himself looking up the alley for any sign of the small strange shadow he'd seen before.

Nothing.

He hurried back into his yard.

Were these things connected? The doll and the shadow? The inexplicable feelings of fear and discomposure he'd been experiencing? He had the sense that they were, but he could not imagine how and he could not begin to comprehend the meaning behind it.

He pushed the barbecue and carried the shovel back into the garage, then walked into the house and washed his hands in the kitchen sink before getting himself a Diet Coke from the fridge. He'd left the television on in the family room and, coincidentally enough, *The Twilight Zone* was on the Sci-Fi channel. It was the episode in which a girl disappeared into the wall of her house, the one he'd always assumed had been the inspiration for *Poltergeist,* and as he watched it for the fiftieth time, alarm bells began going off in his head once again. There was a connection here, something he knew he should be picking up on but just couldn't quite figure out.

He stared at the television, watched the mother and

the father kneel before the wall, calling to their little girl, and it came to him.

The House.

That was it. The House. The home in which he'd been born and where he'd spent the first eleven years of his life. He could remember very little about the House, only flashes of images, portions of events, but there was something about it that reminded him of the girl lost in the walls.

There'd been something scary about the House.

The fact that he could recall almost nothing at all about his childhood home disturbed him. He knew why, of course, and though it wasn't really surprising, it was unsettling to realize just how easily he fit into that clichéd niche, that stereotypical pattern so often exploited by headline-grabbing doctors and the media during sweeps weeks.

He couldn't remember because that was where his mom had died.

He was disappointed in himself that he was so predictable, so typical, and the thought occurred to him that everything else that seemed to be happening—his uneasiness, the shadow, the doll—could all be part of some psychological problem that could be traced back to this one event.

But that wasn't be possible. He'd lived a perfectly normal life all these years. The normal, happy life of a well-adjusted man, a husband, a father. The House had not affected him at all.

Perhaps his long stretch of unemployment had put stress and pressures on him that he couldn't recognize, wasn't able to acknowledge.

He should try to find out if that was the case. A psychiatrist would be the best idea, he supposed, but he was loath to go that route. Despite all the positive propaganda distilled through the media over the past decade, there was still a stigma attached to it in his mind, and he couldn't picture himself lying on a couch, spilling his guts, and letting some stranger give him advice on how he should act and how he should feel and how he should live his life.

Besides, they didn't have the money for it.

And, truth to tell, he didn't really believe that his perceptions *were* off, that what he was thinking, feeling, and experiencing was part of some mental disorder or buried emotional problem.

He *had* seen the shadow.

There *was* something wrong with Tony's doll.

There was a reason for him to feel uneasy.

A psychiatrist might be able to help him remember, though. Might be able to recall his memories of the House.

Why did he think of it as "the House"? he wondered. With a capital "H"? He wasn't sure. He couldn't even get a clear picture in his mind of the House's exterior. Or his bedroom. Or any of the other rooms inside the structure. He could see only a long hallway. And a dark corner with a window seat. And an image of an overflowing bathtub.

Had there been a doll in the House? A doll like Tony's?

He wished his dad were still alive. His dad would help him remember.

Daniel stared at the television as *The Twilight Zone* ended and a commercial came on. It was not normal for him to block out such a large part of his life. And to such an extent. He acknowledged that that was of legitimate concern, but what worried him far more than the fact that he was repressing his childhood memories was the idea that they were somehow connected to what was going on in his life now.

And that Tony was being drawn into it.

Whatever was happening, he wanted it to end. He didn't want to see strange figures or unusual events, and most of all, he did not want anything to happen to his wife or his son.

It had been a long time since he'd gone to church. Several years. But, sitting on the couch, he closed his eyes and folded his hands and, for the first time since he could remember, prayed.

"Dear God," he said softly. "Please keep Margot and Tony safe. Don't let anything happen to them. Help them be healthy and happy and live until they're a hundred years old. Amen."

Margot picked up Tony after school, and they stopped by the grocery store before coming home. Daniel helped his wife carry sacks from the car, while Tony went straight to his bedroom.

He noticed the doll's absence immediately.

"Mom!" He was running out to the kitchen even as Daniel was setting down sacks on the counter and Margot was putting milk in the refrigerator. "Mom!"

Frowning, Margot closed the refrigerator door and looked up. "What?"

"Dad took my project! He stole my project!"

Margot glared at him. "You didn't . . ."

Daniel looked at her, shrugged. "I threw it away."

She glared at him. "Why did you do that? You didn't have to do that."

Yes I did, he wanted to respond, but he kept silent.

"Mom?" Tony said, imploring her with his eyes to somehow bring back the doll.

"Where is it?" Margot demanded. "Where did you put it?"

"It's gone." Daniel turned to face his son. "And that's the end of it."

"Mom!"

"Why is it so important?" Daniel asked him. "What's so important to you about that doll?"

Tony reddened. "It's not a doll!" he yelled.

"It's a doll. And why does it mean so much to you?"

"Daniel," Margot said warningly.

"It's my project!"

"It's not something you're doing for school. Why are you doing it?"

"You can make another one—" Margot began.

"No!" Daniel shouted, and both of them jumped. He pointed at Tony. "You are *not* going to make another one! Do you hear me?"

The boy said nothing, looked to his mom. Margot was silent.

"You are forbidden to make one of those things again.

And if I catch you doing it, you'll be grounded for a month. Do you understand me?"

Tony angrily turned and stalked down the hall, slamming the door to his room.

"I mean it!" Daniel called after him.

"What was that?" Margot demanded. "What the hell is wrong with you?"

He shook his head. "You wouldn't understand."

"Try me."

"I just don't like that doll."

"Why? It's evil?"

He whirled to face her, thrilled that she'd seen it too, but when he met her eyes he saw only anger there. She was being sarcastic, he realized.

"You need to get some help," she told him. "I don't know what's happening with you, but I don't like it. You need to see a psychiatrist."

A psychiatrist.

It was a chance, an opportunity.

But he didn't take it.

"I'm not going to a shrink," he said.

She looked at him. "You need to do something."

"I just don't want a doll like that in our house." He turned without looking at her and walked out to the family room. He switched on the TV, the local news, and a few moments later he heard her angrily slamming cupboards and drawers as she put away the groceries.

SEVEN

Laurie

Laurie sat across from Josh at the small wrought-iron table adjacent to the coffeepot at the rear of the bookstore. She hadn't slept well all week and when he'd called her on it, she told him about the dreams.

In a way, she was grateful. It had not been a conscious thought, but clearly she'd felt the need to talk about what was happening, and when her brother commented on her haggard appearance for the third time and sat her down, demanding Laurie tell him what was wrong, she did. She told him everything, beginning with her encounter with the girl in the alley, giving detailed descriptions of each and every dream, explaining how she'd lain awake as long as possible, not wanting to fall asleep. She was not embarrassed discussing the sexual nature of the dreams with Josh, but she did tone down her reaction, ashamed of how much she had enjoyed the encounters with the child.

The dreams had changed since the first one, evolved. It had happened slowly over the past two weeks, and at first she wasn't even aware of it. The girl had sucked her in with sex, had used intimacy to gain her trust, but the dreams had become increasingly nonerotic, increasingly grotesque and chaotic, and they were now to the point where she considered them nightmares.

Last night, the girl, wearing the same dirty shift she'd had on in the alley, had taken Laurie's hand and led her through a blighted urban landscape, past the rubble of demolished buildings, past trash-can fires warming dirty homeless men, to a tarpaper shack that housed a butcher shop. Inside, a muscular tattooed man in a bloodstained apron was passing a monstrous rat through the blade of his band saw. On the floor were scraps of fat and muscle, the teeth and toes of children. The butcher looked up from his work, smiled at her. "Glad you're home, dear. Take off your clothes and sit on the stump."

And then she'd been in a dark forest, sitting, legs spread, on an upended log, as the girl crouched before her and painfully inserted twigs into her bleeding vagina. "Almost done," the girl kept saying. "Almost done."

The dream had made no sense on any sort of rational level, but there was something about it that rang true to her, that frightened and at the same time spoke to her, and while she did not exactly feel that this was something that *had* happened or *would* happen, Laurie thought it *could* happen, and that was what disturbed her the most.

Josh frowned at her, concerned. "Dreams are not just manifestations of the subconscious," he said. "Sometimes they're the means used to communicate with us, a portal between this world or this plane of existence and others."

It was a cliché, the same type of New Age claptrap she'd made fun of all these years, but it was exactly what she'd been feeling, put into words.

Only it sounded so frightening spoken aloud like this, its implications huge.

"Recurring dreams are scary enough, but the fact that you have a recurring character in your dreams, a figure you saw in reality under what I would say are pretty strange circumstances . . ." He trailed off. "It's scary, Lor."

She smiled wryly. "Tell me about it."

"You have no idea who this girl is? You've never met her before? Never dreamed about her in the past?"

"That's the thing. She seems familiar to me." Laurie paused. "Sort of." She looked across the table at her brother. "I mean, I think I know her from someplace, but I can't for the life of me figure out where. I don't know if she's someone I met or imagined or saw in a movie. There wasn't a girl on our street like that, was there? When we were little?"

"Not when you were with us. But maybe before."

She frowned. "Before?"

"Yeah. If your birth mother was around we could—"

Laurie's heart stopped in her chest. It suddenly seemed impossible to breathe. "My '*birth* mother'?"

"Yeah."

Laurie tried to will the saliva back in her mouth. She felt dizzy.

"I thought . . ." Josh shook his head. "You don't remember?"

"I didn't know."

"You didn't know you were adopted?"

She stared at him numbly. "I thought you were my real brother."

"I am your real brother."

"I mean—"

"We may not be biologically related, but I'm your brother, and Mom and Dad were your parents. We're all family."

"How long have you known?"

"Always." He seemed uncomfortable. "I thought you knew, too. I wouldn't've said anything if—"

"Were you born when they adopted me?"

"Yeah. I was pretty little. You were, I don't know, eight or nine, I guess, when Mom and Dad brought you home. Which meant that I was four or five, but I still sort of remember it."

She stood. For the first time in her life, she knew what writers meant when they described their characters' heads as "spinning." "This is too much to take. I need . . . time. I need to think about this. I need to absorb it."

Josh looked worried. "I still love you, Lor. I couldn't love you more if you were my Siamese twin."

She put a hand on his shoulder. "I know. I love you, too."

"Okay. Let's talk about this, then. Obviously, we need to work this out. I thought you knew all along. I don't know how you could not—"

"I don't want to talk about it." She tried to smile, did not entirely succeed. "Not right now. I think . . . I think I'm going to go for a walk. I need some time to think."

He nodded.

"I'm sorry," he said as she headed toward the door.

She turned, smiled kindly. "You have nothing to be sorry for."

Then she was out of the shop and on the sidewalk, and there were tears in her eyes. She wiped them angrily away. She had nothing to complain about. Her family had been loving, caring, supportive, always there for her. They'd brought her up to be the person she was today.

But it still felt as if her life had suddenly turned upside down, as if the rug had been yanked out from under her. She'd just found out that her brother wasn't her real brother, her parents hadn't been her real parents. She was related to strangers she didn't even know, and she wasn't related to the people she knew and loved.

On the scale of problems, it was low priority. She wasn't a crack-addicted teenager knocked up by her stepfather. She wasn't a battered wife with no education and no prospects. Like anorexia and bulimia, hers was strictly an affluent, upwardly mobile concern.

But it still had a major impact on her life.

Who were her biological parents?

That was the big question. She tried to remember something from before she'd been adopted, some scrap of memory from her previous life, but as hard as she tried to recall the past, her mind remained stubbornly in the present.

She never thought much about her early childhood, she realized, and when she did her thoughts were confined to specific subjects, specific instances, specific images. She'd never stopped to analyze it before, but she understood now that the reason was because most of her early years were a blank.

She frowned. Not noticing that she never thought about her childhood, not wondering why, was as strange as the memory blank itself.

It was *all* strange, and she was tempted to ascribe a deliberate design to it, to recognize a supernatural reason behind it all, but she knew that was stupid. It was probably the dreams that had put her in this frame of mind, that had encouraged her to see anything unusual in this. The truth was, it was probably a perfectly natural reaction for a child to block out memories of parents who had died that early in her life.

Died?

Yes. Her biological parents had died. She knew that much. She could not remember how or why, could not bring to mind any specifics, but the certainty was there, so strong that even though she had no memories or concrete proof, she did not doubt it.

Laurie paused at the corner, thought about crossing the street, but turned right instead. In a kind of daze, she stopped at a coffee stand, bought a mocha, and continued on up the sidewalk.

How had her parents died? she wondered. She had the feeling that they'd both died at once, so it couldn't have been old age or disease. It had to have been catastrophic. Fire? Plane crash? Murder? Had it been something simple or one of those bizarre, convoluted occurrences? Had her father caught her mother with another woman and then joined in the fun only to have the woman's jealous boyfriend kill all three of them? Had her parents been aspiring actors who were conned into doing a snuff film and killed, their murders recorded on camera and now available on video?

She would probably never know.

She slowed to look at the series of newsracks on the side of the street, sipping her coffee as she peered through the faded plastic windows. She'd always been attracted to supernatural stories in lurid tabloids, the more outrageous the headline the better. She told herself that it was camp, a kitsch, postmodern irony, that she liked to read those stories because they were so bad they were funny, so outrageous they were entertaining, but the truth was that she was genuinely interested in the bizarre tales. She felt some sort of affinity for those subjects, and she could not help wondering now if that could be traced back to her first family.

A headline caught her eye: MINISTER'S FAMILY FLEES HAUNTED HOUSE.

She'd lived in a haunted house as a child.

The knowledge came to her not as a revelation, not as a sudden memory breakthrough, but casually, gently, as though it were something she'd always known and often thought about and had just been reminded of by the tabloid. She reread the headline, stared at the obviously fake photograph of a clergyman, his wife, and his daughter looking up at a dilapidated house over which towered a huge horned demon.

Now that she was actively seeking them, memories of her early childhood seemed to be seeping slowly back into her consciousness. But she was no longer sure she wanted to know about life before her adoption. She was curious, of course, but that was balanced by a growing feeling of dread, the impression that there were things in her past she was better off not knowing.

She could see the house in her mind: a dark Victorian mansion located in a clearing in the woods. The surrounding trees were giant, old-growth redwoods, so it must have been in Washington, Oregon, or northern California. As for why the house was haunted, the specifics of it, she had no idea. She knew only that there was something frightening about the house, something she'd sensed even as a young child.

She could not remember having any brothers or sisters, but there'd been another man living with them, hadn't there? An uncle? One of her dad's old army buddies? She could not remember his precise relation to them, could not recall his name, but she could see him in her mind, a nattily dressed man with a thin mustache. She didn't think he was British, but something in her memory of him reminded her of an elegant English actor whose name she did not know.

There *had* been another child, but she had not lived with them, had only come over to visit, to play.

Dawn.

The girl from down the way.

The girl she'd promised to marry.

Laurie remembered her now, remembered her name, but her appearance was confused with that of the girl from the alley, the girl in her dreams. Dawn was the one aspect of her previous life that had not been submerged and buried, that she had not entirely blocked out, but in her reminiscences, the girl had been another hippie kid who lived down the street from where she remembered growing up, and Josh had known her as well. She realized now, though, that her memory had transferred the girl from one place, one time, to another. Dawn had been from before. Before her birth parents had died, before she'd been adopted.

In her mind, she saw Dawn standing between two redwoods, smiling at her, beckoning her toward the forest.

The dimensions of the scene expanded as she mentally reconstructed details of the memory. She had not been allowed to go into the woods surrounding the house. Her parents had instilled within her a fear of the forest, and she'd been aware of the dangers lurking therein since before she'd been allowed to play outside the house. Dawn knew perfectly well that she wasn't supposed to go into the woods, but the other girl tried to lure her in anyway, cajoling her, calling her names, promising her fun, excitement, and lifelong friendship.

Laurie hadn't succumbed—not this time—but Dawn had not quit trying, and it had been a constant battle between her parents' orders and her friend's desires.

Had Dawn had a hand in her parents' deaths?

For some reason, Laurie thought she had. What a small child could have to do with the murder of two adults she did not quite understand, but the feeling was there anyway.

The *murder* of two adults?

Yes.

This was getting a little too creepy.

Laurie finished her coffee, tossed the paper cup into a wastebasket next to the entrance of a small café, and tried to concentrate on the here and now, focusing on the street, on the shops, on the people walking by, trying not to think about her newfound memories.

An hour ago, a half hour ago, she had never even considered the fact that she might be adopted. It was not something that had ever crossed her mind. Now she was recalling a whole other history of herself, a back story she'd never known existed that was already sending out repercussions through the years.

There was too much here, too much to sift through. She couldn't think about it all right now. She needed time to sort things out.

She arrived once again at The Shire. She'd walked around the block, and she pushed open the door and went into the bookstore. Josh was with a customer, a Doug Henning look-alike, but he excused himself and hurried over when he saw her, a worried frown on his face. "Are you all right?"

She smiled weakly. "I'm fine. Go back to your customer."

"He can wait."

She felt the tears welling up in her eyes. Biological relation or not, he was her brother, the only brother she'd ever known, and while he might be a flake and a screwup in many ways, she was lucky to have him, and she couldn't ask for a better or more caring sibling.

She reached out, hugged him. "I love you," she said, the tears rolling down her cheeks. "I love you, Josh."

He hugged her back, held her tight. "I love you, too."

Matt was waiting on the porch when she arrived home.

Her first instinct was to drive on, not stop, keep going and not return until he was gone, but though her hands were shaking and she felt like jelly inside, she forced herself to park the car, get out, stride purposely up the walkway. She fixed the most angrily resolute expression possible on her face.

Matt moved down the steps toward her. "Laurie—"

"I don't want to talk to you," she said firmly.

"I came to apologize."

"You are no longer in my life, there is no connection between us, you have no reason to apologize to me."

"Yes I do, because—"

"Please leave," she said. She took out her key, unlocked and opened the door.

"Laurie!"

She turned to look at him. "Obviously, you don't know me at all. Even after all that time together. Let me spell it out for you: I don't forgive and forget. We're not going to be friends; we're not even going to be acquaintances. At this point, we do not have any relationship at all. It's over. You get one chance with me, and you blew it. I don't give second chances."

He stared up at her.

She glared back.

"Then I guess here's your key." He looked at her deject-edly with that hurt, wounded expression that had always made her feel sorry for him and want to mother him, but she refused to fall for it this time, refused to give in.

She held out her hand, accepted the key, and walked inside without looking back.

Her hands were still shaking as she closed the door, and she turned the lock and threw the dead bolt, leaning against the frame, not wanting him to see her pass in front of the window. She waited. A minute. Two minutes. Three. She hadn't heard him leave, hadn't heard any sound at all, but she figured he had to have left by now and she haz-arded a look around the corner of the curtains.

He was gone.

She had to admit that part of her was gratified that he'd come crawling back, but she was not even remotely tempted to start up with him again. Whatever they'd had was dead and could not be rekindled. He'd killed it. As painful and awkward and horrible as it had been, though, she was glad he'd stopped by. She felt stronger now, more sure of herself, and for the first time, she was happy that the relationship had ended.

The phone rang during dinner, and Laurie let the ma-chine pick up. It was Josh, but she still wasn't in the mood to talk, and she listened to his message as she ate her asparagus.

She tried to arrange what little she remembered from her pre-adoptive years chronologically in her mind but was unable to do so. Her memories remained frag-mented disjointed images, out of context, with only a vague dread linking everything together. She didn't know what was happening to her, what was going on, but she had the feeling that there was something here under the surface, an overarching connection between the past and the present that she couldn't see and wasn't sure she wanted to know about.

She went to bed early, tired.

And she dreamed of the girl.

EIGHT

Norton

Carole's ghost would not go away.

Norton had never believed in ghosts, had always considered those who did to be naive, gullible, and superstitious, the type of people who could be easily separated from their money, but he had had to change his tune.

Carole's ghost would not go away.

He remembered, years ago, taking a group of graduating students on a senior class trip to California. They'd gone to Disneyland, Knott's Berry Farm, Sea World, and in San Diego they'd visited the Whaley House, the first two-story brick home in California. The house was supposed to be haunted, and there was corroboration by generations' worth of witnesses who had claimed to see and hear ghosts, but he'd felt nothing. Some of the girls had gotten scared, one boy had refused to go upstairs, and all of the students later said they'd felt the "vibes" of the place, but he had put it all down to the power of suggestion and had dismissed it. There were no such things as ghosts, he told them.

But there were.

He knew that now.

Carole's ghost had shown up the day after her burial. The funeral had been held at the Presbyterian church adjoining the cemetery, and every pew had been filled. There'd been their friends and her friends and his friends, as well as assorted acquaintances, neighbors, and coworkers, and the whole thing had been nearly overwhelming. He was not a social man by nature—Carole had taken charge of that aspect of the marriage—and this was the time when he felt least like being sociable, felt most like being alone, but he was thrust into the

role of host, having to meet and greet, accepting condolences and offers of support, repeating endlessly that he
was all right, he was okay, he was coping.

It had rained during the burial service, but a canopy
had been set up over the gravesite and while the mourn-
ers were forced to stand a little closer together than was
comfortable, they had remained dry despite the down-
pour. Afterward, people followed him to his house, repeated their condolences, gave him casseroles and Jell-O
and flowers and cards. It had been after eight before the
last person finally left, and he'd gone directly to sleep
after that, not only because he was exhausted, but because he didn't want to be alone, didn't want to have
time to think.

In the morning, Carole's ghost was in the bathroom.

He thought at first that he was hallucinating. She was
naked and standing in front of the sink, apparently looking at herself in the mirror. She had the appearance of
a stereotypical apparition: her form was visible but transparent, a pale see-through representation of solid matter.
He walked into the bathroom—

—and she disappeared.

Despite himself, he felt slightly chilled. His lack of belief
in anything beyond the physical, material world was strong,
but even if its origin was in his own mind, seeing Carole's
form after her death was a little unnerving.

He looked around the bathroom, checked behind the
shower curtain, and, satisfied that there was no one
there, walked over to the toilet to take a leak.

His mind was probably playing tricks on him, he decided. He was so used to seeing Carole that his brain
had filled in the blanks, putting her where he expected
her to be.

But she'd never stood in front of the sink naked. Not
in all the years they'd been married.

It was the stress, he told himself, the shock. It was
making him see things that weren't there.

She was waiting for him ten minutes later in the
kitchen.

Still naked.

This time, he definitely had chills. The nudity, for

some reason, lent credence to the idea that the figure was Carole's ghost. That was one of the problems he'd always had with spirits. People who saw them always claimed they were clothed. Sometimes they were even supposed to be wearing hats. But that made no logical sense. Did the clothes die with the person? Were these the ghosts of their clothes that had accompanied them to the great beyond? Did ghosts somehow conjure up the appearance of clothing so as to not embarrass their earthly counterparts? It had always made more sense to him to assume that if there were such things as ghosts, they would be merely an unformed energy source with no definite shape. The idea that a human soul retained the physical appearance of the body housing it had seemed to him to be a ludicrously illogical idea.

But Carole's ghost looked just like her.

The ghost, again, was standing before the sink, this time the kitchen sink. It was facing him across the length of the room, and it smiled as he entered. He was still clinging to the thought that this was a trick of his mind, but there seemed to be a measurable decrease in temperature as he walked into the kitchen, and he did not think he was imagining that. From behind him came the familiar purr-meow of Hermie begging for his morning Friskies, and the cat jogged between his legs toward the plastic dish next to the stove.

Halfway across the linoleum, Hermie stopped. He stared at the ghost, arched his back, hissed and ran away.

Norton backed up slowly.

Hermie saw her too!

It was not a figment of his imagination, not stress or a hallucination. It was an honest-to-God apparition. He believed that now, and it scared the hell out of him. Outside the window, a bird flew by. He could see it through Carole's head, her insubstantial form obscuring not even the slightest detail of the scene outdoors. In books, it was only evil spirits that were frightening. People claimed to be comforted by the ghosts of relatives and loved ones, as though they felt they were being watched over by a guardian angel.

Norton felt no such thing.

True, he and Carole were probably not as close and loving as they should have been, but even intense hatred would not have accounted for the feeling he got from the figure across the room. It was like nothing he had ever experienced; the emotional knowledge that he was in the presence of something profoundly unnatural, a wrongness so concentrated and powerful that it permeated the room and everything in it, creating within him a sense of complete engulfing dread. The naked, smiling ghost looked like the shade of a human being, a weakened reflection of the person it had been in life, but its aura seemed to be that of something much deeper, much more inexplicable.

It was still Carole, though.

He *knew* that. He could *feel* it.

And that was what scared him.

The figure, still smiling, reached out to him . . . and faded away into nothingness.

He'd taken a week off from work, using his two days of bereavement leave as well as three "personal necessity" days, but he was not sure that had been such a good idea. He felt restless during the day, the suddenly empty house seemed way too large, and he thought that he should have continued working in order to keep himself busy and keep his mind off Carole.

And her ghost.

She did not appear again until the following night. He was in bed, trying to sleep, trying not to focus on the unusual sounds he'd been hearing in the house, on Carole's death or her apparent afterlife, on anything that he'd seen or felt, when, for some reason, he was compelled to open his eyes.

And there she was.

Still naked, the ghost stood on the mattress on Carole's side of the bed, looking down at him. There was no indentation on the mattress, no indication that any weight was being put on the bed despite the fact that the ghost feet were clearly standing flat on the sheet. This close, the detail was amazing. He could make out on the see-through skin the heart-shaped birthmark just below

Carole's right breast. Between the thatch of pellucid pubic hair was the faint suggestion of pale pink lips.

He sat up, but she didn't disappear this time.

His heart was pounding with fear. "Get out!" he screamed. "You're dead! Get out and don't come back!" He'd heard from one parapsychologist on some New Age pseudo-documentary that ghosts were people who were hanging around terrestrial life because they didn't know they had died and weren't ready to move on. He figured it was worth a shot. "You're dead! Leave me alone!"

But the ghost only smiled down at him, lifted her foot, pressed it into his face—

—and disappeared.

He'd seen her several times a day ever since. She was everywhere, all over the house, and he tried ignoring her, tried talking to her, tried yelling at her, tried praying. He tried everything he could think of to get rid of her, but she would not go away.

He was getting desperate, and he considered calling a priest or an exorcist or someone from a tabloid TV show. He had to do something.

She appeared that night in his dream.

It was a kinder, gentler ghost in his dream. There was not that overwhelming sense of wrongness that he'd experienced in the presence of the figure in life. Instead, the ghost was the same as the real Carole—only dead. She was standing in a field, next to a haystack, the kind of haystack that wasn't used anymore, and she was pointing toward a far-off light in the darkness.

"Return," she whispered.

He knew what she was telling him to do, and goose bumps popped up on both his arms. She was telling him to return home, to the house in Oakdale, the house of his birth. He did not know how he knew this, but he did, and even as he accepted its dream logic he was fighting against the request.

"No," he told the ghost.

"Return," she repeated.

Panic welled within him. Not because of Carole's

ghost but at the prospect of returning to the house in Oakdale.

"Return."

Norton awoke, breathing hard, drenched with sweat. He sat up in bed, reached for the cup of water he always kept on the nightstand and drank it all. He hadn't thought about the house in Oakdale for . . . hell, decades. He hadn't consciously *avoided* thinking about it— at least he didn't think he had—but he realized now that that was probably exactly what had happened.

He had not been back to Oakdale since moving forty years ago.

He closed his eyes, took a deep breath. If he'd been so grounded and logical and rational, if he hadn't believed in ghosts, why had he never gone back?

Why had he been *afraid* to go back?

Those were not questions he could answer.

He got out of bed, walked over to the window.

Carole was there.

She was not in his dream now. She was outside, on the grass, next to the tree, her ghost skin absorbing rather than reflecting moonlight.

"Return," she whispered, her words echoing in his head far louder than they had any right to do. "Return."

Frightened, he shivered, turned away.

The next day was Saturday, and he decided to walk across town to Hal Hicks's place. Hal had taught biology and algebra at the high school for thirty years and had retired a few years back when Ralph Stringer came in as principal. He was a good man and Norton's best friend, and if there was anyone he could tell this craziness to it was Hal.

The farther Norton got from the house, the sillier the notion seemed, however, and before he was halfway there he had pretty well decided not to mention anything about Carole's ghost. Around him, men were mowing their lawns, women were weeding flower beds, kids were riding up and down the sidewalk on bikes, trikes, and skates. Ahead, on Main, young couples and middle-aged women were shopping in the downtown business district.

Here, in the real world, around other people, he started to believe again that it was all in his head, a figment of his imagination. There was no such thing as ghosts.

But Hermie had seen it.

He pushed that thought from his mind.

Hal was outside, in his yard, watering his fruit trees.

"Summer's over," Norton said, walking up.

"They still need their water." Hal grinned. "Don't mess with me on biology."

Norton held up his hands in surrender.

"How you holding up?" Hal asked seriously.

He shrugged. Here at his friend's all of a sudden, the events of the past few days no longer seemed quite so silly. He thought once again about telling Hal what was going on.

"Tough time sleeping?"

"Of course," Norton told him.

"You look tired." He put down the hose, walked over to the faucet, turned it off. "Come on in, I'll put on a pot of coffee."

Norton followed his friend into the house. As always, there were piles of newspapers on the couch, leftover dishes on the dining-room table. Books were scattered everywhere.

He wondered if his house would look like this in a few years, as the female influence faded.

Probably.

They walked into the kitchen. Norton sat down at the table in the breakfast nook while Hal dumped the old grounds out of the Mr. Coffee machine and put in a new filter.

Norton just came out and said it: "Do you believe in ghosts?"

He surprised even himself by bringing it up, but he did not backtrack, and he watched Hal's hands as his friend measured out the coffee, not wanting to see the expression on his face.

Hal poured a potful of water into the machine, switched it on, and walked over to the table, wiping his hands on his pants. He sat down, stared at his friend levelly. "Have you felt Carole's presence?"

Norton nodded. He wanted to retract what he'd said, wanted to pretend this was all a joke, wanted to get off this subject, but he couldn't. "Yes."

Hal sighed. "You know, after Mariette died, I thought I felt her presence around the house, too. I didn't tell anyone, didn't talk about it to anybody, but I knew she was here. I *felt* it. I didn't see her or anything, but it was always as if I'd just missed her. I'd walk into the living room, and it'd be like she'd just walked into the kitchen the second before. Or I'd go into the bedroom, and I knew she'd just gone into the bathroom. I can't explain it, but you know how you can tell when a house is occupied, how it feels as if someone's there even though they're in another part of the house and you can't see them? That's what it was like. I never saw her, but I *knew* she was there."

"Why didn't you say anything?"

"Would you have believed me?"

Norton didn't answer.

"I figured everyone'd think I was crazy, want to put me in a home or something. Old widowed man thinking he's being haunted by his wife's ghost?" He shook his head.

Norton was silent for a moment. He cleared his throat. "I haven't just felt her, I've seen her."

Hal raised his eyebrows.

"This isn't just a 'presence.' It's a full-body apparition, a naked apparition, and it appears all over the house, at different times of day, in different places and positions."

"Naked, huh?" Hal chuckled. "Maybe you just need to get yourself a little poon."

Norton frowned at him.

"I'm sorry," Hal said quickly. "I'm sorry. I know it was insensitive and inappropriate. I didn't mean to offend—"

Norton waved him away. "You know me better than that, Hal."

"What is it, then?"

He hesitated. "She asked me to do something. *Told* me to do something."

"You've seen her *and* heard her?"

Norton nodded.

"What'd she say?"

"Well, it was just one word—'Return'—but I understood that she wanted me to go back to Oakdale, to my parents' old house."

"Why?"

"I don't know."

"You believe this? You think it's real?"

He hesitated only a second. "Yes."

Hal thought for a moment. "Maybe you'd better go."

Norton was already shaking his head. "I can't go back there."

"Why?"

"I just can't."

"When was the last time—"

"I haven't seen it since I left."

"How long ago was that?"

"When I went into the army. When I was eighteen."

"I take it you don't have fond memories of the place."

"I'm not going back."

Hal nodded.

They were silent for a moment.

"You get more spiritual as you get older," Hal said. "I don't know if it's because you get scared since you're closer to death, or because you're actually wiser than you used to be, but you start thinking about spiritual things, wondering why we're here, what the point of it all is, whether there's anything else. If I were you, I'd probably go. I'd probably do what the ghost said. There's a reason for it, something we don't understand, and I think I'd have to trust that."

Norton said nothing.

"We've felt these presences or seen these ghosts because we're supposed to. We're not too far from them ourselves, it's almost our time, and who's to say whether this isn't the way it works. Maybe everybody sees ghosts before they go, only they're like me, they're afraid to mention it, afraid to tell anyone."

Norton remained silent.

"This might be a warning. About your death. About

your afterlife. I don't know if you can afford to ignore it."

"I can't go back," Norton repeated.

"Why?"

"Because of what happened."

"In Oakdale?"

Norton looked at him. "In the house," he said.

"What did happen?" Hal asked quietly.

"I don't know," Norton admitted, and a wave of cold passed through him. "I can't remember. But it was bad." He shivered, rubbed his arms. "I know it was bad."

As usual, he was the last person at school save the custodians.

He'd stayed late in the past quite frequently, but it had become a daily routine during the time of Carole's ghost. Now that her spirit was gone, he remained out of habit.

Well, habit and the fact that he wasn't entirely sure she was gone for good.

The ghost had disappeared after that last appearance by the tree, after telling him to return home to Oakdale. It was as if she had done what she had come here to do, had completed her mission and moved on.

Strangely enough, the house seemed even creepier now that she had left. It had been unnerving to see Carole's nude form suddenly appear in a room, stressful to know that she could show up anywhere in the house at any time, without warning. But it had been an extension of her real presence, and though they hadn't always gotten along, it was somehow comforting and reassuring to know that Carole was still in the house.

Now, though, the house seemed . . . what?

He didn't know, couldn't explain it.

On the one hand, it was empty, completely devoid of any activity other than his own. On the other hand, that seemed to be just a temporary state of affairs. He had the feeling that Carole's ghost could return at any moment.

And that she might bring others.

It was impossible to put into words, this feeling, and

it might be simply the mental ravings of a doddering trauma-shocked old man, but he was more afraid of being in the house now than he had been when Carole's ghost was popping up left and right. It was stressful and it made him nervous, and its ripples were infringing on all other aspects of his life. It was even beginning to affect his teaching.

He'd considered selling the place, staying at a boardinghouse or a cheap hotel until he could find a new home or an apartment to rent, but he knew that that would not put an end to it.

There was also Oakdale hanging over his head.

Return.

He'd been thinking a lot about home, about Oakdale lately, but though he had the distinct sense that something horrible had happened there, something that had so alienated him it had kept him away all these years, the only memories he could conjure up were good—

the ants

—and whatever bad memories he had were buried under the layer of years. While he was sure he could uncover those core truths eventually, he was not at all sure he wanted to do so. He'd lived most of his life away from Oakdale, without thinking about it, and he saw no problem with doing the same for whatever years were left to him.

But could he afford to? Whatever was at stake here, it had to be pretty damn important if a ghost had been sent out to harass him.

Sent out by whom?

That was the real question. Although he'd gone to church on and off throughout his life, Norton basically considered himself an agnostic. Well, maybe not exactly an agnostic. A deist, perhaps, like Thomas Jefferson, an adherent to the clockmaker theory. He believed that God had created everything, had set it in motion, but was now on to other projects and other planets, trusting his creation to run in the way he'd intended and not deigning to bother in the affairs of men.

But the appearance of Carole's ghost had thrown him, and for the first time in his life he considered that maybe the fundamentalists were right. Maybe there was a traditional heaven and a traditional hell, and maybe God did take a personal interest in the minutiae of men. Maybe He was an old man with a long white beard who spent all His time monitoring what happened on earth.

Maybe God was trying to communicate with him.

Return.

That was the thought to which he kept coming back, and he had to admit that it frightened him. Hal was right; even if it was not God specifically who was urging him to return to Oakdale, it was some sort of higher power, something able to summon supernatural forces. And who was he to go argue with that? Who was he to go against the wishes of such a being? For all he knew, the fate of the world was at stake and his hesitation and procrastination might doom the human race for eternity. What would have happened if Noah had shirked his duty? What if Moses hadn't been in the mood to lead his people out of Egypt?

Egocentric thinking, he knew. Megalomaniacal even. He wasn't in that kind of position. The world wouldn't end because he refused to go back to Oakdale.

But could he afford to take that chance?

Hal had offered to go back with him, and as simple a gesture as it was, Norton found himself touched by it. He knew how scared his friend was for him, and he was grateful for the support. It was almost enough to tempt him into going.

Almost.

But the bottom line was that he was afraid. Afraid of what might happen, afraid of what he might learn, afraid of what he might remember. If it was God calling him in on this, He'd have to either inject some courage into these old bones or give him another sign of some kind and let him know how important this was and why.

Otherwise, he was staying home.

Norton sighed. Deep down, though, he didn't really believe it was God trying to recruit him. It was interesting to think about, and it was the argument he tried to use on himself, but if God was really trying to get in touch with him, He would have made it a more pleasant experience. He would have used an angel or a bright white light, not the nude ghost of Norton's dead wife. And the message would not have been so ambiguous. It would have been more direct.

If anything, this was a recruitment call not from God but from . . . the other guy.

The devil.

Satan.

There was a knock on the door and Joe Reynolds, the lead custodian, poked his head in the room. "You almost through in here, Mr. Johnson? I need to clean the floors."

Norton tossed a stack of papers and the teacher's edition of the twelfth-grade government textbook into his briefcase. "Just leaving, Joe. Don't mean to hold you up."

"Don't apologize, Mr. Johnson. I think the kids of this town would be a hell of a lot better off if *all* our teachers were as conscientious as you."

Norton smiled at him. "I think you're right."

He walked home the same way he'd walked to work this morning, through the field and over to Fifth Street, but there seemed something different this afternoon and he could not quite put his finger on what it was.

It was chilly once again, and there were red and yellow leaves on the sidewalks and the streets. The sun was not down, but it was low, and the neighborhoods through which he passed were shrouded in shadow. He put down his briefcase, buttoned up his coat against the cold. Fall was here, not officially but in spirit, and that cheered him up. No matter what else was going on, no matter how horrible his life became, there were still things to look forward to, still things to enjoy.

There was a lot to be said for simple pleasures.

At the next intersection, he turned right, onto Clover. Before him, there was a trail of burnt toast on the sidewalk, and he stopped in his tracks, staring at the line of blackened squares stretching out before him.

It came back to him. Not thoughts but feelings. Not images but ambiance.

A cool breeze brushed his cheek.

The burnt toast trail led down the block for as far as he could see, and though he was aware that it could have been placed there by some child as part of a game, he knew that was not the case. It would have taken hours to burn so many pieces of toast, even in the largest toaster, and there was no real point to it. That was too much effort, too much thought, too much work for such a bizarre and meaningless effect.

This was what it had been like in Oakdale, he realized. These were the sorts of things that had happened at home. It had been a world of sudden strangeness, of incongruous juxtapositions, a world in which the irrational was an everyday occurrence.

He stared at the sidewalk in front of him.

No child had done this.

The trail had been meant for him.

It was a sign.

Return.

The breeze was still blowing, but the coldness he felt had nothing to do with the weather. It came from within, and while he could not remember specifics of his life in Oakdale, he had a clearer sense of the overall picture, and he was even more frightened of it than he had been before.

Something was trying to communicate with him, and despite the trepidation he felt, he walked forward, down the sidewalk, following the toast.

The trail led to an empty house in the center of Sterling Avenue, two blocks away. Across the street, a mother standing on her front porch called her bundled daughters in for dinner while their friends continued to play hopscotch on the sidewalk. Several neighbors on both sides of the tree-lined drive waved and called out to each other as they walked their dogs.

No one seemed to notice the unwavering line of burnt bread, and he gathered his courage, took a deep breath, and followed it up the walk and into the open house.

Inside, the rooms were devoid of furniture. The toast trail ended at the porch steps, but there were piles of what looked like strawberry jam in the entryway, the front room, the hall, and the kitchen. Those were all the rooms he could see from the doorway, and he assumed the pattern continued through the bedroom and bathrooms.

He stepped slowly over the threshold, looking around. There was no movement, no sign of people or ghosts or beings of any sort, but the atmosphere was charged with tension and he had the feeling that he could be jumped at any time. The smart thing to do would be to turn back, leave, retreat, but he had to know why he'd been led here and he pressed on.

The girl was waiting for him in the empty back bedroom.

She could not have been more than ten or eleven, and she was wearing a dirty white shift that hung loosely on her thin frame and threatened with every movement to slip off her shoulders. Her filthy hair hung over her forehead in a way that seemed sensuous; not a parody of the posturing of an older girl, but a casually unforced naturalness that was sexy despite her age.

She was standing in front of a window, with the light from the house next door behind her, and he was aware that he could see her legs, backlit through the thin material of the shift, and his eyes were drawn to the meeting place of her thighs.

What the hell was wrong with him? This girl was young enough to be his granddaughter.

Granddaughter?

Great-granddaughter.

The girl smiled at him, and there was something so evil in that smile, something so unnatural and corrupt, that he turned without thinking and ran. It was an instinctive animal reaction. He was absolutely terrified, utterly panic-stricken, and he sped out of the room, down the hall, running faster than he ever had in his life.

In the hall, in the front room, in the entryway, he saw bugs working their way out of the strawberry jam as he leaped over or hurriedly skirted the piles, hundreds of black bodies squirming in the thick red substance, trying to escape.

He jumped off the steps, landing on the cement walkway and scattering the squares of burnt toast. His heart was pounding so furiously and painfully that he thought he might be having a heart attack, but he kept running and did not stop until he was two houses away and almost completely out of breath.

In his mind, he still saw that dirty, sexy little girl, smiling evilly at him. He could not get the image out of his head, and it made him want to keep running, to get as far away from here as quickly as possible, but both his lungs and legs were rebelling, and no matter how frightened he was, he knew he had to rest for a few moments or he wouldn't be getting out of this neighborhood at all.

Across the street, a dog-walking couple was staring at him and frowning, curious, no doubt, as to why an old man had run like hell from an empty house in which he was not supposed to be, and he looked over at them, grimaced, and waved. They turned away, embarrassed, and kept walking.

Norton bent over, resting his hands on his knees and trying to catch his breath. The sun was now almost down, and the shadows had darkened into dusk. He did not want to be on the street when night fell, but he could not afford to push himself any more than he already had. He exhaled deeply, inhaled just as deeply, attempting to regulate and control his breathing.

Jesus, he was in bad shape.

A few minutes later, he straightened, stood. His heart continued to pound, but his breathing had calmed down, and he decided to chance it. He started walking, crossing the street and heading toward Oak Road and Main. He moved slowly, but he didn't have to stop, and five minutes later he was on his own street in his own neighborhood.

The image of the dirty girl was still in his mind, and he started thinking that there was something familiar about her. He had not noticed it at first, but looking back on it, there'd been a spark of recognition in his initial reaction to her, a trace of the known in her appearance.

He had seen her before.

He reached his house, removed his keys from his pocket, unlocked the door, and stepped inside, flipping

on the lights. He'd half expected to see Carole's ghost
again, or some other manifestation, but the house was
empty and for that he was grateful.

He put down his briefcase, walked into the kitchen.

Donna..

That's who the girl reminded him of.

The ants.

Why hadn't he seen it immediately, the resemblance?
It was so obvious now that he thought about it. The
similarity between the two was frightening.

He walked over to the cupboard, took out a shot glass
and a bottle of scotch.

Donna.

The memories flooded back. They'd been friends. At
least it had started out that way. They'd played with
toys, made up games, imagined adventures. But something had changed somewhere along the way. He remembered the two of them beating up other children,
making them cry. Burying a live hamster. Skinning a
dog.

The ants.

It had been fun and he'd enjoyed it, but then things
had changed.

Then had come the sex.

He'd enjoyed that, too. He'd never known anything
like it, and he knew it was something his other friends
weren't getting to do, and it was not only the physical
pleasure it afforded, but the exclusivity of the act and
the air of the forbidden which surrounded it that so
heightened the experience, that made him feel the way
he did.

But then . . .

Then it had gone too far.

Donna had been younger than him but far more
knowledgeable, and as things progressed, she had attempted to entice him into perversity. The sex she'd suggested had been unnatural, the acts she wanted him to
perform with her things he had never even imagined. It
had frightened him and he had pulled away, but he could
not remember what happened after that. His memory

was hazy. Had she moved? Had they simply stopped being friends?

He couldn't recall.

But he had an erection even now, just thinking about it, and for the first time since he'd been a child, he allowed himself to remember what he and Donna had done.

He put down the bottle and the shot glass and walked out of the kitchen, down the hall to the bathroom.

He thought not only of what they'd done, but of what she'd *wanted* to do, of the perverted acts she'd wanted him to engage in, and he recalled the way the girl in the empty house had looked with the window behind her and the meeting of her thighs visible through the thin material of her dirty shift.

He imagined what she looked like without the shift.

Breathing heavily, he pulled down his pants, knelt before the toilet bowl.

He began to masturbate.

NINE

Stormy

Roberta was waiting for him when he got home.

With a lawyer.

The two of them sat on the chairs opposite the coffee table, and Stormy had no choice but to set himself down on the couch. The chairs were higher than the couch, so the two of them looked down on him while he looked up at them. He had to smile. An old movie trick. A visual metaphor. Place the good guys at a slightly higher angle so that there would be a subliminal sense of power and authority on their part, so that they were perceived to have the upper hand and the moral high ground.

It was probably the lawyer's idea.

This was entirely unexpected, completely out of the blue, but he pretended as though it was something he'd been anticipating, and he placed his briefcase on the shag next to the couch and smiled up at Roberta. "Did we have to bring the lawyers in at this stage?"

She frowned. "What the hell are you talking about?"

"Him." He nodded toward the lawyer, though he was suddenly unsure of himself.

"Mr. Reynolds? He's here," she explained patiently, "because the Finnigan brothers declared bankruptcy and you're one of their creditors."

"Is this a bad time?" the lawyer asked, looking from Roberta to Stormy.

Stormy shook his head tiredly. "No, it's fine." He found that he was a little disappointed Roberta was not trying to divorce him, and he tried to pay attention as Reynolds explained that the status of the downtown Albuquerque theater he'd bought with the Finnigan brothers with the intention of turning it into an art theater was now in limbo, but his mind kept wandering. He accepted the forms and folders given him, listened to his options, but figured he'd go over the details later at his leisure.

There were still questions as to whether, as a distributor, he was legally allowed to own a theater, and he'd remained a minority partner, owning forty-nine percent of the enterprise to the Finnigans' fifty-one. There were a lot of cases pending before various courts that addressed this issue and he'd hoped to avoid it entirely, but apparently unless he could get another majority partner, he'd either have to jump in and buy the entire business or forfeit his interest in the project to the bankruptcy court and accept whatever they could get for the theater at auction.

His mind was still on divorce, though. Somehow, this false alarm seemed to have lent him the confidence he'd lacked until now. He realized, for the first time, that an end to the marriage was a realistic possibility. Before now, it had been an abstraction, a fantasy almost, and for some stupid reason he'd assumed that if there was going to be a divorce, it would be initiated by her.

But why?

He could start divorce proceedings himself. He could take an active role in this. Instead of passively waiting for something to happen to him, he could take the initiative and do it himself.

Reynolds stood, handed him a card. "I guess that concludes it. If you have any questions over the next few days, feel free to call."

"I'll talk to my lawyer," Stormy said, "and have him get in touch with you."

Reynolds nodded. "My phone and fax number are on the card."

Stormy saw the other man to the door, watched him get into his black Bronco, and waved good-bye. He shut the door and looked back toward Roberta, who was still standing next to the coffee table.

She stared at him. "You really thought I wanted a divorce?"

He nodded. "Yeah."

She said nothing, only nodded and walked into the kitchen, an unreadable expression on her face.

He drove down to Albuquerque the next day.

Overnight, he'd pretty much given up his dream of owning an art theater. It was an old dream anyway, concocted in L.A. during his college days, when such places were the hip spots for hip students to hang out. Times had changed, though, and cable TV and the multiplexes had pretty well killed off the independently owned art house. Today's viewers were simply not as willing to make the effort to leave their homes and take a chance on quirky, unknown films when they knew they could catch the movies on cable in six months.

Hell, more people saw art films on video today than had ever seen them in a theater.

But it was still depressing.

He pulled up in front of the building and got out of the car to take a last look around. Now that he was out of the project, divorced from the hopes and wishes connected with it, he could see that the idea had been a shaky one. The neighborhood surrounding the theater was not commercial but industrial, having shifted some twenty years ago when downtown retail businesses moved to a newer area of the city. Not the greatest part of town even in the daytime, at night it would be downright spooky to anyone living above the poverty line.

He stared up at the broken marquee and peeling, weathered facade. They'd purchased the building but had not yet started on any of the renovations. Not that there were going to be that many. Art theater patrons liked a dingy, slightly seedy low-tech ambience. It differentiated them from other moviegoers, imparted a feeling of exclusivity to the viewing experience, made them think they were intellectual because they were willing to endure hardship for their love of art.

Still, the building was not up to code and its deteriorated condition was a little too run-down even for the art crowd.

Stormy walked up to the front doors, unlocked and opened them. He was supposed to drop his keys off at

the real-estate office, but he wanted to see his baby one
final time before putting it up for adoption.

He walked into the lobby and immediately the hair
on the back of his neck prickled. It was a physical sensation, a biologic response, not something originating in
his mind. Some instinctive animal part of his nature
sensed danger here, and though he would ordinarily put
such a reaction down to stress or psychological factors
and immediately dismiss it, this time he was not quite
so ready to ignore his response.

He thought of what Ken had said about Tom Utchaca
and his father, about what was happening on the reservation. Once again, the idea of a living doll jogged his
memory, but he couldn't quite recollect what in his past
would provide a correlation.

Maybe there was a doll somewhere in the theater.

His goose bumps doubled, tripled, and he was tempted
to walk out the way he'd come, drive straight to the
real-estate office, and drop off the keys. Even with the
front door open, the lobby was dark, its edges shadowed,
and both the stairway to the balcony and the open door
to the theater proper were pitch-black.

He moved over to the ticket booth, flipped the series
of light switches for the building. Soft yellow bulbs
flickered on but did little to dissipate the gloom.

The idea that there was a kachina doll—a *living* kachina doll—somewhere in the theater was stupid, but the
image was undeniably powerful. In his mind, he could
see one of the strange figures skulking under the projector in the booth, crawling under the seats in the theater,
lurking behind the screen in the storage area.

He'd never been one to let fear get the best of him,
though. If he even suspected he was scared of something,
he'd meet it head-on, fight it and tame it. He'd had a
fear of flying. Now he had a pilot's license. He'd had a
fear of the ocean. He'd taken a cruise to Alaska. This
was smaller, more specific, but that didn't make it any
less acceptable, and he wasn't going to let doubt and
fear and superstition run him out of his own building in
the middle of the day.

He walked forward, through the double doors on the

left side of the concession stand. Before him, rows of red seats sloped slightly downward. He saw no sign of movement in the aisles or on the abbreviated stage below the ripped screen, but he was still chilled, and he stood there for a moment, waiting, watching.

Nothing.

The interior of the theater was quiet, the only sound came from outside, and the silence made him feel a little better. He heard no claws on cement floor, no soft rustling, none of the sounds a doll would make if it was looking for him, coming after him.

If it was looking for him? Coming after him?

Where had he come up with that?

He didn't know.

But he knew the sounds.

He'd heard them before.

The silence was no longer quite so reassuring. He backtracked into the lobby. There was no reason for him to be here. He should lock up, turn in the keys, sign the papers, and get his butt back to Santa Fe before the afternoon rain started.

But he didn't want to feel like he was running away.

He stood for a moment, staring at the dust-covered popcorn machine, then turned and walked upstairs to the balcony.

By rights, this should have been scarier. It was darker, smaller, more claustrophobic, but the tension he'd felt downstairs faded up here, and as he looked down at the screen he felt nothing. It was an old run-down building, that's all. There was nothing unusual here, nothing out of the ordinary.

Why did he think he knew the sounds a doll would make if it was alive and coming after him?

Why did he think he'd heard them before?

He didn't want to even consider that.

He walked slowly back downstairs, intending to lock up and leave. He was past the curve of the stairwell, looking down at his feet, when movement caught his eye. He glanced up from the steps.

And saw the door to the men's rest room closing.

Ten minutes ago, he would've freaked and run out.

But his fear seemed to have fled, and all Stormy thought now was that he'd left the front door open, and some homeless guy had wandered in. He was going to have to find some way to get him out.

Great, he thought.

He hurried down the remaining steps, pushed the restroom door open, and said loudly, "All right—"

And stopped.

There was no one there.

Like the rest of the building, the bathrooms had fallen into a state of serious disrepair, and there were no stalls, no urinals, only a sink and one toilet amid the rubble and pipe fixtures.

The toilet had been used recently. Splashes of water dripped down from the lip, had wet the surrounding floor. Stormy stepped closer. The toilet had not been flushed, but what lay in the bowl water did not look like human waste. It looked like a fruit salad, and there was something about the incongruity of the fruit salad's appearance and its placement that set his already jangled nerves on edge.

He glanced over at the sink, saw a long-stemmed red rose embedded in a chunk of cheddar cheese that protruded from the drain.

This was too weird. This was too fucking creepy. He had no idea what was happening here or what it meant, all he knew was that he did not want to be a part of it. He no longer owned any portion of this building, and at this point he didn't care if they razed it and replaced it with a nuclear power plant. He just wanted to get the hell out.

He stared at the rose.

Living dolls were spooky enough, but they were at least understandable. They were within the range of acknowledged supernatural phenomena, like ghosts and witches and demons. But this was something else entirely. This was . . .

He didn't know what this was.

All he knew was that it scared the shit out of him.

He ran through the deserted lobby and, with trembling

fingers, locked the theater doors. He hurried back to his car.

Maybe this was an isolated occurrence. Maybe this was entirely unconnected to what was going on up at the reservation.

Maybe.

But he didn't think so.

He drove to the real-estate office, turned in his keys, signed the papers, and got the hell out of Albuquerque as quickly as he could.

But the fear followed him all the way to Santa Fe.

And it did not abate that night or the following day.

TEN

Mark

Dry River.

Rounded propane tanks in white trash backyards, tilted clotheslines of rusty pipe, plastic toys in sandy dirt, Dobermans behind chain-link fence. Liquor store, no-name market, Texaco gas station. The familiar hues and shades of the surrounding country: dark against light as the irregular shadows of clouds drifted, shifting, across low desert mountains.

Mark nodded his thanks to the man who'd dropped him off in front of the post office, watching him drive away before turning to survey the town. It was depressingly familiar after all these years, changed hardly at all. Past the bridge that spanned the town's namesake, huge cottonwoods lined the street, shading the buildings below. There were several bicycles parked in front of the small brick library, cars in front of the bar. Two barefoot boys walked toward the trailer park pool, carrying towels. The only noises in the still air were the competing mechanical hums of swamp coolers and air conditioners, and the occasional cry of a high-circling hawk.

Down the road to his left was a new subdivision that had not made it—six identical homes on a dead-end cul-de-sac surrounded by several acres of cleared desert—but other than that, everything seemed to be the same. He started walking, moving past the diner, the tack and feed store, and an empty lot filled with enormous spools of telephone cable, until he could look east toward the ranches.

Sure enough, their house still towered over everything on the plain, its black bulk intimidating even from here.

Kristen.

His gaze swept immediately toward the cemetery on the opposite side of town. Should he go there first? Or should he seek out the mortuary?

No. He wanted to go home before anything. Wanted to see for himself what, if anything, had happened at the house. He hefted his backpack, slipped his arms through the straps, and started off toward Ranch Road.

He passed the high school on his way, saw boys in green and gold football uniforms skirmishing on the field. Saturday morning practice. He remembered it well. He'd joined nearly every school activity imaginable in order to get away from the house, and although he'd been a piss-poor athlete, he'd made it onto all of the varsity sports teams because there wouldn't have been enough alternate players otherwise.

He walked away from town down the ungraded road toward the hulking behemoth that had been his home. It had a powerful effect on him even after all this time, and though it was still several miles away, the dark structure was clearly visible in the flat desert, and he found himself slowing down, not walking so fast, not wanting to reach the house before he had time to mentally prepare himself.

He wished he still had The Power.

There was a roaring, rumbling, clattering sound behind him, and Mark turned to see an old red pickup truck bumping along the road, leaving a cloud of dust in its wake. The operator of the vehicle seemed to be driving erratically, swerving from left to right in order to avoid known potholes and sections of washboard, and Mark moved to the edge of the road, trying to stay out of the truck's way.

With a sliding, dirt-churning stop, the pickup braked to a halt next to him. He waved the swirling dust away from his face, coughing, and saw through brown cloud that the driver was rolling down the passenger window.

Mark moved forward, squinting.

The man was wearing a stained tank top. His lined face was red, his hair thin and greased, combed back. Classic Arizona alky.

Was it someone he knew? Hard to tell. The desert aged people, the sun and the hardscrabble lifestyle combining to add years not yet lived to younger features and faces, but he thought there was something familiar about the man.

"Where you going?" the driver asked.

"The McKinney ranch."

"Kristen's place? Ain't no one out there. She passed on a few days ago."

"I know. I'm her brother."

The alky squinted. "Mark? Is that you?" He laughed, shook his head. "Didn't recognize you, boy."

He knew now who the man was. Dave Bradshaw's older brother, Roy.

"Hop on in. I'll give you a lift."

Mark opened the dented door and climbed into the pickup, pushing his backpack onto the seat between them. He nodded to the driver. "Thanks, Roy. Much obliged."

"Never expected to see you here again. Heard you hit the road and were never comin' back."

"Yeah, well . . ."

Roy shifted into gear and the truck lurched forward. "It's a shame about Kristen. A damn shame."

Mark swallowed, took a deep breath. "Is there going to be a funeral?"

"Already over. Nearly everyone showed up. Kristen was quite a popular gal 'round these parts. Not like your parents." He glanced over at Mark. "No offense."

"None taken." They drove in silence for a few moments, Mark listening to the clatter and roll of the truck on the rough road. "Who found her, Roy? Who . . . discovered that she was dead?"

"Guy who delivered bottled water. She didn't answer the door, he had a hunch and dialed 911. Course, by the time they got out there she was gone."

"Was it—"

"Heart attack. Don't usually happen that way to someone so young, but . . ." He trailed off, shook his head. "It's a damn shame." He reached over Mark's leg, popped open the glove compartment, pulled out a half-finished bottle of rye. "Like a little drink?"

Mark shook his head.

Roy drove for a few seconds with his knees as he expertly opened the bottle, taking the wheel again with his left hand as he used his right to tilt the bottle to his lips. "Aaaah!" he sighed, grinning.

"Dave still in town?" Mark asked.

"Hell, no. Moved to Phoenix after Mom passed on. It's just me and the old man now."

"How're things going here?"

"They're going."

What he really wanted to ask about was Kristen, her funeral, the details of her death, but some of his parents' reticence must have rubbed off on him, because he didn't feel comfortable discussing personal matters, family matters, in public. Especially not with someone like Roy.

Ahead, through the dirty windshield, to the right, the bulk of the house was growing ever bigger, ever closer. *Giant.*

Roy took another swig from his bottle. "You know," he said. "I never did like your house. Never understood why Kristen stayed after your parents passed on. She could've sold it, moved somewhere else, somewhere nice."

Mark didn't understand either, not really, and a slight chill caressed his spine. He licked his lips. "Is Mr. Billings still there?"

Roy frowned. "Billings? Never heard of 'im."

"Hired man? Used to work for my father? Had a retarded daughter?" He tried to jog Roy's memory, but the other man just kept shaking his head.

"Don't ring no bell."

That wasn't entirely surprising. As Roy said, his parents hadn't exactly socialized with their neighbors, and it had been a long time ago. Maybe his father had eventually fired Billings. Or laid him off. Or Billings had simply moved on.

And taken his retarded daughter with him.

"Fuck me in the ass."

He tried to imagine the girl as a teenager; as an adult, but he couldn't. She'd have to be in her mid-twenties now, but Mark could not picture her as anything except the child he remembered.

"Your father does it."

"Kristen didn't live alone, though. She had help—"

"No. Far as I know, she lived by herself."

"No other people came to the funeral? No one you didn't recognize? No . . . hired help?"

"No one 'cept her friends from Dry River." He looked over at Mark. "How'd they ever get in touch with you? I heard tell Frank Neeson was tryin' like hell to find your sorry ass but no one knew where you were. Weren't even in Kristen's phone book or nothing. Guess he finally tracked you down, huh?"

"Yeah," Mark said, not wanting to explain.

"Didn't tell you much, though, did he?"

Mark shook his head. "No."

They reached the ranch gate, and the pickup skidded to a stop. "Here's where I let you off," Roy said. He peered through the open passenger window at the black gabled building. "Still don't like that house," he said.

Mark opened the door and pulled his backpack by one of the shoulder straps. He hopped out and wiped the sweat from his forehead with the back of a sleeve. "Thanks for the lift," he said. "Appreciate it."

"I'll be coming back this way in about an hour or so. Want me to stop by, give you a ride?"

Mark looked up at the hot blue sky, nodded. "Sounds good."

"Be waitin' for me by the gate here. I'll give three honks. If there's no sign of you, I'll head on."

"All right." Mark waved as the pickup took off, but even if Roy had been looking, he wouldn't have been able to see through the dust. Coughing, Mark backed away from the road and turned away. Before him was the closed gate and beyond that the drive that led to the house.

He lifted the latch, swung the gate open, closed it behind him, and stood there for a moment. He was afraid. He'd known that already, of course, but the emotional reality of it had not penetrated until now. He stared at the dark structure, and though the front of the house was facing the sun, there was no glare off the windows. The entire facade of the house was the same flat black, its specific features differentiated only by slight variations in tone. It was as if the building swallowed the sunlight, absorbed it, and Mark noticed that the bushes and plants that were in what would be the perimeter of the house's shadow were all brown and dead.

He was just being overly dramatic. The plants were dead because there was no one here to water them. Without daily attention, everything except cactus and sagebrush died in the desert, and Kristen was no longer here to take care of the property.

That meant that Billings was gone.

It felt as though a weight had been lifted off his chest. From what Roy had said, it sounded as though the assistant was no longer here, but Roy was obviously not the most reliable of witnesses and Mark had always been a hope-for-the-best-and-expect-the-worst kind of guy. There was no way Billings would have allowed the plants to die, though, and to Mark that was as good a proof as any that the assistant was gone.

That meant his daughter wouldn't be here either.

"Fuck me in the ass."

His gaze swept involuntarily to the window where he'd last seen the girl, but it was as flat and lifeless as the rest of the house and he saw nothing there.

He walked slowly forward, rippling heat waves creating a mirage puddle on the drive ahead and filtering the bottom of the house through a wavy mirror. In back of the house and to the side were the chicken coops, but Mark could see even from this far away, even through the heat waves, that they'd fallen into a state of disrepair and were no longer used. More proof that Billings was not here.

Why was he so concerned about the assistant?

Because Billings frightened him. He did not know why, and it had never been the case when he'd lived here, but he was terrified of running into the assistant again. In his mind, Mark saw the man looking exactly the same as he had all those years ago, and that, more than anything else, engendered a feeling of dread within him. The assistant's kindness and bland passivity now seemed to him to be masking an unnatural patience and an unfathomable intent. He could imagine Billings waiting, biding his time, picking off the family one by one until there was only Mark left and he was drawn back to the house.

God, he wished The Power hadn't deserted him.

Even more frightening was the prospect of running into Billings' daughter, of seeing the girl again. He remembered how she hadn't aged before, and he could easily imagine her unchanged, bending over a chair in that dark endless hallway and flipping up her shift.

"I like it hard. Fuck me hard."

He should've gone to the mortuary first, the cemetery, the sheriff's office. It was a mistake to have come here unprepared and all alone. What the hell could he have been thinking?

Still, he continued forward, down the dual-rutted drive with its ever-retreating mirage water, past the sandstone boulders that lined the ragged, shallow, irregularly shaped hole his father had intended to be a pond. The sweat was dripping down the sides of his face, and he had to keep wiping his forehead with his sleeve, but inside he was cold, and the ice within him kept the goose bumps alive on his arms.

He reached the house, walked up the deep porch steps, aware suddenly of how quiet it was. There were no whirs, hums, or other mechanical sounds, none of the noises of civilization. That was to be expected. The ranch was far from town, and the house was empty, everything shut off. But even nature was silent, and that he found more than a little creepy. In this heat, there should have been cicada buzzes, snake rattles, hawk cries.

But there was nothing.

Only the sound of his own feet on the porch boards and the wheeze of his overheated breath.

He no longer had a key for the front door—he'd tossed it off the edge of the Rio Grande Gorge in his own private exorcising ritual several years back—but he knew where his parents had kept a spare, and sure enough, Kristen had continued the tradition. It was on the top of the porch light, just behind the lip edge, and he felt around up there until his fingers found the dusty object.

Once again, he considered turning back, leaving, but he reminded himself that he was not doing this for his own peace of mind, he was doing it for Kristen. He had failed her, and if he was a little uncomfortable at the moment, well, that was just too damn bad. She'd put up with a hell of a lot worse, and it was the least he could do.

The chill in his body intensified as he opened the door and walked inside the house. It was exactly as he'd remembered. Kristen had not altered even the arrangement of the pictures on the walls. Everything was untouched: furniture in place, throw rugs unmoved. It took his breath away, this sudden wholesale immersion in the past, and he stood there for a moment, stunned. The heavy wood, the dark walls and floor and ceiling, all seemed horribly oppressive to him, a reminder of his childhood, and he wondered how his sister had put up with it. Could she have possibly found this atmosphere pleasant? Comforting?

The thought of Kristen living in this unchanging house, all alone, tugged at his heart, and his fear abated somewhat, replaced by an aching sense of loss.

Why hadn't he come back earlier?

Why hadn't he taken her away from this?

He walked slowly forward. To his left, out of the corner of his eye, he saw something out of place in the front sitting room, and he turned in that direction, the blood freezing in his veins even before he recognized what he saw.

Billings.

Sitting in his father's high-backed smoking chair.

As he'd feared, as he'd known, the assistant had not changed at all.

Billings smiled. "Welcome back, Mark. I've been waiting for you."

ELEVEN

Daniel

It was raining, a heavy fall Pennsylvania rain that drew a curtain over the city and blurred even the houses across the street into indistinct shadows of gray. The snow would be coming soon, and Daniel knew that as tough as it was trying to find a job in good weather, it was absolute hell in the winter. He might as well just write off the next five months and hibernate until spring.

From down the hall, he heard Margot and Tony laughing about something. He'd been getting the cold shoulder from both of them ever since he'd disposed of the doll, and he was getting pretty damn sick of it. He and Margot hadn't made love in a week, and she seemed to be dead serious about wanting him to seek psychological help. He'd tried to explain to her how he felt, what he'd seen, why he was acting this way, but his far-flung concerns had no connections, there were no discernible bridges between the disparate elements of his only partially tied-together tale, and he had to admit that his story sounded loony even to himself.

Tony seemed to be afraid of him.

Daniel sighed. Maybe he did need help. Maybe everything was in his mind, and nothing out of the ordinary was going on. The world was a logical, rational straightforward place, and the thoughts he'd been thinking had a place only in pulp fiction and B movies.

Margot walked into the kitchen, looked at him, and for the first time this week, the sight of him did not knock the smile off her face. She was finally beginning to thaw. He attempted a halfhearted grin and was grateful when she passed by and touched his shoulder.

"Are we pals again?" he asked.

"We're always pals."

He reached for her hand, gave it a small squeeze. There was a lot more he wanted to say, a lot more he wanted to ask, a lot more he wanted to tell her, but while he was in her good graces again, it was only by a slim margin, and the slightest misstep could send him back. He'd have to broach things slowly, subtly, carefully for the next few days.

Margot opened the refrigerator, took out a plastic bag of tomatoes from the vegetable drawer. "Brian's coming over for dinner tonight," she said.

The last thing he wanted right now was to spend the evening with her brother, but he smiled and nodded and said, "Great."

The evening didn't turn out to be that bad. Brian didn't bring up Daniel's job status even once, and he left early, just after nine-thirty. While he was there, he was pleasant, playful with Tony, cheerful with Margot, and after dinner, when the two of them were alone—Tony having disappeared into his bedroom, Margot washing the dishes—even he found Brian entertaining and fun to be around. The two of them would never be best buds, but Daniel thought that he'd probably been too hard on his brother-in-law, and he vowed to be nicer to him in the future.

It was still raining pretty heavily outside, and he wanted to go to bed and get into some makeup sex, but Margot said she wasn't tired and wanted to stay awake a little longer. There was nothing on HBO or any of the other channels, so he ran through their videotape titles. None of the movies sounded good, and they finally settled on watching some episodes of *Fawlty Towers,* Margot's favorite TV show of all time.

She went off to go to the bathroom while he fast-forwarded to an episode they hadn't seen in a while, the one with Manuel's rat. On an impulse, he walked back to Tony's room. The door was closed, and he pressed his ear to it but could hear nothing. Margot was still in the bathroom, and he paused a moment, then pushed open his son's door.

A half-finished doll lay on the center of Tony's bed. This one, if possible, was even worse than the one before. Like its predecessor, it was made up of junk-food cups and plastic straws, toilet-paper tubes and toothpicks. But the newspaper photographs that had been cut out and taped together to form its composite face were angry and wild: widely staring eyes, flared nostrils, screaming mouth. The effect was one of discordance and derangement, and Daniel looked from the doll to his surprised son, who belatedly moved his body in front of the figure to hide it.

Daniel stared at the boy, felt the anger rise within him. "I warned you, didn't I?"

"There's nothing wrong with it!" Tony replied defensively. "It's just my project!"

Daniel crossed the room in two steps, moved the boy aside with one arm, grabbed the doll with the other.

Did Margot know about this?

If she did, he'd get into it with her. Sticking up for her son in an argument was one thing, but deliberately going behind his back and helping Tony to deceive him was another.

The doll felt strange in his hand. Heavier than it should. More solid. He squeezed it hard, tried to crumple it, but only succeeded in creating two slight indentations in the cup body.

He shook the doll at his son. "I told you you couldn't do this, didn't I?"

Tony cowered before him. "You don't have to go crazy."

He was a little more out of control than he should be, more adamant than he wanted, and he tried to calm down. "I specifically told you—"

"Mom!"

Daniel turned to see Margot standing in the doorway.

She *hadn't* known about the doll. There was a split-second expression of surprise upon her face, then what looked like fear crossed her features as her gaze passed over the figure. Her eyes met Daniel's, and the two of them exchanged a wordless understanding.

Margot stepped into the room, her face set. "Your father told you not to make another one of those dolls."

"It's not a doll!"

"You purposely disobeyed him."

"But, Mom!"

"No 'buts,' " Daniel said. He was still holding the doll in his hand, but he wanted to drop it, get rid of it. The irrational fear that it would come to life and suddenly attack him, biting his face with its newsprint mouth, had come over him and refused to be dislodged from his brain. He could not let his son see that he was afraid of the figure, though, and he shook it again at the boy. "You're grounded for a week. And if I ever catch you doing this again, you're going to be in big, big trouble."

Margot looked at him again, her eyes worried, before turning once more toward Tony. "Why is this thing so important to you? Why are you doing this?"

Tony stared down at his shoes. "Nothing," he said.

"The answer to 'why?' is never 'nothing.' "

"I don't know."

"Look at me, young man." He glanced up at his mother. "There's something going on here that you're not telling us."

"I'm sorry. I won't do it again."

"What is the big deal about this doll?"

"It's not—"

"It's a doll," she said flatly.

"Where did you learn how to make it?" Daniel asked.

"Doneen," Tony said reluctantly. "Doneen taught me how to do it."

Doneen?

Margot's expression was blank. She'd obviously never heard of anyone named Doneen.

But he had.

In the House.

"Who's Doneen?" he asked.

"A new girl. She lives over on Edgecomb."

"When did you meet her?" Margot asked. "And why haven't you said anything to us about her?"

Tony shrugged uncomfortably.

"Is she in your class?"

"Not exactly."

Daniel felt cold. "You can't see her anymore," he said. "You understand me?"

"Why not?"

"I don't want you to."

"She's a nice girl."

"I don't care."

"Her dad said he wanted to talk to you."

"Her dad?"

"Mr. Billingsly."

The coldness intensified.

Billingsly.

He'd heard that name before, too.

Daniel dropped the doll in the trash can, wary of holding on to it any longer. He'd pick it up later and make sure it was destroyed. He sat down on the bed next to Tony, putting an arm around his son's shoulders. "Look," he said. "Whether you believe it or not, we're doing this for your own good."

"But—"

Daniel held up his hand. "Let me finish. I'll go talk to this Mr. Billingsly tomorrow, but until your mother or I tell you otherwise, you are not to see this girl Doneen and you are not to make any more dolls."

Tony stared up at him. There was no duplicity in the boy's eyes, no indication that he was lying or intentionally trying to deceive them. Daniel had the feeling that his son didn't really know why the doll was so important to him or why he was so compelled to work on the object.

He found that frightening.

His anger had abated somewhat, and for the first time he saw both himself and Tony as pawns, small players in a much larger game. He had no clue as to what that game was or who was playing it or what its purpose might be, but he was determined to find out before anything happened to his family.

He glanced up at Margot, saw both concern and confusion in her eyes.

"I'm sorry," Tony said.

"You're off the hook this time," Daniel told him. "Just don't let it happen again."

They lay in bed, reading their respective magazines. Or pretending to. The television murmured softly in the background.

Margot put down her *Time* and shifted in the bed, turning toward Daniel. "I'm scared," she said.

He wrapped a protective arm around her shoulder. "I thought you were overreacting about Tony's . . . 'project.' I'm sorry I didn't back you up. I didn't realize it was this obsession with him."

"At least it's not drugs."

"I almost wish it were," she said softly. "At least we'd know how to deal with it."

"You don't mean that," Daniel said.

She sighed. "I suppose not. But it's not normal, his fixation on making this doll. It's like he *has* to do it, like he's driven to do it. And he has to use exactly the same things to make it with." She twisted her neck to meet his eyes. "And what's with this girl and her father?"

"I don't know."

"The father of the girl who taught him to make this doll wants to meet you? What's that all about?"

He shook his head, hoping his face didn't betray the unease he felt.

Margot's voice was flat. "Maybe he's involved in a cult," she said. "Maybe he's turning into one of those suburban kids who are into devil worship."

"I don't think so."

"What is it then?" Margot asked.

It was his chance to come clean, to tell her about the shadow and what he remembered about the House, what he thought and what he suspected, everything. But he wanted to protect her, didn't want her involved.

"I don't know," he said.

Doneen and Billingsly.

Daniel started the car, turned on the windshield wipers. The names were connected in his mind with the House, but he could not recall their origins or put a face to either of them. He'd heard the names before, though. Of that he was sure, and he pulled out of the driveway and drove around the block to Edgecomb Avenue.

The rain had abated during the night, but it had started up again a half hour ago, and he drove slowly through the puddle at the intersection, careful not to splash a pair of raincoated kids waiting on the sidewalk to cross.

Tony had stuck to his story about the girl and her father, had insisted that Mr. Billingsly wanted to talk to him, but it was obvious that his son did not want him to go over and meet either of them. He was purposely vague about which house the Billingslys lived in, and he kept insisting that it was over, he'd learned his lesson, he'd never make another doll again.

Something was going on here.

Daniel vowed that he'd find the Billingslys if he had to knock on every door and ask every single person in every single house on Edgecomb.

He parked at the end of the street and got out of the car, opening his umbrella. The rain was back down to a drizzle. Daniel was grateful for that, and he hopped over the running gutter onto the sidewalk. He felt a little strange walking up to the door of the first house, a little foolish, but by the time he reached the fifth house, he had his spiel down pat and his embarrassment had given way to uneasiness.

Before he'd finished with the first side of the street, he knew the truth.

There was no one named Billingsly living on Edgecomb.

No one had seen or heard of a girl named Doneen.

He went up the opposite side of the street just in case, but the result was the same. Neither adult nor child knew anything about Tony's mysterious acquaintances.

Daniel got back into the car and sat for a moment behind the steering wheel, staring out the windshield at the rainy street.

What bothered him the most was that he knew his son was not lying. Doneen was not simply a made-up person or a figment of Tony's imagination. She and her father were real. Or, rather, Tony had really met them.

How did he know that? How could he be so sure?

Because he'd met them himself as a child.

There it was again, on the tip of his consciousness, just that side of recollection. He knew he'd met them but could not recall any specifics. He tried not to derail this train of thought, tried to keep his mind on that narrow track, but other thoughts intruded, expanding his concentration outward, and his brief tenuous grasp of the past slipped, any hope he had of pinning down those memories gone. There remained only the certainty, not backed up by detail, that he had once met Doneen and Mr. Billingsly, and that Tony had too.

He started the car, pulled out into the street. Rather than back up or execute a three-point turn in the rain, he drove down to the end of Edgecomb and turned left, intending to drive around the block and return to their street.

He was halfway down Edgecomb when he saw it.

There, in the rain, in the middle of the street, a small shadow, the same shadow he'd seen before in the alley.

Doneen?

He braked to a halt, jumped out of the car, but it was gone. The street was empty, the sidewalks vacant, no sign of anyone or anything out of the ordinary. The rain chose that moment to stop entirely, and through a thin curtain of white amid the dark clouds above, the light of the sun poked through, illuminating the neighborhood.

Nothing.

That was it, the last straw. This was enough. He had to know. He'd had his fill of these half remembrances and partial sightings and nebulous portents. He wanted to know about the House. He wanted to know what had happened to him there and what it had to do with Margot and Tony. He wanted to know why he couldn't remember his past. He wanted to know what the hell was going on.

He'd talk to Margot about it, call a psychiatrist tomorrow, one that specialized in hypnosis and regression therapy. Her insurance had to have some type of mental health provisions. He could say he suspected that he'd been molested as a child. Hell, he could just tell the truth, explain what he'd been seeing and hearing and thinking, and he'd have no problem finding a shrink willing to uncover the dark secrets of his past.

He didn't have to go to a psychiatrist, though.

It came back on its own.

All of it.

TWELVE

Laurie

Laurie dug through the box of her parents' photographs looking for a clue, trying to find some documentation of her previous life, some hint of her pre-adoptive days. Josh sat next to her on the floor, sorting through additional piles of pictures, attempting to help her reconstruct a past that neither of them knew anything about.

She stared at a photo of herself and Josh at Disneyland, waving and smiling in front of It's A Small World.

She was adopted.

It shouldn't have affected anything, but it did, and already she felt distanced from Josh, not as close to him as she had been before. She'd give anything in the world to bring back her old feelings, but the knowledge that they were not really related had completely changed the emotional dynamics of their relationship, and she felt simultaneously as if a weight had been lifted from her shoulders and as if she were floating off into space, her tether broken.

She had to bear in mind that it was only *her* feelings that had changed. He had known all along, so his perception of her was exactly the same as it had always been.

He loved her like a sister.

She felt guilty that she was allowing the concrete sciences of biology and genetics to affect the fragile nature of her own feelings and emotions.

"Hey," Josh said excitedly. "I think we have something here. Look at this."

He scooted next to her on the floor, handing her an old black-and-white photo.

Their parents were standing with her biological parents.

In front of the house.

It was everything at once, in one picture, and she stared at it dumbly, taking it all in. There was the forest behind the house: old growth redwoods, holding in darkness. The Victorian mansion: black gables and shuttered windows and wraparound porch, retaining even in the photo the aura of spookiness she so clearly remembered.

In front of the house, on the circular dirt drive, were her parents.

All four of them.

The ones who had brought her up, the only parents she knew, Josh's parents, were smiling for the camera, their flowered paisley clothes loud even in black-and-white, a large trunk on the ground to the left of them. On the other side of the trunk, unsmiling, wearing formal clothes and equally formal expressions, were her real parents, her biological parents.

She looked closely at first her mother's face, then her father's, then back again. She recognized the faces now, but they engendered no response, triggered no emotion within her. She didn't know what she'd expected—some cathartic rush of long pent-up feeling perhaps—but she wasn't prepared for this detached, objective reaction. As she stared at the photo, her feelings were for her other parents, her adoptive parents, and for the first time since she'd learned what had happened to her, she was glad Josh's parents had adopted her, glad she had not grown up with this sober, grimly humorless couple.

She looked over at Josh, and once again he felt like her real brother.

She focused her attention on the photograph. It was all familiar to her, everything in the picture, and, despite her lack of feeling for the man and woman who had brought her into this world, the relentless curiosity about her past and compulsive thirst for self-knowledge that had been driving her for the past several days, ever since she found out she'd been adopted, had not abated at all. If anything, those impulses were stronger, and her desire to know what had happened to her, why she'd been adopted—

why her parents had been murdered

—was a palpable hunger, almost a physical need. She felt strongly that whatever had happened at that house, whatever cataclysm had destroyed her family, was connected with the dreams she was having now, with the girl.

Dawn.

"Do you know this place?" she asked, pointing at the photo. "Do you know where it is?"

Josh nodded. "I remember that house." He thought for a moment, turned to her. "Do you?"

She shivered. "How could anyone forget it?"

"It's on a vortex," he said.

Cut out the New Age crap, she wanted to tell him, but something kept her from it.

"Of course, we didn't know what that was back then. Especially not me. I was what? Four? But even I could tell there was something . . . *powerful* about that house."

"You mean it was haunted."

"Is that what you remember?"

She nodded.

He took the photo from her. "That's how I remember it, too."

"Do you know where it is?" she repeated.

He stared at the picture. "I was pretty young, but I know we were traveling around northern California for a month or so. I can't recall if we were on a vacation or just bumming around—you know how Mom and Dad were—but we'd stopped in this small gold-rush town somewhere in the Sierras. I don't remember the name, but I'd probably be able to pick it out if I saw a map or something."

She smiled at him, punched his arm playfully. "And you were only four years old? That's pretty impressive."

"I grew up to be an underachiever."

"So what happened?"

"We stayed in town for a day or so, then we went out to visit these people. They might've been friends of Mom and Dad's or maybe someone in town told them about them. I can't remember. All I know is that pretty soon we were driving down this winding little road through the forest, looking for these people who sold lamb's wool blankets. We passed through a clearing where there were people selling juice and fruit from a little roadside stand, and Dad bought me some blackberry juice. That part's pretty clear. Then the next thing I remember is being at this big giant house in the middle of nowhere." He tapped a finger on the picture. "*This* house." He frowned. "Come to think of it, I think they might've been friends. It seemed like they knew each other from somewhere before, because they greeted each other like they were old pals."

"Did you stay there?"

"Oh, yeah. For several days."

Laurie shook her head wonderingly. "How come I don't remember any of this?"

"That's the funny thing. I don't remember you either. I mean, you must've been there, but I just remember this weird old couple—" He looked at her. "Sorry. No offense—and this . . . overpowering house. I mean, I know now that the house was on a vortex, but back then I just thought it was scary."

"So you don't remember me at all?"

He shook his head.

What about the man who'd lived with them? she wondered. Her father's friend. She thought hard, tried to remember his name. She could see his face, hear his voice, but she couldn't quite—

Billington.

That was it.

"Do you remember anyone else?" she asked.

He frowned. "No . . ." he said slowly. "I don't think so."

"Who took the picture?"

He looked at it again. "I don't remember. A man, I think."

"Was his name Billington or something like that?"

"I don't remember."

"Did you see anyone else while you were there?" She licked her lips. "A girl maybe?"

He picked up on it instantly, glancing sharply at her. "The girl in your dreams?"

She nodded a reluctant acknowledgment. "I think her name was Dawn."

"And that's the same girl you saw in the alley?"

Already there were goose bumps on her arm. "I think so."

"Why didn't you tell me this before?"

"I didn't know before. I just sort of . . . It's coming back slowly. And I can't remember half as much as you remember. And you were younger than me." She paused. "Trauma, probably."

"Trauma?"

"I think my parents were killed."

A pause. "I figured it was probably something like that."

"You don't remember anyone except my parents?"

"Sorry." He shook his head. "But I want to know more about this girl. Dawn. When you saw her in the alley, when you dreamed about her, she looked like she did . . . then?"

"She looked exactly the same."

"You think she was killed, too?"

"I don't know. I don't think so."

"You think you saw a ghost?"

"No."

"A hallucination?'

"No."

They were both silent for a moment.

"So what happened while you were there?" Laurie asked finally. "What else do you remember?"

Josh chewed his lower lip, a thinking habit he'd had since childhood. "I remember being scared. I remember a long hallway. With dark wood and red velvet. Like a Victorian whorehouse. I remember not being able to sleep because I kept hearing weird noises. A tapping. Like someone was knocking on my door, trying to get in. I remember that I thought your parents didn't really seem happy to see us. Like we'd come at a bad time or something. Like they were fighting but had to pretend to get along because they had company." He met her eyes. "And I remember that your dad got really mad at me because I was late for breakfast. I was tired and Mom and Dad let me oversleep, and your dad went crazy. My parents and your parents almost got in a screaming match, and I felt really guilty. I'd already woken up and come downstairs to eat, and I heard them fighting and I started crying. Mom and Dad tried to comfort me, but your dad said something like, 'That's what he deserves.'" Josh's voice had fallen almost to a whisper. "Your dad scared me. I didn't like him."

Laurie hugged her brother. "I don't think I would've either." She smiled at him. "I'm glad Mom and Dad adopted me."

"I am too."

She pulled away. "What else?"

"That's it, really. I think we did buy some blankets from them, although I'm not sure that's why we really went over there."

"Then what?"

He shrugged. "We left. Continued on with our vacation or our travels or whatever it was. We finally settled in Thripp's Crossing, and a couple months later, you showed up."

"I just showed up?"

"Well no, not literally. Mom and Dad left. I stayed with Mrs. Kylie, and when they came back they had you."

"They never told you why? Never explained why you suddenly had a new sister?"

"Nope."

Laurie sighed. "I don't remember any of that at all. I wish I did, but it's all a big blank."

Josh handed her back the photo. "I never put two and two together before this. I never realized that those people were your real parents. I remembered them, I remembered the trip, but I don't remember you there, so I never connected it. When I saw that picture, though . . . something clicked."

"For me too." She grabbed another handful of photographs out of the box. "Let's see if we can find some other ones."

"There's one more thing," Josh said slowly.

Laurie looked up, and she realized that she was already holding her breath.

"I've never told this to anyone before, and I don't know if it really happened or if I just dreamed it or . . ." He trailed off.

"What?"

"I might've just imagined it."

"What?"

"I think I watched your mother kill a lamb."

She shook her head, confused. "I don't . . . I don't understand. You watched her slaughter a lamb?"

"No. The lamb was in my room. I don't know why. It wasn't night, it was daytime, but it was always dark inside that house and there wasn't much difference. I'd just come in from outside and I was going to . . . I don't know, get a comic book out of my suitcase or something. I ran upstairs as fast as I could because I wanted to get back down to where Mom and Dad were as quickly as possible, and there was this lamb in my bed. Just standing there on the mattress. The covers were pulled down, and it was just . . . baaing. It couldn't really move because it was heavy and the mattress wasn't that stable, and it looked at me and cried.

"And then your mom came out of my closet and told me she was sorry, the lamb wasn't supposed to be in my room, and she lifted it off the bed and . . . slammed it onto the ground."

Laurie could not believe she'd heard right. "What?"

"She lifted the lamb over her head, like a weight lifter or something, and threw it down on the floor as hard as she could and . . . killed it. It didn't move, didn't make any noise, and she picked it up and smiled at me and apologized again and carried it out of the room. There was blood dribbling out of its mouth, but the carpeting was dark red already and you couldn't really see where it dripped. Like I said, I don't know if that was a nightmare and I imagined it or if it really happened, but I never told Mom and Dad and I never said a word about it to anyone until now."

Laurie picked up the photo again, looked at the face of the grim woman who had been her mother.

She could see her throwing a lamb down hard enough to kill it.

"I dreamed about Dawn and a butcher. You saw my mom slaughter a lamb. This is just too close for comfort."

Josh nodded. "I agree."

"I want to see the house," Laurie said. "I want to go there. You said you'd recognize the name of the town if you saw it?"

"I just need something to jog my memory."

"Let's find a map, then."

"All right." Josh looked at her. "Let's do it."

They left before dawn, and it was still only midmorning by the time they reached the town of Pine Creek.

The country here was beautiful. Wooded foothills, redwoods, the snowcapped Sierras high to the east. The two-lane road wound through valleys and skirted canyons, twin borders of green leafy ferns hemming in both sides, low gray clouds providing a ceiling to the forest, light mist shrouding the shadowed areas between the trees.

But Laurie barely registered the scenery flying by the windows. She kept trying to remember exactly how her parents had been killed. They'd been murdered—of that she was fairly sure—but the details remained hazy, the specifics unspecific, and try as she might, she could not mentally reconstruct the events that had led to her adoption. She had only a vague feeling that the girl, Dawn, was involved somehow and that the grim couple in the photograph whom she knew to be her biological parents had died a horrible, gruesomely unnatural death.

It all came back to her when she saw the house.

They drove out of Pine Creek and down a narrow winding road. Josh said nearly everything had changed in the years since he'd been there. There'd been no McDonald's in town then, no Wal-Mart, no Holiday Inn, and the condos that had sprung up on seemingly every side of Pine Creek had certainly not been there.

But he grew quiet as they drove into the countryside,

as they moved farther away from town. He recognized this road, he said. He recognized this area. And Laurie could tell from his tone of voice that he felt the same oppressive dread she did as the car sped beneath the overhanging branches of the trees.

They drove up and down side roads, pulling in and backing out of long dirt drives, and after an hour or so, through this process of trial and error, they finally found it.

The house.

It looked exactly as they both remembered. It had not been repainted or refurbished. It had not deteriorated or gone to seed. It looked just as it had all those years ago.

And everything came back to her.

It was as if an entirely new door had been opened in her mind. Memories suddenly flooded in: knowledge, emotions, events, sensations. Things so thoroughly forgotten that she'd been unaware she'd ever known them, their presence in her mind having left not even a residual trace.

She recalled the meal rituals, the way they'd all held hands and hummed before eating breakfasts that corresponded precisely to the dawn, dinners that always accompanied sundown.

She remembered Mr. Billington, the man who lived with them, the man who was supposed to have been her father's friend but of whom her father had always seemed afraid and who apparently had no intention of ever leaving.

She remembered the animals. The way her mother had incorporated their unpredictable disappearances and sometimes terrifying reappearances into children's stories designed to make her feel that this was normal and not something of which she should be afraid.

She remembered her parents' deaths.

She'd been playing with Dawn, not in the woods, where Dawn wanted to play, but in the barn, which was also supposed to be off-limits. They were practicing their marriage ceremony, Dawn as usual taking the role of both minister and groom. For rings, they had Coke can pull-tabs and were wearing wreaths they'd woven from weeds. Laurie pretended to be enjoying the game, but there was something unsettling about it all, about Dawn's solemnity and almost ferocious dedication to strict marriage tradition.

Dawn had just pronounced them husband and wife and had given herself permission to kiss the bride when they heard a softly muttered "Shit!" from the yard outside.

"Hide!" Dawn ordered.

Laurie hurriedly ducked into the tool closet, closing the door. It was her father, and she knew he'd take the strap to her if he caught her in the barn after he'd specifically told her she was never to go near it.

She expected Dawn to follow her or to find a hiding place of her own, but her friend stood her ground as the big door opened and her father entered.

"Hello, Ralph," Dawn said.

Ralph! She dared to call him by his first name?

Against all odds, her father didn't seem to mind. Didn't seem to even notice. To Laurie's shock and surprise, her father chuckled, and in a voice more tender than any she'd ever heard him use with her mother or herself, he said, "Dawn."

There was whispering then, whispering and low murmuring, and what sounded like her father's belt buckle being unfastened.

Was Dawn going to get the strap?

Laurie knew it was dangerous, knew she should remain still and quiet, but she could not resist, she had to know what was going on, and she pushed open the door a fraction of an inch and peeked through the crack.

She didn't know what she'd expected to see, but it was definitely not this.

This was something she could not have thought up in her wildest imaginings.

Her father stood there, in the center of the barn, and his pants were pulled down. Dawn was kneeling before him and his hands were on her head and his peepee was in her mouth.

Laurie grimaced with distaste, not crying out in disgust only because of the fear that now filled her completely.

She did not know what was going on out there, she did not understand what was happening, but it made her sick inside and she felt like throwing up. Holding her fingers against the door, she slowly let it close.

She was suddenly certain that Dawn had known this would happen, had known her father was coming to the barn.

And had wanted her to see it.

The tool closet had another door at its opposite end, one that led outside to the yard, and carefully, quietly, Laurie inched toward it, careful not to touch or disturb the scythes and machetes, rakes and clippers hanging on the walls. Her father was saying something, murmuring in a low soothing voice, and she did not want to hear it, she did not want to know what it was.

There was no lock on the rough wooden door, no catch, but the hinges were squeaky, and she pushed the door open slowly, slowly, trying to prevent the escape of a single sound. When there was enough room between the door and the jamb for her to sneak out, she slid through and, just as slowly, closed the door once again.

She hurried across the open yard and was almost to the house when she saw her mother emerging from the garage, carrying what looked like the can of gasoline her father used for the tractor. Laurie was about to call out, but she changed her mind when she saw the look of grim determination and single-minded purpose on her mother's face.

The feelings of shock and disgust within her were replaced by a feeling of dread, the overwhelming sense that her mother knew what was going on in the barn and was going to do something about it.

Laurie wanted to hide, to run upstairs to her room and pretend that none of this was going on and play with her dolls until her mother called her for lunch, but she knew that ignoring what was happening would not make it go away, and she was not at all sure that her mother would even be making lunch today.

She was not sure that her mother—or her father— would still be alive come lunchtime.

She had no idea where that came from, but it grew from a fear into a certainty as she saw her mother stride over to the barn and throw open the big door.

Laurie dashed back across the trampled grass. Her mother had run into the barn and opened up the can and was furiously splashing gasoline over the bodies of Dawn and her father, now on the dirt floor without their clothes. Her father was sputtering angrily, yelling sounds that were supposed to be words, but Dawn was laughing, and it was that high tinkling musical sound that scared Laurie more than anything else.

"No!" Laurie cried. "Stop!" But no one seemed to hear her, and her mother tossed the gasoline can aside and pulled out a matchbook and lit a match. Screaming crazily, she threw the lit match onto the gasoline-covered bodies.

"You bastard!" she yelled. "She's mine! She's mine!"

There was a huge rush of flame, a sucking explosion that simultaneously drew in air and expelled agonizing heat.

"Mom!" Laurie cried.

Her mother pushed her aside and, stone-faced, strode through the door and across the yard toward the house.

Laurie saw Dawn's hair catch fire, the skin of her face darken and crinkle. Her father's back blistered and peeled open, his blood bubbling black the second it hit the flames. They were both writhing and rolling on the dirt, trying to get away, but the fire was not around them, it was on them, and there was no way they could escape from it.

Laurie ran around to the side of the barn, got the hose, turned it on full blast, and squirted water on the fire, but it didn't do any good, didn't make a dent, and she ran sobbing back to the house to tell Mr. Billington to call the firemen, knowing even as she did so that they would not arrive in time to save her father, Dawn, or the barn.

"Mr. Billington!" she screamed. "Mr. Billington!"

Her father's friend was nowhere to be seen, but her mother was lying on her back on the floor of the kitchen, her skirts hiked up.

With Dawn.

The girl was naked, but she was not burned and not dead, and the shock of seeing her here, alive, only seconds after watching her burn in the barn, overrode for a second the shock of what was happening.

Then Laurie noticed what was going on.

"Yes," her mother was saying, and Dawn's head was between her legs, moving slowly around. Laurie screamed at the top of her lungs, a desperate cry for help from someone, anyone.

All of a sudden, as her mother moaned in pleasure, the girl became a goat, arms turning to legs, gray hair growing over skin, and she started bucking, shoving her head forward with animal roughness, the horns spearing through the bare flesh of her mother's stomach, as her mother's expression of happiness and bliss changed instantly to one of horror and agony.

"Mom!" Laurie screamed.

For the first time since seeing her mother in the yard with the can of gasoline, her mom seemed to hear her, recognize her, acknowledge her. She was screaming in pain, trying to push the bucking goat away, but her eyes were hopeless, sad and despairing, filled with agonized regret, and they kept darting between Laurie and the door, and Laurie took the hint and ran.

She did not know where to go. The barn fire had not spread as she'd expected but seemed to have gone out, and that seemed ominous. Laurie ran unthinkingly, away from the barn, away from the house. Part of her wanted to find Mr. Billington, but another part of her, a deeper truer part, knew that he was somehow involved in this, so she did not call his name, did not call out anything, but simply ran.

She could not go into the woods—Laurie knew that much—but she was afraid to stay near the house, so she headed through the trees that paralleled the drive, heading toward the road. She heard Mr. Billington call her name, from somewhere far behind her, but she kept running.

She slept that night in a ditch by the side of the road, and the next day made it into Pine Creek, where she

stumbled into the police station and blurted out everything that had happened.

No one believed her, of course. Or at least they didn't
believe all of it, but they found the bodies of her parents—her father's charred corpse, her mother's gutted
form—and Laurie spent several weeks in a foster home
until one day, somehow, some way, Josh's parents showed
up and took her away to live permanently with them.

Laurie glanced over at Josh and, not for the first time,
she was grateful that she'd been adopted. What had happened to her real parents was terrible, horrifying, but as
emotionally scarring as it had been, she was aware of
the fact that she'd been better off without them, better
off away from the house, better off with Josh and his
parents.

Their parents.

Yes. Their parents. No matter who had sired her, they
had raised her and it was their love, their values, their
influence that had shaped her into the woman she was
today.

"Are you all right?" Josh asked, looking over at her.

Not trusting herself to speak, she nodded.

Josh parked the car in front of the garage. Laurie got
out silently, looked to her right at the barn, to her left
at the house. Nothing had changed in all those years. It
was as if the place had remained frozen in time, waiting
for her return.

She thought of Dawn. Shivered.

"Where do we start?" Josh asked, squinting against
the early afternoon sun. He stared up at the house.
"Damn. This place is as creepy as I remember it."

Laurie smiled wryly. "Tell me about it."

She walked toward the front of the house, saw in real
life the angle they'd seen in the photograph.

"It *is* a place of power," Josh said.

She ignored him. She wasn't in the mood for metaphysical chats, and though she wasn't exactly sure what
she hoped to find here or what she hoped to accomplish,
she knew she wanted to get it all done this afternoon.

She did not want to be anywhere near the house when
night fell.

Taking a deep breath, Laurie walked forward, gravel crunching beneath her feet. She reached the porch stairs, and it was as if her body were on automatic pilot. She grabbed a corner of the banister, leaned on it, then trailed her fingers along the wooden railing as she walked the four steps. It was the way she'd walked up these stairs as a child, and though the movements were instinctive, she was acutely aware of them, and she found it disconcerting to think that even though her mind had forgotten about the place for many years, her body apparently had not.

Josh followed close behind her, and the two of them stood on the porch for a moment, looking out at the yard, the drive, the surrounding trees. Everything seemed perfectly kept, well maintained, as though someone had been caring for the place all these years.

Mr. Billington.

No. That was impossible.

Still, the thought of it gave her a chill, and brave modern businesswoman that she was, she was glad Josh was here to protect her. Just in case.

She turned, looked at the front door. Dark brown wood with a small leaded-glass web window up above. What if it was locked? Neither she nor Josh had a key.

It wouldn't be locked.

She knew that.

Laurie hesitated for a moment. She wanted to go inside, but what did she hope to see, what did she hope to find, what did she hope to discover? Did she really think that answers to the questions she had would be found within the house's empty rooms? It was pointless, really, to go inside. They'd probably learn more by talking to neighbors, hunting down members of the local historical society.

An alarm was going off in her head, some hunch or intuition telling her to stay out, but that was exactly why she had to push on. There *was* something in the house. She didn't know what it was or how she knew of its existence, but she knew that she could only find out what she needed to know by going into her old home.

She tried the door handle. It *wasn't* locked, and she

glanced over her shoulder at Josh. "Let's go in," she said.

She walked through the doorway.

And the door slammed shut behind her.

"Josh!" she screamed.

The door had obviously caught him as he was trying to enter. There was a thin line of blood on the edge of the wood, a small clump of hair at head level. Her heart was pounding crazily, and from the other side of the door she heard her brother scream.

"Josh!" she yelled. She tried the door, but now it *was* locked, and the pounding of her heart, the thumping of blood in her head, was almost as loud as her pounding on the door.

"Josh!" she demanded. "Are you all right?"

"I'm okay!"

She heard his voice as if from a distance, as if more than simply a closed door separated them. It was a strange sensation and a frightening one, and she kept talking to him, telling him to push on the door the same time she pulled, as his voice grew fainter and fainter and then finally disappeared entirely.

She yanked once more on the door handle, then looked frantically around. There were no windows in the entryway save for the one high above the door, no way she could look out and see her brother, so she ran around to the front sitting room to look out the window, but when she pushed aside the lace curtains and pulled up the shade, she saw not the drive, not the yard, not the trees, not the porch, not Josh, but thick white fog that pressed flat against the glass, obscuring the entire world beyond.

She felt like a child again, like a little girl, scared and frightened and alone, and she wished that, dreams or no dreams, strange experiences or no strange experiences, they'd never come up here.

There was the sound of movement, the quiet shuffle of shoes on hardwood floor. A chill stabbed through her, but she did not turn around.

The clearing of a throat.

A man's voice.

She recognized it, and though she didn't want to, she knew that she had to look behind her.

She turned, faced him.

It was exactly who she'd known it would be.

"Laurie," he said quietly. "It's so nice to see you again."

THIRTEEN

Norton

When Norton awoke, his bed was covered with burnt toast.

Pieces fell as he stirred, dropped off the bed as he sat up, but he could tell that someone—

something

—sometime during the night had placed burnt toast over every square inch of his bed: the quilt on top of him, the empty pillow next to him, the spaces of open mattress.

Donna.

For some reason, he did not suspect Carole's ghost. It was that evil little girl whom he believed had covered his bed. A burnt toast trail had led him to her, had been laid for him to follow, and he assumed that the consistent use of the toast here was purposeful, was meant to send him a message.

The pressure was being increased. Whatever lay behind this campaign desperately wanted him to hurry up and get back to Oakdale.

Return.

He picked up a piece of toast, smelled it, tentatively touched it to his tongue. It was real. It was burnt bread, not some sort of disguised alien substance or supernatural manifestation.

What was the significance of it? he wondered. What did it symbolize? What did it mean?

He got out of bed, searching through the house for something else out of the ordinary or out of place, but everything was normal, everything was as it should be. He walked back into the bedroom to get dressed, saw the blackened squares on the bed and the surrounding floor, and he imagined that evil child placing them there, her slight shift blowing in the cold night breeze that passed through his perpetually open window, and he found himself becoming aroused.

Norton walked into the bathroom, looked at his unshaven face in the mirror, at his baggy eyes and wildly uncombed white hair. He was still erect, and he considered masturbating in the shower, but he resisted the temptation.

This couldn't go on, he realized. The pressure was only going to escalate and sooner or later he was going to have to return to Oakdale. He did not know why, he did not know what would happen, but as frightening and intimidating as he found the prospect, it also offered the only relief he could see from this dark situation in which he found himself.

He shaved, combed his hair, dressed, then called the district office. No one was there yet, so he left a message on the answering machine, telling them he was sick and specifically asking for Gail Doig to be his substitute. Gail was an ex-student, and she'd subbed for him last year on the one day he'd been ill and had done an excellent job.

It was still early, only six-thirty, so he made himself breakfast—no toast—and ate it, reading the morning paper, before giving Hal a call.

His friend was already up, had been up for several hours. Norton hadn't told Hal about his encounter with the girl, but he told him now and he described waking up with the burnt toast covering his bed.

He took a deep breath. "I have to go," he said. "Back to Oakdale. Will you come with me?"

Hal sounded annoyed. "I told you I would, didn't I?"

"It's far. It'll be almost a day's drive, and I don't know what's going to happen when I get there or how long I'll be staying—"

"Are you deaf? I told you I'm going with you."

"What's the bee in your bonnet?"

There was silence on the other end of the line.

"Hal?"

Norton heard his friend sigh even over the phone. "I felt Mariette's presence in the house."

"Did you see her?"

"No. It was like before. I could just tell that she was here."

"You think it's connected to what's happening to me?"

"I don't know," Hal said tiredly. "Maybe it's because we're both going to die soon. Hell, I don't know. But . . ." He trailed off.

"But?" Norton prompted.

"Her presence isn't comforting like it was before. It's . . . scary."

"What does that have to do with me?"

"Nothing, asshole! I just want to get out of the house and get away from here! Is that all right with you?"

"Jesus, bite my head off."

"Do you want me to come or not?"

"Of course I do. That's why I called."

"Then when are we going to go?"

Norton looked up at the clock. Seven-ten. "I'll pick you up in an hour. Bring a suitcase and a couple days' clothes just in case."

"I'll be ready."

There was a click on the other end and Norton gingerly put the receiver back on its hook. Hal sounded shaken, and he found that a little disconcerting. He also didn't like the fact that Hal believed the ghost of his wife had returned. It was too close to be unrelated, and he didn't like the idea that whatever supernatural forces were trained on him had also focused their attention on his friend. Hal was frightened, and he didn't think he'd known Hal ever to be frightened.

Oakdale loomed before him. And the house.

He knew that whatever had happened there was bad, that its horror was so overpowering and overwhelming it had erased any trace of its existence from his mind, blanking out his memory. Within the past weeks, his worldview, his belief system, the rational tenets of thought that had supported his intellectual life for the past half century, had been turned upside down, and now he was seeing ghosts and encountering evil children and witnessing unexplainable events, but he had the feeling that that change was minuscule compared to what lay ahead.

He was terrified by the thought of returning to Oakdale, and only the fact that Hal was accompanying him, would be there to offer moral, intellectual, spiritual, and, weak as it was, physical support, kept him from feeling totally incapacitated in the face of his fear.

But Hal was being targeted. By telling Hal what had happened, by bringing him into this, Norton had quite possibly put his friend in danger. A danger that neither of them understood.

Maybe he should call it off, wait it out, see what transpired. There was no real reason for him to go back to Oakdale, to the house.

Yes there was.

He didn't know what that reason could be, but it was there, and Norton could not let his own cowardice prevent him from doing what he knew was right, what he knew had to be done. He'd spent his entire professional life lecturing students about history, going over the past and second-guessing, making moral judgments about decisions that were made, and telling both his students and himself that they should have been made differently.

Well, now was his opportunity to put his money where his mouth was. He had a decision to make here, and he knew what needed to be done. Did he have the guts to do it?

Yes.

But he could not drag Hal into this. As grateful as he was for his friend's advice and support, for his willingness to share the burdens to be borne, he knew deep down that the responsibility was his own. This was something he had to do himself. He could not risk endangering Hal.

He walked into the bedroom, threw the blanket and the toast atop it to the floor, and got his suitcase out of the closet, throwing it onto the mattress. He began packing underwear and socks, shirts and pants.

No, he decided. He would not pick up Hal. He would leave his friend behind.

He would go back to the house alone.

*   *   *

There were signs along the way.

It was remarkable how quickly and completely his thinking, his mindset, his outlook had changed. He who had always been so literal and logical and concrete, who had never entertained the possibility that anything outside the material world existed, was now reading import into roadside occurrences, seeing omens in passing phenomena glimpsed through the windshield of his car. It was egocentric, this thinking, this belief that supernatural forces were creating portents out of landscapes and natural objects just for his sake.

But he knew that's what was happening.

Over the town of Magruder, he saw a black rainbow. No clouds, no rain, only the black-banded arch, stretching across the clear blue sky.

It began in a pasture this side of the town.

Its end appeared to be somewhere in the vicinity of Oakdale.

There were other signs as well. In Shaw: bodies of dead squirrels piled into a pyramid on the empty front island of an abandoned gas station. In Edison: a sycamore that had been carved into the shape of a girl bearing an eerie resemblance to a thin and stretched-out Donna. In Haytown: a bearded wild-haired hitchhiker by the side of the road, holding a homemade sign that read: "Return."

He almost chickened out. Driving into Oakdale from the east side of town, he could see the weather vane on the roof of the house's central gable, visible even above the bank building. He passed through the downtown, grown from two blocks to five in the intervening years and now populated with fast-food restaurants and gas stations, and emerged into open farmland. Ahead, off the road, was the house, its dark bulk contrasting sharply with the low white buildings of the other farms.

The black rainbow ended at the foot of the drive.

It disappeared almost instantly, and his first instinct was to make a U-turn and head back to Finley.

But then he thought of Carole's ghost and the trail of

toast and the dirty girl in the empty house and he knew he had to go forward.

Return.

He drove down the road, up the drive, to the house.

There was a plucked chicken waiting for him.

It was on a stick in the center of the drive, speared through the buttocks, and though there was no sign or message taped to it, he knew that it had been meant as a greeting. The animal looked freshly killed, had obviously not been sitting out too long in the Midwest sun, and the orange beak in its naked face made it look as though it were smiling.

One featherless wing pointed toward the house.

His gaze followed the pointing wing, and as he scanned the length of the front porch and the various darkened windows, he realized that he was holding his breath.

He was expecting to see Donna.

Donna.

It returned to him all of a sudden in vivid detail, what had happened to his family, and Norton sat there, staring at the chicken, trembling.

Donna.

He could see her face clearly in his mind, her overbright eyes and sly smile and tanned dirty skin. He could not remember when he'd first met the girl, but it seemed as though she'd always been around. They'd played together as children. The house had no close neighbors, and both his brother and two sisters were considerably older than he was, so he really had no other playmates until he began going to school. Even then, Donna remained his best friend.

They'd done typical children's things at first—built forts and dug tunnels and played imaginary games—but, gradually, things changed. Even now, Norton did not know how it had happened or why he'd gone along with it. He knew what he was doing was wrong even at the time, and he felt guilty and ashamed. He was smart enough to keep it from his family, smart enough not to tell his parents or his brother or his sisters, but he was not smart enough to avoid doing it, not smart enough to keep from getting involved.

It started with a group of ants. Donna had found an anthill out in back of the house, in the area between the house and the silo. She showed it to him, then stepped on it, and they both laughed as they watched the ants scurry around. Then she told him to wait and ran off into the house. She returned a few moments later with a kerosene lamp and a match. He knew what she wanted to do, and he didn't like the idea—he knew they'd get in trouble for it—but she smiled at him and told him to gather some dry weeds and twigs, and he did. He tossed the sticks and weeds on top of the flattened anthill, and Donna dribbled some of the kerosene on top of it, set down the lamp, and lit the match.

It was like a little explosion. The twigs and weeds went up instantly, and all of the ants stopped dead in their tracks and shriveled into tiny black balls. Donna crouched down next to the fire and watched, laughing and pointing, and while he knew it was wrong, he also thought it looked kind of neat, and he helped her pick up some of the stray ants that had escaped, the ones outside the fire range, and drop them into the flames. They crackled and popped as they burned, and the two of them spread out, looking for other bugs. Donna found a beetle and threw it in. He kicked a grasshopper across the dirt and into the fire. They tossed in a whole bunch of spiders and crickets. Donna found a kitten and was about to drop it onto the blaze, but by that time the flames had died down to almost nothing, and the animal got away.

He was glad.

It went on from there, though, and it got worse over the next year or so. They buried a hamster alive. They skinned a dog. He remembered holding a neighbor girl down while Donna . . . assaulted her with a stick.

She loved it, all the violence, all the torture, all the death. It excited her. As kids today would say, she "got off" on it.

Then she started demanding sex.

They did it and he loved it, but even there things

changed, got rougher, and the type of sex she wanted became more unusual, more exotic.

Unnatural.

He was tempted to try what she wanted, of course. But he was more frightened than anything else. She scared him, and that was what finally brought him back to his senses and made him realize that what they were doing was wrong. They'd never been caught, never gotten in trouble for anything they'd done, no one had ever told. But he knew it wasn't right, and he latched on to this as a way to put a stop to it all, to end the whole thing and just . . . backtrack.

So he broke it off. He stopped seeing her. She'd want to play and he'd be busy; she'd try to sneak into his room and he'd make sure his doors and windows were locked. Eventually, she just . . . went away. He was not sure how, exactly. There was no final fight, no big to-do, they simply stopped seeing each other, and then one day he noticed he didn't have to make an effort to avoid her anymore. She was gone.

He did not see her again until he was eighteen.

He'd been drafted into the army, and just before he was scheduled to go into basic training, he went into town to buy a card, a sort of Don't-Forget-Me card for Darcy Wallace, his girlfriend at the time. He returned home, and the second he walked through the door, he could smell something burning. He called out but no one answered. He thought maybe his mother had left something in the oven and forgotten about it. She'd done that before. His brother, who was already in the army, and his sisters, who were living together in an apartment in Toledo where they were both going to secretarial school, were supposed to come home for the big going-away party, and he figured his mother was making something special, a roast or a turkey.

He rushed into the kitchen, pushed open the swinging door. The entire room was filled with smoke. Black smoke that smelled like—

burnt toast.

He didn't know what had happened at first. He shut off the oven and opened the windows and the back door.

Donna was standing in the yard in her dirty shift, staring back at him, unmoving, but he didn't have time to fool around with her, and he hurried back over to the stove.

She'd killed them and cut off their heads and put their heads in the oven.

All of them.

His parents, his brother, his sisters.

He was fanning out the smoke when he saw his father's burned head, sitting on the middle rack. The old man's eyes were gone and his lips were flattened and all of the fat and flesh seemed to have melted off, but Norton recognized who it was. Next to that, his mother's head had fallen over and parts of her were sticking to the grill. His brother's and sisters' heads were smoldering in the back, all lumped together.

They reminded him of the burned ants.

He never saw Donna again. Just that last look through the door, through the smoke. And when he thought back on it, later, he realized that she looked the same as she had before. She hadn't aged at all. She still looked twelve.

Now Norton sucked in a deep breath and looked up at the house, then turned back toward the plucked chicken and its pointing wing. Was this a joke or a warning? Was it meant to be threatening or welcoming? It was impossible to tell; the mind behind it was so alien to his own. Nevertheless, he got out of the car and walked purposely toward the house, up the porch. He thought he heard a child laughing.

A girl.

Donna.

He pressed down on his erection.

The front door opened even before he had a chance to knock, and their old hired hand stood there, within the dark entryway, smiling at him, looking exactly the same as he had all those years ago.

"Hello, Billingson," Norton said, trying to keep the quiver from his voice. "May I come in?"

FOURTEEN

Stormy

Roberta was gone.

There'd been no hint, no warning, no indication that she'd been planning on leaving him. She'd been even colder and more diffident to him than usual after the misunderstanding with the Finnigan brothers' bankruptcy lawyer, but that wasn't a drastic departure from her typical pattern of behavior, and it had hardly registered on his emotional radar.

But he'd come home on Monday and she hadn't been there, and now she'd been gone for three days. There'd been no note, he hadn't heard from her, and since she'd packed several suitcases and taken the Saab, he assumed that she'd left him.

And he found that he didn't really care.

He cared about the hanging threads, of course. The unresolved details. He didn't like loose ends, didn't like having anything hanging over his head. But he assumed she'd talk to a lawyer at some point and the lawyer would contact him and they'd work out some sort of settlement.

Then he'd be free.

It was a strange feeling and he wasn't entirely used to it yet. Everyone was telling him good riddance, even Joan, and both Rance and Ken had offered to reintroduce him to the singles' scene, teach him the ropes, but the truth was that he was not ready to start dating again. Not yet. His friends' descriptions of one-night stands with young nubile women willing to do anything, no matter how kinky, were admittedly tempting, and even at his fringe of the entertainment industry the opportunities were there, but he just didn't seem to be in the mood to immediately jump back into the social whirl, to begin forming new emotional attachments. He felt tired, drained, a little burned out, and he wanted to collect himself, charge his batteries a bit before starting up again.

Fruit salad in the toilet.

Rose and cheese in the sink drain.

Those images had never been very far from his mind, and he supposed that was one reason why he was so reluctant to commit to anything new. He'd been haunted by his experience in the theater. He'd been having dreams ever since that day, dreams of his parents' old house in Chicago. Nightmares filled with recurring images: living dolls and walking dead fathers and dirty sex-crazed children.

But it was what he had seen in the theater that scared him the most. Ghosts and zombies and the other traditional trappings of horror were indeed frightening—particularly in real life, outside the make-believe context of film—but it was the irrational incomprehensibility of what he'd seen in the demolished bathroom that made him feel truly afraid. For these were things that were not categorized or recognized, that were not part of fiction or folklore, and they made him realize how ignorant and inconsequential he really was.

There was meaning in what he had seen—of that he was sure—but the fact that he could not begin to even grasp the superficialities of intent shook him to the core of his being.

Something was going on, something just underneath the surface realities, something so huge and all-encompassing that it was breaking through in unexpected places and in unfathomable ways.

Once again, he thought about the events on the reservation and the idea that these supernatural occurrences were spreading outward from a common cause over an epic area of ground.

It terrified him, but a perenially practical part of his mind told him that it might not make for a bad movie.

There was a knock on his door frame, and Russ Madsen, this semester's intern, poked his head into the office. "Mr. Salinger? Could I speak to you for a moment?"

Stormy nodded, waved him in. Like most of the interns he'd had over the past two years, Russ was terminally overeager and far too obsequious for his own good. He was a nice kid, but Stormy had entered into an agreement with the university in Albuquerque because, as he understood it, the kids would get real world experience, he'd get free workers, and the school would collect tuition without having to teach. From his perspective, though, the internship program had turned out to be more trouble than it was worth. The students who came to his company were all wannabe filmmakers and they seemed to spend most of their time trying to impress him with their knowledge and talent rather than doing the jobs he assigned them.

Russ was a little better than the others. He was just as adept at brown-nosing, and he tried just as hard to impress, but he did actually do the work and he completed the assignments given him.

Stormy smiled at the intern. "What is it, Russ?"

"I have a tape I think you might like." He placed a videocassette on the desk. "It's an unreleased feature by a local filmmaker, and I think it's terrific. It's sort of a horror movie, but it's . . . different. I don't really know how to explain it. But I thought you might want to take a look at it."

"Your film?"

"No." He smiled. "That would be conflict of interest."

"Excellent answer." Stormy reached for the tape, picked it up. The title on the label was *Butchery.*

"Good title," Stormy observed.

"Good film. I know I'm just an intern, but I think it has potential. I watched it last night, and I was so blown away that I had to let you see it. I lied and told the guy who gave it to me that I hadn't watched it yet and asked if I could hold on to it for another day so I could get it to you."

Stormy looked over at Russ. He'd never really talked to the boy before, and he was impressed by what appeared to be his genuine love and enthusiasm for movies. Most of his other interns had been closer in temperament to his old L.A. cronies, film snobs who would probably end up in businesses entirely unrelated to the industry but who still looked down on the direct-to-video market and considered their time here to be a form of slumming. Russ seemed to be more like himself, and he thought that maybe he'd been a little too quick to rush to judgment.

"You do have a film of your own, though? Right?"

"Yeah," the intern admitted.

"Something you think we'd be interested in here?"

"I think so. It's an action flick and I made it on a shoestring budget, but the production values are pretty good, and the female lead's a real find. I think the actors are really impressive.

"I'd like to see it sometime."

"That'd be great! I'm in post now, but I'd love to let you look at it when I'm done. Any help or advice you could give me would be . . . I mean, I'd really appreciate it."

"All right," Stormy said, smiling. He held up the video-cassette. "Thanks for dropping this off, and I'll take a look at it today."

Russ understood that the meeting was over, and he awkwardly excused himself and hurriedly left the office.

Butchery.

Stormy toyed with the tape in his hand. With all of the other things going on, it might be relaxing to view a little video carnage. It might take a little of the edge off what passed for reality these days. There was a lot of paperwork he had to do, some agreements he had to go over that would allow a few of his more explicit titles to be sold in Canada, but he was having a difficult time concentrating on work this morning, and he told Joan to hold all his calls, closed the door, popped the tape in his VCR, settling back in his chair to watch the movie.

The title was misleading. There was no butchery in the film. There was not even any blood. There was instead a gothic mansion and an ambiguously manipulative butler and a misunderstood young boy with a crazy grand-mother and two emotionally distant parents.

Stormy felt increasingly cold as he watched the film, filled with a growing sense of dread.

He knew this house.

He knew this story.

It was his parents' place in Chicago, and the unnamed boy was himself as a child, navigating the treacherous waters of the unstable household, trying to maintain for himself a normal existence despite the continuous unde-fined threats of the strange insular world around him. He'd forgotten a lot of this, forgotten the butler, forgot-ten the intimidating house, forgotten the feeling of being always off balance, always nervous, always floundering, but it came back to him now as he watched the movie, and when the boy was seduced by the butler's sly daugh-ter, posing as a homeless street urchin, Stormy mouthed the girl's name.

"Donielle."

If the film fell into any genre, it would be psychologi-cal horror, but that limiting label did not begin to convey the scope of the work. Russ was right. The film was amazingly accomplished. As good as the Hopi kid's flick. It created an unsettling universe of its own, and despite the rather slow pace of the movie, it drew the viewer in, and it made one care deeply about the fate of its protagonist.

It was not the film's artistic merit, however, but the personal connection, the references to himself, to his own life, to his childhood, that gripped Stormy, that left him staring at the snow filled screen for several minutes after the movie had ended.

It meant something, he knew, but again he didn't know what.

He thought of what he'd seen in the theater, and the connection was made.

Theater.

Film.

There was a thread linking his childhood in that horri-ble frightening house to the disappearing figure, the fruit salad in the toilet, the rose in the cheese in the sink drain. It was a connective tissue so fine as to be almost nonexistent, but it was there, and it was extant, and he was suddenly possessed by the need to meet the person who had made this movie.

There was a feeling of urgency about it, an imperative sense that, like a house of cards, it all might fall apart and whatever tentative connections had been established would disappear.

He burst out of his office. Joan, at her desk, jumped. "Where's Russ?" he demanded.

"Duping room."

Stormy strode down the hall to the technical facilities and held up the videocassette. "Where did you get this film?" he demanded.

Russ looked up from the equipment, startled. "A, uh, friend of mine gave it to me. He got it from P. P. Rodman, the guy who made it."

"Where is this Rodman?"

"Do you want to buy the distribution rights?"

"I want to meet the person who made this film."

"He lives on the reservation."

The reservation.

It *was* all connected, the house and the dolls and the theater and Tom Utchaca's dead dad, and Stormy's almost frantic need to meet this filmmaker immediately intensified. Whatever was going on here, it was big, something that he could only barely imagine, but he was filled with the unfounded, absurd but unshakable conviction that if he could figure out the core cause of all of this craziness, he could put a stop to it before anything catastrophic happened.

Catastrophic?

Where had that come from?

"Do you have Rodman's phone number?" he asked.

Russ shook his head. "He doesn't have a phone."

"Do you know how to get in touch with him?"

"My friend carpools with him to school. I could give him a call."

"Do it."

Stormy hurried back to his office, gave Ken a quick call. Ken was more familiar with the reservation than he was, knew quite a few people there, and Stormy gave a thumbnail sketch of where he was going and why and asked his friend if he'd come along.

"I'm at the office. Pick me up on the way."

Russ knocked on the door frame. "Doug says P.P. doesn't have classes today. He should be home."

"You have an address?"

"I know where it is."

"You're coming with me, then. Let's go."

A half hour later, Stormy, Russ, and Ken were bumping along the dusty road across the mesa that led to the pueblo serving as tribal headquarters.

Ken's accounts of supernatural occurrences were not exaggerated. If anything, they'd underrepresented the degree of infiltration. Stormy pulled to a stop in front of the headquarters. Kachina dolls were indeed walking around, and they were doing so in the open. There were dozens of them on the flat ground in front of the pueblo, lurching, waddling, and crawling in different directions. Several stood like sentries on the ledge above the door, swiveling about. On the other side of the creek that bisected the open gathering area, a group of dead men were standing in a circle, apparently speaking among themselves.

Stormy sat for a moment in the car. The extent of what was happening here was overwhelming, and he marveled at how the few people he saw walking about completely ignored the dolls and the dead. Human beings, he thought, can get used to anything.

But perhaps whatever was behind all this knew that. Maybe it was starting here because the Native American culture was more open in regard to the supernatural, more readily accepting of the nonmaterial world. Maybe this was the first assault in a full-fledged invasion of ghosts and spirits and demons and monsters. Maybe they were easing in gradually, getting people used to them before they . . . What? Took over the world?

He'd seen too many movies.

But movies were the only real reference point for what was going on. There was no parallel in the real world, no factual, historical correspondence.

Ken hopped out of the car. "I'll be back in a sec," he

said, running into the tribal office. "I'm just going to tell them we're here."

Stormy turned, looked at Russ in the backseat. The intern's face was white, blanched.

"What's going on?" Russ asked.

Stormy shook his head. "I don't know."

The dolls were not as frightening to him as he'd thought they'd be. He supposed it was because they were out in the open, in the daylight, with people around. There was an old saw in the horror film industry about ghosts and monsters being more frightening when they were juxtaposed against normal, everyday life, but he had never believed that to be true. A ghost in a mall was nowhere near as scary as a ghost in an old dark house, and the same thing was true here. The kachinas were obviously alive, their wooden bodies and feathered faces were moving in a terrifyingly unnatural way, a way that shouldn't be possible, but they were nowhere near as frightening to him as the thought he'd had of a lone doll sneaking around—

the house

—the inside of the abandoned theater.

Ken came running back. "It's cool. Let's go."

"Two streets down," Russ said from the back. "The white house."

Stormy put the car into gear. "Pretty fucking spooky," he said.

Ken nodded. "You're telling me." He glanced at the circle of dead men as they drove by. "I'd like to get a close-up look at one of them," he said.

Stormy shivered. "No you wouldn't."

"What's going on?" Russ asked again.

Neither of them answered him.

It was like driving through a foreign country, Stormy thought. Or an alien landscape. No, it was more surreal than that. Like passing through a Fellini world or a David Lynch world or . . . No. Even film analogies broke down here.

On the side of the road, a woman popped into existence. She hadn't been there a second before, and then she was, and she smiled and waved at them.

"Turn here," Russ said, pointing. "That's his house."

Stormy braked to a halt in the middle of a short dirt driveway in front of a small dilapidated home. P. P. Rodman was already out the front door and walking toward the car before Stormy had even shut off the engine. The filmmaker was a scrawny little half-and-half who looked as though he was about sixteen. Russ had told him that Rodman was in grad school, but had he not known, he would have guessed high school freshman.

Stormy got out of the car and walked toward the filmmaker, hand extended. "Hello," he said. "I'm Stormy Salinger—"

"President of Monster Distribution." Rodman nodded, "I know."

"Russ here gave me a tape of *Butchery*, and I have to say, I was very impressed."

Rodman squinted against the sun. "Thanks."

"Did you write the film?" Stormy asked.

"Wrote and directed it," Rodman said proudly.

"Where'd you get the idea?"

The kid frowned. "It came to me in a dream."

A dream.

Stormy tried to maintain the bland expression on his face. "I thought it might have been inspired by"—he motioned toward the land surrounding them—"everything that was happening."

"Are you kidding? I wrote the original draft two years ago. It took me a year to film it."

Two years. That was even more unsettling. He could not get the thought out of his mind that the movie had been made specifically for him, that an unknown power had inspired this kid, knowing he would make this film and that his friend would pass it to *his* friend and that that person would be working for Stormy's company and would show him the video. It was a frighteningly comprehensive plan, hidden behind an apparent series of coincidences, and Stormy found himself intimidated by the sheer scope of it all, by the complex and concentrated linkages.

He didn't know if he was being warned or threatened, but the idea that this kid was just a messenger, his film the message, and that it had been meant for him and him alone, remained strong in his mind.

He licked his lips. "Where's the house?" he asked.

"Special effect," the filmmaker said. "It's a model. I based it on the house in my dream."

Stormy was sweating. "How close is the film to your dream?"

"I thought you were interested in distributing my movie."

"Humor me," Stormy told him. "How close?"

"It's almost the same."

"Was there anything in your dream that you didn't put in the movie? Any additional images you cut out because they'd interrupt the narrative flow?"

"What narrative flow?"

"Was there anything you cut out?"

"No."

He continued questioning Rodman, but the kid was a blank, and Stormy understood that whatever meaning he was supposed to get from this, he was supposed to get from the film itself.

"Have you seen any of the dead?" he asked before they left.

Rodman snorted. "Who hasn't?"

"What's it mean?"

"You tell me."

They left after that. Stormy was just as in the dark as he had been before the visit, and he felt both frightened and frustrated. He intended to watch the videotape again, but he had the distinct feeling that there was something else he was supposed to be doing. Should he return to the theater? Get the keys back from the real-estate agent and check the bathroom again?

What would that do? He'd seen the kachinas, seen talking dead men and a reappearing woman, and he hadn't learned anything from that. Was there anything else that could be learned from the theater?

He needed to go back home.

It was as if he were a cartoon character and a lightbulb had suddenly gone off above his head. That was exactly what he was supposed to do. Why hadn't he seen it before? Everything he'd felt or experienced or heard about pointed in that direction. He'd just been too dumb to pick up on it. He needed to go back to Chicago, back to the house. The answer was there.

The answer to what?

He didn't know.

He dropped Ken off at the County building, drove back to his own offices. Russ returned to the duping room and the tapes on which he'd been working, and Stormy had Joan make reservations for him on a flight to Chicago tomorrow.

He locked his office and watched *Butchery* once again.

The flight was booked for noon, with an open-ended return ticket, and he stayed late, instructing his employees on what they were to work on in case he was gone for more than a few days, going over the agreements and contracts that needed his immediate signature. It was nearly nine when he finally arrived home, and he turned on all the lights in the house before collapsing into a chair.

Even his house seemed creepy.

He was not sure that his old home in Chicago was still standing, but he assumed that it was and he wondered what it would be like as he absently sorted through his mail. In his mind, it looked just like the house in *Butchery*, a dark forbidding mansion, but it must have been repainted and remodeled since his childhood.

At least he hoped it had.

He stopped shuffling the envelopes in his hand, not breathing, certain that he had heard something, a knock from the back of the house, but it was not repeated and when he walked carefully through the rooms he saw nothing unusual.

Most of his mail was either bills or ads, but one envelope was postmarked Brentwood, California, and the name on the return address was Phillip Emmons. Phillip was an old writer friend from L.A., and Stormy opened the envelope, curious. It contained a cryptic yet tantalizing note stating that Phillip had been writing narration for a PBS documentary on Benjamin Franklin and had run across something in his research that he thought Stormy might be interested in.

"It's an entry from Thomas Jefferson's diary," Phillip wrote, "and it concerns some sort of haunted doll. Thought you might like to see it."

Haunted doll?

That was the weird thing about Phillip. He always seemed to have his finger on the pulse of his friends' lives and psyches, always seemed to provide just the object or scrap of knowledge needed. He was one of those people who, by accident or design, were always in the right place at the right time. Phillip's fiction ran toward hard-edged serial killer stories or sex-and-blood horror, and to Stormy's way of thinking, his real life seemed to dovetail with like subjects far more often than should have been the case.

He'd always liked Phillip, but he had to admit, he'd always been a little afraid of him.

He looked down at the enclosed Xerox, started reading:

From Thomas Jefferson's Diary:
April 15

I am Awake again well before Dawn because of that Infernal Dream engendered by the Figure Shown to Me by Franklin. It is the Fifth Time I have Had the Dream. Did I not Know Franklin so well, I would Believe Him a Practitioner of Witchcraft and the Black Arts.

The Doll, if Doll it Be, Appeared to be Made from Twigs and Straw and Pieces of Human Hair and Toenail. The Totality was Glued together by what seemed an Unsavory Substance that Franklin and I Took to be Dried Seed from the Male Sex.

Franklin Claims that He has Seen a Similar Figure in his Travels although He Cannot Remember Where. For My Part, I would Never have Forgotten such an Object or Whence I first Discovered It, as I Will Not Forget It Now.

Against My Wishes and Advice, Franklin has Taken the Doll into his House. He Intends to Keep It in his

Study so that He may Perform some of his Experiments upon It. I Bade Him Leave it in the Spirit House in which He Discovered It, but Franklin is not a Man who Takes Readily to Suggestion.

I am Frightened for Franklin and, indeed, for All of Us.

At the bottom of the diary entry was a detailed piece of artwork in Jefferson's own hand. A detailed rendering that was clearly identifiable and instantly recognizable.

It was a drawing of the house.

His plane landed at O'Hare just after noon, and Stormy immediately picked up his rental car and drove home.

He could not remember the last time he'd been to the old neighborhood or seen the old house, but it had obviously been a while. The street had changed completely. Redevelopment had obliterated an entire block, replacing old tenements with newer tenements. The tough Polish gang members who used to hang out on the street corners in front of the liquor stores had been replaced by tough black gang members who hung out on the street corners in front of the liquor stores. A lot of the buildings he remembered were either condemned or gone.

The house, though, had stayed exactly the same. It was as if it were enclosed within a force field or clear protective barrier. The detritus of the street did not reach it. There was no graffiti on its walls, no garbage thrown on its lawn. The handful of homes remaining around it had deteriorated tremendously and were now as dilapidated as the surrounding apartment buildings, but the house remained unchanged.

There was something spooky about that.

Butchery.

He realized that he had never asked the kid why he had called his film *Butchery*. Sitting there in his rental car, in the middle of the slummy neighborhood, staring at his unchanged home, that suddenly seemed important.

The early afternoon sun was blocked by buildings, but

its light shone through the broken windows of an empty fire-gutted structure across the street, casting bizarre shadows on the face of the house, shadows that were too abstract to resemble anything real but that nonetheless jogged some recess of his memory.

Stormy got out of the car. He felt like a flea standing before a tidal wave. If whatever was happening encompassed this house in Chicago, the theater in Albuquerque, the reservation, and God knew what else, he was a dust speck in the face of it. It made no sense for him to even be here. The thought that he could do something, that he could make a difference, that he could possibly have an influence over anything was ludicrous. He'd been drawn here, called perhaps, summoned, but he understood now that for him to try to intervene was pointless.

Still, he opened the small gate and walked through the well-tended yard to the porch.

It was a warm afternoon, but the air was cold in the shadow of the house, and he remembered that from before. He felt like a kid again, powerless, at the mercy of things he didn't understand. He knew his grandmother and parents were dead, understood it intellectually, but emotionally it felt to him as though they were inside, waiting for him, waiting to criticize him, waiting to punish him, and he wiped his sweaty palms on his pants.

He had no key, but the front door was unlocked, and he opened it, walked inside. He was wrong: the house *had* changed. Not the building itself, not the walls or the floors or the ceilings or the furnishings. Those were exactly as they had been thirty years before. Almost eerily so. But the mood of the house seemed different, the air of regal formality that had reigned previously, that had so permeated every inch of this place, was gone, replaced with a graceless foreboding. He walked forward, turned right. The long hallway in which he had played as a child now seemed grim and intimidating, its opposite end fading into a gloomy darkness that for some reason frightened him.

There was no way he'd be able to muster the bravery to even attempt to go upstairs.

He turned around, walked back through the entryway, saw movement in the sitting room. It was afternoon outside, but little daylight penetrated into the house, and, nervously, his hand fumbled for a light switch. He found it, flipped it on.

The butler was standing just inside the doorway.

"Billingham," Stormy said, not entirely surprised.

The butler smiled at him, bowed. "Stormy."

FIFTEEN

Daniel

The summer stretched before them, new, ripe with the possibility of adventure, its inevitable end so far in the future that it was almost inconceivable. The days were long and hot, and he and his friends filled the hours with projects. Making sand candles: melting real candles they'd stolen from Jim's house, letting the wax drip around slices of string into holes they'd dug in the dirt of the backyard. Selling Kool-Aid: using Paul's dad's folding card table, having Jim's sister draw them a sign, sitting for hours in the burning sun, adding more and more ice to the pitcher until the Kool-Aid was so watered down even they couldn't drink it. Egging mailboxes: stealing two eggs from each of their refrigerators, playing paper-scissors-rock to determine who would rush up to their neighbors' mailboxes and slam the eggs in.

It was a perfect existence. Nothing had to be planned, nothing had to be completed, they did what they wanted when they wanted, following their whims through the free and open days.

But something was wrong at home. Daniel could feel it. His parents didn't say anything, but he sensed a subtle difference in their relationship, perceived the loss of something he hadn't even known existed. At night, at the dinner table, there was anger beneath his father's surface pleasantry, sadness underlying his mother's cheerfulness, and he was glad it was summer and he could stay out late and he didn't have to spend as much time with his family as he ordinarily would.

As the days passed, however, as the memory of school receded and the rhythms of summer became less tentative, more reliable, he came to believe—no, to know—that it *was neither his mother's fault nor his father's fault that things were falling apart between them. They were victims. They were like him, able to see what was happening but unable to do anything about it, forced to watch as it occurred.*

It was the fault of their servant, Billingsly.

And his dirty little daughter.

Daniel did not know what made him think that, but he knew it was true, and while he'd never really given it much thought before, he realized that those two scared him. He was not sure why; Billingsly had always been polite and deferential to him—too polite and too deferential—while Doneen had always been shy and elusive and seemed to have a crush on him. But he was afraid of them, he realized, and he began making a concerted effort to stay out of their way, to not come into contact with them, to avoid them whenever possible.

His parents, he noticed, did the same.

What was going on here? Why didn't his father just fire Billingsly?

Because it wasn't only the servant and his daughter. It was the house as well. Something about their home seemed threatening and confining and unnatural, as if . . .

As if it was haunted.

That was it exactly. It was as if the building itself were alive, controlling everything within its borders—who slept where, what time they ate their meals, where they could go and what they could do—and they were merely its pawns. It was a strange thought, he knew, but it was the way he felt, and it explained why his father, who had always been lord of the manor, the king of his castle, walked around these days like a beaten man, a guest in his own home.

No, not a guest.

A prisoner.

If he'd been braver, if he'd been older, he would have talked to his parents about it, would have asked what was wrong and why and whether they could do anything about the situation, but that was not the way the dynamics of their family worked. They did not talk out problems, did not confront them directly, but hinted around about them, trying to get their individual points across with oblique references and small suggestions, hoping the other members of the family would understand what they meant without having to come out and explain.

So he stayed out as much as possible, played with his friends, concentrated on summer and fun and tried not to think about the changes at home. He and Jim and Paul and Madson built a clubhouse in the woods behind Paul's backyard. They made a go-cart that they took turns racing down State Street. They panned for gold in the creek. They watched game shows on Jim's family's color TV set. They camped out in the park.

Outside the walls of the house, it was a great summer. But inside . . .

It started one night after he and his friends had spent the day downtown at the movie theater, sitting twice through a double feature of two Disney movies: Snowball Express and $1,000,000 Duck. They'd emerged tired and gorged with candy, and they'd gone home to their respective houses. His parents had been waiting for him—they always ate dinner together, that was a family rule—and he'd eaten and then gone upstairs to take a bath.

He'd been successfully avoiding Billingsly and his daughter for several weeks, had only seen the servant at dinner and had not seen Doneen at all, but he was still taking no chances and he made sure that the servant was still in the kitchen and carefully checked the hallways for his daughter before grabbing pajamas from his bedroom and locking himself in the bathroom.

She walked in while he was washing himself in the tub.

"Hey!" he said.

He had locked the door, he was sure of it, and the fact that the girl had still been able to get in frightened him.

She slipped off her dirty nightgown, got into the water.

He jumped up, splashing water on the floor, frantically calling for his mom, his dad, as he grabbed the towel and scrambled away from the tub, trying not to slip on the tile.

Doneen giggled at him.

"Get out of here!" he screamed at her.

"You don't really want me to leave." Still giggling, she pointed at his penis, and he quickly covered it with the *towel, embarrassed. He couldn't help it; he had an erection. It was exciting to see a naked girl, but it was even more frightening, and he backed against the door, reaching for the knob and trying to turn it.*

It was locked.

He didn't want to turn his back on Doneen, was not sure what she could or would do, but he had no choice and he turned, unlocking the door.

"Your mother can't live," the girl said behind him.

He whirled around. "What?"

"She's going to have to die."

There was something about the matter-of-fact tone in the girl's voice that scared the shit out of him, and he ran out of the bathroom and down the long hallway. He wanted to go into his bedroom, get his clothes, get dressed, but he was afraid to do so, afraid she might be able to sneak in there as easily as she'd entered the bathroom, so he ran downstairs, still covering himself with the towel. His parents had remained at the dinner table, and when his mother looked up in surprise and he saw the mingled expression of concern, worry, and fear cross her face, he burst into tears. He had not cried in a long time—crying was for babies— but he was crying now, and she stood up and allowed him to hug her, and he kept repeating, "I don't want you to die!"

"I'm not going to die," she told him. But her voice was not as reassuring as it should have been, and it only made him cry harder.

Afterward, he was embarrassed. He should not have been—there were more important things at stake here than embarrassment—but that was the way he felt, and although he told his parents he'd been scared upstairs, in the bathroom, he did not tell them why or what had really happened. Still, he made them accompany him back up, hoping that Doneen would still be there, and made his father search his bedroom closets and the other rooms off the hallway before putting on his pajamas and telling them to go downstairs, he was all right.

It was the crying that had embarrassed him the most, and he thought that if he had not burst into tears like a little girl, he might have been able to broach the subject

*of the servant's daughter and what she'd said. But he'd
been naked and crying into his mother's blouse, and he
could not bring himself to compound that humiliation
with the admission of what must seem like a lunatic fear—
no matter how serious the consequences might be.*

*He would just have to stay alert, keep an eye on his
mother, make sure nothing happened.*

*He stopped playing outside, stopped going places with
his friends. He told them that he was grounded, that his
parents would not let him go out. He told his mother that
Jim's and Paul's families had gone on vacation and that
Madson was grounded.*

And he stayed in the house.

Stayed near his mother.

*He still avoided Billingsly as much as possible, but he
did not have to make an effort to stay away from Doneen.
Either her father or his parents had talked to her, or she
had decided on her own to keep her distance, and he saw
only occasional glimpses of her in hallways or rooms or
outside in the yard, and that was fine by him.*

*A few evenings later, his father was cutting his hair,
and the idea that he should save the cut hair occurred to
him. He did not know why, did not know where this
notion had come from, but almost as soon as it had
flashed into his mind, it had solidified into a necessity, a
priority, and after his father finished trimming his bangs
and tossed away the newspapers that had been spread on
the floor underneath his chair, Daniel snuck into the
kitchen, took the crumpled paper with its cache of cut
hair, and brought everything back up into his room.*

*Over the next week, he collected other things: used
Kleenex, discarded toothpicks, peach pits, chicken bones,
an apple core. It became almost an obsession, this search
for specific objects, and while he never knew exactly what
he was looking for, he always recognized it when he
found it.*

*He understood that he was supposed to take all of the
elements and combine them, make them into a cohesive
whole, construct a figure that would serve as a talisman
against . . . Against what?*

He did not know, but he worked on the figure nonethe-

less, adding his newest acquisitions to it at night before he went to bed, reshaping them in the morning when he awoke.

He destroyed the figure as soon as he finished it. He had not noticed until the very end, until every element was in place, exactly what he'd been making, but when he saw the expression he'd created on the figure's face, saw the threatening stance and intimidating structure of the object, he realized instantly that he had not created a talisman to ward against *something* but had made a figure designed to attract *something*.

Something bad.

This was just what Doneen and her father and the house had wanted him to do, and he tore it up immediately, stomping and flattening the pieces, throwing them in a paper bag and taking the sack out to the backyard and burning it.

He heard whispers that night. And his father came into his room and told him in a worried voice not to get out of bed, not even if he had to go to the bathroom, until the sun came out the next morning.

He wet his bed for the first time since kindergarten, but he wasn't embarrassed and didn't get in trouble for it, and when he walked into the dining room for breakfast, he heard a portion of a conversation that ended instantly the second he walked through the door:

"What are we going to do?" Mother.

"Nothing we can do. They're back." Father.

That night, again, he was told not to get out of bed, but something made him disobey those orders, and he crept silently across the floor of his room and slowly opened the door, peeking out.

It emerged from the shadows, a small squat figure of dust and hair, paper clip and tape, bread crumb and lint. Gathered material from the rug underneath the furniture. A living counterpart to the static figure he had created and destroyed.

Daniel stood in the doorway of his room, frozen, unable to even suck in a breath, watching as the horrible creature moved away from him, down the hall.

To his parents' room.

Their bedroom door opened. Closed.

"No!" he screamed.

"Daniel?" his father called from downstairs.

His parents had not come up yet! They were safe from that . . . whatever it was.

A relief so powerful that it seemed to weaken his muscles flooded over him, through him. He started left, toward the stairwell, when he heard the sound of a crash from his parents' room. The sound of something falling.

And a partial yelp.

"Mother!" he screamed, running.

"Daniel!" his father bellowed from downstairs.

He heard his father's heavy elephant tread from somewhere on the floor below, but he didn't, couldn't wait, and he rushed down the hall to his parents' bedroom and threw open the door.

The creature was on the bed.

His mother, naked, thrashed about, bucking wildly, as the figure forced itself into her open mouth. Daniel was screaming for his father, screaming at the top of his lungs, but he could not take his eyes off the bed, where his mother tried to first yank the figure from her mouth, then began beating herself violently in the face, trying to dislodge it. He knew he should do something, but he didn't know what, had no idea how he could help, and a moment later, before he could spur himself into action, his father was thundering down the hall and rushing through the open door and running up to the bed.

The figure's feet disappeared down his mother's throat.

"Help me!" his father ordered. He picked her up, began pounding her on the back. "Help me!"

Daniel didn't know what to do, didn't know how to help, but he rushed over and his father had him grab his mother's arms and hold them up while he attempted to stick his fingers down her throat and pull out the creature.

Her face was already turning blue, and the weak wheezy gasps that had been issuing from her mouth had silenced. Her too-wide eyes stared blankly straight ahead, and only the open-close-open-close fish motion of her lips indicated that she was still alive.

Screaming crazily, a primal bellow of rage and pain,

*his father grabbed his mother around the waist, turned
her upside down, and, holding her ankles, thumped his
knee against her back in an effort to dislodge the dust
creature.*

*It was to no avail. His mother died in front of their
eyes, not professing her love for them, not reassuring
them with last words, but gasping silently like a fish out
of water, jerking and twitching spasmodically.*

*The next week was a blur. There were doctors and
police and morticians and other men in uniforms and
suits who came in and out of the house. An autopsy was
performed on his mother's body and he wanted to ask if
they found the dust monster within her, but he was told
that the cause of death was heart failure, and he figured
that the creature had either gotten out or had simply dissipated and come apart within her system.*

*He knew, though. And his father knew. And the two
of them started packing up their belongings, planning to
leave.*

"Where are we going?" Daniel asked.

*"Anywhere," his father said in the defeated monotone
that had become his normal voice.*

*But they were only in the very earliest stages of packing
when they were confronted by Billingsly. The servant
knocked on the frame of the open doorway as usual and
stood deferentially outside the room, and Daniel was immediately filled with a deep cold fear at the sight of him.
He glanced over at his father and saw that his father
appeared frightened as well. He'd put down the jewelry
box he'd been holding and stood staring at the servant.*

"You can't go," Billingsly said quietly.

Daniel's father said nothing.

"You have a responsibility to uphold."

*For the first time since his mother's death, Daniel saw
tears in his father's eyes. The sight made him uncomfortable and, on some level, frightened, but though he wanted
to look away, he did not.*

"I can't," his father said.

*"You must," Billingsly insisted. He looked at them.
"You both have to stay."*

They did stay. For several more years. Until Daniel

entered high school. They remained in the house, battered and victimized by the same unseen forces that had killed his mother, each of them maintaining three bedrooms, never sure when one bed might be overrun by colored worms or stained with black water, or when the furniture might decide to shift shape or a room disappear altogether. They never talked about it—any of it—this was simply the way they lived, and his mother's death became by unspoken agreement a secret memory, not discussed or referenced or even alluded to, part of an alternate history that did not conform to the lie they lived.

And then, one day, they left. They packed nothing, took nothing with them. Daniel just received a call slip from the office on the first day of his freshman year in high school, and when he walked over, his father was waiting for him.

The two of them got in the car and left.

To Pennsylvania.

They found an apartment, his father found a job, and although Daniel wanted to ask his father what had happened, how they had been able to escape, he was afraid to do so.

His father died several years later, when he was a sophomore in college. They'd never mentioned or discussed the house after they'd left it, and by that time the memory of his other life had been completely buried and repressed. As amazing as it seemed, he'd forgotten all about Billingsly and Doneen and what had happened to his mother, and when he thought about his mother, which was rarely, his mind skipped over her death. If pressed, he would have had to admit that he did not know exactly how she'd died.

It seemed strange even to him, and while most of the circumstances of his childhood had been buried in his memory over the years, not all of them had been completely forgotten. He had, for example, been dimly aware on some level that they'd had a servant in their house. It had never occurred to him to wonder how his family had been able to afford a servant, however, and even now the specifics of that arrangement eluded him.

Probably the same way the Brady Bunch could afford their maid.

No. It was nothing so benign as that.

And Billingsly had been much more than just a servant.

Daniel stood before his wife, adamant but ashamed, dead set on the course of action he'd chosen but embarrassed by the melodrama of its origin, the potboiler nature of its cause.

"I have to go," he said.

Margot simply stared at him.

"I know it sounds irrational. I know it sounds crazy, but trust me, that's what happened, and . . . whatever it was, it's starting again. And it's trying to involve Tony."

She was silent for a moment. "I believe you," she said finally. "That's the scary part."

He looked at her, stunned. "You do?"

"Well, not completely maybe. But enough so that I trust your instincts." She paused. "Don't forget, I saw that doll, too. I know something's going on. And if you can somehow . . . exorcise this whatever-it-is and keep it away from Tony, well then I'm all for it."

Daniel stared at his wife. It wasn't supposed to work this way, it wasn't supposed to be this easy. In books and movies, things worked out like this, but in real life it was supposed to be tougher. No one believed in ghosts and demons and the supernatural, and they didn't just accept someone's word on something like that. He tried to imagine what he would do, how he would react if Margot came to him with some wild story about seeing a UFO or something. He wasn't sure he'd buy into it or even if he'd automatically be on her side. He'd probably agree with her for love's sake, but he'd figure out some way to test her—or some way for her to get help. He doubted that he would completely change his worldview and suddenly believe in things he had never believed in before merely on the word of someone else.

Even if that other person was Margot.

He understood for the first time how truly lucky he was to have this woman for his wife.

"It's in Maine," he said. "The town's called Matty

Groves and I'm not even sure exactly where it is, but I know it's probably a day's drive from here. I know I shouldn't—"

She put a firm arm on his, looked into his eyes.

"Go," she told him.

It was indeed almost a day's drive, and Daniel reached Matty Groves just as the sun was setting. He should've left earlier—he'd set the alarm for five this morning—but he hadn't wanted to part from Margot and Tony, and he'd ended up staying through breakfast.

He was filled with the absurd conviction that this was the last time he'd ever see them.

Although maybe, he thought as he approached the house, the idea wasn't so absurd.

Against its cheerful forested backdrop, the three-storied building looked even gloomier and more gothic, like a stereotypical haunted mansion. Its slatted wooden walls were a dark gray; the trim, door, and shutters black. Even the glass in the windows seemed dusky, although that may just have been a trick of the dying light. It was an imposing structure, with some of the same off-putting air of impenetrability as a medieval fortress or cathedral, and Daniel stood in front of it, goose bumps on his arms. He had not seen the house since he and his father had fled, and had managed until now to block out all memory of it entirely, but once again he was here, and it was as though the house had been waiting for his return.

So it could punish him.

That was ridiculous.

Was it? Whatever it was, whatever lived here, whatever made this house its home, had found him, over distance, over time, and it had reached out to his son, to Tony, had introduced the boy to Billingsly and Doneen, had taught the boy how to make the doll.

It was crazy. All of it.

But there was nothing there he doubted.

He got out of the car, stared up at the dark building, taking it all in. The twin chimneys. The gables. The high window of his mother's corner bedroom. The wraparound porch where he and his friends had so often played, remaining always in the front because they were afraid of the sides and back of the house.

Where were his friends? he wondered. What had happened to them? What did they remember?

Something caught his eye. Movement in one of the lower windows. A dark face?

A dust doll?

He wanted to leave, wanted to turn tail and run, and if it had not been for Margot and Tony, he would have done exactly that. But he was not here only for himself. He was here to find out what was infiltrating his life and put a stop to it, to intercept and end the supernatural harassment of his family.

Supernatural.

He hadn't thought of it in precisely those terms before, but that was exactly what was going on.

He supposed, on some level, he'd always been subtly aware that despite his comfortably normal mainstream existence, there was more to the universe than the material, physical world, that despite the life he had made for himself, there was something else that was somehow . . . influencing him, guiding him. He'd repressed all memory of his childhood and had never seen any overt example or evidence of the supernatural, but all along there'd been small instances of déjà vu, coincidences and coordinations that did not make any kind of logical sense but nonetheless bespoke Truth. It was as if he were a cog in a great machine and every once in a while he was allowed to glance over and see nearly identical cogs performing nearly identical functions. There were connections he could not understand but knew existed, and he knew now that it was all tied to whatever existed inside that house.

Another small dark face at another low window.

His entire body seemed to be covered with gooseflesh and his heart was pounding harder than he'd known it could, but Daniel steeled himself and pressed forward. Night appeared to be falling quicker than usual, sundown and dusk fairly speeding by, and if he had learned that this was a phenomenon which only happened here, that the power within the house somehow had the ability to influence the sun, he would not have been surprised.

He walked up the porch steps, knocked on the heavy oak door.

It was opened instantly.

By Billingsly.

Daniel sucked in his breath at the sight of the man. He was no longer a child and the servant an adult—they were both grown men of approximately the same size—but the balance of power had not shifted in all these years, and Daniel instinctively stepped back. Billingsly was still a frighteningly intimidating figure, alien and unknowable in his proper attire, the blankness in his eyes impossible to read. He bowed, smiling enigmatically. "You are the last."

"What?" Daniel said.

"I trust you had a pleasant trip?" The servant stepped aside, motioning him in.

Daniel stepped over the threshold, acutely aware of the symbolism of that simple act.

The door shut immediately behind him.

PART II

Inside

ONE

Mark

He was scared shitless, but he tried not to let it show.

It was not merely the circumstances of his arrival or the air of menace that overhung the house which left him feeling so terrified, but the fact that he wasn't exactly a guest, wasn't exactly a prisoner, but seemed to be somewhere in-between—and he had no idea what to do about it.

Mark glanced nervously around the sitting room. It was strange being back, seeing the high-vaulted ceilings and the patterned hardwood floors, all of the familiar furniture in all of the familiar places, mileposts of his childhood that were indelibly ingrained in his memory. It was the *smell* of the house that affected him most strongly, though, the familiar odors of old flowers and fireplace smoke and dust; scents of his past that lingered in the room and remained behind, present but invisible, like ghosts.

Mark stared at Billings. What was he? Ghost? Demon? Monster? None of them seemed to hit the mark, but they were all close, they were all within the ballpark.

Feigning a bravery he did not feel, he turned his back on the assistant and walked across the sitting room, pulling open the drapes covering the window. He tried peering out, but it was night outside and he could see nothing.

"I should be able to see the lights of Dry River," he said.

"Curious, isn't it?"

Mark dropped the drapes. "What's going on here?" he demanded.

Billings chuckled.

"Who are you?"

"You know who I am, Marky boy."

Mark felt cold. "All right, then. *What* are you?"

"I'm the assistant."

"What do you want from me?"

"Me? Nothing. It's the House that called you back."

"Called me back?"

"You are to live here again."

Mark shook his head. "I don't know what the fuck you're talking about, but I came back here because Kristen died and I wanted to find out what happened to her. And for your information, I came back for a visit, not to stay."

"But stay you shall. The House needs occupants."

"For what?"

"Why, to maintain the border, of course."

Mark didn't like the sound of that, and he tried not to let his fear show.

"The House," Billings continued, "was built as a barrier, to maintain the border between this world, the material world, and the other world, the Other Side."

Mark's mouth felt dry. "The 'Other Side'?"

Billings's eyes were flat, unreadable. "The hereafter, the world of the dead, the world of magic and the supernatural, the world of spirits. It is the opposite of this world, your world, and it is a horrific place, a world of terrors and abominations the likes of which you have never seen nor ever dreamed. The House was built to keep the two separate, and it is the only reason your people, your world, are still here. Otherwise, you would have been overrun long ago."

Mark said nothing.

"The House is like an electrified fence or, more precisely, like a battery supplying power to that fence. And it is charged by people living within it. That is why you were called back. For the first time, the House is empty. There is no one living here, and the barriers are coming down. On both sides." He looked at Mark. "Ever since Kristen passed on."

Mark turned away, didn't respond. His heart was

pumping crazily, and his body was drenched with a sheen of fear sweat.

"The border is a semipervious membrane. It is not a solid wall, and without a strong barrier to separate the two worlds, they will inevitably collide. And that," he said, "would be catastrophic."

"So I'm here to recharge the battery?"

"If you will."

"What happens if I refuse?"

"You have not refused. You have come."

"What if I leave?"

"You can't leave."

"Who's going to stop me if I break one of these windows and jump out and run away?"

Billings looked at him. "The House."

There was silence between them after that.

"Where did the house come from?" Mark asked finally. "Who built it?"

"The Ones Who Went Before."

The name, with its ambiguity and intimations of tremendous age, frightened him, and he listened quietly as Mr. Billings described the early days, after the barrier was erected, the days of miracles, when gods and monsters roamed the earth, when seas were parted, when oracles foretold the future, when miraculous beings and the resurrected dead mingled with ordinary men. After the House became occupied, he explained, as it gained strength and became more efficient, more attuned to its purpose, those "leaks" were plugged, all access to the Other Side was sealed off.

"Nothing is perfect," the assistant said. "And, in the past, isolated spirits have made it through. But the House was built to maintain the laws of reason and rationality, and those exceptions had no influence or bearing upon that purpose. The Other Side was eventually forgotten about, passing into the realm of myth and fiction, and the occasionally sighted monster, the occasional haunted house, the occasional ghost became an aberration, entertainment, a story that was interesting but not to be believed.

"Now, however, the House is failing. Elements of the

other world are breaking through to this world, the material world, and elements of your world are breaking into it."

Mark desperately wanted a drink. "How long have you been here?" he asked. "In the House?"

"I have always been here."

He didn't like that answer.

"What about your daughter?"

The assistant frowned. "What?"

"Is she still here?" He saw in his mind the child's sly corrupt face, and he shivered even as he acknowledged the faint sensual stirring within him.

Billings blinked, puzzled, and an expression closely related to fear crossed his features.

"I have no daughter," he said.

TWO

Norton

For the first time since he'd arrived, for the first time in his memory, Billingson appeared to be rattled, and Norton felt a small twinge of satisfaction. It was petty, he knew, and should have been beneath him, but the hired hand's discomfort made him feel good.

At the same time, he was terrified.

He didn't know what he'd expected to find here when he returned. A haunted house? Yes. Ghosts from his past? Yes. But not this wide-ranging, elaborate, *epic* situation.

Did he believe it?

There was no doubt in his mind that the hired hand spoke the truth. Nothing else made sense. But the story was so all-inclusive as to be completely overwhelming. A demon possessed a peasant in Bangladesh, or a hiker in the Himalayas caught a glimpse of the abominable snowman, and it was because he didn't live in the Oakdale house anymore? Such a causal connection seemed on the face of it impossible, but Billingson's simple explanation tied it all together in a way that seemed to him entirely believable.

And what about the girl?

As happy as he was to see Billingson so shaken, it frightened him to realize that the hired hand knew nothing about the child who was supposed to have been his daughter.

Donna.

He felt a stirring in his groin just thinking about her. But the fact that Billingson, who seemed to know everything, who seemed to be at the center of all that was going on, was completely unaware of the girl's existence disturbed him in a way he could not explain. As terrifying as the House was, there seemed to be a logic to it, a coherent theory or controlling power behind it. But the girl existed outside of that. She was a wild card, and her existence threw everything off balance, darkening and complicating an already dark and complex picture.

The conversation, the lecture, had been derailed by the revelation that he had seen Billingson's daughter, but the hired hand, while clearly shaken, faced Norton calmly, once again perfectly composed, and said, "It's getting late. I think we should finish this discussion in the morning."

Norton glanced around the sitting room. Until this point, his time in the House had been spent in the sitting room, like a variation of *No Exit,* and his first thought was that he was going to have to sleep here—on the couch or the love seat or the chairs or the floor—and was never going to be able to leave the room.

But when he asked, "Where am I going to sleep?" Billingson replied, "Your room is waiting for you."

Indeed, his bedroom was exactly where it had always been: halfway down the third-story hall. There were numerous doors lining both sides of the dark corridor and Norton realized that even as a child he had never known what was in most of those other rooms. Their doors had always been closed or locked, and he had never even wondered what was inside them.

There are other dimensions besides space and time.

It was what Billingson had said when quizzed about the exact placement of the House vis-á-vis the "Other Side," and though Norton had said nothing at the time, the statement had frightened him and stuck with him.

He was way out of his depth here, and he wished to God he had never come. It was the coward's response, he knew, but he had no problem answering to that description. He would rather have put up with a million monstrous manifestations on the streets of Finley than be trapped here in this House. Those were intrusions of horror into the normal everyday world. Here, horror was the normal everyday occurrence.

Billingson led him to his bedroom door, opened it for

him, and smiled. "Sweet dreams, Nort," he said before bowing theatrically and heading down the hall.

It was what his father used to say to him each night before tucking him into bed.

Norton took a deep breath, walked into the bedroom. Everything looked precisely as it had half a century ago.

It was not exactly a surprise, but the extent of his immersion into the past was still staggering. There was the low bed with the red-checkered bedspread, the small corner desk covered with finished and half-finished airplane models, the photos of Buck and Roy Rogers tacked to the wall, the cigar box on the nightstand that he'd used to store his valuables. He looked up. Above the door was the upside-down horseshoe he'd nailed there for good luck.

Good luck.

He smiled wryly. That was a joke. He'd never had anything remotely approaching good luck in this House.

He was bigger and the room and its contents were smaller, but there was none of the awkwardness usually associated with revisiting scenes from childhood. Instead, he felt perfectly at home here. He sat down on the bed, and his body's memory kicked in, remembering the contours of the mattress and the texture of the bedspread, snuggling into a physical familiarity with the room.

He sat for a few moments on the bed, looking around, taking it all in, then rummaged through the cigar box and the drawers of the desk, picking up and touching objects with which he was intimately familiar but had neither seen nor thought about for many decades.

It depressed him, being in this room again, made him sad. The fear was still there, constant beneath his other layers of feeling, but he also felt pensive and melancholic. Being here reminded him of what he'd thought as a child, what he'd planned, and the realization that the future he'd been so eagerly awaiting had already passed left him somewhat heavy-hearted. For the first time in his life, he truly felt his age.

He walked to the window, looked out. It was still dark out, but it wasn't night. There were no stars, no moon, no town lights or road lights. It was as black as if the window glass had been painted, but the darkness had depth, and he knew there was a world outside the window.

He just wasn't sure he wanted to know what that world was.

Sighing, he turned away. He felt dirty, filthy from both the long trip and the cold-sweat stress of everything he'd experienced since, and although the bathroom, if he remembered correctly, was halfway down the hall, he decided to take a shower before bed. He'd brought no robe, though, no pajamas, and his extra clothes were still in the car. Strange. He'd always intended to stay overnight in Oakdale, maybe stay several nights, and he had no explanation for why he had not packed appropriately.

That was not like him.

He found it worrisome.

He decided to simply walk down the hall, take his shower, put his clothes back on afterward, and then sleep in his underwear and wear the clothes again tomorrow. He considered calling for Billingson, asking for a towel and washcloth, but he didn't relish the idea of seeing the hired hand again, and he figured he'd check the bathroom first, see if he couldn't find what he needed on his own.

He took off his shoes and his belt, emptied the contents of his pockets on the nightstand. He heard no noise from any of the other rooms as he walked down the hall, but the silence was more unnerving than sound would have been, and he considered calling off the shower and retreating to his bedroom, hiding until morning. The hallway was dark, the silence unnerving and oppressive, but he wasn't about to be intimidated by the House or anything in it. He might feel fear, but he wouldn't show it, and he purposely kept his gait as easy and natural as he could.

Unlike in the hallway and, to a lesser extent, his bedroom, the light in the bathroom was bright, modern, fluorescent. This was one room that had obviously been updated and remodeled since his day. He flipped on the switch and clear white light illuminated every corner of the small functional space.

The modern bathroom made him feel good, gave him hope. It was an island of normalcy in the surreal landscape of the House, and its matter-of-fact concreteness kept him grounded and tethered, kept him in touch with the ordinary everyday world.

There were indeed towels and washcloths and soap, and Norton closed and locked the door, taking off his clothes and placing them on the closed lid of the toilet. There was not a separate shower and bathtub but a combined shower bath, and he pulled aside the beige plastic shower curtain and stepped into the tub, closing it behind him. Bending down to turn on the water, he saw movement out of the corner of his eye. He straightened, stood. Beneath the edge of the shower curtain, dark against the whiteness of the tub, were what looked like thousands of thin hairs—whiskers or spider legs—moving crazily, jerkily, and he flattened against the tiled wall and stared at the wildly twisting strands.

The fear that was triggered within him came from the very core of his being. There was no thought, no conscious determination of danger, only an instinctive terror of the thin hairs, an irrational alarm.

The water was on, and for that he was grateful.

He did not want to hear the noise the hairs were making.

He found himself thinking of the ants he'd burned with Donna. For some reason, the crinkling of their bodies, their spasms of death, reminded him on a subliminal level of the wildly whipping whiskers, and the thought occurred to him that this was some sort of retribution, some decades-delayed revenge for that long-ago act.

The hairs had been moving crazily, independently, but he saw now that they were moving together, swishing and sweeping back and forth, from side to side. They extended below the curtain for the entire length of the tub, there was no empty space, and his panicked racing mind tried to think of how he could possibly escape. He didn't know whether the whiskers were independent entities or part of some larger creature, but either way he didn't want to open the curtain, didn't want to see any more than the few inches already visible against the wall of the tub.

He was about to scream for help when the hairs pulled up and were gone. They were visible for a second in the air above the shower rod, waving in that even swish above the plastic curtain, and then they disappeared completely. He waited for a moment, still flattened against the wall, then, detecting no movement, carefully pulled open one side of the curtain.

The bathroom was empty.

There were no whiskers or hairs or spider legs or creatures near the toilet or the sink or the counter or the towel rack. The door was closed and locked.

He still felt dirty, still wanted to take a shower, but he was shaking and afraid, and he quickly shut off the water, pulled his pants back on, and, grabbing the rest of his clothes, ran back down the hall to his room.

He sat on his bed, breathing heavily.

What would happen in the middle of the night if he had to take a leak?

He'd hang his dick out the window and piss in the open air.

There was no way in hell he was going back into that bathroom.

He closed his eyes, saw again those twitching hairs, and shivered. He longed for the benign manifestations he'd seen before, for ghosts or burnt toast.

But he changed his mind about that.

Ghosts did come.

Later.

And he longed for the benign manifestation of hairs in the bathtub.

THREE

Daniel

Billingsly looked different in the morning. Better, healthier, as though he were suddenly well again after a long illness.

He himself looked like hell.

He'd had a bad night.

Daniel had been almost asleep when the doll had come to visit. He was tired from driving and from stress, and he'd lain down on the bed, intending only to close his eyes and rest for a moment before attempting to find an escape route out of this loony bin, but when he felt himself drifting off, he figured he might as well pack it in for the night and wait for morning, when he'd have a clear mind and refreshed body and his chances would be better. He took off his clothes, crawled under the covers, closed his eyes.

And heard something scuttling in the corner.

He jerked up in bed, eyes wide open, heart pounding. He recognized that sound, and he glanced immediately toward the corner of the room from which the noise had come, but it was too dark for him to see anything.

He flipped on the nightstand lamp, then rushed over to the door and turned on the overhead light.

There it was, between a wastepaper basket and his toy chest.

The doll.

It stared at him with feather eyes, its head a mass of dust and hair strands, its open mouth an empty hole crisscrossed by broken toothpicks. It was not quite the doll he remembered from the past, not quite the figure Tony had been making, but some unwholesome hybrid. He stayed by the door, hand still on the light switch, afraid to move. Fully dressed and wearing protective combat gear, he still would have felt unprepared to face the small figure; barefoot and naked, he felt completely vulnerable. It stared at him from its corner with an intensity and malevolence he had never seen before, and the thought occurred to him that it knew he had destroyed its brethren, Tony's creations.

And it wanted revenge.

That was stupid, he told himself.

But he could not make himself believe it.

The horrid figure shifted against the toy chest, its feather eyes never once leaving his. What had the doll been planning? To kill him the way his mother had been killed, to stuff itself down his throat as he slept? Daniel trembled as he thought of how close he had come to that fate. He was so dead tired tonight that if he had fallen fully asleep, nothing could have awakened him. By the time he was roused, it would have been too late.

He glanced around for a weapon, saw the handle of his old baseball bat peeking out from beneath the bed. Did he dare try for it? It was a good five steps away. He'd have to rush halfway across the room, duck down and grab it. What would the doll be able to do in that time?

It didn't matter. Unless he wanted to run out into the hallway naked and let the doll escape to boot, the bat was his only hope.

The good thing was that the bat was sticking out from under the foot of the bed, the part nearest the door. It would be difficult to grab, but not impossible, and even if the doll ran for the door while he was grabbing the weapon, it would not have time to open the door and he would be able to whale on it and destroy it before it could escape.

What if it attacked him instead?

He did not even want to think about that.

Daniel shot one more glance at the dark shifting figure, then moved quickly, dashing across the carpet. He bent down, acutely aware of the vulnerability of his dangling genitals, and braced himself for an attack as he reached under the bed and hurriedly grasped the familiar tape-covered handle.

The door clicked open behind him, and he whirled around to see the doll running out of the bedroom, laughing in a whispery sibilant way that reminded him of the sound of broom bristles on hardwood floor.

He followed it into the hall. He was still naked, but embarrassment was the least of his concerns, and, grunting, he swung the bat low, as hard as he could, hoping the doll had not gotten too far away and that he'd be able to hit it.

No such luck.

Still laughing, the figure hurried down the dark hallway, blending in with the shadows against the sideboard, disappearing into the gloom.

"Damn!" he said.

He looked up, and on the far wall, in a dim half circle of what appeared to be reflected moonlight, he thought he saw a shadow.

The shadow of a girl.

Doneen.

Beckoning him.

He'd gone back into his room after that, locking his door, and although he dozed off eventually, he tried to stay awake all night, and what little sleep he did get was troubled and intermittent. He was as tired when he woke up as he had been the night before.

Daniel walked into the dining room. Billingsly smiled cheerfully at him and, lifting a silver pot, said, "Coffee?"

The butler had laid out an elaborate breakfast on the oversized banquet table, and Daniel sat down at its foot, nodding his acknowledgment.

He felt like shit. Billingsly, by contrast, was in peak condition. If yesterday he had accentuated the spookiness of the House with his pale, cadaverous appearance, today he complemented it with his visible robustness. He was no less creepy for his newfound vigor, however, and improved health only served to emphasize those things that were so disturbing about him in the first place.

Daniel looked from the rejuvenated Billingsly to his

own enervated reflection in a mirror above the side-board. The dichotomy was too striking not to notice.

Maybe Billingsly was a vampire. Maybe the butler was feeding off him, sucking the life out of him for his own nourishment.

No. More likely, the butler's health was connected with that of the House. And now that the House was getting charged back up, old Billingsly was receiving a power boost as well.

Billingsly smirked at him as he poured his coffee. "I trust you had a pleasant evening?"

Daniel smiled sweetly up at him. "Couldn't have been better." He sipped the hot drink. It tasted wonderful. "So why didn't you recruit new people to live in the House? I assume that's what you did before. I know my family didn't live here for generations."

"No, they didn't. But they knew why they were here, they knew what they were doing. They were recruited by the previous occupants, specifically selected to maintain the barrier, and they did so, following all of the rules and rituals bequeathed them by their predecessors." His expression hardened suddenly, and the change in expression was so quick and complete that Daniel nearly spilled his coffee. "As you remember, Danny boy, breakfast is promptly at six. No later. You will be allowed to slide today, but tomorrow . . ." His voice trailed off, an implied threat.

Daniel's heart was pounding, but he feigned nonchalance, tried to keep the tremble out of his hand. "Your daughter," he found himself saying. "She predicted my mother's death. And she was somehow involved with it." His eyes met Billingsly's. "I thought you were, too."

The butler shook his head. "No."

"Then why did you force us to stay, me and my dad?"

"As I told you, the House needed occupants."

"But you knew she died?"

"I did not know how."

"A doll, a doll made out of dust and lint and gum wrappers, shoved itself down her throat and strangled her."

The butler's voice remained even. "I did not know that."

"You didn't know that I was making one of those dolls, too? You don't know that my son saw her and she taught him how to make them, as well?"

"She was obviously trying to keep you from the House, trying to remind you of what had happened and scare you away."

"And you? Tony said he saw you, too."

"I was trying to entice you back."

"And you knew nothing about her? This is all news to you?"

Billingsly nodded.

Daniel angrily grabbed a bagel, dug into the eggs and sausage on his plate. Billingsly moved unobtrusively around the table, refilling Daniel's coffee cup, taking dishes back to the kitchen, and it was only after Daniel had finished his breakfast that the butler finally asked a question: "Have you had sex with this . . . being?"

"No." Daniel was firm. "She wanted me to, but I refused. Like I said, that's why I left."

Billingsly nodded. "I don't know who or what this child is, but I assure you that I have never seen her, and until now I've been entirely unaware of her existence."

It was true, Daniel thought. He had never seen the two of them together. He'd just *assumed* Doneen was Billingsly's daughter.

Or perhaps she'd told him that.

"Apparently, she was successful in her efforts to drive you away from the House," Billingsly said. "And, indeed, that weakened the barrier. I assume that was her goal, to open the border." The butler smiled reassuringly. "But if she was here, she is gone now—at least in that guise. You have come back, the House is once again returning to its intended state, and all attempts to thwart the House in its intended purpose have failed."

"My son saw her," Daniel reminded him. "I think I've seen her, too. And I thought I saw one of those . . . dolls in the window when I drove up. I'm pretty sure she's still around."

Billingsly smiled again, and this time there was some-

thing predatory in the gesture, an intensity and cold
unnatural fierceness completely unlike any human expression. For the first time, Daniel thought, he was
seeing the real butler, and he could not look upon the
sight, he had to turn away.

Billingsly placed his coffeepot back on its tray and
surveyed the table. "Are we all finished with breakfast?"
he asked innocently.

He was acting as though nothing was wrong, as though
nothing unusual had occurred or been discussed, and
Daniel wasn't sure if that was good or bad.

"I think so," he said.

"Very well. Dinner is at six sharp. You may eat lunch
or not, as is your wont, but you must appear for dinner."
His eyes were hard. "On time."

"What am I supposed to do all day? Can I leave,
go shopping?"

Billingsly laughed, and for the first time there seemed
to be real humor in it. "I'm afraid not."

"What then?"

The butler began walking around the table. "Whatever you want. This is your home now, explore it. Get
to know it."

"I do know it," Daniel said. "I spent half my fucking
life here."

Billingsly smiled. "I think you'll be surprised."

There was nothing threatening in either Billingsly's
words or his tone of voice but Daniel still felt chilled.

"I don't want to be surprised," he said softly.

But the butler had walked into the kitchen and did
not hear him.

FOUR

Stormy

Stormy strode out of the dining room into the sitting room. He was determined not to simply fall into line and do whatever Billingham told him to do. That snotty servant had rubbed him the wrong way even as a child, and while he'd always been afraid of and intimidated by him, he'd always resented it. He wasn't about to capitulate now, to give in and give up and blindly follow orders. If anything, he was more determined than ever to stand up to the butler and the House.

Butchery.

He kept thinking of the movie.

He kept thinking about a lot of movies. Now that he knew the world wasn't going to end, he was anxious to get the hell out of here and get back to work. He didn't know how long he'd been here—with the wacky time that seemed to affect this place, who could tell?—but even if it had just been a day or two, he needed to get back. He had things to do. He had the Taos festival to prepare for.

Had he been reported missing? he wondered. Were people looking for him? Would anybody be able to find him?

Doubtful. He didn't know where he was himself. To paraphrase Dorothy, he had the feeling he wasn't in Chicago anymore.

He wondered if the dead who had come back to life were still hanging around the reservation. Or if his return home and the fact that the House was once again occupied had put a stop to that. Had they disappeared, the living dead? Had they simply fallen in their tracks? Had they rotted away and turned to dust like Dracula?

He hoped Rodman had been out there with his camera, documenting it. It would make a hell of a film.

He had to get out of here. He had to escape.

But what if the butler was right? What if he *was* the only thing protecting the world, the universe, from demons and monsters, from this "Other Side." Didn't he owe it to . . . to humanity to do everything he could to—how did Billingham put it—"maintain the barrier"?

No.

There were bound to be people willing to give up their lives for this, to devote all of their time for the greater good. The same people who joined the Peace Corps and spent all of their free time helping the homeless.

But he was not one of them.

He knew it was selfish, but he had things he wanted to do, too. He had his own life to live. Let Billingham find someone else to staff his fucking House. From what Stormy could tell, all that was needed was a warm body. Anyone would do. It didn't have to be him. He wasn't bringing any special skills or abilities to the table.

Stormy glanced back toward the dining room. The first question he had to ask himself was: Did he believe Billingham about the House?

Yes.

He didn't know why—he'd seen no evidence to support the butler's wild claims—but he supposed it was because he'd experienced his own examples of that other world bleeding into this one. And Billingham offered an easy one-stop explanation.

Time for the next question: Who was Billingham? *What* was he?

That one was a little harder.

Maybe he was God.

God was his family's servant? He found that hard to believe.

But it worked from an objective, interpretive standpoint. If this was a film, the girl would obviously represent the devil, evil, temptation. You didn't have to be Antonioni to figure that out.

And that would make Billingham God.

No, Stormy thought. He didn't buy it. The butler clearly didn't know about the girl.

But maybe he wasn't the final word here. Maybe he was a good guy, but the power didn't rest with him. Maybe he and the girl were both puppets.

With the House pulling the strings.

Stormy took a deep breath. The first thing he had to determine was what he wanted to do. Obviously, Billingham was not very forthcoming on these subjects. He didn't think he was going to get a whole lot more out of him than what he'd gotten already. So should he confront the butler or go around him? Should he accept fate and do as he was told—or try to escape?

Stormy picked up a lamp off the small table next to the love seat and yanked out its extension cord.

He voted for escape.

He threw the lamp at the front window as hard as he could. He expected it to either break the glass or bounce back, but instead it disappeared into the window, as though it were sinking in a pool of water—

—and instantly appeared back on the table.

He glanced wildly around the room, found a marble cameo box in the center of the long coffee table, picked it up, and heaved it with all of his might at the window.

Same result.

Fuck it. Billingham had told him to explore, and he was going to explore, goddamn it. And he'd find another way out of here if it killed him.

He remembered what the butler had said: *I think you'll be surprised.*

A chill passed through him.

He ignored it, pushed all reservations to the back of his mind. Where should he start?

The doors. He'd tried to get out through the front door almost immediately after he'd arrived, but he hadn't tried it since. And if he remembered right, there was a side door off the kitchen and a door leading from the den to the back porch.

If that didn't work, he'd start with the basement and work his way up.

He walked out of the sitting room into the entryway.

The front door was still locked. Not just locked. Frozen. The latch on the handle did not rattle, and there was not even the slightest give as he tried to yank the door open.

Billingham was in the kitchen, humming to himself, some song that nagged on Stormy's brain with its familiarity but which he could not quite place, so he left that one for later and went into the den.

It had been a long time since he'd been in this room, but he remembered it perfectly: its look, its smell, the way sunlight seemed to die somewhere along the way from the windows to the dark wood walls. Even the books on the shelves were exactly as he remembered them—he recognized the titles.

The den windows *had* looked out onto the extensive gardens in the backyard, but the windows now looked out on nothing. Light came through them, clear bright light obviously generated by the sun, but it appeared to be either smoggy or foggy behind the glass and there was only white and only light and no detail of the world beyond could be made out.

He increased the speed of his step as he approached the back door. He reached for the knob, and it turned in his hand. It was unlocked.

He opened the door.

And stepped over the threshold to the Other Side.

It was not at all what he'd expected. There were no ghosts or animated corpses, no black sky or barren landscape, no skeletons or witches or drooling befanged demons. Instead, he was in a house structurally identical to the one he had just left, but with all of its insides scooped out. There were no rooms or staircases or hallways or interior walls, just a giant, single three-story room that took up the entire building. Its unadorned interior was a color that had no counterpart in the known universe, an entirely new hue that bore no relation to red, yellow, blue, black, white, or any of the colors of the spectrum. High above, clouds floated near the top of the three gables, the whitish wisps floating back and forth just beneath the ceiling, as if searching for a way out.

It was a compelling sight, beautiful in its way, but his

attention was captured by a figure against the far wall:
a bald woman, naked, sitting in a huge straw nest atop
an egg the size of a medicine ball.

His mother.

Stormy stood rooted in place, staring, unable to move.

His mother waved at him, smiled broadly. "Stormy!"

There were tears in his eyes, and part of him wanted
to run over to her and throw his arms around her and
hug her so hard that she could never get away from him.
But another part of him, a more rational part, was not
sure that it would be such a good idea. The egg and the
nest and the baldness threw him off, and while he had
no doubt that this really was his mother, something kept
him from wholeheartedly embracing her.

"Stormy!" she called again.

Was this what it would be like if the border was
down? Conversing with the dead, maintaining a relationship with someone even after they passed away?

And was that so bad?

He didn't think so. Death was responsible for most of
the sadness in the world, and if loved ones were still
around after they died, if ghosts weren't considered
frighteningly unnatural, weren't demonized by myth and
religions but were accepted as merely another form of
being, all of that grieving and mourning and anguish and
depression would be immediately eliminated.

But were the living and the dead supposed to mix?

They had at one time. Before the House.

According to Billingham, though, if they'd continued
to do so, his world would have long since been engulfed
and would no longer exist.

Was this heaven? he wondered.

Or hell?

Maybe it was both.

Through the windows, he could see other houses of
the same unknown color, an endless line of them, like
repeating images in a hall of mirrors, stretching endlessly
to either side.

In front was whiteness.

In back was black.

Was this the afterlife? Was this where people went

when they died? It seemed kind of small and limiting, kind of barren. He had never really given much thought to what would happen to him after death, and if pressed he probably would have said that his brain would stop and that would be it, he would cease to exist. He had never really believed in a heaven or hell.

But clearly, the soul, the spirit, the essence of a person, did live on after death.

Only . . .

Only he found it kind of depressing. If he *had* imagined a hereafter, it would have been more expansive than this, more luxurious, more along the lines of traditional conceptions. But if his mother died only to become a bald lady sitting on a nest in an empty house . . .

Well, simply having his brain stop and ceasing to exist didn't seem quite so bad.

But that feeling disappeared as he gathered his courage and began walking toward her. She called his name again, and waved to him, but as he drew closer she seemed to fade and grow insubstantial. Her form became slim and wavery, and as he reached the nest, she floated upward, joining the clouds at the top of the house. Only they weren't clouds, he saw now. They were spirits. The wisps had faces, faint traces of eyes and mouths that shifted and changed as they moved.

As one, all of the clouds, all of the spirits, flew out of the window of the center gable, into the whiteness, where they became a rainbow and then were gone.

Stormy was filled with an almost joyous sense of wonder, and the realization that the afterlife was not limited to this row of houses, that it encompassed a world far beyond what he could see or understand, cheered him up immensely. He looked around the empty house with awe.

The egg and the nest still remained, and he patted the egg a few times. It felt warm, leathery, and he wondered what was in it.

But he was not sure he really wanted to know.

He walked carefully around the nest, examining it, touching it, then looked about him. There were no doors aside from the one he'd come through, and after walking slowly around the perimeter of the open oversized room, he found himself back at the entrance to the den. He returned through it, closing the door behind him.

Apparently Billingham had been telling the truth. The House was definitely on the border, and it probably did keep that border sealed.

But was that good? What he'd seen wasn't horrible or awful. Maybe *some* of the things in that world would turn out to be so, but it was clear that it was not all evil.

Maybe the House *shouldn't* be manned, he thought. Maybe its occupancy had been allowed to lapse for a reason. Maybe it was time for the borders to come down. He'd only thought that the Other Side was bad because he'd been *told* it was bad, he'd been told it was wrong. Yes, it was scary to imagine coexisting with the dead, with shapeshifters and ghosts and God knew what else, but that was only because he'd been conditioned to think that way. Maybe this was how things were supposed to be. Maybe this was the natural way of things. Maybe keeping the two worlds apart was what was wrong, and it was the House that was unnatural.

Maybe the House was evil.

He looked back at the closed door. The House had not been exactly saintly, he had to admit. His family had been torn apart. He'd been lied to and was now being held prisoner against his will. And for what? So the House could maintain its power? He shook his head. The end did not justify the means. Evil acts could not be performed for the greater good.

And from where he stood, all of the horrifying, terrible things that had happened so far had been the work of the House.

No, that was not true.

They were the work of Donielle.

The girl was evil.

It was true. Moral relativism might be a safe intellectual refuge when confronted with something like the afterlife, but the girl, in either world, was indeed evil. He didn't know how he knew, but he did, and all of a sudden he felt the need to get out of the den, to get back to the sitting room or the dining room or someplace close to Billingham.

A chime rang through the House, a light musical sound that had no specific point of origin but seemed to come from everywhere.

The den door opened, and Billingham, in the hallway, poked his head into the room. "Wash up," he said. "It's time for dinner." He smiled. "We have guests."

FIVE

Laurie

There were other people at the dining-room table.

Laurie stopped short and stood in the doorway, staring. Four men were seated around the table, empty seats between each, as though they all wanted their own space or were wary of getting too close.

They looked . . . normal. She did not get the impression that they were denizens of the House, that they were manifestations or ghosts or Billington's peers. They seemed more like her, and there was an almost uniform wariness in their expressions that led her to believe they were prisoners of the House as well.

She experienced a sudden exhilarating rush of energy. Ever since she'd arrived here, ever since Billington's little speech, ever since she'd known she'd been lured back to stay and was not going to be allowed to leave, she'd felt uncharacteristically powerless. Both demoralized and dispirited. She'd tried her damnedest to find a way out of the House, to somehow contact the outside world. She'd even attempted one of Josh's silly astral projection exercises in a vain effort to contact her brother. But nothing had worked, nothing had come of any of it, and she'd just about given up, resigning herself to the fact that the House was more powerful than she was.

But with five of them . . .

Five heads were better than one, as the saying went, and between them, they might be able to come up with an escape plan. She felt a renewed sense of hope as she looked at the men in front of her.

With a theatrical flourish, Billington introduced them, moving clockwise around the table. "This is Daniel Anderson, this is Norton Johnson, this is Stormy Salinger, and this is Mark McKinney."

They all smiled at Laurie awkwardly, acknowledging her nodded greeting.

Billington bowed in her direction. "This, everyone, is Laurie Mitchell."

Nods again.

The assistant looked happily around the dining room, and his smile broadened in a way that she found extremely unnerving. "We're all together at last." He bowed again. "I will prepare tonight's repast and leave you kiddies alone to get acquainted."

He retreated through the swinging doors into the kitchen, and the second he was out of the room, the five of them started talking. None of them were under the impression that they had really been left alone, that they were not being watched and spied upon, but that took a backseat to their more immediate and pressing concerns.

It was Stormy who was the first to articulate the question at the forefront of all of their minds: "What the fuck is going on here?"

They all began talking at once, and after several loud confusing minutes Laurie raised her hands and said, "Quiet! One at a time, please!"

The others shut up, looked at her, and with that she was thrust into the role of de facto leader. She didn't mind—if there was one thing she'd learned in business it was that if anything was ever going to get done there had to be only one person in charge—but she felt just as lost as the rest of them and singularly unqualified to take control of their efforts to . . . what? Escape? Find out what was at the heart of the House? She was not sure what the others wanted.

Still, she could preside over the discussion, she could maintain some semblance of order and bring some organizational skills to the table, and she looked from one face to another. "All right," she said. "Who wants to go first?"

They'd all, it seemed, known Billington or Billingsly or Billings or whoever the hell he was when they were children. As Stormy described his experiences in New

Mexico, there were nods of recognition all around. While the specifics of his story might have been different from hers, the underlying thread of it was not, and Laurie knew exactly what he had gone through.

The same was true for Mark, hitching throughout the West; Norton, in Iowa; and Daniel, in Pennsylvania.

Then she told her story.

And everyone understood.

She felt an immediate kinship with the others. It wasn't quite as if they were siblings separated at birth who had suddenly found family, but it was along those lines and there was a definite connection between them.

Only Mark stood apart. He was younger than the rest of them and although that could have accounted for it, she didn't think so. He seemed . . . different somehow, more unfazed by it all, as though he accepted, even, on some level, understood what was happening. None of this seemed to be as alien to him as it was to the rest of them, and while she did not doubt his loyalties, while she knew he was as much a victim as the rest of them, he was the only one whose story she did not entirely believe. She did not think he was lying, but she had the feeling he was keeping something back, not telling the whole truth.

And that kept him at arm's length.

They were no closer to knowing what was going on after they'd spilled their guts than they had been before. They could empathize with each other, they could sympathize, but understanding eluded them. Their stories might all be similar in tone, but on the most basic level, the narrative level, they were contradictory and did not mesh.

In addition to the obvious disparities of location, there were the times of arrival. Daniel had been the first to pick up on that, and after Mark had finished his story, he asked, "How long have you been here?"

Mark shrugged. "Since yesterday."

"What day was that?" Daniel pressed him.

"What are you talking about?"

"What day did you arrive here?"

"Saturday."

"It's Friday," Daniel said quietly.

"What's the date?" Stormy asked. He reached in his pocket, pulled out a plane ticket. "To me, it's Thursday. I flew into Chicago yesterday. September ninth."

"It's Friday the eighteenth," Daniel told him.

"Oh, shit." Mark sat down hard on the couch.

"You think you've only been here for a day, but by my watch it's been over a week."

Laurie's head hurt. No matter how much they talked, they were still in the dark. They could not pull their stories together, could not create coherence out of the chaos.

"So where are we?" she said quietly. "*When* are we?"

The door to the kitchen swung open and Billington? Billingson? Billings? Billingsly? Billingham? walked in, carrying a tray of hors d'oeuvres.

Daniel turned toward him. "What is this?" he demanded.

The other man chuckled.

"And what's your name?" Norton asked. "We seem to have conflicting reports."

"We'll just call him Mr. Bill," Stormy said.

Laurie felt a little bit better. Humor leavened the seriousness of the situation, made it not seem so scary, so solemn, so grave.

Grave.

"You can call me Mr. Billings," the assistant said in a voice that brooked no argument. "That is the name by which I am currently known." He put the tray down on the table.

"What's going on?" Daniel asked.

"You want to know what's happening? You want to know why you entered a House in Dry River, Arizona"—he nodded at Mark—"and you entered a House in Chicago, Illinois"—Stormy—"and yet you're both here? Along with everyone else?"

"It had crossed our minds," Stormy said dryly.

"It's because the Houses are getting stronger. They are almost at full strength."

Laurie stared at the assistant. She had to keep reminding herself that he was five different men, a different person to each of them, and that was a hard thing to fully comprehend. There were similarities, obviously, but there were differences as well: different dynamics in their relationships with him, different memories and histories, different names. It was, she supposed, like looking at the individual facets of a giant diamond from five angles. Or like the old blind-men-and-the-elephant story.

"I didn't know there were other Houses," Daniel said.

Billings smiled. "Perhaps I forgot to mention that."

Stormy snorted. "I guess each House is a post of your electrified fence, huh?"

"Not a bad analogy, Stormy boy." His expression darkened. "But lose the sarcasm, and please refrain from speaking to me in that manner. I am less than happy with that attitude."

Stormy shut up.

"So where are we?" Laurie asked. "Whose House are we in?"

"All of them."

"That doesn't make any sense."

He smiled at her. "It doesn't have to."

Laurie thought about what she'd seen on the Other Side, in that empty hollowed House through the den door, and the conversation she'd had with her mother—her adoptive mother, she amended, although that coldly matter-of-fact description did not in any way do justice to their relationship. They'd talked about family things, about her father and Josh, and although they had not had time to discuss the House before her mother had flown away, she'd told Laurie that she had come to visit "while you were here," and Laurie put the most positive spin on that statement and took it to mean that there was a possibility of escape.

But nothing made sense, nothing fit together in any sort of logical manner. She'd been thrilled to see her mother again, emotionally overwhelmed, but her mother's physical appearance had been truly bizarre, and the conversation they'd had had been filled with disconcerting non sequiturs.

"So we don't need to understand anything," Daniel

said. "We just need to live here and charge up the
batteries."

The assistant grinned. "Bingo."

"What about when they're fully charged again?" Norton asked. "Can we leave then? Will our jobs be done?"

"Oh, no. You can never leave."

"Why not?"

"The Houses don't want you to."

"So we're supposed to just—"

"Make the best of it."

Laurie listened silently to this exchange. She was still
not sure how she felt about Billington—Billings—and
that was one thing she wanted to talk to the others
about. He was clearly not affiliated with Dawn—he
hadn't even been aware of the girl's existence until she'd
told him about her—but even though the girl was evil,
did that automatically make Billings good? She wasn't
sure. He didn't seem . . . bad, exactly. But he was not a
knight in shining armor, either. And the fact that he was
keeping them here against their will, or was aiding the
House in doing so, suggested that his motives were not
all that pure.

Billings pointed toward the tray of hors d'oeuvres.
"Eat up," he said. "There's plenty more where that
came from." He smiled at them, headed toward the
kitchen. "You can talk behind my back for a few minutes. I'll return in a moment with your meals."

They did not talk behind his back, though. They were
afraid to. And when he returned soon after with a tray
of roast beef, they were eating in silence.

SIX

Norton

After serving dinner and clearing off their plates, Billings disappeared, and the rest of them quickly tried the kitchen door and the cellar door to see if either of them offered a way to get out of the House, but it was to no avail. Outside each of the windows, the world was dark, pitch-black, and Norton found himself wondering if the windows looked out onto the other world or were simply facing the blankness of the border in between.

Neither thought was particularly comforting.

They spent some time comparing notes, comparing theories, hashing over some of their concerns, but they did not seem to be making much headway, and when Norton's wristwatch had—correctly or incorrectly—informed him that it was ten o'clock, he said he was tired, excused himself, and went upstairs to his bedroom. As he climbed the stairs, he heard Stormy complain loudly about not having a television or radio, and Norton had to admit that he himself would appreciate having something to read. If they were going to be stuck in here with only each other for company and no entertainment or intellectual stimulation of any sort, nerves were going to get awfully frayed awfully fast. They were already starting to grate on each other. They had the Houses in common, yes, and their current predicament, but they were also five separate people from five different walks of life, and even under the best of circumstances that was not always a recipe for harmony.

And these were far from the best of circumstances.

He lay in his bed, unable to sleep, staring upward at the ceiling. He'd lied. He wasn't tired. He'd just wanted some time alone, some time to think. Even if everything

the butler said was true, there were still gaps, still things
he didn't understand, and he wanted to be able to sort
through it all and see if he couldn't somehow make sense
of it.

A half hour passed. An hour. He heard Mark walk
down the hallway to his room. Another hour passed.
Two. He tried to go to sleep. Couldn't. Tossing and turning, he closed his eyes, lying first on his back, then on
his stomach, then on his side, but sleep would not come.
Sighing, he turned his head on the pillow, looked toward
the window. He saw the moon outside, stars. A typical
night sky.

A typical night sky?

His heart pounding, excited but afraid to get his hopes
up, he sat up in bed, threw off the covers. He stood,
walked over to the window, and looked out.

Lights.

The lights of Oakdale.

He could make out the blinking red light atop the
water tower, assorted streetlights, the glowing orange
ball of the 76 station.

Was it over? Were they free? Norton quickly pulled
on his pants and shirt, unlocked his bedroom door. He
hurried out into the hall. It was long after midnight and
he would have expected there to be only quiet, but the
House was far from silent. He heard low whispers at the
far end of the shadowed hall, occasional thumping from
somewhere downstairs. Above, in the attic perhaps,
there was a noise that sounded like a child's laugh, a
high continuous chuckle that did not pause for breath
but went on nonstop.

The typical sounds of a haunted house.

There were goose bumps on his arms, but he resisted
his instinctive impulse to turn back and flee into the
safety of his room. This was too important, and he might
not get another chance like it. This burst of reality might
be only temporary. Hell, it might even be only a joke,
something to tempt him.

No matter what it was, he had to act on it, had to
assume that it was real, and he ignored the slithery whispers around him as he sped down the hall to Mark's

room and knocked quietly. "Mark!" he whispered.
"Mark!"

No response.

He knocked a little louder, raised his voice. "Mark!"
No answer.

"Mark!" he yelled.

Nothing.

There were several possibilities. Mark could be sound
asleep, he might not be able to hear through the thick
door, he could have left the room and gone downstairs—

he could be dead

—or this could all be a dream.

He didn't have time to find out, though. Time was a-
wasting. Norton turned away from the closed door.

And something rushed by him in the hall. A small
dark figure that did not even come up to his knee but
traveled on two feet like a man.

A doll.

He did not want to think about it, and he kept his
attention focused on what he'd seen out the window as
he hurried down the hall toward the stairway, ignoring
the unidentifiable noises that dogged him through the
semidarkness.

There were footsteps other than his own on the stairs
as he took the steps two at a time, but he ignored them
as well.

Of course the front door was locked, but he'd known
that would be the case, and after a quick cursory try he
headed down the dark corridor that led past the dining
room, kitchen, pantry to the den. The air was cold but
he was sweating, perspiring more from nervous tension
than fear. If he'd known where Daniel and Stormy and
Laurie were sleeping, where their bedrooms were, he
would've tried to rouse them, but he didn't feel he had
time to hunt them down. The House was too big and
this was too good an opportunity to waste.

He could come back for them later, rescue them.

Rescue them?

Who was he kidding? That was a crock and he knew
it. He was running now on pure coward's energy, and
despite all of his moral superiority, his lofty talk about

sacrificing individual desires for the greater good, when push came to shove he was just like anyone else. A good Nazi. Willing to save his own ass at the expense of others. Hell, at *any* cost.

He walked faster.

He'd been the one playing devil's advocate, taking Billings' side, defending the purpose of the Houses, suggesting that they be content with their lot, that they accept the roles fate selected for them because they had been chosen to do important work, to not only save the free world but to protect the structural integrity of the entire universe. Had it all been rationalization, merely his own way of attempting to make the best of a bad situation? He didn't think so. He had believed it—at least some of it. But he also had to admit that the prospect of escaping, of actually being able to get away from this prison filled him with a joy and hope he had not experienced in . . . years.

If ever.

Freedom became so much more precious when it was taken away.

He stopped in front of the den. The door was open and through the windows of the room he could see the lights of the next farm over.

It was as if a great weight had been lifted from his chest.

He walked quickly into the den, not bothering to turn on the light. The door he'd gone through before was locked, but he could still see farmland through the windows, hay bales lit blue by the moon. He remembered what Stormy had told them about trying to break a window, and though it hadn't worked for Stormy, Norton figured it was worth another try. He glanced around the den, looking for something he could use to smash the glass. His gaze alighted on a small three-legged table next to a high-backed leather smoking chair. There was a heavy ashtray atop the table, and he tried that first, cocking his arm back and throwing the ashtray as hard as he could at one of the windows.

It sank into the glass, reappeared on top of the table. He picked up the table itself, letting the ashtray fall to the floor. Using both hands to grasp two of the table's legs, he stationed himself to the left of the window, pulled back, and swung the table as hard as he could into the glass. He did not let go of the legs, and there was a strange liquidy tremor as the tabletop hit the window, a wobbling transmitted by the wooden legs that he could feel throughout his entire body.

A portion of the table reappeared next to the chair.

He stared at the window. He could still see farmland, hay bales, the Iowa sky, but everything was blurry, indistinct, as though the glass had been soaped over or smeared with Vaseline. The legs of the table and one corner of its top were still visible on this side of the window, but they had no counterpart beyond it, and he released his grip, let the legs go. The rest of the table was immediately sucked into the window and the entire piece of furniture returned to its normal location in the room.

His spirits sank. It was a mirage, an illusion. There was no Iowa outside. There was no way he could escape from the House into that farmland and make his way back to Oakdale.

He turned. There were new shadows in the den now, shadows that had not been there before, sleek, furtive swaths of darkness that had no distinct features but that he knew were watching him. One on top of a bookcase. One in the fireplace. One beneath the pool table. They moved, switched positions, changed shape.

Something passed by him, brushed him.

He felt tickling hairs, whiskers.

He instinctively backed up, not screaming only through a sheer effort of will.

The light was switched on.

Billings was standing in the doorway.

The butler was smiling at him, and something in that smile made Norton take a step back. His heart was pounding painfully and he wondered if he was having a heart attack.

It would serve him right if he did.

"Is the door locked?" Billings asked.

Norton stared at him.

"It's not supposed to be. Not at this hour."

The butler strode across the room, removing a full key chain from his pocket. Sorting through keys, he found the one he was looking for and placed it in the small keyhole beneath the doorknob, turning it.

He pocketed the key chain. "It's open," he said, gesturing toward the door.

Norton remained unmoving. This was a trick. It had to be.

Billings smiled at him.

Norton swiveled around, reached out, grasped the knob. It turned in his hand.

He yanked open the door, felt the coolness of night on his face, smelled the fertile scent of a newly plowed field.

There was a jolt like a small earthquake, a tremor that passed through the house, swinging the chandelier, knocking a bust of Plato to the floor. It was accompanied by an electronic hum, a low sustained tone that hurt his ears and made his stomach feel queasy.

Billings smiled. "The House is ready," he said, and his skin appeared suddenly tanned. His eyes were sparkling. "It has finally regained its full strength."

He bowed toward Norton. "Thank you."

It was then that the doors and windows were sealed shut.

SEVEN

Daniel

They met in the entryway.

They'd all been awakened by the shaking of the House, by the earthquake or whatever it was, and they'd rushed downstairs, panicked and frightened. A veteran of several major California quakes, Laurie appeared to be a little less rattled than the rest of them, but the fact that the shaking had occurred here, in the House, had obviously put her on guard as well.

Norton was already downstairs. They were staring at where the front door had been when he emerged from the den, walking down the hall toward them. His face was white, his hands shaking, and he explained what had happened, describing his first view of Oakdale through the bedroom window, his attempt to wake up Mark, his experience in the den.

Daniel looked around the entryway as Norton talked. Where window had been was only wall. The door had become a decorative piece of solid oak, an extension of the wainscoting.

"So the doors and windows were just . . . sealed up?" Laurie asked. "The walls came down over them?"

"Yeah. Basically."

"But what caused it to happen? Did Billings say something or do something?"

"I told you. I . . . I just opened the door. And I guess that triggered it."

Laurie shook her head. "But that doesn't make sense."

"Like he said, it doesn't have to make sense." Mark's voice was low. "Magic isn't logical. It follows its own logic."

They all turned toward him. He'd been so quiet until now, had spoken so rarely, that it was something of an event when he talked, and Daniel wondered if that wasn't on purpose. A passive-aggressive attention-grabber.

Then he looked into the young man's face, saw the anguish there, and immediately felt guilty for harboring such a thought. They were all going through enough without ascribing petty motives to each other's words and actions. More than anything else, they needed to stick together.

"Where did Billings go?" Daniel asked.

Norton shrugged. "I don't know. One minute he was there and the next minute he was gone."

Stormy snickered. "Was he wearing his PJs?"

"I don't think he sleeps," Norton said. "He was wearing his uniform. As always." He paused. "Only . . . he looked different. Tan. Happy."

"He's been looking better ever since I got here," Daniel said.

Stormy smiled. "I guess we've been charging his battery too, huh?"

Daniel grinned at him. "Speak for yourself, nancy boy."

There was another low rumble, more sound than movement this time. Lights in the House began switching on and off: the candle-shaped bulbs on the wall of the landing above them extinguishing, the swinging chandelier in the sitting room flicking on, the globe light in the hallway winking off, a light in the dining room flaring brightly.

It should not have been that scary. They'd all been through much worse, and the fact that they were together should have offered some reassurance and comfort. But Daniel's pulse was racing, and more than at any time since he'd walked through the front door into the House, he wished he were out of here. The rapidly flickering lights had the effect of a strobe used in a Halloween haunted house, darkening everything around them, making the building—particularly the upstairs—seem much bigger and more vast than it was.

Noises accompanied the sudden light shifts.

Whispers from the shadows,

High-pitched laughter from above.

There was another low rumble, and as quickly as it had started, everything stopped. The lights that were on stayed on, the lights that were off stayed off, and there was no more noise. The House was silent.

"Come on," Laurie said, taking charge. "Let's check out the den."

She started down the hall, lit now by only a brief sliver of yellow that spilled out from the partially open pantry door. Daniel quickly fell into step behind her, the others following.

The den door was closed. Laurie tried to open it, Daniel tried, Stormy tried, Mark tried, even Norton tried, but it was locked and nothing they did could get it open. Stormy attempted to kick the door, warning everyone to stay back in typical movie fashion, but his cowboy boot had absolutely no effect and even the sound of contact was flat, muffled, and ineffectual.

"Billings!" Norton called, pounding on the door with his fists.

Stormy took up the cry: "Billings!"

A door opened slowly at the far end of the hallway.

Daniel stared, trying to ignore the feeling of fear that filled him as he watched the slowly opening door. He racked his brain, trying to remember what was in that room, but he had no childhood memory of it, he had not made it to that end of the hall in his earlier explorations, and he could not for the life of him figure out what was in there.

The door was now open all the way, and through the rectangular entrance dark tangled shadows were visible against pale bluish light.

This time, he was the one who took the lead.

He realized what lay behind the door even before they reached it.

It was a solarium.

Or a lunarium.

For the plants in it were obviously night-blooming. Daniel entered the room and stopped just inside the door. They were on the west side of the building, though he could not recall ever seeing anything like a green-house in that location before. The ceiling, a skylight, was two stories above their heads, the wall of windows opposite them frosted, translucent, letting in light but not offering a view. The plants, on rows of shelves and oversized pots, were all impossibly exotic, comprised of shapes and colors that did not match.

He found himself wondering where they had come from.

And who tended them.

Slowly, the five of them began spreading out, drawn by their individual eyes and interests to particular flowers or shrubs. Daniel stood by a sort of cactus that looked like a headless human skeleton covered with yellowish skin and spiny needles.

Stormy had walked over to the wall of windows and was gingerly touching the glass. "Feels solid," he said, looking back. He knocked on the glass, and Daniel heard a recognizable clink-clink-clink sound. "Might as well try." Stormy glanced around him, picked up a decent-sized potted plant, and threw it at the window.

It disappeared.

Reappeared.

"What would happen if someone kicked one of those windowpanes?" Daniel wondered, walking over. "Would his foot get caught in that . . . whatever it is, and then show up again in here?"

"You want to try it?" Stormy asked.

Daniel held up his hands. "Not me. I'm just wondering."

"I guess you'll keep on wondering. I'm not trying it either."

"Hey, guys!"

Both of them turned to see Norton standing before a peculiarly sparse bush with unusually large dark leaves. They walked over and saw as they drew closer that even though there was no wind in the greenhouse, no air-conditioning, no breeze, the leaves of the bush were moving, twitching, twisting in the air.

There seemed something obscene about the plant's

movements, an unnatural and aggressive sexuality to the
motions that reminded Daniel of

Doneen

He looked over at Norton, Stormy, and saw the same
look of recognition in both of their eyes. Laurie and
Mark were heading over as well, and he could tell from
the expression on their faces that they had the same
reaction to the plant.

A branch reached for him, drew back, reached again,
drew back, its strange leaves curving in on themselves
invitingly. At the tip of the branch was a small round
berry.

Eve and the apple.

That's what it reminded him of, and for the first time,
he thought that perhaps their earlier talk of God and
the devil wasn't that far off.

"What's the point of this?" Laurie asked. "Why were
we led here?"

Daniel shrugged. "You got me."

Behind Laurie, another plant was moving, a series of
skinny stalks topped by orchidlike flowers. Following his
gaze, she turned. The red engorged stamen of the closest
flower wiggled at her, lengthened to its quivering full
extension, a drop of dew dripping from its tip.

"Let's get out of here," she said disgustedly.

"Fine by me."

"Let's hit it," Stormy agreed.

All five of them moved back out the open doorway
the way they'd come, Daniel bringing up the rear, keeping his eyes peeled for anything unusual, but nothing
happened, even the plants had stopped moving, and
when they were all back in the hallway the door
slammed shut.

"What was that all about?" Stormy asked. "Obviously
we were supposed to go in there. Obviously we were
supposed to see something. But what?"

No one had an answer.

It was still the dead of night—two o'clock according
to one watch, three-thirty according to another—and
they were all pretty tired, so after a short discussion in
which they vowed to confront Billings in the morning

and demand to know what had happened tonight, why the House had been sealed off, they returned to their rooms.

"Anything unusual," Laurie said as they walked up the stairs, "call for help. Don't try to take on anything alone."

"Anything *unusual*?" Stormy asked.

Laurie smiled. "Anything more unusual than usual."

Mark and Norton headed up to the third floor. Stormy stopped off at his room, and Daniel accompanied Laurie to her door before walking down to his own bedroom and locking the door behind him.

He stripped off his clothes, hit the sheets, and fell asleep almost immediately.

He dreamed of Doneen.

He awoke, by the Batman clock on his dresser, at six. He heard the chime calling them to breakfast, sounding from its unspecific source somewhere nearby. There was no light other than the small desk lamp he'd turned on before sleeping because flat wood now covered the spot where his window used to be, and he realized that they were now living in a world without natural light.

Maybe that's why they'd been shown the greenhouse—because it was the only room left that had windows.

The chime sounded once again.

Daniel remained in bed. Fuck Billings. He was going back to sleep. If punctual communal meals assisted the Houses in their regeneration of power, then he wasn't going to do anything to help. Besides, he was still tired and didn't want to wake up. And they'd have all day—hell, all year—to interrogate the butler.

There was a knock on his door. "Daniel?"

Laurie.

"Just a minute." Sighing, he got out of bed, pulled on his pants, and opened the door.

She stood in the hall, dressed, hair combed, and he unconsciously ran a hand through his own hair. "May I come in?" she asked.

He nodded, stepped back. She closed the door behind her, and his first thought was that he ought to remind her that he was married. But she seemed oblivious to that potential in the situation and pulled his small chair away from the desk, sitting down. "I know we haven't had a chance to talk one-on-one," she said. "None of us have. But I've been doing some thinking and . . . well . . ." She met his eyes. "What do you think of Mark?"

"Mark? I . . . I don't know. Why?"

"Come on. Cut the crap. There's no reason to be diplomatic here. What are your feelings about Mark? Your gut reaction."

"No reason to be diplomatic?" He smiled. "The way I see it, we may be stuck with each other for the rest of our lives. And beyond. I should try to get along with as many people as I can."

"I'm being serious," Laurie said.

He nodded, sitting down on the side of the unmade bed. "I know. What are you getting at?"

"There's something . . . not right about him."

"Well, he's not a real talkative guy, but—"

"Not that." She sighed. "What if he's a spy?"

"What?"

"Just hear me out."

"That's crazy."

"Is it? I don't think he's been totally honest with us—"

"Come on! Everyone has secrets. You think I'd completely spill my guts to a bunch of strangers? You think I told you guys everything about me?"

"No, but I think you were honest enough to tell us everything that you thought pertained to this situation. I'm not so sure Mark did. I think he's keeping something from us."

"And that makes him—what?—a House agent?"

"I don't know. I'm not saying he's monitoring our conversations and reporting back to Billings or whoever. I'm just saying that I don't entirely trust him."

"Why did you come to me? Why are you telling me this?"

"You seem . . . I feel like we maybe have more in common than some of the others. I don't want your ego to get too swollen, but you seem smart. Confident. Straightforward. And I guess the bottom line is that I trust you the most."

Daniel couldn't help smiling. "I'm flattered."

"Look. Just think about it. Just keep your eyes open. That's all I'm saying." She stood up. "It's getting late. We'd better go down to breakfast."

"I'm not hungry," Daniel said.

"But—"

"But what? Our faithful servant will get mad at me? Let him."

Laurie nodded, understanding dawning in her eyes. "Maybe these rituals give the Houses power."

"It's a possibility."

"I'll tell the others."

"You going to skip breakfast too?"

"Starting tomorrow." She smiled embarrassedly. "I'm hungry."

Daniel laughed. "Go on, then. I'll see you guys later."

But he couldn't fall back asleep, and after a fruitless forty-five minutes tossing and turning restlessly, he put on his clothes and headed downstairs to the dining room.

The table was set, but there was no food on it and no one was eating. Whatever conversation there had been had died, and Laurie, Mark, Norton, and Stormy sat in separate sections of the long table, playing with their silverware or staring into space.

"Where's Billings?" Daniel asked, sitting down.

Stormy shrugged. "That's the big question."

"Has anyone tried to look for him?"

"I did," Laurie said. "No sign of him. On this floor at least."

"So . . . what? We're going to starve?"

Stormy stood. "I'll make the damn breakfast." He looked around the table. "But we're switching off. This is not my regular gig."

"I'll take dinner," Laurie said.

"And we can each make our own lunch." Daniel smiled. "I know the schedule."

"You'd better like scrambled eggs," Stormy said. "It's all I can make." He disappeared into the kitchen and emerged a moment later, looking perplexed, carrying a tray of bacon and a pitcher of orange juice.

"It's ready," he said.

"What?"

"Our breakfast is in there. It's all cooked and ready."

"It wasn't there before," Laurie said. "I checked."

"Somebody want to come in here and give me a hand?"

They all stood, followed him into the kitchen, picked up assorted dishes. There were pancakes and bagels, muffins and fresh fruit. Neither the stove nor the oven appeared to have been used, and there were no dirty knives or cooking utensils on the counters or in the sink. It was as if the food had just . . . appeared.

Daniel picked up the coffeepot and a plate of sausage and headed back to the dining room. He couldn't put his finger on it, but there seemed something different about the kitchen. It seemed larger than he remembered, the positioning of its elements changed slightly. He wondered if the room was a composite of all of their old kitchens and if a modification or remodeling on the part of one of the families had thrown it off a little bit. Until now, everything in the House looked exactly the same as it had in Matty Groves.

Maybe that was knowledge that could be used to their advantage.

They ate, for the most part, in silence, occasional mini-conversations breaking out and then dying. He did find himself watching Mark, paying attention to what the young man did and the few things he said, and he was angry with Laurie for planting the seeds of doubt in his mind.

But he couldn't be too angry with her. He really was flattered that she trusted him, that she respected his honesty and intelligence, and had chosen him to confide in. He smiled to himself. Anyone with perceptions that astute couldn't be completely wrong.

But it was a bad precedent. They'd only been together for, what? Twelve hours, House time? What would it be like in a week? A month?

Hopefully, they wouldn't be here by then. Hopefully, they would have found a way out by that time.

But if they hadn't?

They'd probably be at each other's throats, like that old *Twilight Zone* episode, "The Monsters Are Due on Maple Street," where a group of aliens shut off water and power and watched the residents of a neighborhood scapegoat each other, blame each other, distrust each other, finally kill each other.

He glanced over at Laurie. She gave him a wan smile.

They had to get out of here.

They spent the day exploring the House: the basement to the attic, and the three floors in between. He would have thought that sealing off the windows, removing all trace of the world—or worlds—outside the House would make it seem more claustrophobic, smaller, but that was not the case. Instead, it seemed even bigger, its corridors more labyrinthine, the number of rooms greater.

Except he knew that wasn't true. He knew where all of the room doors were, knew what was behind most of them, and there were no more than there had been when he'd lived here as a child.

So why did the interior of the House seem to be expanding?

He did not know and he did not want to know, and after the maddening frustration of their fruitless day, he was grateful when he was finally able to retire to his room.

He took off his clothes. Were they really going to be trapped inside this damn House for the rest of their lives?

Margot and Tony had never been far from his mind, but seeing Laurie in his room this morning had reminded him even more acutely how much he missed his wife and how desperately he needed to get back to her. The thought that he might never see her again stabbed at his heart.

He folded his pants and shirt, hanging them over a chair, thinking that he was going to have to wash them soon, that if he did not do so they'd be so encrusted with filth he wouldn't be able to fold them at all.

But his mind returned to Margot as he slipped under the covers, and he thought of how she looked while she was sleeping, the cute sound of her little half snore, the comforting feel of her warm body snuggling next to his in the middle of the cold night. He missed her, he wanted her, he needed her, and for the first time since he'd been a child in the House, he cried himself to sleep.

EIGHT

Mark

Mark lay on his bed staring up at the ceiling. He was exhausted and drenched with sweat, having tried in vain for the past half hour to once again access The Power, to focus his mind and concentrate completely on reviving the abilities he'd possessed and, until recently, taken for granted.

He wiped the perspiration from his forehead, felt a small rivulet trickle down the side of his face into his ear. What was he doing here? What did he have in common with these residents of other Houses? He felt closer to Billings than he did to Norton or Laurie—and the servant scared the living shit out of him.

Was he even supposed to be here or was it all some fluke of bad timing? Because the fact remained that although Billings had obviously been expecting him when he arrived, he was the only one who hadn't been specifically summoned.

He was the only one who hadn't had a recent encounter with the girl.

That was at the root of his concern, and he found himself wondering if maybe some *other* force had led him back here, had compelled him to return home.

No, it was Kristen's death. There was no higher power pushing him. No overall design. He'd come back simply because his sister had died and he wanted to find out what had happened to her.

Whatever the reason, though, he was here, a prisoner like the rest of them, and he felt that it was his responsibility to get them out of this. He had not mentioned The Power to anyone, and while he knew he should have come clean instantly, that time was past. It would be too awkward now, would raise too many questions. None of them seemed to have ever possessed any sort of extra-sensory abilities or to suspect that he had.

Did Billings even know?

He wasn't sure.

That might give him an advantage.

He decided to try again. If anything was going to help him get them out of here and escape, it would be The Power. If he could just get an opportunity to *read* Billings, to scan the House . . .

He took a deep breath.

Concentrated hard.

Nothing.

His head hurt, the blood pounding in his temples, and his muscles were starting to ache from the strain as his body grew rigid and relaxed, rigid and relaxed. He wiped the sweat from his face, looked upward once again, and *pushed* until it felt as though his eyes were going to pop from his head.

And a figure flickered into existence at the foot of his bed.

He saw the form at the bottom of his peripheral vision, and he sat up instantly, facing it full on.

Kristen.

She was older, the way she must have looked when she died, but he recognized her instantly. She was not solid, not flesh, but she was not transparent either. Instead, she seemed to be sort of . . . glowing. And translucent. Like a computer-generated specter in a big-budget movie.

He was suspicious of that at first, not believing that reality would hew so closely to the middle-of-the-road imaginations of anonymous film craftsmen, but then she turned her head, craned her neck, looking around as if uncertain for a second where she was, and her eyes alighted on Mark.

She smiled, her entire face lighting up.

And he knew it was her.

"We've still got it," she said to him, and there was a playfulness to the smile on her lips. Her hand reached out to touch his foot and he felt not pressure but a pleasant warmth, as though a ray of sunlight had been concentrated on that section of his skin. "How are you, Mark?"

He nodded, not knowing what to say.

"It's not your fault," she said. "About me dying, I mean."

"I never—"

"Yes you did." She laughed, a sound that reminded him of tinkling chimes, the wind in the trees. "I know you, Mark."

"I should've come back for you. I should've been there."

"You made your choices. I made mine."

He swung his legs off the bed, stood up, and walked over to where she stood. Reaching out to touch her face, his fingers passed through her form and he felt only that pleasant warmth.

He took a deep breath. "How did you die?" he asked. It was why he had come here. It was what he most wanted to know.

A frown crossed her features. "I can't talk about that."

"Kristen!"

"That's not why I'm here. That's not why I came back."

"Did I bring you back?"

She smiled again. "You helped."

"How did you die?"

"I told you—"

"I need to know!" His eyes did not leave hers, and he saw a struggle there.

"I'm not supposed to talk to you about that."

"Kristen . . ."

She glanced furtively around, as if checking to make sure no one was eavesdropping. "You know how," she said and looked at him meaningfully.

Her warmth was replaced by a wave of cold that came entirely from within him. "The girl?" he said.

She nodded.

"I knew it! What happened?"

"I can't—"

"Kristen . . ."

Another furtive look around. "She sat on my face. And smothered me."

"Jesus!"

"She was always wanting to have sex with me. And I always refused. And I guess, finally, she took the initiative. I was sleeping and when I woke up she was sitting on my face and I couldn't breathe. I tried to push her off me, but even though she's still a child, she weighed as much as a sumo wrestler. I couldn't get her off. I tried to hit her, tried to buck her off, tried to roll over, but she just sat there on top of me, and finally I passed out. And I died."

"I should've been there," Mark said. "I should've come back after Dad died."

"There's nothing you could've done."

"I could've protected you."

"Not unless you slept with me every night. And I don't think even you're *that* weird." She smiled teasingly, and he had to smile back.

"I miss you," he said.

"I miss you."

"Did you ever try to get her out of the House? Her or Billings?"

Kristen shook her head. "They're part of the House."

"But did you ever try?"

"I didn't know how. I just avoided them. Like we used to."

"And now we're both trapped here."

"Maybe," she said.

"Come on. Billings won't let us leave."

"First of all, I'm not really here. I'm . . . visiting."

"Then he's trapped *me* here."

"You're trapped," she told him, "but Billings hasn't done it to you. He's not keeping you here. Any of you. You're keeping yourselves here. As long as you remain tied to your homes, as long as you have unresolved issues with those on the Other Side, you will remain on the border. It is the only hold the Houses have over you, this connection to the past, to the dead."

"Unresolved issues?"

Kristen nodded.

"With you?"

She shook her head, smiled. "We always understood one another," she said. She touched his cheek, and he felt the warmth of sunshine. "We still do."

"Who, then?"

She paused. "Mother. Father."

Mark grew silent.

"That is why you can't leave."

"Because I never came back and made it up with Mom and Dad?"

She nodded.

"I can't believe this."

"The House keeps them tied the same way. Those threads that bind you to the House and to the Other Side bind them to the House as well."

"What if those threads are broken?"

"It is complicated."

"What happens?"

She shook her head.

"Will the barrier be . . . weakened?"

"Possibly."

"Is that good or bad?" he asked.

Her luminescent face grew grave. "It is bad," she said. "The two sides must not mix."

Mark smiled. "You'd be able to visit more often," he said.

Kristen laughed, that tinkling musical sound that wasn't quite human. "Mark," she said fondly. "I really do miss you."

"I know," he said, and he felt the tears welling up as he looked at her face. She was as beautiful as he'd known she'd be, and she'd grown from a gawky teenager into a confident self-assured woman. God, if she'd only been allowed to live . . .

He wiped his eyes. "So that's it. I'm stuck here. We're all stuck here. We're screwed."

"No, that's not it," Kristen said.

"What, then?"

"The Houses do need people," she admitted. "But that doesn't necessarily mean it has to be you. It could be anyone. And if you guys leave, someone will come to take your place. Nature, as they say, abhors a vacuum." She paused. "But when someone else comes, it will be voluntary. It will be their decision. They won't be coerced or forced or held prisoner against their will. They'll be like I was."

"But how can we leave?"

"Resolve your problems."

"And how do we do that?"

"It will come of its own."

"What will?"

"You'll see."

"What? Can't you say?"

"No. But you will have that chance. Be prepared for it when it happens."

He didn't like the vagueness of her answer, and every opportunity that he could come up with for reconciling with his parents filled him full of dread.

He did not want to see his dead mother or father.

"There's one other thing you have to do, though," Kristen said.

"What's that?"

"Kill her." And there was a look of uncharacteristic fierceness on her face. "Kill the bitch. She's the one who's doing this, who's perverted the Houses for her own purposes, who's tried to bring down the barrier. Once she's out of the way, everything will return to normal and will be back the way it should, with voluntary border guards and the Other Side safely separated."

"She's evil," Mark said.

Kristen nodded, and for the first time she looked afraid. "Yes," she said. "She's evil."

"I'll do it," Mark told her.

There was a slight gasp, and an expression of pain crossed Kristen's face. She hugged him, but she was already fading quickly, her warmth cooling into nothingness. "I love you," she whispered, her voice barely audible.

"I love you too," he said.

But before he reached the word "love," she was gone.

NINE

Stormy

So where was Billings?

They hadn't seen the butler all day yesterday, and now he was missing again this morning. It was pretty obvious that something had happened to him, and they were at a loss as to what to do about it. None of them liked the butler, and they all seemed to be afraid of him, but he was their link to the House, the translator between themselves and the hórrific impersonality of the events that occurred here.

Maybe he'd served his purpose, Norton suggested. Maybe he was only needed to lure them here and to keep them imprisoned until the House was charged up again. It sounded plausible, but Stormy didn't quite buy it. Nothing logical happened here, and even the most benign and minor events inevitably had ominous implications.

He figured the butler had been captured by the girl.

Or killed.

Or both.

Stormy sipped his coffee. Once again, breakfast had been made for them. Just as dinner had been last night. They'd had to serve themselves, but someone—or something—else had cooked and prepared the food. Laurie suggested that one of them stake out the kitchen this afternoon, an hour or so before dinner, to try and find out who or what was making their meals, and Mark volunteered for a tour of duty.

They'd finished eating for the most part, but they remained in the dining room, sipping juice and coffee, nibbling on muffin crumbs, bored, having run out of things to do and having a difficult time thinking of things to

say. He'd felt an instinctive camaraderie with the others
the instant he met them, but that feeling had been fading
ever since. These weren't really people with whom he'd
choose to spend his time if he had a choice.

God, he wished he could watch a morning show or
listen to Howard Stern or . . . something.

"What's happening outside this House?" Stormy said.
"In the real world? That's what I'd like to know. Why
can't we have a TV or a radio in this fucking place?"
He pushed his chair away from the table, stood, and
began pacing. "I'm getting tired of this shit."

"Who isn't?" Norton said.

"Can't we at least have a newspaper delivered with
our breakfast?"

"The Ghostly Gazette?" Daniel suggested.

"Very funny."

Laurie stood. "We'd better stop here before we really
start getting on each other's nerves. Let's clear the table.
I'll wash the dishes."

"I'll dry," Daniel offered.

"Where's that leave the rest of us?" Stormy asked.

Daniel grinned. "Free to do as you choose."

"Great," he muttered.

There was nothing they had planned, nothing they had
to do. They'd searched the entire House yesterday, and
today loomed before them, a huge monolith of time.
Stormy carried his cup and plate into the kitchen. Last
night, he'd begun a sort of journal—notes for a possible
movie, actually—with pen and paper he'd found in his
room. He had some other ideas he wanted to write
down, so rather than plop his ass on a seat in the sitting
room and stare at the damn wall, he got himself some
ice cubes and a big old glass of water and, excusing himself, went back upstairs.

Where there was a TV in his room.

A TV!

Excitedly, he ran over, flipped it on. Channel 2 was
static and snow. The same with channels 4, 5, 6, 7, and
8. The only channel that came in was 13, and it was
showing some type of documentary, but he didn't care.
Any audiovisual contact with the outside world was like

a crust of bread to a starving man at this point, and he
was even grateful for the simple physical presence of the
television in his room. He'd never realized before how
completely and utterly dependent he was on mass com-
munications and he promised himself that if he ever
started thinking about chucking it all, moving to a cabin
in Montana and living off the land, as he periodically
did when business was down and the pressure was up,
he'd kick his own ass.

He sat down on the side of the bed and stared at the
screen. He didn't know what he was watching, but it
definitely had a documentary feel, a gritty unstaged look
that gave it the appearance of reality, a verisimilitude
only reinforced by the generic synthesized music that
accompanied the montage of pan shots. It was film, not
video, a travel show or nature show or Indian show, and
it had obviously been shot in New Mexico—he recognized the familiar blue sky and massive clouds as well
as the adobe ruins of Bandelier. He'd heard no' voice-
over since turning on the television, but he knew from
the rhythm of the piece that narration would kick in at
any second, and he lay down on his side and piled both
pillows beneath his head to watch.

The program did not play out the way he expected,
however. There was no narration, and the panoramic
vistas and beautifully shot ruins gave way to uninspired
and routinely lensed footage of high-desert brush along
the side of a flat dirt road. The music disappeared, and
the camera panned down to a low, heavily eroded ditch
by the side of the road, where a dead body lay twisted
against the exposed roots of a palo verde.

Roberta.

Stormy sat up at the sight of his wife, all of the air in
his body seeming to escape in one violently exhaled
breath. She was wearing only torn panties and a dirty
bra. Her right arm, bloody, a section of skin torn off
and blackened with dried blood, lay twisted behind her
back at an impossible angle.

In her hand was a piece of cheddar cheese with a rose
embedded in it.

The camera panned up her body, and Stormy saw that

there was a trail of black dots stretched across her forehead and her wildly staring eyes that looked like—

burned ants.

He stood, intending to get Norton and bring him back
here, to find out why their lives and experiences were
crossing all of a sudden, but he could not leave before
the program ended, and he yelled "Norton! Norton!" at
the top of his lungs as he stared at the screen and
watched a lingering shot of what looked like a rotting
full-sized marlin lying in the ditch next to her.

The House started to shake.

It was not merely a rumble or single jolt this time but
a full-scale quake that rocked the foundations of the
House and tilted the floor as though it were the deck of
a storm-tossed ship. The television winked off instantly,
but the lights in the room remained operational, and he
could at least see what was happening as he was knocked
off his feet by the force of the temblor and sent flying
into the wall beneath where the window used to be.

Stormy scurried across the floor, half crawling. The
door had been thrown open, and he scrambled into
the hallway.

It looked like a low-budget earthquake scene from a
bad direct-to-video flick, the camera shaking, blurring,
and doubling everything in the scene.

Except that there was no camera. And the blurring
and doubling were not due to some optical trick but to
the fact that the walls and floor and ceiling actually
seemed to be physically separating, splitting like cells
into identical twins of themselves.

There was a cry from off to his left, and Stormy turned
his head to look down the hall. Norton had obviously
heeded his call and was at the top of the stairs, holding
tightly to the banister to keep from falling onto the landing below.

Stormy stood, bracing himself in the doorway.
"What's happening?" he yelled.

"I think the Houses are separating!"

Why hadn't he seen that? Around him, that strange
mitosis was continuing. He was still recognizably situated
in a tangible, material House, but the transparent out-

lines of other Houses could be seen emerging from it. The doorway in which he was standing was quadrupled, and seeing four ghostly doorways surrounded by four ghostly walls receding into the solid reality of his corporeal House was not only disorienting but dizzying. He turned toward Norton again, and the old man looked transparent as well.

Holy shit. He was going to be left alone here again. They were all going to be alone. It was bad enough being trapped in one House together. But trapped in separate Houses . . .

And without Billings?

He didn't think he could survive that.

The adrenaline that had been revving up his heart on account of the shaking kicked into overdrive, and he scrambled desperately toward the staircase at the end of the hall, crying with fear and frustration. He wanted to grab Norton, to hold on to him so they wouldn't be separated, but the old man's figure was fading into the wainscoting.

"No!" he screamed.

But the transparent Norton couldn't hear him.

And then the earthquake was over and the other Houses were gone.

TEN

Daniel

Where was he? In what House? In what time period? Everything was confused, and Daniel shook his head as if to clear it. He stood alone in what had been the entryway, staring down the hall. The dark corridor was endless. There seemed to be literally hundreds of doors stretching out as far as he could see, with no discernible end. This was not the House he remembered, not any House he had ever seen, and he wondered exactly what had happened. He and Laurie had been in the kitchen, starting the dishes, when the shaking started. Following her lead, he'd stood in the doorway, and then . . .

What?

His recollection of what happened next was hazy. He seemed to recall seeing Mark duck under the dining-room table. But then there were two dining-room tables. And two dining rooms.

And then three. Four. Five.

He'd remained in place, anchored to this House, while Mark and Laurie broke off into different directions and faded away with their respective dwellings.

Had they been real at all, he wondered, or were they just manifestations of the House? Had he been alone all along, only thinking there were others here with him? Was this some sort of head trip the House was playing with him, some way of getting information from him or testing his reactions?

He didn't think so. It was possible, but his gut reaction was that the others were real, that what Billings had told them was the truth, and that now that the Houses were back at full power, they had the strength to merge and separate at will.

So was his House the true House? He was pretty sure it was. He was the one who had remained in place, who had remained here in the House they'd all shared, while Laurie and Mark—and, presumably, Norton and Stormy—had spun off elsewhere.

Except he hadn't really remained in place, had he? Because this House had changed, too. Gone were any pretexts that this was the exact same home he and his father had fled all those years ago. There were similarities, of course, but there were differences as well, and he stared down the endless hallway wondering exactly where he was now, trying to gather the courage to try some of the doors before him, to explore the House alone.

The sound of whispering from the sitting room behind him and a partial glimpse of a small dark figure—

a doll

—ducking behind the love seat spurred him into action, and he moved forward, started down the hall.

He was about to try and open the first door on the right, when he saw, a hundred yards or so down the corridor, an unmoving lump in the center of the floor. There were no bright fluorescent lights, only dim flame-shaped yellow bulbs on silver fixtures spaced far apart on opposite walls, and he took a few steps forward, squinting, trying to make out what it was.

It looked like a dead body.

He thought he saw the black-on-white of a formal butler's uniform.

Daniel ran down the hallway. Even running at full speed, it took him a minute or so to reach the body, and the end of the hallway was still nowhere in sight. Breathing heavily, he stared down at the form on the floor.

It was Billings. The butler was lying faceup, and while there were no visible signs of violence and the white shirt remained unsoiled, the hardwood floor around the body was soaked with drying blood. Billings's eyes were wide open, as was his mouth. There was a small lipstick kiss on his white forehead.

God is dead, Daniel thought crazily. God is dead. *Satan lives.*

Where was the girl? Where was Doneen? He looked anxiously around, expecting to see her jump out at any moment, to leap from behind one of the doors or come running up from the murk shrouding the far end of the hall. But there was no sign of her, and he dropped to one knee and picked up the butler's cold right hand to feel for a pulse.

Nothing.

Had there ever been a pulse? Daniel didn't know. Billings claimed to have been here as long as the House had, and all five of them had remembered him from their childhoods and he had not changed one bit. Perhaps he had never been alive. He was certainly not human.

What could kill him?

That was something he didn't even want to think about, and with a last look at the puddled blood on the floor, Daniel stood. He was about to start walking back up the hall when something caught his eye. A dark spot in the blood by Billings' left foot.

Daniel bent down, looked closely.

Hair and lint.

In the shape of a small footprint.

From somewhere in the House came an echo of high laughter.

He had to get out of here. Whether that meant finding a legitimate exit or exorcising Doneen or taking apart this fucking House board by board, he had to escape. He had to extricate himself from this situation and get his butt back to Margot and Tony.

There had to be an answer or a clue or a hint or something behind one of these doors, and he walked over to the closest one, grabbed the handle, and yanked it open.

A mirror stared back at him, reflecting his own anguished face.

He strode down to the next door, pulled it open.

A linen closet.

The next: a library.

He crossed the hall, pulled open a door on the opposite side.

And there was his mother's Victorian bedroom.

She was lying in bed, next to his father, and they were both alive, both young, younger than he was right now. His father whispered something, and his mother laughed. He had not heard her laugh since he was in grammar school, and the sound brought back an entire world to him. Chills passed through his body, chills not of fear but of pure raw emotion: love, longing, recognition, remembrance, discovery.

"Hey, Daniel." His father waved him over. "Come in. Shut the door."

His mother smiled at him, and he smiled back.

He wanted to go in, wanted to jump on the bed the way he had as a child and snuggle between the two of them, but he was acutely aware of the fact that he was an adult, older than they were, and that they were probably naked under the heavy blankets.

Besides, what was this? A time tunnel? A vision? A joke? His gut told him that these were his real parents and they were calling to him, but his mind could not quite buy it. He thought it was probably a trick of the House. They weren't seriously altered, the way Laurie and Stormy said their mothers had been in the House on the Other Side, and they didn't have the insubstantial forms of ghosts. They looked exactly the way they had thirty years ago, and that made Daniel suspicious.

His mother held out her arms. "Danny."

He closed the door on them.

He had the sense that he was doing something wrong, that he should be in there, talking to them, that taking this tack would not lead him where he wanted to go, but he had nothing he really wanted to say to his parents—if those figures *were* his parents—and he ignored that section of his mind and the nagging doubt lapsed into silence.

He moved on to the next door. Behind it was a small anteroom and yet another door. He walked in, opened the second door—

and was home, in Pennsylvania, in Tyler, in his kitchen. Tony was sitting at the dinner table doing his homework and Margot was stirring a pot on the stove. He could smell the delicious aroma of beef stew, could feel the warmth from the stove. Outside it was raining, and the windows were fogged with condensation.

There was no doubt here, no suspicion in his mind. This seemed completely real to him, on all levels, and he tried to rush over to Margot and hug her, but was stopped by what felt like a Plexiglas wall. He moved toward Tony, was stopped again.

He began pounding on the invisible barrier. "Margot!" he yelled at the top of his lungs. He started jumping up and down, waving his arms wildly. "Margot! Tony!"

They couldn't see him or hear him.

Maybe he was a ghost.

Maybe *they* were the ghosts.

The thought sent a chill through his heart.

No. Most likely, the House had not transported him back home but was simply allowing him to see, to smell, to hear, to experience what was happening there.

But why?

He folded his arms, stood in place, watched, listened.

Tony looked up from his homework. "When's Dad coming back?" he asked.

He saw the look of worried concern that crossed Margot's face, and his heart ached for her. "I don't know," she said.

"He didn't . . . leave us, did he?"

Margot turned around. "What made you think that?"

He shrugged. "I don't know."

"Of course not. I told you, your father's visiting his old house in Maine for a few days."

"How come he didn't take us?"

"Because I have to work and you have school."

"How come he doesn't call?"

"I don't know," Margot admitted.

"Maybe something happened to him."

"Don't even joke about something like that."

"I'm not joking."

Margot turned down the heat on the stove, her mouth tightening. "Put your books away," she told him. "And wash up. It's time to eat."

Tony folded his homework, put it in his history textbook, picked up his pen and pencil, and carried everything back to his room. He returned a moment later, helped his mother set the table, poured himself a glass of milk, and the two of them sat down to eat.

Daniel walked around the table, periodically reaching out and trying to touch either his wife or his son, but the barrier was always there. Margot and Tony ate dinner in silence, the only noise the occasional clink of silverware against plate and the quiet sounds of chewing and swallowing. The unspoken emotion between them was heartrending. Tired, frustrated, Daniel sat down on the floor of the kitchen. He felt almost like crying, and it was only the fact that he had to keep his wits about him and remain sharp, ready for anything, that kept him from doing so.

Immediately after finishing his meal, Tony excused himself and went out to the living room to watch TV. Margot sighed, stared down into her nearly empty bowl, pushed a piece of carrot around with her spoon.

Daniel concentrated hard. "Margot," he said, thought.

No response.

He kept trying as she cleared the table, washed the dishes, but there was no contact and he only ended up with a headache.

He walked out with her to the living room, and together he, his wife, and his son watched an old Humphrey Bogart movie.

Almost like a real family.

This time he did cry. He couldn't help it. Maybe that's what the House wanted, maybe he was falling right into the trap that had been set for him, but he didn't give a shit. He sat on the floor, next to the couch, and let the tears flow.

After the movie, both Margot and Tony went to bed. It was early for Margot, past Tony's bedtime, but these obviously weren't ordinary circumstances, and Daniel walked with them, standing next to Margot as she watched Tony brush his teeth and then kissed him good night.

He followed her into the bedroom, watched her take off her clothes and then climb into bed, forgoing her usual shower. She pulled the covers up to her neck, clasped her hands.

Prayed.

That surprised him. To his knowledge, his wife had never been a religious woman, and he did not think he had ever seen her pray in all their years of marriage. Had she always done so, hiding it from him, doing it when he was asleep or out of the room? Or had she only started recently, after his abrupt departure? Either way, he was oddly touched by her actions. He wished he could kiss her, even if it was just a simple peck on the forehead, but the barrier was still in place.

Margot had closed the bedroom door, and he walked over to see if he could open it. He could not, but it was as if the door were not there for him and he passed right through it. Could he walk through walls too? He tried it, got a bump on the head for his attempt.

His headache even worse now, he walked down the short hallway, passed through Tony's door.

His son was making another doll.

Daniel stared in horror as he watched the boy open the closet door, glance furtively around, and pull out a new doll. This one had a body made from a McDonald's sack tied with rubber bands. Its arms and legs were twigs, its head a scruffy and nearly bald tennis ball with carefully pasted string segments positioned into crudely simplistic facial features.

Tony carried the figure to the bed, placed it on his pillow. He withdrew from his pocket a folded Baggie filled with what looked like dead spiders. Smiling to himself, he reached into the plastic sandwich bag, tore off the legs of a dead daddy longlegs, and placed them on a strip of exposed tape atop the doll's head.

He was making hair.

"Tony!" Daniel screamed. "Goddamn it, Tony!"

The boy's concentration was focused completely on the doll. Daniel looked back at the door, saw that it was locked. He hurried outside, back to Margot, hoping that she'd be awakened by Tony's movements or at least alerted on some psychic level to what was going on in the next room, but she was sound asleep, a mild frown furrowing her brow.

Daniel sped back to Tony's bedroom. The overhead light was off, the only illumination an orangish circle emanating from the small desk lamp, and it looked like a spotlight was being trained on the boy and the doll.

"Tony!" he screamed again.

The boy did not even hesitate, kept applying spider legs to the doll head.

There was a loud creak from somewhere else in the house, settling engendered by temperature and humidity and the contrast between the wet rainy world outside and the dry warm world inside. Tony froze, not even daring to breathe, his eyes staring at the closed bedroom door as he waited to see whether his mother was on her way.

Daniel caught a hint of movement out of the corner of his eye and adjusted his focus. He found himself staring at the doll.

The figure turned its head, looked at him, grinned, the corners of its string mouth turning up.

Daniel grabbed for the doll, but again it, like everything in the room, was behind Plexiglas. His hand hit an invisible border and pain flared up his arm, across his shoulders. He wiggled his fingers weakly, felt searing flashes of agony that corresponded precisely to the movements, and realized that he'd broken or sprained at least three of his fingers.

Tony was already back at work on the hair, not noticing the new tilt of the figure's head, the new expression on its face, and Daniel wanted to scream with rage.

What the hell was going on here? Tony couldn't see him but that thing could? What was that all about?

Maybe he *was* a ghost.

"No!" he said aloud.

"I can help you."

At the sound of the voice, Daniel jerked his head to the right.

Doneen was sitting on Tony's desk chair. She was seated like a man, flat-footed, leg spread, and even in the dim orangish light he could see up her dirty ragged shift to the nearly hairless cleft between her thighs. He knew what she wanted—

You don't really want me to leave

—and although he found himself, against his will and as sick as it was, tempted, he suppressed those thoughts and faced the girl. She was smiling at him, that same mocking derisive smile she'd had for him when he'd leaped out of the bathtub as a child, and anger helped hold the fear at bay. "Get out of here," he ordered.

She stood, walked slowly toward him. Tony, oblivious to both of them, placed the last two spider legs on the strip of tape. "I can take this away from him," she said softly, "He'll never see me again or make another doll."

"Get out of here," Daniel repeated.

Doneen giggled. "He'll never see Mr. Billings again So that part of your nightmare's taken care of." She reached him, rubbed a hand between his legs.

Daniel pulled back.

"There's only me to contend with now, and I can put your lives back to normal just like"—she snapped her fingers—"that."

He grimaced distastefully. "What do you want?"

"What do *you* want?"

He shook his head. "I'm not playing this."

"You do something for me, and I'll do something for you."

"What?"

"Lick me." She bent over, pulled up her shift. "Lick me clean."

"No," he said.

She looked over her shoulder at him, smiled "We never finished what we started."

"And we never will."

She remained bent over, trailed a languorous finger over the smooth skin of her buttocks, let it slide down her crack. "It would be a shame if Tony woke up to find his doll shoving its way down his mommy's throat."

"You little bitch!" He reached for her, found that he could grab her; there was no barrier between them. His fingers dug into the soft flesh of her arm.

She flinched, moaned. "Rape me," she whispered. "Take me any way you want."

He let go, pushed her away. She laughed. "What's the matter? Not man enough?"

"I'm not going to do it, and I'm not going to let you goad me into it."

She stood, suddenly serious, smoothing down her dirty shift. "Fine."

"And if anything happens to them . . ."

"There is another way," she said matter-of-factly.

"What?"

"There's no sex involved."

"What is it?"

"The only thing is: you're going to have to do something you might not like."

"What's that?"

She smiled, and a cold shiver ran down his spine. "Trust me," she said.

ELEVEN

Laurie

When Laurie came to, she was lying on the bed. She'd been in the doorway of the kitchen when the Houses separated, and she must have gotten hit on the head or fainted or something because she could remember no further than that. Someone had obviously carried her up to her bedroom, though, and for that she was grateful.

She sat up warily. Her head hurt, but when she felt around, there were no bumps or blood. She didn't know what was going on and she was about to search the House, see if any of the others had remained with her, find out who had brought her to her room, when her question was answered.

"Laurie! Come down here!"

It was her mother.

Her biological mother.

She recognized the voice though she hadn't heard it since early childhood. Her recent remembrances had rendered everything from that time period as sharp and immediate as if they had happened yesterday, and her mother's voice brought the feelings back as well. She was suddenly anxious to obey, filled with an almost Pavlovian compulsion to respond. She still wasn't sure if she was here as an observer or a participant, if her mother was yelling at *her* or at a younger version of her that was also around somewhere, but when her mother called "Laurie!" once again and there was no answer, she hollered back "Coming!"

That response seemed to satisfy. There were no more shouted demands, and Laurie rolled out of bed, trying to ignore the pounding in her head. She suddenly realized that her room had a window again, and she walked over to it. Outside, she was not surprised to see the garage, the barn.

It was daytime. She breathed deeply, smelled mist and mulch, redwood and grass. This was not the House in which she had been trapped for the past few days. This was the House in which she'd been born, the House of her childhood. She was herself, she was an adult, but all traces of her contemporary life had been erased and she was thrust back completely into the past.

Her past.

The feelings of childhood were back as well. The fears she'd been experiencing recently had been merely echoes of the originals, but now she was once again in the thick of it, her feelings sharp with the edge of immediacy.

There was danger here.

She stared for a moment at the barn, then turned, walked out of the bedroom. She headed downstairs, uncertain of what to expect.

"Laurie?"

At the bottom of the stairway, she saw her mother beckoning from the sitting room. It was unsettling and disorienting, being treated like a child when she was an adult, but she forced herself to smile and walked into the room.

Her parents, all four of them, were seated on the couch. The sight nearly took her breath away. It wasn't all that shocking, really. But the emotional impact was far greater than she could have ever imagined. She remained standing in the doorway, staring, trying to hold back the tears that were welling up in her eyes as she looked upon the living faces of dead loved ones she'd never expected to see again.

Sitting between their parents, she saw Josh, a cute alert-eyed little boy with the hair of a little girl, and she wanted to rush over and grab him, hug him, hold him, but like his mother and father, he stared at her with only mild open friendliness. None of them, obviously, had any idea who she was.

"Ken?" her biological mother said. "Lisa? This is our daughter Laurie."

It broke her heart to see the impartial distance of the unacquainted on faces she loved and knew so well, so intimately.

She sat with her biological parents, pretending she was a child listening politely while the grown-ups talked. Though she was obviously an adult and taller than her mother, no one acted as though it were anything out of the ordinary. She found herself looking at Josh, studying him, but he offered no clue as to what was going on. Why was she here? Had she been sent back in time? Had the past been sent up to her? Were these people real? It was impossible to tell, and she decided to just let everything play out and see what happened.

Her parents talked about nothing: the weather, gardening, her adoptive parents' trip up here. There was no subtext to the conversation. It was what it was: an ordinary, everyday discussion between casual acquaintances.

When her mother excused herself to make lunch, Laurie followed her into the kitchen. Another full-fledged blast from the past. She recognized a salad bowl she'd forgotten about, remembered the pattern on the sandwich plates and iced tea glasses.

"Can I help?" she asked.

"Just stay out of the way."

Laurie took a deep breath. "I'm going to go outside."

Her mother looked at her. "Don't go too far. We'll be eating in a few minutes."

Laurie's heart was thumping with excitement. It was the first time she'd been out of the House in three days, and whether this world held or disappeared when she walked through that door, she was intoxicated with the thought that she could once again go outside.

She'd taken only one step when a goat appeared in the center of the kitchen, directly behind her mother. The air was suddenly filled with the smell of fresh daisies. Smoothly, easily, almost without thought, her mother grabbed a long knife from the counter, turned, and in one quick movement skillfully slit the goat's throat. She picked up the spasming animal and, kicking open the screen door, tossed it into the yard. Without pausing, she unrolled a sizable length of paper towel,

ran a portion of the perforated sheet through sink water,
and began wiping up the blood on the floor. She looked
up at Laurie as she scrubbed. "If you're going to go
outside, go. It's almost time to eat."

She was tempted to ask her mother if Billington would
be joining them for lunch, but more than anything she
wanted outside, wanted to leave the House, and she
walked over to the screen door, pushed it open.

And was out.

The air was fresh, clean, glorious. She'd smelled it
from the window, but that wasn't the same as being in
it, of it, surrounded by it, engulfed by it. At the bottom
of the steps was the broken body of the goat, so Laurie
walked instead along the wraparound porch, toward the
front of the House.

Billington was nowhere to be seen, but Dawn was
waiting for her around the corner of the House, playing
with a nasty-looking doll made from dried weeds and
twigs.

Laurie stopped in her tracks, stared at the dirty figure
in the girl's hand.

She thought of Daniel, shivered.

"About time," Dawn said, standing, brushing dust off
her shift. She dropped the doll, picked up a tin cup from
the porch next to her, walked over to Laurie. "I've been
waiting out here for ages."

Laurie looked through the window to her right, into
the sitting room. Josh and their parents and her biological father were still seated, still talking over mundane
matters, and she understood that she would not learn
anything from her brother or either set of parents. For
all she knew, they were the psychic equivalent of tape
loops; unchanging and unalterable reflections of what
had once occurred, endlessly repeating.

But Dawn was different. Dawn was definitely real, of
her time, of her House, and Laurie vowed that she
would find out what she could from the girl.

"What are you drinking?" she asked politely.

Grinning, Dawn held out her cup. "I like wood chips
in my water."

Sure enough, the water in the cup was dirty, filled

with dead floating leaves, splintered wood, and oversized pieces of sawdust. The girl pressed the cup to her lips, tilted it, drank the remaining contents. She smiled at Laurie, flakes of sawdust caught between her teeth, and that smile put Laurie on guard. There was lust in it, lust and some other emotion she didn't recognize, and she had to remind herself that this was not really a little girl, this was not merely a manifestation of the House, a puppet. This was . . . something else.

"Do you want to play?" Dawn asked.

Laurie nodded. She realized that there was import beyond the immediate in the question, but the time had come to jump in, to sink or swim.

Dawn giggled. "Let's do it in the woods."

Laurie took a deep breath, looked into the window again, then turned toward the girl. "All right," she said. "Let's do it in the woods."

TWELVE

Stormy

Stormy walked slowly downstairs, past the banister where Norton had disappeared, past the first landing. Already he could sense that things were different. The House looked the same as far as he could tell, but there was a new vibe to it, a sense of instability, a feeling he recognized from the past.

His mother was waiting for him at the bottom of the stairs.

She was not bald but looked exactly as she had when he was a child, only she was wearing one of his father's old suits, the legs of the pants and the arms of the jacket raggedly cut to fit her form.

He stopped several steps above her. There was an expression of almost manic excitement on her face, and she was staring at him in a way that he found disconcerting. She looked quickly around—behind her, to the left, to the right—in order to make sure they were alone. "Stormy!" she said in a loud whisper. "Get down here! There's something I have to show you!"

He remained in place. "What is it?"

She frowned, her brow furrowing in an exaggerated manner that looked like either bad acting or emotional disturbance. "Get down here now!"

"What is it?" he asked again.

"I found the monster."

She turned, started toward the hall, and Stormy hurried after her. He didn't know what she was talking about, what was going on here, whether he was in the present or the past or some House-bred amalgam of the two, but he figured the best idea was probably just to roll with it.

His mother stopped halfway down the hall and opened a door. She let him catch up with her, and the two of them walked through the doorway into another, narrower hall. This one had no flocked wallpaper, no expensive wainscoting. There was only unadorned bare wood walls and a single exposed bulb in the center of the ceiling. At the opposite end was another door, and his mother took a key from her raggedly cut suit, unlocked the door and opened it.

"It's a bone monster," she said, whispered. Her eyes looked bright, feverish.

He hadn't remembered this, and he looked into the closet at his grandfather's skeleton in the wheelchair. The bones were clean save for a patch of dried skin and hair on the left side of the skull, and something about that rang a bell, seemed vaguely familiar. Had this actually happened? Had he dreamed this?

Butchery.

Had it been in the movie?

No. The film had been more subtle. There's been nothing this overt, nothing this traditionally horrific.

Maybe he did remember it from childhood.

Stormy looked over at his mother. "A bone monster," she said, staring at her father's skeleton, talking more to herself than him.

It was amazing how much he'd blocked out. Even the film didn't come close to capturing the craziness of the household, the unsettling irrationality of its workings. It was coming back to him now, what it had been like living here. Not just the broad brush strokes but the details, not just the events that had occurred but the feelings they generated within him.

He realized now why he had hated living here so much.

And why the one family vacation they'd taken, their trip to New Mexico, had been so important to him, had made such a big impression.

His mother grasped his shoulder, pointed at the skeleton. "That's the monster," she said. "It's a bone monster."

"Yeah." He pulled away from her, started back down the narrow hidden hallway to the House proper.

He could already hear his father bellowing from the study, and Stormy made his way over there, pushing apart the sliding wooden doors that opened onto the hallway.

"Billingham!" his father ordered. "I want a knife and a sack of cotton balls—" He paused, frowned, looked at Stormy. "I didn't call for you. I called for Billingham."

"Sorry," Stormy said.

"Billingham!" his father yelled. He paused, waited. "Billingham!"

The butler did not come.

Stormy looked behind him, saw only empty hallway. Billingham had never, to his knowledge, failed to come on his father's order, had never had to be called more than once, and Stormy saw here the present intruding on the past. Whatever had happened to the butler in the House he'd shared with Norton and Mark and Daniel and Laurie, whatever had caused his absence for the past two days, was affecting life in this House, too.

It was a pretty good indication that the butler was dead.

That worried him. Like the others, he had originally believed that the butler and the girl were allies, working together. But though both were intimately and inexorably connected with the Houses, he now saw them as antagonists, opposing forces, and the idea that the butler was dead, that the girl was now free to do as she chose, with no one to stop her, frightened him to the core.

A door opened in the hallway behind him, and Stormy turned to look, hoping and praying for it to be Billingham, but it was his grandmother who emerged from one of the bathrooms, hobbling out with the assistance of a bone-handled cane.

"Hi, Grandma," he said, but the old lady ignored him, turned the other direction, walked away.

"Billingham!" his father bellowed again.

Facing forward, Stormy glanced around the study. He had seldom been asked in here as a child, and he had always been too afraid of his father to take the initiative and enter on his own, so his memories of the room were hazy. One whole wall, he saw now, was covered with floor to-ceiling bookshelves. A big picture window on the opposite wall looked out onto the back garden. There was a desk and a pair of identical leather chairs. Two dark wood filing cabinets. A potted palm.

And a doll.

Stormy's breath caught in his throat. It was lying on the floor directly behind his father, as though his father had dropped it there. The face was upside down, but the wide white eyes seemed to be staring into his, the disturbing inverted smile trained directly on him. He didn't know why he hadn't seen the figure immediately, and the thought occurred to him that his father had been holding it behind his back, hiding it.

He met his father's eyes, and the old man looked quickly and guiltily away.

Stormy knew now what had happened in this House, though he had not understood it as a child. They'd been corrupted in their purpose, his parents. His entire family. They'd been seduced by Donielle and had neglected their duties, their responsibilities, defecting under the watchful but naive and uncomprehending eyes of Billingham. It had affected their relationship with him, their own son, had erected the barrier between them that had stood for the rest of their lives, and the fact that they'd allowed themselves to be drawn in by the girl, that they had so easily been manipulated by her, had led him to disassociate himself from them. He might not have been able to articulate it at the time, but subliminally, subconsciously, he'd been able to read the signs even then, and it was why he'd never really had any respect for his parents. He'd been afraid of them, intimidated by them, but he hadn't respected them.

And it was why he had eventually left and moved west.

He had changed, though. He had grown over the years, and he was no longer the hesitant, easily cowed, easily intimidated child he had been. He'd come back to the House, to his family, a new person, an adult, a successful businessman and entrepreneur, and he would no longer be bullied into submission by his father's words, by his mother's demands.

Maybe he'd been given the opportunity to right the wrongs of the past. Maybe he'd been sent back here to stop the girl early, before she was able to do any major damage. To head her off at the pass, as it were.

Whatever the reason, whatever the motive, he felt he had the chance to change things, to do things differently, and it was not a chance he was going to waste. He walked across the study, bent down, and picked up the doll. "What's this?" he asked.

His father snatched the figure from him. "Don't you dare touch that!"

Behind him, he heard his mother enter the room.

Good. Both of them needed to hear this.

He faced his father. "Why are we here?" he asked. "In this House?"

"This is our home!"

"We're here for a reason," Stormy said patiently. "And it's not to fuck that little urchin girl."

"Oh!" his mother gasped.

His father glared at him. "I will not be spoken to that way by my own son!"

"Why don't you want me to see her, then? Why can't I see Donielle?"

His father hesitated. "Because . . . because she's a bad influence on you."

"And she's a bad influence on you, too. She's a bad influence on all of us." He met his parents' eyes. Both of them looked away, embarrassed.

"Does Billingham know about Donielle?"

"Billingham?" His parents exchanged a quick look. "What does Billingham have to do with this?"

"You know."

"Stormy—"

"You know why the House must be maintained. You know what it does. And you know you're not supposed to do anything to jeopardize that." He pointed at the doll, still clutched in his father's fingers. "What's that, Dad?"

"It's none of your damn business."

"*She* gave it to you. It's hers. You're busy trying to keep me from going anywhere or doing anything with her, pretending that she's not good enough for our family, and you're seeing her behind my back. She's a child, Dad. A child."

His father shook his head. He looked suddenly old. "She's no child," he said.

"And we're only trying to protect you," his mother said. "She *is* a bad influence."

"Then how come you keep seeing her yourselves?"

Neither of them answered.

"Don't you want it back the way it was? The way it used to be?"

"It can't go back," his father said.

"Why not?"

"Because it's gone too far."

"No," Stormy said. "Not yet it hasn't."

"You're wrong." His father looked down at the doll in his hand. "You don't understand."

"What don't I understand?"

"I fucked her, okay?" There was anger in his voice. "I fucked her ass."

Stormy stared at him.

His voice dropped to a whisper. "Now I'm hers forever."

"No." Stormy grabbed the doll from his father, threw it onto the ground. He felt shaken, sickened. It was one thing to suspect something or to know it deductively, and it was quite another to be confronted with its specifics outright, but still he pressed on. "You have a choice, Dad. You always have a choice. Right now, you're just choosing to give up, choosing to give in. You can break free if you want to. There's nothing binding you to Donielle. Tell her to fuck off. Take control of your life, for God's sake."

"I can't," his father said weakly.

"Look at Mom." He motioned toward his mother, wearing the oversized cutoff suit. "Look what's happened to her, what she's become. And you know why! You know what's done this to her! Don't you even care enough about her to put a stop to this?"

On the floor, the doll shifted, rolled onto its side. Stormy was not sure whether it had moved of its own

accord or it had simply landed on a precarious angle and
was settling, but the motion frightened him anyway, and
he kicked the doll as hard as he could, watching it slide
across the hardwood floor and under the desk. There
were goose bumps on his arms, and he saw that both of
his parents were looking under the desk at the figure.

"Donielle asked me to marry her," Stormy said.

That brought them back.

His father's gaze snapped onto his, and there was
anger on his face, confusion beneath the anger, fear beneath the confusion. His mother gasped, clapped a hand
to her mouth.

"She knows you forbid me to talk to her, and she
suggested we elope. She said she wants to take me away
from the House"—he paused—"and away from you."

"She . . . she can't!" his father exclaimed.

His mother began quietly sobbing.

"She thinks she can," Stormy said, but he was suddenly uncertain as to whether his parents were upset
because they didn't want to lose him—or didn't want to
lose *her*.

He took a deep breath. "Is she more important to you
than me?"

"No!" his mother said, shocked.

"Of course not, son."

"Then what if I told you that you had to choose?
What if I said it's either her or me?"

His father's face clouded over. "She's trying to break
up the family."

"Who would you choose?"

"It's not that little slut who's causing all the problems," his mother announced.

Stormy turned to her. "Who is it, then?"

"It's the bone monster," she said, eyes widening.

His father stared at him silently, looking lost.

"Would you choose me, Dad?"

A tear rolled down his father's right cheek. "I would
if I could."

Stormy smiled at them sadly. "I love you," he said.
"I love you both."

For a moment, his mother's gaze was lucid, his father's

expression softened. "We love you, too," his mother told him, putting her arms around him. His father nodded.

A chime rang out, a deeply resonant almost churchy sound. The doorbell.

"Billingham!" his father bellowed.

His mother pulled away from him.

Another chime.

"Billingham!"

Stormy sighed. "I'll get it," he said.

He walked out of the den and down the hall to the foyer. The doorbell rang again, and he sped up, unlocking and opening the door.

A girl was standing on the porch in front of him.

Donielle.

He caught his breath at the sight of her. He was an adult now and she was a child, but the feelings she evoked within him were the same as those engendered all those years ago. His heart was racing, and there was a pleasant tingling in his groin. Despite everything he knew, despite everything that had happened, the attraction was still there, and his first impulse was to reach out and grab her hands and hold them in his. He wanted to touch her, but he held back, remained holding on to the door. "Yes?" he said coldly.

"Oh, Stormy!" She rushed forward, threw her arms around him, and against his will his body responded. Beneath his jeans, his growing penis pressed against her midsection, and she held him tighter, rubbing herself against it.

Stormy grabbed her arms, pulled her away from him.

"What's the matter?" she said, looking up at him. Her eyes were full of hurt innocence.

He steeled himself. "You know what's the matter."

"I love you, Stormy."

He held on to her arms, looked away from her face. "I don't love you."

"I—"

"I don't like what you're trying to do."

"I'm on your side! I'm the one who told you you have to stand up for yourself, you can't let your family boss you around and make all your decisions!"

"I am standing up for myself."

"That's why your family hates me!"

"And I'm standing up for my family."

"I have nothing against them," she said, and tears welled up in her eyes. "They're the ones who don't like me! They don't like me because I'm poor. They don't like me because I love you more than they do and I think about your feelings and what's good for you and not just what'll look good and save face for the family."

"They don't want me to see you anymore," he said. "And I don't want to see you either."

"Fuck your family," Donielle told him.

"No," he said. "Fuck you."

The tears stopped flowing, her face hardened. "What did you say?"

"You heard me."

"That's the way you want it?"

"That's the way it's going to be. Get out of here. I never want to see you again."

"What you want and what you'll get are two different things." With a flip of her hair, she turned and walked away, and he thought that from behind she didn't look like a child at all, she looked like a dwarf.

That lessened the attraction somewhat.

Lessened it.

But did not get rid of it.

He closed the door. Behind him he heard the click-tap of his grandmother's cane on the floor, and he turned to see her standing by the foot of the stairs.

"I can't find Billingham," she said.

"I . . . I think he's gone," Stormy told her.

There was a brief flash of lucidity, a quick second in which he saw panic and fear and incomprehension on her face. She knew the butler had been part of the House, and she knew that if he was gone, something was seriously amiss. Then her usual tight expression of stoic immobility settled into place, and she said, "You will have to serve in his place, then."

Stormy nodded. "Do you want me to help you up the stairs?"

"No," she told him. "I want you to draw my bath. I

will bathe tonight in blood. Have my tub filled with goat's blood. Temperature tepid."

He nodded dumbly, watched her struggle up the steps. From far down the first-floor hall, he heard his mother wailing, heard his father bellow, "Billingham!"

He stood in the foyer, unmoving. What had he accomplished? Nothing. He'd tried his damnedest and confronted his parents, put it all on the line, and they had remained unmovable, entrenched, fatalistically resigned to things as they were. Everything was exactly the same as it was before.

He sighed. You really couldn't go home again.

Still, he felt better for having talked to his parents, for having confronted them, for having at least tried to stop their abandonment of Billingham and the House, to change their increasing reliance on Donielle.

If he had it to do over again, he would not run away from home. He would stay in the House with his parents, and try to work things out with them.

There was no sign of his grandmother on the stairs, he could not hear the tapping of her cane, so he walked up the steps to make sure she was all right. She was not in the second- or third-floor hallways, and he knocked on the door of her bedroom. "Grandma?"

No answer.

He tried to open the door, but it was locked.

He knocked on the door of her bathroom, but again there was no answer, and he put his ear to the wood, listening for sound.

Nothing.

Could she have gone somewhere else? He started toward the stairs again, but his eye was caught by the open door to his bedroom. Had it been open before? He didn't think so.

"Hello?" he called out tentatively. He poked his head into the room, and there was a sudden shift of atmosphere and air pressure, a lightening of mood. He saw earthquake debris strewn across the floor of the bedroom, and against the opposite wall, a broken television.

He was back.

THIRTEEN

Norton

Norton understood the change immediately.

After the shaking stopped, he let go of the banister and stood, glancing around. The restrained House in which he'd spent the last several days, the House he'd shared with Laurie and Daniel and Stormy and Mark, was gone. This was the House of old, the wildly unpredictable House in which he'd grown up, and the sudden electric silence, the thick heavy air, the undefinable undercurrent that ran like a river of sludge beneath the surface reality around him, all told him that he was home.

Just to make sure, he walked down the hall to the room in which Stormy had been staying. The door was open, but there was no sign of Stormy or anyone else. The room was what it had been in his childhood: a sewing room for his mother.

With an almost audible snap, the wall of silence was broken, and from farther down the hall he heard sound, noise. Low conversation. Laughter.

It was coming from the library, and he moved quietly, carefully, down the corridor. The lights were low, the hallway dark, and while the shadows provided him with cover, they also added to the already spooky and intimidating atmosphere. He wiped his sweaty palms on his pants and tried not to breathe too loudly as he walked past Darren's room, past the bathroom, and to the library.

He stopped just before the door, poked his head around the edge of the door frame.

And saw his family.

He ducked quickly back, his heart pounding. It was suddenly hard to breathe; he felt as though he'd been punched in the stomach, and try as he might, he could not seem to suck enough air into his lungs. It was not a surprise, seeing his family. In fact, it was exactly what he'd expected. But somehow the reality of it carried an emotional weight no amount of imagining or intellectual preparation could anticipate.

They were playing Parcheesi, seated around the game table in the center of the room, and they looked the way they had when he was about twelve or so. His sisters were both wearing the calico party dresses their mother had made for them and which they'd worn, with a little letting-out, through most of their teens. Bella, the eldest, was feigning an air of disinterest in the game, as though family activities like this were juvenile and beneath her, but both his other sister Estelle and his brother Darren were laughing and joking with each other in an obviously competitive way. His parents, still in their early forties, sat across from each other, separating the sisters, smiling amusedly.

It was the type of evening they'd often spent at home together, after a hard day apart working and going to school, only there was something wrong this time, something out of place, and it took him a moment to realize what it was.

There were no books in the library.

How could he have not noticed something so obvious? The floor-to-ceiling shelves were all empty. The dark wood wall behind the blank shelves lent the room the same air of formality it had possessed with the books, but it was as though they were playing Parcheesi in an empty house, an abandoned house, and the effect was creepy.

What had happened to the books? he wondered. Where had they gone? All of his father's books had been in place downstairs, in the den.

But that had been back at the other House, the current House.

He was confused. Was he on the Other Side now? Was the House allowing him to visit the ghosts, the souls, the spirits of his murdered family? Or, with the bizarre concept of time that seemed to exist in the House, were

all time periods still extant? Could the House pop him
in and out of different eras at will?

Either way, he could not face his family now, could
not meet them. He would do so later, when he felt
stronger, but for now he needed to be alone, to think,
to sort things out.

One thing he'd always tried to impart to his students
was the effect of the past on the present, the extent to
which actions had reactions and events had repercussions that rippled forward into the future. Perhaps that
was at the root of what was happening to him now.
Maybe the House was giving him an opportunity to discover the source of the ripples that had spread outward
to resurrect Carole and affect the lives of Daniel and
Stormy and Laurie and Mark.

Maybe it was giving him a chance to change it.

The thought was at once exciting and terrifying, but
both emotions were small and intensely personal. If what
Billingson—Billings—said was true, if the House—the
Houses—really did maintain a barrier protecting the
physical material world from the intrusion of the Other
Side, then this was as big as . . . no, *bigger* than . . .
being granted the chance to go back into time and kill
the pre-Nazi Hitler.

But emotionally it didn't feel that way. He supposed
it was because these were things he had just learned and
the enormity of Nazi Germany and World War II had
been validated by society, by the world, and had been
drilled into him for over half a century, but the fact
remained that this seemed much smaller in scope, much
more personal and localized.

Considering the consequences, he supposed that was
a good thing.

Norton moved away from the doorway, back down
the hall, careful not to make a sound. Even after all
these years, he remembered the location of the creaky
spots in the floor, and he made a concerted effort to
avoid them.

Once again, he found himself at the top of the stairs.
He started down, but when he glanced up from the steps,
he saw graffiti on the wall of the stairwell ahead of him,

a huge blue chalk drawing of a face, a simplistic rendering that looked as though it had been done by a not
particularly talented five-year-old.

The chalk figure winked at him.

Smiled.

There was only one tooth in its poorly drawn mouth
and that should have made it look goofy, comical, but
instead it lent the face an air of wildness, and Norton
was afraid to continue down the steps, afraid to pass
beneath the gaze of the face. It was a strange facet of
human nature, but horror was much more frightening on
a small scale than a large one. More than all of the
talk of the Other Side and the afterlife, more than the
possibility of dire epic consequences, it was the intimate
simplicity of this chalk drawing that spoke directly to his
fear center, that dried up the saliva in his mouth and
made his heart pound wildly, his blood run cold.

The round face tilted to the left, to the right, its single-
toothed mouth opening and closing.

It was laughing.

Norton ran. He did it without thinking, without planning, without pausing to consider his options and weigh
the outcomes. At that second, he wanted only to get
away from that horrible drawing and its terrifying movements, and he bolted back up the few steps he'd de-
scended and took off down the hallway as fast as his
old legs would carry him. He considered stopping before
reaching the library, not wanting to see his family or let
them know he was here, but he could still visualize in
his mind the rocking movement of the laughing face, the
opening and closing mouth, and in his imagination it
was making a horrible clicking noise, like a school film
projector, the individual sounds synchronized precisely
with the drawing's movements, and that made him run
all the faster.

He sped by the library door, hoping no one saw him
but not pausing to check. His plan was to go down the
back stairs, but here, finally, he stopped, afraid he'd see
another graffiti drawing on this back wall. There was
nothing there, though. At least nothing he could see in

the dim light. He took a deep breath, gathered his courage, and ran downstairs.

He reached the bottom of the steps without incident, and immediately moved away from the stairwell. His heart was still thumping in his chest so hard that he felt as if he would go into cardiac arrest any second, but already he was ashamed of himself for running, and even as he backed away from the staircase, he swore that he would not give in to fear again. He'd panicked, acted on instinct, and he was determined that next time he would stand his ground, would think before he acted.

Next time?

Yes. There would be a next time.

Norton looked around. He'd lived in this House until he was eighteen, had spent the last few days in it (or a reasonable facsimile thereof), but right now he could not say precisely where in the House he was. The intersecting corridors and closed doors did not look familiar to him, and his sense of direction seemed to be off. He could not get his bearings. If he remembered right, the back stairs ended near the laundry and storage rooms. This certainly didn't look like the laundry area, but he walked over to the closed door opposite him and pulled it open.

The room before him was huge, twice the size of the library, as big as the sitting room and the dining room combined. No pictures hung on its bare walls. There was no furniture.

The room was completely empty except for the books.

Still holding on to the doorknob, Norton stared. Books, hundreds of them, had been placed on end and stood next to each other like dominoes, making a trail that snaked through an elaborate design covering almost the entire floor of the massive space, twisting and curving, circling around, making sudden sharp turns at sharp angles.

He didn't know whether it was what he was supposed to do or not supposed to do, but it was what he *wanted* to do, and he kicked over the first book, the one closest to the door, and watched as the rest of them all went down sequentially, the room suddenly echoing with a series of rapid-fire slaps and muffled thuds, dust jacket hitting dust jacket, cover smacking cover, everything hitting the floor.

It took a good two minutes for all of the books to go down, for the wave to pass through the room, and he stood there unmoving, his eyes following the falling books as the pattern wound around the opposite side of the room and then finally returned to the area near the door.

Now that the books were flat, he could see the design they had been arranged to make.

The same face as the chalk drawing.

The single-toothed mouth grinned crazily upward at the ceiling.

Norton backed away. Again, his first instinct was to run, but he checked that impulse and instead breathed deeply, forcing himself to remain in place. This face did not move, did not wink, did not laugh, showed no sign of animation. He thought for a moment, then walked into the room, kicking books to the right and to the left, destroying the carefully wrought pattern. He strode all the way to the opposite wall and all the way back, and when he was through it looked as though the books had simply been dumped into this room haphazardly, without any thought to their placement, and he closed the door behind him and started off down the hall toward where he thought the front of the House should be.

He ended up in another junction of two corridors. He turned left, and now he recognized where he was. *This* hallway led to the foyer and the front of the House.

A snake slithered across the floor in front of him—a green snake with a pale, barely visible underbelly—and he thought of Laurie. Where were the others now? He wondered. In their own childhood Houses? Going through their own tests and trials and tribulations?

He watched the snake flatten, slide through the thin space under the bathroom door.

It was amazing how quickly he'd fallen back into the rhythm of the House. He was scared—he couldn't claim to be unaffected by the manifestations thrown at him— but they did not really surprise him, and he did not question them. He accepted their existence, considered them as much a part of the House as the wallpaper and light fixtures.

Just as he had all those decades ago.

He knew now that it was because the House was on the border, that it was the mixing of the material world and the . . . other world which created these surreal shifts in reality, but this understanding was on a purely intellectual level. As a child, long before he'd been made aware of the purpose of the House, he had adjusted to its wild displays and bizarre juxtapositions, and acceptance had been achieved long before understanding.

There was a noise behind him, a tapping. He turned—

And it was Carole.

Seeing her ghost was almost like seeing an old friend. In life, they hadn't gotten along particularly well. At least not for the past half decade or so. And after her death, seeing her ghost around their home and last night, especially, had been frightening and disturbing. But his life had taken a 180-degree turn, and here, in this House, he was glad to see her ghost. It was comforting, a pleasant surprise, and he looked at her naked form and found himself smiling. "Carole," he said.

She did not smile back. "Your family is waiting for you."

He shook his head as though he had not heard correctly. "What?"

"You need to talk to your family. Your parents. Your brother. Your sisters."

There was no expression on her face, only a dispassionate blankness, and his own smile had completely disappeared. The last thing he wanted to do was talk to his family. "Why?" he asked.

"That is why you are here."

"To meet with them?"

The ghost nodded.

"I will," he said. "Eventually."

"No you won't."

He met her eyes. "Maybe I won't."

"You can't keep avoiding them," Carole said.

"Watch me."

The two of them faced each other, and he realized suddenly that the reason he was so apprehensive about meeting his family again was because he felt responsible for their deaths. It was his fault they had been killed. If he had not stopped seeing Donna, if he had not dumped her, she would not have taken this revenge on him. Hell, if he hadn't gotten involved with her in the first place, if he had not *started* seeing her, he would not have had to stop seeing her. No matter which way he sliced it, it was his fault that his parents, his brother, and his sisters had been murdered, and that was why he had been unwilling to talk to them, to meet them, why he had been so uncomfortable even seeing them again. He didn't know if this version of his family knew what had happened to them or what would happen to them, but he was afraid that they'd confront him about it, that they'd blame him, and while he could handle supernatural snakes and recurring ghosts and book-faces, he did not think he would be able to handle that.

"Talk to them," Carole urged.

Norton cleared his throat, and though all of those years, all of those decades had gone by, he felt like a little boy again, nervous and afraid. "I can't," he said.

"You have to."

"I can't."

"Have you seen Billings?" she asked.

He shook his head. Where *was* the hired hand? he wondered.

"He's dead," she said, and he heard a tremor of fear in her voice. "She had him killed."

"She?"

"Donna."

Norton felt the cold wash over him.

"Talk to your parents," Carole said. "Talk to your family."

She left then, not floating away, not fading into nothingness, but somehow . . . dispersing, her form devolving into separate elements and components that were absorbed into the floor, the walls, the ceiling, changing color, changing shape, blending in and disappearing.

He looked around, then stared at the spot where she'd been. Was she real? Or was she a part of the House? Or both?

He didn't know, and he supposed in the end it didn't really matter. He believed her, she'd spoken the truth, and the important thing was that her message had gotten across. As much as he dreaded the idea, as much as he didn't want to do it, he knew that he had to meet with his family, he had to talk to them. About what, he didn't know. But he supposed that would work itself out.

As if on cue, he heard the sound of voices coming from up ahead. He recognized Darren's laugh, Estelle's whine. He moved forward, walking slowly, wiping his sweaty hands on his pants and trying desperately to think of what he would say to them.

Light spilled into the hall from an open doorway up ahead, and taking a fortifying breath, he stepped into the light.

They were all in the family room now: his sisters and brother on the floor in their pajamas, gathered around the radio; his mother in her chair next to the unlit fireplace, crocheting; his father in his chair next to the light, reading a book. In his mind, he saw their heads in the oven, blackened, peeling, stuck together, and he closed his eyes for a moment, breathing deeply, trying to will the image away.

When he opened his eyes, they were all looking at him. His mother's crocheting had stopped in mid-weave; his father had put down his book. He knew this couldn't be real—a few minutes ago, they'd all been upstairs playing Parcheesi in the empty library, and there was no way they could have gotten downstairs and changed their clothes and settled into these new positions that fast— but it *felt* real, and he understood that even if the physical specifics weren't what they were supposed to be, the underlying emotional realities were. He looked from his father to his mother. "Hello," he said.

"Where've you been?" his father asked gruffly. He picked up his book, settled down to read.

"Fibber McGee's on," his mother said, motioning toward the radio.

He was thrown a little off balance. He'd been expecting something . . . different. But his parents were treating him as though he were still a child and this was an ordinary evening, and he'd simply shown up late to listen to his favorite radio show. He wasn't sure what he should do, how he should react. Should he play along, pretend as though he were a child and try to fit into this cozy little scene? Or should he break the spell, be who he really was, say what he wanted to say, ask what he wanted to ask?

He thought for a moment, then walked across the family room to the radio, turning it off. His brother and sisters looked up at him, annoyed, but he ignored them and turned to face his parents. "We need to talk," he said. "We need to talk about Donna."

Once again, his father put his book down. His mother let her crocheting fall into her lap.

"She's a bad girl," Norton said.

His father nodded.

"She's nasty," Bella piped up. "She likes to play sex games."

He expected his parents to shush his sister, chastise her, tell her not to talk about such obscenities, but they did not even flinch, and their serious gazes remained focused on his.

He swallowed hard. "She *is* nasty," he said. "She *does* like to play sex games."

His parents looked at each other.

He was an old man, older than his father had ever lived to be, but he felt as embarrassed saying this in front of his family as he would have at ten years of age. He felt hot, flushed, and he knew his face was beet red. "I know because I've done it with her," he said, not meeting their eyes. "But I . . . I stopped. She didn't like that. Now she plans to—" He cleared his throat. "She plans to kill you. All of you."

"She likes to play blood games," Bella said.

He looked from his father, to his mother, to his brother and sisters. "Don't you understand what I'm saying here? You are in danger. If you don't do something, you'll end up dead, your heads chopped off."

"What do you expect me to do?" his father said calmly.

"I don't know!" Norton was growing increasingly exasperated. "Hunt her down! Kill her!"

"Kill Donna? Your little friend? Billingson's daughter?"

Norton pressed forward, finger pointed in the air in the classic lecturing position. "She's not Billingson's daughter," he said. "The two aren't even related."

For the first time, something like worry crossed his parents' faces.

"Of course she's his daughter," his mother said.

"Did he ever say that? Did he ever tell you that? Have you ever seen the two of them together?"

"Well, no. But . . ." She trailed off, obviously thinking.

Now he had his father's attention. "How do you know this?"

"He told me. Billingson. Before he disappeared."

"Disappeared? He's—"

"He's gone. She killed him. Or had him killed." He knelt down on the floor in front of his father. "You know what this House is. You know what it does. You know why we're here—"

His father fixed his mother with a look of black rage. "I told you not to—"

"She didn't say anything. I found out on my own." He looked into his father's eyes. "*She's* the one who told you not to say anything. *She's* the one who told you not to tell us, right?"

His father nodded reluctantly.

"She's evil."

"I know that! This whole House is evil!"

"No, it's not."

Darren and Bella and Estelle had been quiet all this time, and Norton glanced over at them. They looked scared, but not exactly surprised, as though what they'd feared had turned out to be true.

"She likes to play blood games," Bella repeated softly.

Their father nodded. "Yes," he said tiredly. "She does."

They talked. For the first and only time, he and his parents and his brother and his sisters talked like families in movies and on TV talked—openly, honestly—and it was a liberating experience. He felt as though a great weight had been lifted from his shoulders, and he learned that Donna had approached all of them, had appealed to each of them, had offered herself to his mother and father, had presented herself as a friend to his sisters, a girlfriend to his brother.

He himself was the only one who had taken the bait, and while they'd all known about it, while she'd practically flaunted it in front of them, they had never mentioned it to him, never brought it up between themselves. Such things just weren't talked about in that family in that time in that place, and it was the lack of communication as much as his own weakness and stupidity that had inflamed the situation and led to its inevitable end.

Was that end still inevitable?

He didn't know, but he thought not. He felt good, he felt free, he felt closer to his family than he ever had before, and while it might not be the case, he had the distinct impression that merely by talking, merely by hashing things out, they had changed the course of events, they had avoided a repeat of what had happened the first time.

It was several hours later that his mother yawned, placed her crocheting needles into her sewing basket, rolled up the afghan on which she was working, and said, "It's time for bed. I think we've had enough startling revelations for one night."

The kids, tired, nodded and stood, heading off unbidden to their respective bedrooms.

His father stood as well, and offered his hand to Norton, who took it and shook. He could not remember ever shaking his father's hand before, and the action made him feel more like a grown-up than anything else in his life ever had.

"We'll find her," he promised. "All of us. And then we'll decide what to do."

Norton nodded. He was feeling tired himself, and he walked out of the family room and, waving good night, went down the hall to the entryway and started up the stairs to his bedroom. The unfamiliar expansiveness he'd experienced earlier was gone, and the House seemed cozy and comfortable, not frightening or forbidding at all but . . . homey.

He wasn't quite brave enough to take a shower yet, but he did walk into the bathroom to wash his face. The water that came out of the sink faucet was red and thick, and no doubt he was supposed to believe it was blood, but it smelled like water, and it rolled off his hands, leaving no stain, and he bent down and splashed it onto his face, enjoying the cool refreshing wetness.

He fell asleep happy.

FOURTEEN

Mark

Mark opened his eyes.

And was sitting on the porch.

It was night. To the north, a domed semicircle of orange—the lights of Dry River—shone like a beacon in the desert darkness. There were other lights, individual lights, spread across the plain to the south, east, and west: the ranches of their neighbors. Above, the sky was moonless, but he could make out familiar constellations in the star-crowded sky.

On the bench swing opposite his chair, his parents sat, heads together, rocking slowly back and forth. On the top porch step, to his right, sat Kristen.

The family was all together.

Unresolved issues.

He squinted through the darkness at his sister, but though the only illumination came from the pale square of sitting-room light shining from a window some ten feet down the porch, he could still see Kristen clearly, and he understood that this was her as a child, this was the Kristen he had known, not the Kristen he had only recently met.

She said something, obviously a reply to a question someone else had asked, and he realized that they were in the middle of a conversation, one of those slow languorous summer-night conversations where thoughts were mulled over before spoken and long lapses between question and answer were the rule rather than the exception. They'd had these conversations often when he was little, and it was when he had felt closest to his parents. This was the time after the day's chores and rituals had been completed, when there was nothing that had to be done and the requirements of the day were finished until tomorrow, and it was the only time when his parents seemed truly relaxed, not overworked or overburdened or under stress.

It was the only time that they weren't working for the House, the only time they'd been allowed to be themselves.

He hadn't known that then, but perhaps he'd sensed it. These porch sessions had been almost sacrosanct to him, set off in his mind from the daylight life of his family, from their life inside the House, and it was why he was now so reluctant to bring up Billings and the girl and everything else. He knew he had to talk to his parents about it, but he did not want to shatter the mood, and he decided to wait until he could naturally broach the subject within the context of the conversation.

The night air was cool, the day's heat dissipated, and above the ever-present odor of the chickens, he could smell mesquite and a whole host of night-blooming desert flowers.

He listened to his mom, listened to his dad, listened to Kristen, and it was so nice to be here with them again, alone with them. His parents told stories of the past, laid out plans for the future, and they were still talking when he drifted off to sleep.

When he awoke, it was morning.

He'd been left where he'd fallen asleep, in the chair, but someone had given him a blanket and he was wrapped up in it, curled like a shrimp. The sun was high in the sky, and he heard the sound of his father's truck clattering up the drive, so it was obviously past breakfast time, and he wondered why he hadn't been awakened and forced to eat his meal in the proper manner at the proper hour.

They'd never gotten around to discussing the girl. They hadn't discussed Billings or the House, either. He roused himself, pushed off the blanket, stretched out, and stood up. His muscles were sore, and there was a hard crick in his neck. Yawning tiredly, he walked over to the front door and walked inside. He expected to smell breakfast, or at least the remnants of breakfast, but even as he walked through the dining room into the kitchen, there were no odors of food. The dishes in the sink were all from last night.

"Mom!" he called. "Kristen!"

"Mom went to town for groceries."

His sister was standing in the doorway, staring at him, and he had a quick flash of déjà vu. He'd been here before, standing in this exact same spot, with Kristen standing in the exact same spot and saying exactly the same thing. He wondered if this whole experience at the House had been cobbled from preexisting events, edited together like a videotape or a CD-ROM game.

No. Kristen walked into the kitchen, took a sack of bread out of the refrigerator, and popped two slices into the toaster. He knew nothing like that had ever happened at *their* House; snacks had never been allowed and meals had always been eaten together.

This was really happening.

"Dad's outside," Kristen said. "I think he's unloading the feed. He probably wants you to help him."

Mark nodded dumbly, then walked outside, pushing open the kitchen door and stepping onto the side porch. He thought of grabbing a bite to eat, but he really wasn't hungry. He'd eaten breakfast with Daniel and Laurie and Norton and Stormy, then found himself on the porch at night after the Houses split, and slept for a while, so even though it was morning here, it felt like lunchtime to his body. And he usually skipped lunch.

He stepped off the porch, walked across the dirt and around back. The already hot air was heavy with the muted sound of thousands of chickens, clucking and moving rustlingly in their cages. The four chicken coops, long low buildings of tin roofs and unpainted slat walls, stretched away from the House on a slight grade.

His father's pickup was parked next to the second coop, on this side of the metal silo, and Mark walked over, the gradual slope causing him to unintentionally increase the speed of his step.

He saw the retarded girl in the doorway of the chicken coop behind his father.

The old man was unloading pallets of feed, lifting

them off the pickup and piling them on the ground next
to the sagging slatted building. She would hide whenever
he faced in her direction, retreating into the coop, but
the second he turned his back on her, she would jump
into the doorway and pull up her shift, exposing herself
and thrusting her thin dirty hips out suggestively.

It was the first time Mark had seen her since he'd
come back, and he felt the same rush of cold fear he'd
experienced before. This was outside, in the sunlight and
open air, with his father hard at work between them,
but he felt the same way he had years ago, alone in the
dark hallway.

Scared.

His father put down a pallet, reached into his back
pocket, and grabbed a handkerchief to wipe the sweat
from his forehead. He noticed Mark standing there and
motioned him over. "I was wondering when you were
going to wake up. Why don't you give me a hand here.
My back's killing me."

Mark nodded, moved forward. His attention was still
on the girl in the doorway.

Your father does it.

He looked away from her, and tried to concentrate on
the task at hand, he and his father each taking one end
of the remaining pallets and stacking them on the
ground, but he kept seeing her out of the corner of his
eye, kept seeing her dirty shift flip up, and he wondered
if the old man saw it too and was just pretending not to.

He makes it hurt.

Finally, they finished. His father wiped the sweat from
his forehead once again. "I'm going into town to pick
up another load and get your mother. Don't wander too
far. I'm going to need your help when I get back."

Mark nodded as his father opened the driver's door
of the pickup and climbed in. The engine rattled to life,
and Mark stood there as the truck bounced up the slight
slope to the drive.

He turned back toward the chicken coop.

The girl was still in the doorway, but now she was
unmoving, staring at him. "Mark," she said, and he re-

membered that voice, remembered the way she'd said his name, and a chill surfed down his spine.

She moved slowly forward, away from the coop, toward him, and he took an involuntary step backward.

She stopped. And then she was on the dirt, on her hands and knees, shift flipped up, and just as before, she looked slyly over her shoulder. "I still like it best up the ass."

He had no desire to copulate with her in any shape, form, or manner, but he was seriously tempted to kick her as hard as he could. The thought of his boot connecting with her midsection, knocking her over, knocking that smile off her face, hurting her, making her pay for what she'd done, tempted him sorely, but he knew it would not really accomplish anything. She would not really be hurt—whatever she was—and he would only be showing his hand, revealing his true emotions.

And that, he figured, was probably the most dangerous thing he could do.

So he remained in place, staring impassively at the girl, and she laughed obscenely, a dirty nasty sound that was at once seductive and derisive, dismissal and promise. She thrust her buttocks out at him, and he turned away, began walking back toward the House, and the wild sound of her obscene laughter followed him all the way.

He was waiting for his parents in the kitchen when they returned.

Both his mother and father walked in, each of them carrying a sack of groceries.

He took a deep breath. "Mom. Dad. We need to talk."

His parents looked at each other, then looked at him. It was his father who spoke. "What about, son?"

"About the House."

"I still have those pallets to unload. I thought you could help me—"

"About the girl."

Again, his parents looked at each other.

"Sit down," Mark said, motioning toward the seats he'd pulled out for them at the kitchen table.

They talked.

He did not press his father on the girl, but he described what had happened to him in the hallway, and made it clear that that was why he'd wanted to get out of the House, to run away. And that was exactly what *she* wanted, he explained. She wanted to weaken the House, wanted to break apart their family, wanted to get them out.

"But I'm not going to let her," he said. "I love you. I love you both."

"I love you, too," his mother said.

His father nodded, put a hand on his arm.

Mark started crying, and tears obscured his vision, and he closed his eyes and rubbed them, and when he opened them again he was alone in the kitchen. The windows had remained, but there was no porch outside, no chicken coops, only a white blanket of fog, and he understood that he had returned.

He felt warmth on the back of his neck, and he jumped up and turned around, but it was Kristen, standing there, smiling at him.

"You did good," Kristen said. "You did fine."

He smiled wryly. "Is everything resolved?"

"Do you still resent them?"

"No."

"Then I guess so." She hugged him, and he felt warm sunlight, but he thought he could hear, from somewhere in the whiteness outside, an echo of that wild, obscene laugh, and he was not sure that it was entirely in his head.

Kristen pulled back, looked at him.

"Only one more thing," she said.

He faced her. "What's that?"

"You have to find the bitch," she said. "And kill her."

FIFTEEN

Daniel

Daniel followed Doneen out of the house into the rain. There were no barriers keeping him from leaving the building, and once outside he could feel the chill, feel the wind, feel the water against his skin. The air even *smelled* like his street during a rainstorm, and it was these tactile sensations more than anything else that killed any idea he might have had that this was not really his house, that none of this was really happening.

"Where are we going?" he asked.

"To see someone."

"Who?"

"I told you: you're going to have to trust me."

"And you'll leave Tony and Margot alone?"

"That's the deal."

He followed the girl through the small yard, through the gate, to the sidewalk. There was a gang of young toughs leaning against the wall, huddling together in the rain, too cool to use umbrellas but not too cool to wear heavy jackets. They seemed to be waiting for someone.

Daniel thought of Margot and Tony inside the house and wanted to tell these hoods to hit the road, find someplace else to hang out, but he knew they would not be able to hear him.

Then Doneen skipped ahead, turned left on the sidewalk, stepped up to the gang of youths, and to Daniel's surprise, started talking to them. They gathered around her in a semicircle, leaning down to listen.

They could hear her!

The tallest one straightened, turned toward him, and Daniel's heart skipped a beat as he saw wild purple eyes beneath unnatural, impossibly thick hair. The creature smiled, and his overlarge mouth was filled with tiny sharpened teeth.

She'd tricked him, he realized. She'd set him up.

He turned and tried to run back toward the house, but was stopped halfway down the walk by another invisible barrier that split open his nose and lip and knocked him flat on the ground.

"Kill him!" Doneen yelled from the sidewalk. "Kill him!"

He was too stunned to even lurch back to his feet before the gang surrounded him. They were from the Other Side, he knew. He saw strange hair and strange faces and unbelievable colors in their eyes. He lashed out, tried to kick the closest one, but the creature avoided him easily, and then they were attacking him. He was kicked and punched and clawed, but he was too busy trying to protect his face and stomach to clearly see what was going on.

Then he was picked up, several strong arms lifting him into the air, and they started biting him.

He screamed as fangs tore into his forearm, as razor-teeth ripped the flesh of his cheeks. The pain was unbearable, unbelievable, and an artery in his leg started gushing as sharp teeth chewed through his thigh.

Doneen grinned at him as he was eaten alive. He saw her through the pain, through the faces, through the blood, and if he had one last wish that could be granted, it would be to see her killed.

But he was granted no last wish.

He felt his body die, felt the life within him stop as his heart ceased pumping and his brain functions ended, but beyond the shock and pain there was a lightening, a lessening of weight as his spirit pulled free of its heavy fleshy host and emerged unburdened into the open air. It was not a transformation, this transition from life to death; there were no disruptions in his thoughts, no change in his self. It was more like kicking off a pair of shoes and going barefoot. Or stripping off clothes and walking naked. The difference was all external, the loss one of accoutrements, not essence.

He saw his body beneath him, saw the jacketed creatures eating his remains, saw Doneen staring at him with victorious glee. She could still see him, and she waved mockingly as he felt a tug on his form, a power drawing him like a magnet. He thought of Margot and was immediately in her bedroom, in her bed, next to her. There was no longer a barrier between them, and for a brief fraction of a second, he smelled her skin, touched her face, felt the smoothness of her breasts.

And then he was yanked back, pulled into and through the House into a House on the Other Side.

It happened in an instant. There was no flight through space, no view of the Eastern Seaboard beneath him, no surrounding blackness through which he passed, simply a sensation of vacuumlike suction and what looked like a split-section transformation of their bedroom into the House, before he was flat on the floor on the Other Side.

He jumped up. The House in which he found himself was identical to the one he'd entered via the den door, the one in which he'd seen his mother. There were no walls or rooms, only that big open space in that color he did not recognize. Above him were the wispy spirits he had seen before, but though they now looked like individual beings to him rather than clouds, apparently he was not yet one of them. He could neither fly nor float, and he had to run across the floor to the corner, where his mother, still bald, was once again sitting on an egg in a nest.

She smiled at him as he approached.

"I'm dead!" he cried.

She nodded.

He fell into the nest, hugged her, and she felt solid to him, real, and there was something comforting in that. "Margot's a widow! Tony has no father!"

"Time passes quickly here," his mother said. "They'll be with you soon enough."

The sticks of the nest were hard and uncomfortable against his side, but his mother's arms were soft and warm, her smile welcoming. There were a million questions swirling in his mind. He wanted to know where his father was, where the centuries' worth of other dead people were, whether there was a God or a heaven or a hell, whether he was going to be reincarnated or live here or move on to someplace else, but overpowering everything was the desire for revenge, the burning need to get back at Doneen and punish her, make her pay for what she'd done. He might be dead, but he had not lost his capacity for human emotions. He had not been filled with peace and love and a warm sense of contentment.

He hated the bitch.

He wanted her dead.

"Why am I here?" he asked his mother. "Is this where I'm supposed to spend my . . . afterlife?"

She picked up a rose from somewhere in the nest to the right of her and chewed on it thoughtfully.

"You're still in the House," she said. "It doesn't seem to want to let you go."

"Is that good or bad?"

"It's . . . interesting."

"What happened to you?"

"After I was killed?"

He nodded.

"I was freed instantly."

"Did you go . . . here?"

She shook her head, laughing, and her laugh was like music. "I am not here even now."

"Where are you?"

"I am on the Other Side."

"Where is this, then? I thought this was the Other Side."

"The border. The Other Side of the border, but the border nevertheless. Until you are fully on the Other Side, you can still go back. You may be dead, but you are not yet completely free from . . . that world. That's what makes it interesting."

"I thought the Houses were charged up again. I thought the barrier was in place and you . . . we . . . couldn't go back and forth."

"You're still part of the House." She looked at him. "You're not bound by the border. Apparently, the House still needs you."

"But the barrier is up, right? Things aren't . . . leaking out anymore, are they?"

"No." She stroked his hair.

"What about those . . . things that killed me?"

"They must've been trapped out there when the border closed."

He blinked. "Jesus, Margot and Tony!"

She placed a calming hand on his. "Those creatures probably burnt themselves out fighting you. They're like fish out of water there. They don't last long. The worlds . . . aren't really compatible." She smiled at him.

"Good."

She nodded. "Yes."

"So where's Billings?"

His mother's face fell, and for the first time, she looked worried. "He's gone."

"I know he's dead. I mean, where's his ghost or his spirit or—"

"He's *gone*," she said. "There's nothing left of him."

"He—"

"They're not like us, the butler and the girl."

Understanding dawned on him. "Then if he can be killed, she can be killed."

His mother nodded.

"Is that why I'm still part of the House?"

"Perhaps," she mused. She thought for a moment. "You can capture her, you know."

"Can I kill her?"

She shook her head. "No. Not anymore. You could have if you were alive. But dead you can only hold her, restrain her. You can still bring her back, though. You can return her to the House and keep her here, keep her away from your wife and son." She looked at him as though she'd just thought of it for the first time. "Your son," she said wonderingly. "My grandson."

He smiled at her. "Tony."

"Tony."

"I think you'd like him, Mom."

"I'm sure I will."

The egg shook, rumbled, and Daniel leaped to his feet, tottering on the unstable branches of the nest. His mother moved off the egg, and helped him out of the nest.

It shook again, vibrated, jerked.

Suddenly the egg cracked open, and from it emerged . . . nothing.

A beatific smile crossed his mother's face, and she started to fade. As she grew slowly insubstantial, her hair seemed to return, and she looked more like the mother he remembered. He reached out to her, but their hands passed through each other.

"I love you," his mother said. "We all love you."

"I love you, too."

"I'll see you in—" she began.

And she was gone.

The House darkened, the interior dimming as if a light had been switched off, the blank world outside growing indistinct. He felt panicky, didn't know what he was supposed to do, but he thought of Margot, thought of Tony—

and he was back home, in their bedroom, standing at the foot of the bed and staring down at a sleeping Margot.

He felt lost, confused. He supposed, in the back of his mind, despite all of the surface layers of skepticism modern life had heaped on him, he had assumed that all would be revealed after death, that the answers to the cosmic questions and metaphysical concerns that had bedeviled mankind since the beginning of history and provided the impetus for every religion would be instantly supplied to him and he would become some sort of wise, enlightened, loving being, far different and far superior to the ordinary average guy he'd been.

But he was the same person as before, no different, no smarter, no more enlightened.

Just dead.

Piecing together what he knew and what he could infer, Doneen had driven out or killed all of the residents of all of the Houses, leaving the Houses empty, in an attempt to bring down the barrier and open the border, allowing the dead and various beings from the Other Side to invade the material, physical world. Billings, the attendant of the Houses, had doggedly kept on, plugging away as the Houses faded, the barrier weakened, entirely unaware of the girl's existence. Despite Doneen's best efforts to scare them and keep them away, Billings and the Houses had called them back, and once again the integrity of the border was restored, the two worlds separated. But the girl had killed Billings and was now systematically trying to destroy the rest of them. Why? What was the reason? What did she hope to gain? What were her ultimate goals? He didn't know, couldn't say.

He thought of what Mark had said: *Magic isn't logical.* The observation was wiser than he'd given it credit for being, and he had the feeling that there was no rational reason for what she was doing, that her object was not something he could ever hope to understand.

Whatever her purpose, though, he knew it was evil, knew it was wrong.

He wondered what had happened to Mark, to Stormy and Norton, to Laurie. Had they all been tricked into death as he had been? Had they all been murdered? His mother said that Doneen could not be killed by someone who was dead, that it would take a living human being to stop her, and he assumed that Doneen's immediate plan was to kill them all, to make sure they could not harm her. Why she hadn't murdered them outright, why she'd let them get this far, why she hadn't killed them before they even returned to their Houses, was a mystery. Perhaps Billings had been protecting them. Perhaps the Houses had. Maybe her power to inflict harm did not extend beyond the Houses' walls.

He looked down at Margot, sleeping soundly, completely unaware of the fact that he was dead and would never return. He was filled with a deep profound sadness, and he felt like crying, but he was not sure if it was for her or himself. It was for both of them, he supposed, for the forced death of their relationship.

He could not cry, though. The emotion was there, but not the physical capability, and he stood there looking down at her, unable to express what he was experiencing.

He reached down to stroke her cheek. His hand did not pass through her, his fingers were stopped by her skin, but there was no sensation of feeling. He felt neither the warmth of her body nor the softness of her face. Her cheek was merely an impediment to him. But there was no more wall between them, and though he could no longer feel her the way he had in that split second before he'd been pulled back to the House, just the fact that he could be close to her made him feel better, made him feel good.

He bent down even farther to kiss her, and he realized that when he pressed his cheek to hers, he could hear her sleeping thoughts. She was dreaming about him, planning their reunion, thinking about their future life together, and he had to pull away; it was too painful, too raw. He wished he could talk to her, wished he could communicate, but when he tried to nudge her and wake her up, he found that he could not move her. He could touch her form but was unable to exert any pressure against it. He said her name. Softly first, then louder, but she did not awaken.

He straightened, turned toward the door. Tony was the real reason he'd returned, Tony and Doneen, and he took one last look at Margot's sleeping form, then walked out of the bedroom. He could not only pass through the door now but through the wall, and he walked directly into Tony's room through the back of the closet.

Doneen was on the bed talking to Tony, sitting next to him. The boy could obviously see her, obviously hear her, and there was an expression on his son's face as he listened to the girl that made Daniel feel extremely uneasy. It was a look he'd never seen before, an insidious, unwholesomely cunning look that seemed totally out of place on Tony and only served to accentuate the influence Doneen was exerting on him.

A doll lay between the two of them.

"Tony!" Daniel yelled.

The boy gave no indication that he could hear.

"Tony!"

Doneen's eyes flicked up at him for a brief second,

but she continued talking to his son in a low, steady, even voice, not pausing, and the boy did not turn or even flinch when he screamed his name again.

"TONY!"

Daniel moved closer, grabbed his son's arm, but though his hand closed around the boy's wrist, he could not move the arm, no matter how hard he tried. He put all of his muscles, all of his weight into it, but it was like trying to lift a mountain, he was not able to pull his son even a fraction of an inch.

"Use your mother's teeth for the mouth next time," Doneen was saying. She pointed to the figure's half-finished face. "Knock them out while she's asleep and use as many of them as you can on the project."

For the first time since he'd come into the room, Daniel saw hesitancy in his son's face.

"No, Tony!" he yelled, though he knew his son could not hear him. "Don't listen to her!"

"I don't want to do that," Tony said.

"That's okay," Doneen assured him quickly. "That's all right. Maybe the teeth of someone else. Someone you don't like. Someone at school, maybe."

"Maybe," he said, doubtfully.

She patted his hand, reached between his legs, and gave his crotch a small squeeze. "Just keep on doing what you're doing," she said. "It's a fine job."

"Okay."

Doneen looked up at Daniel again. "You can work on the hands a bit," she told Tony. "I'll be back in a minute."

He nodded mechanically.

Doneen stood, walked over to the desk. Daniel let go of his son's arm and followed her.

She turned to face him. "I thought I had you killed," she said softly, and even though he was already dead, there was something about her tone of voice that frightened him. He could not be threatened with death or physical harm anymore, but in the core of his being he feared her, and he moved back a step.

"What do you think you can do to me? Why are you

here?" She stared at him fiercely. "I eat ghosts like you for breakfast."

He kept his voice steady. "You lied. You said you'd leave him alone."

"Yes. I lied."

He reached out and slapped her. His hand connected with her cheek, and her head rocked back.

A look of doubt crossed her features, disappearing as quickly as it had come.

He stared at the red imprint of his hand across her cheek, and thought of what his mother had said.

He could bring her back to the House.

He wasn't exactly sure how to do that. He wasn't sure how he had come back here, for one thing. He'd simply thought about being home and . . . here he was. Was that all there was to it? Could he just think about the House and be returned there?

It was worth a try.

Doneen was scowling at him, and Daniel realized that he might have only one chance.

He'd better make it count.

"I'll kill—" she began.

And he lunged forward.

He grabbed her, tackled her. Concentrating hard, he cleared his mind and thought about where he wanted to go.

They were sucked out of the house and out of the world to the Other Side.

SIXTEEN

Laurie

They walked together into the woods, holding hands. Dawn's fingers and palm felt slimy in hers, greasy, and Laurie wanted to pull away, but she dared not. She wasn't sure exactly where they were going or what they were going to do, but she was smart enough to know that if she kept quiet, kept her mouth shut and her eyes and ears open, she just might learn something.

Around them, the trees and bushes grew thicker. The path on which they'd started walking had narrowed and dwindled until it was now less a clearly defined trail than a section of forest that was not quite as overgrown as the rest. They'd stopped talking several minutes before, and the only sounds were the crunching of their shoes on the mulchy ground and the far-off calls of increasingly bizarre-sounding birds.

Laurie didn't like the woods. She kept thinking she saw movement in the bushes to the sides, shadows amid the ferns, figures that ducked behind tree trunks whenever she turned in their direction. It was unsettling being here, and she was sorry she'd come.

To her left, there was a face formed from the tangle of branches. She did not know if it was really there or if it was a trick of the leaf-filtered sunlight, but the small random shadows on the bare intertwined twigs highlighted a cruel, pointed-nosed face.

She glanced over at Dawn.

Who smiled.

They continued deeper into the woods, and her apprehension increased.

"We're almost there," Dawn said.

"Where?"

"You'll see."

Laurie stopped. "I don't want to see," she said. "I want to go back. The fun's over."

Dawn's smile took on a strange secretive quality. "The fun hasn't even started yet."

"I'm out of here." Laurie turned, started back the way they'd come, but she immediately slipped on one of the slimy leaves, fell, and before she could get up, Dawn was crouching above her, squatting down. Laurie saw a pink-slitted vagina beneath the dirty tattered slip. Screaming, she rolled away, jumped to her feet.

Dawn tapped the pull tab on her finger. "I'm your husband," she said.

What the hell was she supposed to do? How was she supposed to get out of here? Laurie glanced quickly around, saw only thick brush and unfamiliar forest. Above, the sun was blocked by layers of tree leaves and branches.

"It's time to do your wifely duty." The girl lifted the hem of her tattered garment, revealing the split-V of her crotch. "Get on your knees," she said. "And lick it. Lick it clean."

Laurie took off.

She wasn't going to learn anything here, she wasn't going to find out anything that would help her. She was going to end up dead, and she ran as fast as she could away from the girl, through a copse of overgrown manzanita, the red branches scraping the skin of her arms, the small thin leaves slapping against her face. She turned, ran parallel to the path on which they'd come, but nothing looked familiar to her, and when she adjusted her course, running at an angle to intercept the path, she found nothing.

She stopped, breathing heavily, drenched with sweat from the humid air, and looked wildly about. Her sense of direction was completely screwed up, and she did not know which way was the House. Her heart leaped in her chest as she saw the figure of a man in a derby in her peripheral vision, but when she whirled to face the figure, she saw that it was only a skinny sapling with a bushy and irregularly shaped top. From somewhere behind her, Dawn called out her name in an amused, playful voice.

"Lau-rie!"

That's why her parents had forbid her to come here. The woods were *hers*.

"Lau-rie!"

She started running again, heading in the direction in which she *thought* they'd come. There was still no sign of the path, but whatever direction she was traveling, she was getting farther away from Dawn, and at this point that was the most important thing.

Ahead was an indentation in the ground, what looked like a partially filled pit, and as she raced around it, Laurie glanced in and saw the bones of cats and rats and other small animals emerging from furry reddish brown mud. There was a partially eviscerated goat as well, lying lengthwise across the bones, and the stem of a red rose protruded from between its clenched teeth.

She continued on without slowing. She was horrendously out of shape, and not only did her lungs feel as though they were going to burst, but the muscles in her legs were cramping, and she knew she would not be able to go on much longer.

"Lau-rie!" Dawn yelled.

Her voice sounded closer.

She was almost ready to give up and give in, to try to fight it out with the girl if it came to that, but ahead she saw light through the trees, a thinning of brush, and what looked like the black bulk of the House against the sky. She increased her speed, utilizing her last remaining reserves of strength, and ran out from between the trees.

Both of her mothers and both of her fathers, standing on the ground next to the back steps of the porch, turned toward her as she dashed across the open space toward them. "Oh, there you are," her biological mother called out.

Laurie turned around to see Dawn standing at the edge of the trees, stomping her feet, gnashing her teeth.

And then—

she was gone.

Laurie stared at the place where the girl had been and

saw only overgrown weeds. She did not stop, did not slow down, kept running toward the House, but she could not help wondering what had happened. Had Dawn gone back into the woods? Had she somehow transported herself someplace else, back to the House perhaps? Laurie had the feeling that the disappearance was not intentional, that it had been forced or imposed upon the girl rather than instigated by her, and she hoped that was true.

She was almost to the back porch, and this close she could see that all four of the adults were frowning at her.

"What's wrong?" her biological father asked.

"Oh, Mother!" Laurie cried, but she ran into the arms of Josh's mom, not her own birth mother. She recognized the feel of the woman as she hugged her, the smell of her, and a whole host of memories flooded back, and whether it was that or the release of tension from her escape in the woods, she started crying. She sobbed into her mother's blouse, and the woman held her, patted her back, told her everything was all right.

"Are you okay?" Josh asked, and she remembered his baby voice, remembered when he had talked this way, and that instigated another flood of tears. She pulled away from her mother, wiped her eyes, smiled through her sobs, and dropped to one knee to hug her brother. Although he was obviously confused, he did not struggle against her and there was something that looked like understanding in his eyes. Neither he nor his parents broke character—they all pretended as though she were the daughter of the people they'd come to visit, a girl they liked and felt sorry for but didn't really know—but more was at work here than that, and beneath that surface level was an underlying complicity, an acknowledgment that something else was going on.

Her biological mother offered a grim smile. "We were looking for you. It's time for lunch."

"I'm starving!" Her father clapped his hands together. "Let's eat!"

Laurie felt suddenly embarrassed, self-conscious, and she dropped back behind the rest of them as they walked up the steps to the porch.

"It's such a beautiful place you have," Josh's mother said, turning and looking around the property from over the railing.

Her father, her biological father, nodded proudly. "We like it."

Lunch was already on the table, and they ate soup and salad and sandwiches, the adults engaging in polite conversation and completely ignoring what had just happened outside. Laurie and Josh ate in silence.

After they finished, her mother collected all the plates, refusing an offer of assistance from Josh's mom, and promised to return with glasses of homemade lemonade for everyone.

"You should taste her lemonade," her father said. "Best in California."

Conversation started up again, the war this time, and she excused herself from the table and walked into the kitchen, where her mother was using an ice pick to chop ice on the sink counter.

She took a deep breath. "We have to talk," she said.

Her mother did not even look up. "About what?"

"You have to stop seeing that girl," she said. "Stop seeing Dawn."

A moment of silence.

"So you know," her mother said flatly.

Laurie nodded.

Her mother continued to chop ice. "I can't."

"What do you mean, 'you can't'?"

"I don't want to." Her mother faced her, not embarrassed but defiant, the expression giving her already too-serious face an even grimmer cast.

"Jesus."

"She does for me what your father can't do anymore."

"The girl is evil," she told her mother.

Her mother looked away, continued chopping. "You don't think I know that?"

"Then why—"

"I am the mother here. You are the daughter. I do not want to talk about this with you."

Laurie pounded a fist on the counter. "We have to talk about it!"

Her mother looked up at her, surprised, apparently taken aback by the vehemence of her response.

"I don't know if you've noticed, Mother, but I'm not a child anymore. I'm an adult. Aren't you even a little curious why that is?"

Her mother said nothing.

Laurie reached out, grabbed her mother's hand. "Dawn will kill you," she said. "She wants us all out of the House, she wants to leave the House unattended, and she will do whatever it takes to make that happen."

"Billington won't let that happen."

"Billington is gone!" Laurie said. "He's probably dead! She probably killed him!"

There was silence between them.

Her mother coughed. "You don't understand."

"No, *you* don't understand! You think Dawn's doing this for her health? You think she cares about you? She wants you out of the House. And if that means she has to kill you, then so be it."

Her mother was already shaking her head.

"Father's seeing her, too."

At that, her mother stiffened. Laurie had not been intending to reveal that fact, had not planned to say anything about it, had been hoping she could talk to both parents individually and get them each to stop seeing the girl, and she instantly regretted spilling the beans. The horrible thought occurred to her that she was the one responsible for sending her mother after her father, for setting into motion the events that led to her parents' deaths.

Had she done Dawn's work for her?

"Mother," she said earnestly. "You have to put a stop to this. You can't let her run your life. You're just a pawn to her. She'll use you up and toss you aside."

"It's okay," her mother said, and patted her hand. "I know you mean well, but you don't understand everything." She put a finger over Laurie's lips before she could respond. "I know you think you do, but believe me, you don't."

She didn't know what to say, didn't know what to do. She wanted to cry from frustration.

"No matter what happens, I want you to always remember that I love you."

"I love you, too," Laurie said, although even as she spoke the words she was thinking that she loved her other mother more.

Love wasn't perfect, she realized. It didn't cure all ills and didn't solve all problems and wasn't always what was needed. It also wasn't equal. There was a hierarchy of love, some people you loved more than others, and it *did* make a difference. Sometimes just loving someone was not enough. Sometimes you had to love someone *enough*.

Would she have really traded her childhood and her new family for a life with this family in the House?

No.

Her father, her biological father, walked into the kitchen. "What's going on in here?" he asked. "What's taking so long? We're thirsty out there."

Her mother stared at him with a blank, unreadable expression, and whatever else he'd been intending to say died in his throat. "Go back out there with our guests," she said. "I'll bring the lemonade out in a minute."

He nodded.

"Father?" Laurie said.

"Yes?"

"Stop seeing her. Stop seeing Dawn."

His face reddened, tensed, and he was about to say something, to respond angrily, but he glanced over at her mother's face and closed his mouth.

"She's evil," Laurie said.

He nodded tiredly, started to turn away.

They were doomed, she saw now. There was no way she could change anything, no way any of their future could be avoided. Still, she was glad she'd talked to them, and she felt a little bit better knowing that she'd at least made an effort.

"Go out there with your father," her mother said. "I'll bring the drinks in a minute."

Laurie nodded, gave her mother's hand a small squeeze, and she and her father walked back into the dining room where her future family waited.

SEVENTEEN

Daniel

The Other Side.

It was not something he could have anticipated, not even from those views through the windows of the other House.

It was not like any afterlife he had ever imagined. There were no blue skies or fields of green, no cloud palaces, no geographical distinctions at all. There were no hydras or unicorns or banshees, no gods or monsters, no recognizable beings. Occasional indistinct blobs of blackness flew by, shooting past him as though shot from a cannon, but for the most part this world was empty, barren, devoid of even the smallest sign of life or movement.

He was floating in nothingness.

Doneen kneed him in the midsection, trying to dislodge his grip, but he held tightly on to her, ignoring her shrieks and cries, her hideous yelps and growls, wrestling with her in the open air, clutching her close to his chest. He felt no pain, but she was as strong or stronger than he was, and even if she could not hurt him, she could get away from him.

He had no idea what to do with her. He'd wanted only to get her as far away from Tony and Margot as possible, and the Other Side seemed perfect for that, but what was next? Was he supposed to fight with her forever, to wrestle here with her for years in order to keep her occupied and give Tony a chance to grow up? He had to admit that he felt no flagging of his energy, no decrease in strength, and he had no doubt that he *could* continue tangling with her through eternity without becoming fatigued. But he did not want to. He wanted to do something with her, to get rid of her, to imprison her or put her out of commission.

To kill her.

His anger had not flagged either, and he tried to think of some way he could stop her permanently. His mother had said that he could restrain her but not destroy her, and he tried to find some loophole in that, tried to come up with some means to do her in. That would solve not only his family problem but the problems of Laurie and Norton and Stormy and Mark. Doneen was the only real threat to the Houses, and if he could put a stop to her once and for all, everything would go back to the way it was supposed to be.

She squirmed in his grasp, was able to bend her arm and twist her hand in front of his face. Sharp claws snapped out from the ends of her fingers, and his first instinct was to push her away from him, but instead he butted her forehead with his, and used all of his strength and weight and the leverage granted him by size to twist her arm around her back.

She screamed wildly.

He still seemed to be tethered to the House, and for that he was grateful. He could see a line of Houses, far in the distance, the only discernible shapes in this horribly empty universe. There were a lot more than five of them. They stretched infinitely across what passed for a horizon, and although they appeared to be identical, one House, *his* House, blinked periodically from the highest window in its highest gable, an attic window, and at each pulse of light he felt a slight tug, as though it were pulling on some sort of invisible cord connecting him to it.

That connection was the only thing keeping him from defeatism and despair.

God, he wished Billings were still alive.

He could've used some help.

Doneen changed in his hands, her left arm transforming into a green snake, her head morphing into that of Tony's first doll. He was supposed to be scared, frightened away, but he wasn't. She was the only constant in the world floating by them, her transformations at least contextually understandable and recognizable, and he continued to hold on to her as tightly as he could, as the doll head became a goat's head and snapped at him. He kicked her crotch, was gratified to see her snap back into human form and howl in what sounded like pain.

In the opposite direction of the Houses, there were flashes of light in the far distance, flashes that looked like multicolored popcorn. Instead of flaring and fading, they remained, piled onto each other, slowly growing into something approximating a mountain. Both sky and ground were colors he did not recognize, but simply having a "sky" and a "ground," an up and a down, identifiable directions, was reassuring.

Where were his mother and father and all of the other generations of human dead? This world had seemed more hospitable before, and he was both puzzled and troubled by the absence of any presences. The thought occurred to him that there was not just the *Other* Side, that there were *many* sides, and that this one was *her* world, her hereafter.

This was where her kind went when they died.

The thought was not at all comforting.

She snarled at him, spit, and she was no longer a she but a he. A long red penis snaked up between them, its engorged head and wet slitted opening pressing against his closed lips, and he was tempted to open his mouth and bite it off, but he had the feeling that's what she wanted him to do, so he turned his head and maintained his pressure on her wrists, kicking at her lower section as hard as he could with his feet, sending them both tumbling head over heels.

The color of the sky changed as she transformed from female to male and back again, the only indication that she and this terrifyingly empty world were connected.

He maneuvered his hands until he was finally able to reach her neck. He let go of her hands, and she punched him, clawed at him, but he felt nothing and her blows did no damage. His fingers were firmly around her throat, and he tried to squeeze shut her windpipe, to strangle her, but his efforts had no discernible effect. He was not sure if she *could* be strangled, if she were breathing or if she even *had* to breathe, but he knew that it would not make any difference either way. His mother had been right, he could not kill her.

She understood what he was trying to do, and she stopped struggling for a moment, long enough to laugh at him.

"You should've fucked me when you had the chance," she said.

She pushed him hard away with both feet and both hands.

He was holding on to her only by the neck, and the sudden application of force sent him flying back.

"They're mine," she said, grinning. "They're all mine."

And she was gone.

EIGHTEEN

Norton

Norton awoke in the present.

The past was gone. He was back in the House that he'd shared with the others, only now he was alone. There was no sign of Daniel or Laurie or Stormy or Mark, no indication that they were here or that they had ever been here. He was somewhere upstairs, somewhere in the center of the House that he didn't recognize. To his left, a hallway lined with opposing sets of closed doors stretched into the dimness. To his right, the same. Behind him was a wall, and ahead of him another hallway, shorter, with no doors opening onto it, ending in a blue room.

He walked slowly forward, down the short hallway. The air grew colder with each step, and by the time he reached the room he could see his breath. It felt like a meat locker, he thought, and that analogy left him feeling unsettled.

The room was empty, but to the right of the door, in the opposite wall, was another doorway, leading to another room, this one a lighter shade of blue. He passed through the vestibule, and the temperature went up a few degrees. Once again, there was another doorway, this one on the left wall, and it led into yet another room, an even lighter shade of blue.

Norton stood, looking around. There were no lamps or light fixtures, but the rooms were somehow illuminated, and that made him nervous.

It was one of the many things that made him nervous. These rooms did not seem to him like part of the House. They were, he knew, but until now everything within the House had had a counterpart with the past,

with his childhood. The solarium had been new, but like
the bathroom, he had accepted it as part of the remodeling that must have occurred over the past half century.

These rooms did not seem like they had ever been a
part of the House.

Maybe he wasn't in the present but in some future
time. Or even some outside time. He definitely wasn't
in the past, though. He knew that. He could *feel* it.

Perhaps this was some sort of test. Maybe he'd passed
the first part of the test, with his family, and now he was
being tested again.

Maybe if he successfully completed this part, he'd be
allowed to go free.

It was that hope, that possibility, that pushed him
forward.

The next room, a white room, was warmer.

There were nine rooms all together. It was like a
maze, and he didn't understand how the center of the
House could contain this much space, but he walked
through increasingly warm chambers, until, finally, he
reached the last room.

It was empty save for the girl.

She was naked, and she smiled slyly at Norton, slowly
bending over, grabbing her ankles. "Kiss my ass," she
said.

He stared at her.

"Kiss my ass," she repeated softly, sensuously. "You
know you want to."

He *did* want to—even after all he'd been through,
even after all that had happened. He could see the small
pink puckering between her spread buttocks and he
longed to place his mouth there, to touch it with his
tongue.

Wasn't that how the devil was supposed to have sealed
his covenant with witches?

Norton closed his eyes. He didn't know what to think
anymore. He was sweating, and he wiped his perspiring
brow with the back of his hand. There were no other
doors in this room, no way out save for the way he'd
come in.

"I'm not the enemy," she said. "It's the Houses that are the enemies."

"Th-that's not true," he said.

Her smile grew wider, and it not only looked sensuous to him but curiously friendly. "Yes it is. You know it is. We're both trapped here. We're both prisoners. Why do you think you were lured back? You honestly think that the forces of good kidnapped you and planned to make you live out the rest of your life here? Because you're the only one who can save the world? Does that make any sense at all? Be serious."

The expression on her face seemed open and honest to him, and he found himself following her logic. Maybe he and the others had been wrong. Maybe they'd been brainwashed by Billings and his Houses.

"I never touched your parents or anyone in your family. I was the one who tried to save them. It was Mr. Billings who did them in. And he's been trying to keep us apart ever since because he knew I'd tell you the truth."

The ants.

He pushed that thought out of his mind.

She ran a finger slowly down the opened crack of her buttocks. "Come on," she said softly. "Kiss it. Kiss my ass. What can it hurt?"

He licked his dry lips and found himself nodding.

"I've been waiting for this for a long time, Norton."

He moved forward, knelt behind her, placed his face between the cheeks of her buttocks, closed his eyes, and began licking.

The girl moaned.

When he opened his eyes, he was in a black room, his face buried between two red pillows on the floor. He looked up and saw a marble table set up like an altar.

Strapped down, lying on top of the table, was Billings.

The assistant, hired hand, butler, whatever-he-was, was straining against his bonds. There was defiance in his face but no fear, and Norton walked slowly over and looked down at him. Billings was still in his formal attire, and even under these circumstances he seemed to retain a sense of dignity. He stared up at Norton, and it was clear that he wanted to be released, but he was not about to beg, and he said nothing.

There was a tug on his arm, and Norton looked down to see Donna pulling on his sleeve. "Come here," she said softly, and a slight smile played about her lips. "Come look."

He noticed for the first time that the room was crowded, filled with tables and display cases and huge heavy pieces of furniture that served functions he did not understand. He saw what looked like severed hands and genitalia lying on a long glass shelf on one wall. Something small and dark and furry ran past his feet, chattering to itself.

He did not see either a door or a window, an entrance or an exit to the room.

Donna pulled him around a large stationary object of mirror and wood that he did not recognize, and he found himself in a corner area even more jumbled and chaotic than the rest of the room. There was no furniture here, though.

There were bodies.

And body parts.

His first instinct was to back away. The floor was sticky with blood, and what looked like deflated clouds, the pale empty husks of the ghosts he'd seen in the House on the Other Side, hung from staggered hooks on the black wall. The torso of some unknown rainbow-colored creature sat atop a cube made from interlocking bones, next to the discarded head of an evil-looking old woman. The stench was horrendous, and he held his hand to his nose, gagging.

But Donna would not let him go. She held tightly to his wrist, her strength both unforced and unnatural, and she talked to him softly. There was no true death, she said. There was only a transformation from one form into another, a passage from one world to the next. Why should he hold on to his outdated notions of morality, his prudish small-town conceptions of what was right? There was nothing wrong with killing. It only facilitated the inevitable.

He heard her, understood her, and though he should

have had arguments with which to dispute her, he did
not. She led him through the abattoir, still softly talking,
lovingly touching the remains of the dispatched.

There was beauty in the bones, he saw now, a poetry
in the eviscerated flesh.

Donna reached the wall, and from a skin sheath hanging from a spike, she withdrew a dull rusty knife. She
handed it to him. "Mr. Billings is yours."

"What?"

"It's time for him to move on, and you have been
chosen to assist him." She pressed the knife into his
hand. It felt heavy, good. "It's an opportunity for you."

She led him back through the furniture to the marble
table, and he looked at Billings, strapped down and unable to move. Norton shook his head. He could not go
through with this. He understood that death was not the
end, but he still could not bring himself to kill someone,
to murder in cold blood.

Donna must have sensed his hesitancy because she
rubbed against him, placed a hand between his legs. "It's
his time," she said. "He *wants* to go."

Billings did not look like he wanted to go. Norton
glanced down at the defiant face and turned quickly
away.

Donna faced him. Her legs were slightly spread, the
thin material of her dirty shift stretched tight, and he
found himself wishing she'd bend over again, wishing
she'd let him between her thighs.

One of the wispy ghosts had been pinned to the wall
behind the table and was weakly fluttering, its blue-gray
essence seeping slowly out from a slit in the fabric of its
being and floating into the girl's mouth even as she
spoke, even as she whispered the words he wanted to
hear.

"I'll drink your sperm and drink your piss and drink
your blood. I'll take everything you give me and do anything you want me to. All you have to do is take care
of Mr. Billings."

Norton nodded. He didn't know why he was doing
what he was doing, but he held out the knife, walked
up to the marble table.

"Do it," Donna said.

He did.

Even as Billings screamed, as he inserted the knife in the assistant's groin and jerked upward, Norton understood that he was the reason Billings had disappeared. Wherever he was—whenever he was—it was after he had met Daniel and Laurie and Stormy and Mark but before the Houses had split apart. He had not known it then because his own life unfolded sequentially, no matter what happened, but the Houses did not follow such a conventional timetable, were not so circumscribed, and he had been wrenched back and forth, forced to be at the Houses' beck and call, to respond to whatever they put in front of him.

Donna was right. It was the Houses that were evil.

But he realized the fallacy of that reasoning even as it occurred to him. Billings' screams were now silent, his mouth frozen wide open, his eyes bulging with agony, and Norton knew with a certainty that could not be denied that he'd been right the first time, that his initial instincts had been correct. The girl was the evil one.

"Yes," Donna said, egging him on. And there was hunger in her eyes. "Gut the fucker!"

He stopped then and there. He pulled the knife out and dropped it, knowing that it was too late, that he had been corrupted by the girl—

Kiss my ass

—that he had been caught in her web, that he was lost. He heard the knife hit the floor, and he stared down at his hands, covered to the elbows with hot blood, and he started to cry, but Donna knelt before him and, smiling up at him, unfastened the snaps on his pants.

"I'll take care of you," she promised. "I'll reward you."

He pulled back from her, jerked away. "What have you done?" he screamed at her.

She smiled up at him. "What have *you* done?"

"You didn't kill my family," he said, understanding finally dawning on him, "because you couldn't kill them."

Donna smiled. "Darcy did just as good a job. I was very proud of her."

Norton's stomach dropped. "No," he whispered, shaking his head. He thought of his old girlfriend, and though he didn't want to be able to imagine her cutting off heads and cooking them in the oven, he could.

But how had she done it? His father and Darren and his sisters—hell, even his mother—could have easily beaten Darcy in a fight. And all of them together would certainly have been able to not only resist her but overpower her.

Donna had made them sacrifice themselves.

It made perfect sense.

He stared at her with horror.

"But I can kill," she said. "You're wrong about that. I can fuck and I can kill."

"Then why do you make other people do it for you?"

She smiled. "Because it's fun."

He backed away from her.

"I killed Darcy after that. Skinned her in the garage. And Mark's sister Kristen? The last true resident of the House? I sat on her face, made her eat me, suffocated her with my hot pussy. And—"

"Why didn't you kill Billings?"

Her face clouded over. "That's different."

"Why?"

"Because."

"You couldn't do it?"

"No, I needed you."

He looked back at the assistant's bloody, unmoving form on the table. "What have I done?" he cried.

"You've helped me."

And even as he screamed his anguish into the black and bone-cluttered room, she was on her knees in front of him, pulling down his pants.

NINETEEN

Stormy

The windows were back.

That was the first thing he noticed.

But the world outside was foggy and featureless, and although the front door of the House opened when he tried it, he was afraid to go out into that murk.

Stormy closed the door and looked around the entryway, down the hall. "Daniel!" he called. "Daniel!"

No answer.

"Norton! Laurie! . . . Mark!"

His voice died without echo in the heavy oppressive air, and there was no answering noise from anywhere else in the House.

Funny. He could have sworn he was back in the same House he'd shared with his compatriots. It certainly looked and felt that way to him. But he seemed to be completely alone, and he wondered if they'd been trapped somewhere else. In their own pasts, perhaps.

Or if they'd been killed.

He hoped to God that wasn't the case.

Stormy walked into the dining room, into the kitchen. There were crackers in one of the cupboards, and he took out the box, grabbing a handful. He was hungry, he realized. He felt as though he'd been running a marathon or working out in a gym. He was drained, enervated, and he felt the need to bolster himself with nourishment. He searched through all of the other cupboards as well as the refrigerator, but he found only two other items.

A can of fruit cocktail.

And a hunk of cheddar cheese.

He ate neither, left them in the cupboard and refrigerator, respectively, feeling chilled.

He finished off the box of crackers, poured himself a glass of water.

So what was next?

It was clear that he had done something, accomplished something. He'd been set down in the household of his childhood for a reason, and while that reason was still unclear, the fact that he was back, had been returned, meant that he had completed whatever it was he'd been expected to do.

But the purpose of it was still unknown, even the assumptions behind it nebulous. How could changing the specifics of his own past life affect anything having to do with the Houses and this border that was supposed to protect—what?—the known universe from supernatural forces?

It was the mixture of the cosmic and the personal that he found so hard to accept. He had never bought into the Christian idea that God would ignore wars and atrocities and holocausts yet intervene on behalf of a housewife with marital problems. It seemed absurd and inconsistent to him. Highly illogical, to quote the great Mr. Spock.

But he knew now that the Infinite was illogical, that the epic and the intimate were inexorably intertwined, and while it might be hard to grasp and difficult to adjust to, a missed appointment could have as much consequence as the troop movements of an army a thousand soldiers strong, could *lead* to the movement of an army a thousand soldiers strong. In the grand scheme of things, individual actions and large-scale events were both equally important. Here in the House and on the Other Side, that truism seemed to be even more pronounced. Feelings and emotions were as tangible as actions, and while he might not understand the specifics of it, he knew that reconnecting with his parents and confronting Donielle had somehow had a profound impact on the House and therefore the world.

He looked out the kitchen windows at the white fog that obscured whatever lay outside.

The Ones Who Went Before.

For the first time since Billings had spoken that terrifying name to him, Stormy thought about the builders of the Houses. What did they look like? Did they have a definite shape and form? He would never know and was not sure that he wanted to know.

What about the Houses themselves? If they had been around as long as Billings had intimated, they could not have always looked like this. What had been here before them? Teepees? Caves?

It was a creepy line of thought, and Stormy forced himself to back away from it. There would be time for that later. There were more immediate concerns at present. He needed to find out where he was, when he was, where the others were, and how they were going to escape from here.

Crackers were stuck between his teeth, and he poured himself another glass of water and rinsed his mouth out in the sink before embarking on a floor-by-floor search of the House.

He went through every room on the first floor, then wandered upstairs, looking for one of the others, looking for . . . something. He saw nothing unusual until he reached the third story. There, across the hall from his bedroom, was a door that had not been there before, a door he did not remember. He felt suddenly nervous and was not sure he wanted to look inside, especially not alone, but he forced himself to be brave, opened the door, and peeked into the room.

"Oh, Jesus," he breathed.

Butchery.

This deserved the title. The black room before him was the site of almost unbelievable carnage. Faces hung from hooks on the wall like hats, the drooping, sagging skin contorting their former shapes into stretched mockeries of human forms. Bones and skulls and pieces of flesh lay strewn across the blood-spattered floor next to a pile of discarded gossamer that looked like the empty bodies of the cloudlike ghosts he'd seen on the Other Side. Metal instruments that could only be tools of torture were scattered about the room.

On the top of a marble table was Billings.

The butler had been stabbed. No, not just stabbed. Slit open. His mouth was frozen in a rictus of agony, and his eyes were wide, staring. The red imprint of a kiss—lipstick? blood?—could be seen on his white forehead.

Stormy remained in the doorway, afraid to enter the room. He didn't know what this meant, where it fit into anything, but it scared the hell out of him, and the confirmation that Billings was dead hit him much harder than expected.

What were they going to do now? Their guiding light was gone.

What was *he* going to do now? That was the big question. Because the others weren't anywhere to be found. For all he knew, they had been killed as well and their bloody corpses awaited him in some other room of the House.

He thought he detected movement to the right of Billings' body, and immediately he shifted his attention in that direction. At first he saw nothing, but he squinted his eyes, looked more carefully.

A shade, a shadow—Norton?—was standing near the foot of the table, its indistinct form covered with blood, staring at its own outstretched hands with an expression that could be read as horror, could be read as awe. The face was obscure, faded into transparency, but there was something about the shape of its body, its stance, the movement of its head and arms, that reminded him of Norton, and he was suddenly sure that the old man was dead.

He called out Norton's name, tried to communicate with the ghost or whatever it was, but no matter what he said or how much he gesticulated, he could not seem to capture the figure's attention.

There was additional movement in the far corner of the dark room, a flash of white in his peripheral vision, and Stormy quickly glanced over at that area.

Donielle.

She had no trouble seeing him. The girl smiled in his direction, and her lips were bright crimson, there were flecks of blood on her teeth. She lifted her shift, and he saw smears of red on her crotch where she'd been . . . touching herself. "Come and get it," she said, giggling. Her voice seemed to come from far away.

Looking at her now, Stormy could not understand how he had ever even been tempted.

She turned around and bent over, still giggling. "Kiss it!" she said.

He slammed the door of the room as hard as he could, backing toward his bedroom across the hall. More than anything, he needed time to think, time to sort things out, but he had the feeling that was exactly what he was not going to get. He was filled with the sudden conviction that things were coming to a head, that whatever it had all been building toward had arrived, that the girl had almost achieved her goal.

That he was next.

Reaching behind him, his hands felt the jamb of his bedroom doorway and he turned around. But it was not his room. It was the black room again, and amid the bloody mayhem, Donielle stood at the foot of Billings's table with her shift hiked up and rubbed herself with bloody hands.

He turned, and the door he had slammed shut was now open again, and he saw the identical room across the hall. He tried to think of what he should do, how he could get out of this, but his mind was a blank.

"You can't escape," Donielle said.

And advanced on him from both directions.

TWENTY

Mark

He walked slowly through the House, looking for the girl.

Mark trod carefully down the halls, hyper-aware of each shadow and sound. He wished he had a weapon, but he did not think it would make any difference if he did. Traditional concepts did not apply here, and though it would have made him feel slightly more secure having something to hold in his hand, he knew that was just a mental crutch.

He had no idea how he was going to fight her, but years of being on the road had made him pretty good at thinking quickly on his feet, and he trusted himself to figure something out when the time came.

Ahead was the door that led to the solarium. The hall around it was dark, a single candle bulb in a candelabra wall fixture throwing a weak light onto the door itself, leaving the surrounding space in blackness.

He wished Kristen had come with him. Or that Daniel or Laurie or Norton or Stormy were here.

He wished Billings were around.

Mark never would have thought he'd actually desire the assistant's company, but his mindset had gone through some hard changes since he'd learned Kristen had died and returned to the House. Almost everything he'd thought growing up had turned out to be wrong, his reality had been reversed, and he could not help thinking that all of this could have been avoided had he and his parents or he and Billings just talked, just communicated.

He reached the door, hesitating before opening it. Did he really think he could kill the girl? Kristen seemed to believe that he could, and he supposed that's what gave him the little confidence he had. Her belief in him might be nothing more than faith or hope, but it was reassuring nonetheless, and it made him feel that he at least had a fighting chance.

He reached for the door handle. Turned it. Pulled.

The solarium was gone. The door opened onto a black room with blood-spattered walls, floor, and ceiling. The room was empty, but smeared swaths of blood, and scrapes and scratches on the floor, made it look as though heavy objects had been recently moved out. There was an aura of corruption and violent depravity about the room, a sensation so clear and strong that for a second Mark thought The Power had returned. But he realized almost instantly that the evil here was so thick and concentrated that even the most dull and unimaginative man would have no trouble detecting it.

There was no one in the room, though, and despite its unbearable atmosphere and visible remnants of past atrocities, there was nothing for him here, no sign of the girl, and he gratefully closed the door.

He walked back down the hall.

The Power.

He'd feel better if he still had it, and he found himself wondering why only he and Kristen, out of all of the residents in all the Houses, had been granted such extra-sensory abilities. It seemed strange to him, and he wondered if it wasn't a fluke, a mistake.

Maybe he'd been chosen.

That made no sense. Chosen that long ago? Selected as a child? Why? So that he could one day go up against the girl? It seemed both absurd and stupid to him that the House would know all of this was going to happen, would prepare for it by *grooming* him, yet would do nothing to prevent any of it from occurring.

Still, the idea was not inconceivable, and he could not quite believe that his possession of The Power had been accidental.

But why had it been taken from him?

Maybe *she* had taken it.

He should have asked Kristen.

Mark forced himself to stop thinking, to concentrate only on the House around him and the task ahead of him. He could not allow himself to be distracted. One false move could cost him whatever small advantage he might have. He had to remain focused.

Slowly, he climbed the stairs to the second floor.

He stopped for a moment at the top of the stairs, hesitated. The mood up here was familiar, the ambience one of palpable malevolence. It was exactly the same thing he'd felt that day when he'd been alone in the house with the retarded girl, and it was everything he could do to keep from running back down the stairs. He felt like a kid again, a scared kid, and he forced that feeling into submission, knowing it was what she wanted, knowing it would give her the edge she needed.

He moved carefully down the hall, alert for any sign that anything was out of the ordinary, and froze as he heard the sound of a child laughing. It was a chilling sound, the timbre that of a pre-adolescent but the cadence informed with the experience of an adult.

It was coming from halfway down the hall.

From Kristen's room.

Mark could smell the sour stench of his own sweat as he approached the closed door. His hands were clenched, the palms sweaty. He still had no plan, no idea of what he was going to do or even what he should do. There was no choice but to plow ahead, however, and he stood before the door, took a deep breath, reached out.

And opened it.

The retarded girl was seated cross-legged on Kristen's bed. She looked over at him, and he saw for the first time that she looked exactly like Kristen had as a child. He'd never noticed that before.

Had it been true before?

He wasn't sure, couldn't remember.

"Mark," the girl said.

There were dolls surrounding her. Dozens of them. She'd been making them out of lint and fiber, thread and dust, and they covered the floor, the hope chest, the bed. Each was unique, with eyes and mouths of different materials, but there was an underlying uniformity to them all, a bedrock constant that marked them as her creations.

They were all staring at him.

And smiling.

"You know how I like it," she said.

In answer, he kicked the nearest doll. He kicked it as hard as he could, but there was no weight to it, no heft, no bulk, and instead of flying across the room, the figure flopped to the floor less than a foot away.

The girl shook her head, and she no longer looked like his sister. "Good-bye," she said.

She smiled at him, disappeared, but reappeared instantly, struggling against the binding arms of . . . Daniel?

It was him, but he was like Kristen, glowing and translucent, a Hollywood special effect, and Mark realized at that instant that Daniel was dead. The girl screamed, spit, tried to bite the glowing arm holding her. She must have fled to the Other Side, and Daniel had been there to capture her and bring her back. Once again Mark thought that there was no coincidence in all of this, that everything had been mapped out and planned ahead of time.

By who or what he didn't know, but he didn't have time to speculate on it. The dolls were coming after him, moving quickly. Daniel and the girl still struggled atop the bed, and Mark faced the scurrying, crawling, leaping creatures, bracing himself for the onslaught.

The first doll reached him, clambering up his leg. He tried to grab it, but there was nothing to grab, no skeleton or solid center. His fingers closed around a soft wispy mass of hair and met his palm on the other side. He felt the sharp prick of a needle on the skin of his forearm and saw that the doll was bending over to bite him. He grabbed the feet of the creature with his right hand, its head with his left, and pulled, ripping it apart. The individual elements devolved into their original components, separating, whatever power or force that held them together dissipating and disappearing.

He pulled the needle out of his skin, and saw that the

doll no longer even had a shape, was just a tangled, elongated mass of hair and lint and trash.

The second doll reached him, and he tore it apart as well, his hands working crazily, arms flailing. He ripped it into pieces before it could even get a hold on him.

He looked up, over at the bed, but Daniel was gone. The girl was jumping up and down on the mattress, pointing at him and gibbering excitedly in a language he did not understand. He didn't know whether she had beaten Daniel or he had accomplished what he'd set out to do and left on his own, but he didn't have time to dwell on it. More dolls had reached him, six or seven of them, and he lit into them, grabbing what he could and pulling, rending, severing, not knowing what he was grabbing or how many of them he was separating.

They were easier to fight off than he would have thought, and although there were occasional pinpricks and scrapes, the dolls were unable to do any serious damage to him.

They also weren't nearly as frightening as he had been led to believe.

Paper tigers.

Several of them *were* partially made of paper, and he found himself wondering if all of the girl's threats were like this, if they'd always been more illusionary than real, more psychological than physical. Perhaps the only hold she'd ever had on any of them was her ability to exploit their own fears.

No. She'd killed Kristen. And she'd probably killed Daniel.

He still had to be careful. He couldn't underestimate her.

He destroyed all of the dolls. The girl did not jump in at any point and try to help, and Mark thought that odd. She could have attacked him while he was busy and distracted. She could probably have gained serious advantage. But she remained on the bed, jumping up and down and screaming in that strange unnatural tongue.

He tore the head off the last doll, ripped out the punch holes that had been its eyes, and stood amid the pile of dust and dirt and hair and trash. He glanced over, stared at the girl.

She was afraid of him!

The realization surprised him. He did not know why or how this had happened, did not know to what he should attribute this sudden empowerment, but he knew enough to take advantage of it, and before his nerve failed, he rushed the bed.

She tried to get away, but she wasn't fast enough. She hadn't anticipated this move, and he tackled her around the midsection, slamming her into the wall. She was stronger than he was, he could *feel* the strength in her muscles, could sense the coiled power within her, but surprise and her own apprehension had given him the momentary advantage, and he kneed her in the crotch and elbowed her in the chest and got his arms around her throat.

He'd been waiting for this, wanting it. It was what Kristen had told him to do, what Daniel and the others obviously desired. But his hands were around her neck and he was about to twist them—

—and he couldn't.

As evil as she was, as many problems as she had caused over the years, over the centuries perhaps, he could not bring himself to kill her. When all was said and done, she was a child. As evil as she might be, she was still not an adult, and that made a difference. He knew now why inner-city gangs used kids to commit some of their hits. No matter how heinous the crime they committed might be, it was almost impossible to sentence children to death, and their punishment was invariably lightened because of their juvenile status.

She wasn't a child, though. Not really. She was much more than that.

But when he looked down at her face, felt the smallness of her form beneath him, he could not bring himself to finish her off.

She looked up at him, all innocence, and then that innocence was slowly washed away. She smiled at him lewdly, wickedness and a base sensuality creeping across her corrupt features, and he finally understood emotionally, not just intellectually, that she was *not* a child. That she had never been a child.

His grip tightened around her neck, and he wondered why she had done that, why she had revealed herself to him. Did she *want* him to kill her? Would that somehow make her stronger? Or was she simply teasing him, playing with him, leading him on before finally doing him in?

He felt her muscles tighten beneath him, felt a surge of strength in her chest.

There was a sudden flash of brightness, an abrupt incandescence at the side of the bed that distracted her attention for a second.

And Mark snapped her neck.

He saw knowledge flood into her face in that last second, as the life drained from her, and he thought that she had not expected this, had not even considered its possibility.

She spit at him with her last breath.

Daniel stood by the side of the bed, the source of the brightness. "Quick thinking," he said.

Mark looked at the ghost of the other man. He had not had time to determine the source of that flaring incandescence, had assumed it was something she had created and was going to use against him, and he'd moved quickly only because of his certainty that this would be his final chance. He had not expected it to be a diversion intentionally created by Daniel's ghost, and he climbed off the bed and the girl's lifeless body, facing the glowing form.

"Daniel?"

"In the flesh." The ghost smiled. "Well . . . in the spirit."

"You're dead, aren't you?"

Daniel laughed, and the sound was like music, like Kristen's laugh. "Oh, yes."

"What's it like?"

"Being dead?"

Mark nodded.

"I don't know," Daniel said thoughtfully.

"You don't know?"

"It's confusing. I'm just as in the dark as I was before.

Even more so, really. Because at least I knew how living worked. I knew what I had to do and where I could go. I knew my body's needs and limits. I knew about the world I lived in. Now . . . I'm just lost. There's no handbook, no guide, no one to really explain anything to me. I'm just . . . I'm trying to sort it all out right now."

"Did she kill you?"

"Yes." Daniel explained what had happened, how he'd been back at home with his wife and son, how she'd tricked him into death by promising to stay away from his boy, how he'd met his mother and she'd told him he could bring the girl back to the House, how he'd done that and had ended up in some sort of limbo, how the girl had escaped, and how she'd suddenly reappeared in the other House and he'd brought her back.

"What was she?" Mark asked.

Daniel shrugged. "You got me."

"Is it over now? Is that it?"

"I hope so."

Mark looked over at the girl's corpse, still lying on the bed. In death, it looked like the body of a child. There was nothing unusual about it, nothing out of the ordinary, nothing to indicate that it had been anything other than a little girl. He met Daniel's eyes, saw understanding there.

The two of them were silent for several moments.

"Did it hurt when she killed you?" Mark asked finally. "When you died?"

"My body hurt. But once I was out of it, I felt no pain."

Mark nodded, thought of his sister. "So what's on the Other Side? Beyond the Houses, I mean."

"I don't know. I haven't seen it yet."

"What do you mean you haven't seen it? You're dead!"

"I seem to be . . . trapped. In the Houses. That's all I've seen. What I told you."

"Have you met my sister, Kristen?"

Daniel shook his head. "I haven't met anybody. I've seen my mother. That's it. I suppose all that comes next. I don't really know."

"You haven't disappeared yet. You're still here."

"I know," Daniel said worriedly.

"So what are you going to do now?" Mark asked.

"Go home," Daniel said. "If I can."

"And if you can't?"

He shrugged.

"Is there . . ." Mark cleared his throat awkwardly. "Is there anything we should, you know, tell your wife? Or your son?"

Daniel was shaking his head. "No. Don't . . ." He trailed off, thought for a moment. "Tell my wife . . . tell Margot . . . tell her . . . I don't know, tell her something she can believe and she can understand. And let her know that I love her and that she and Tony were what I was thinking about and concerned about."

Mark nodded.

"Make sure she knows that I love her."

"Where does she live?"

Daniel gave him the address.

They stood there for a few moments longer, but they had nothing left to say to each other. There was an awkward silence between them, and finally Daniel said, "I'm going to try to go home, try to see Margot and Tony myself."

"Good luck," Mark told him.

Daniel smiled, nodded.

And before Mark could say another word, he was gone.

He was left alone in the room, the broken-necked body on the bed, the floor strewn with lint and dust and the other ingredients that had made up the dolls. He didn't know what was supposed to happen now, where he was to go from here, and he closed his eyes for a moment.

"Hello, Mark."

He opened his eyes.

It was Kristen.

She was standing next to him, and she put an arm around his shoulder, and he felt warmth, sunlight. "I'm proud of you, big brother."

"I thought I was a goner there for a sec."

She smiled. "I wasn't worried."

"You didn't think she could take me?"

Kristen shook her head. "Things can only work out the way they do."

Before he had time to ask her about that deterministic statement, she had moved over to the bed and was staring down at the girl's body.

Mark followed her, joined her. "Billings and the girl," he said. "What were they?"

"Meddlers in the natural process."

"Stormy thought maybe he was God and she was the devil."

"They have been called that."

He blinked. "So . . . so God really is dead?"

"Not exactly."

"What do you mean, 'not exactly'?"

"They were merely representatives of other, higher forces. Pawns. You could call them good and evil, but good and evil are not all there is. There is something beyond all that."

"What?"

"I can't tell you."

"And I wouldn't understand?"

She nodded, smiling. "And you wouldn't understand."

"Do you?"

"Not completely. Not yet."

"But it's over now?"

"Nothing's ever over."

"You're more annoying dead than alive. Do you know that?"

Kristen laughed, and he laughed with her. It was the first time he'd allowed himself to laugh in a long, long while, and it felt good, it felt right.

When he stopped laughing, he saw that the girl's body was gone. It had disappeared. He turned toward his sister. "Where did she go?"

"She's still here."

"I don't see her."

"Think of her as a sacrifice. A sacrifice to the House."

"The House demands sacrifices?"

Kristen smiled. "No."

"I don't—"

"You don't need to."

"So what happens now?"

"That's up to you."

"Are the others—?"

"You'll see them in a minute."

"And then what?"

"That's up to you." She kissed his cheek, and a flood of pleasant feelings passed through him. "You can leave now if you want. The doors are open."

"Kristen," he said.

He reached for her.

And she was gone.

TWENTY-ONE

Stormy

There was no earthquake this time, only a silent temporary blurring of wall and floor and ceiling as the Houses came together.

He'd been standing in that previously unknown room—

Butchery

—facing the oncoming Donielle, and she had suddenly stopped in place, eyes widening. She fell to the floor, flailing about, then stiffened and was still. He'd turned around, and the other Donielle was lying on the floor, too. He remained there for a moment, unmoving, then walked toward her to make sure she was dead.

She was.

They both were.

He felt for a pulse, looked for any indication that there was life within the still bodies, and was gratified to learn that there were none. He was still in one of those black rooms, still staring at the girl's body, but when the change occurred, when the Houses again came together, he was in the sitting room, and the girl's body was nowhere in sight.

Once more, the House felt different. He didn't know why, didn't know how, but the aura of dread that had been in the background, like white noise, since he'd first stepped through the door of the House, was gone, replaced with a surprisingly benign sense of calm.

The windows of the sitting room were fogged with condensation, but there was light outside and shapes behind the obscuring blur of the glass.

He had the feeling that the real world was once again within reach.

Laurie walked in from the dining room, followed by
Mark. Norton emerged from the entryway.

The four of them stood staring at each other for a
long moment.

It was Mark who broke the silence. "Daniel's dead,"
he said. "She killed him. Or had him killed."

He explained what had happened, how he had confronted her in his sister's bedroom, how he had killed
her and Daniel had helped.

The rest of them remained silent through his story,
not interrupting, and even after he had finished none of
them had any questions.

Stormy sighed tiredly. "I guess it's my turn."

They each described what had happened in their absence. As before, while the details were different, the
stories were remarkably similar Also, as before, Norton's
was the most horrific.

Stormy was shocked by the old man's confession, and
he found that he was disgusted, horrified, and slightly
afraid of the teacher. He'd been surprised to see Norton
alive, and happy about it at first, but as the other man
related the events that had befallen him, Stormy recalled
that bloody transparent figure he'd seen in the black
room, and he understood what had happened there.

He did not like Norton, he realized, and as embarrassed and apologetic as the old man was, Stormy detected something hard and dark beneath that surface
contrition, and he felt uncomfortable being in the same
room with him.

He edged a little closer to Laurie.

"So what next?" Laurie asked after Norton had finished talking. She gestured toward the sitting-room window. "It's light out there. Anybody want to try to go
outside? See if we can finally get out of here?"

"Count me in," Stormy told her.

"The doors are open," Mark said. "There's nothing
holding you here. You can go."

Laurie looked at him. " 'You'?"

Mark cleared his throat nervously. "I'm staying."

They looked at him.

"What?" Stormy said, incredulous.

Norton sucked in a deep breath. "I am, too."

"This is crazy!" Stormy looked from one man to the other. "Have you both lost your fucking minds? Billings is dead. Donielle's dead. The Houses are open. There's nothing keeping us here. We're free! We can go back to our normal lives and pretend this never happened!"

Mark's voice was quiet. "Yes, Billings and the girl are gone, but we don't know what that means. What we *do* know, is that with someone living in at least one of the Houses, the barrier holds."

"You still want to stay? After everything that's happened to you here?"

"Especially after everything that's happened. Think of what we've seen. Think of what we know. Can you leave here with a clear conscience, knowing that if the Houses are empty it'll all happen again? You had dead people popping up on your Indian reservation. And that kind of shit was happening all over the country, all over the world maybe. You know what would happen if the border fell entirely?" He shook his head. "I can't let that occur."

"We've been prisoners here!"

Norton smiled sadly. "I'm not a prisoner anymore. This time it's my choice. And perhaps, in some small way, I can make up for . . . for what happened before."

Laurie faced him. "Penance?"

"If you like."

Stormy waved his arms, exasperated. "But maybe normal people can live here and it'll do the same thing. Hell, they don't even need to know about it—"

"It's still on the borderline," Mark said. "They'll still see things they can't understand. It'll still be haunted."

Norton shrugged. "Besides, I'm up for it. I'd like to explore this border. I'm not that far away from passing over to the Other Side myself, and I'd like to know where I'm going, I'd like to find out a little bit about it first."

"Well, my duty as border guard is over. I'm through with this shit."

Laurie smiled sympathetically. "I'm getting out of here, too, if I can. I've spent enough of my life in this

House. I don't want to spend any more of it here." She looked at Norton. "You I can understand." She turned toward Mark. "But you're still young. You have your whole life ahead of you. Don't you want to do something with it?"

"I am," he said.

They were silent for a moment.

"Well," Laurie said. "At least you won't be trapped inside anymore. It'll be more like when we were kids, probably. You'll be able to go outside, go into town, leave whenever you want. This'll just be . . . your home."

"Yeah," Mark said.

Silence settled over them, and Stormy cleared his throat. It was rude, perhaps, but he didn't want to hang around here one more second. As far as he was concerned, this little adventure was over, and it was time for him to get the hell out of here and back to his real life. The rest of them could go or stay or do whatever they wanted to do, but he wanted to get as far away from the Houses as he could, as quickly as he could. "It's been fun," he said. "But I have important things to do."

Laurie smiled. "Videos?"

"You got it."

"Wait up," she said. "I'm coming with you."

All four of them walked out to the entryway and stood awkwardly a moment before the door. Were they supposed to hug, cry, shake hands? Stormy felt like doing none of those things. Oddly enough, he'd felt closer to the others when he'd first met them than he did now, and before anyone else could initiate some sort of bogus parting gesture, he opened the front door. The sun, white and hot, was shining in his eyes, its brightness obscuring the view outside.

"Later," he said. He waved good-bye, stepped through the doorway—

—and emerged alone onto the porch. Across the street was the fire-gutted building. Next to the curb, in front of the House, right where he'd left it, was his rental car.

He was in Chicago.

He turned to look behind him, but there were no other people in the entryway of the House. There was only a dirty dusty floor in a foyer that looked as though it had been abandoned for years. The only footprints in the dust were his own.

He hurried down the steps and off the porch, feeling cold. There were goose bumps on his arms, hair prickling on the back of his neck. He strode quickly down the walk, trying to get away from the House as fast as possible. He still did not understand where the House in which they'd met was located, but he did not really care, he did not want to find out.

He walked around the front of his car, fumbled in his pocket for the keys, quickly opened the driver's door.

On the seat of his car was a rose.

He hesitated less than a second, then tossed the flower onto the floor.

For the first time since he'd seen the television in his bedroom, he thought of Roberta. Was she really dead? he wondered. Or had that been part of the show put on for him?

He had the feeling that she *was* dead, and though he knew their marriage was over and that no matter what happened they would never get together again, he hoped that she was all right, he hoped that she was unharmed. He didn't love her, but he still cared about her in a way, and the thought that anything from the House, anything to which he was remotely connected, had hurt Roberta or had caused her death made him feel sick inside.

But he'd find out about all that when he got back to New Mexico. Right now, he just wanted to get away from the House and get out of Chicago.

He closed the door, turned the key in the ignition, and put the car into gear. Grinding the rose underneath the heel of his boot, he sped down the street as fast as his rental car would accelerate.

TWENTY-TWO

Laurie

Josh was waiting for her when she emerged from the House.

As was a crew of firefighters and several policemen and an ambulance.

They hadn't yet tried to break into the House, but it was clear that was what they intended to do, and two firemen carrying axes stopped when they saw her walk out onto the porch. She turned back, looking through the open door the way she'd come, but as she'd expected, as she'd known, there was no sign of either Mark or Norton.

Josh leaped up the steps, grabbed her, hugged her. "Thank God you're all right!"

"How long was I in there?" she asked.

"A long time. At least three or four hours. I thought you might be dead."

"Three or four hours?" She shook her head. " 'The spirits have done it all in one night.' "

"What?"

She shook her head. "Nothing."

There was a bandage on the side of Josh's head where he'd been clipped by the door, and a circle of red had leaked through the white. He looked back at the firemen. "I didn't want to leave you in there alone, but I yelled and yelled and I couldn't hear you anymore. I tried to get in, but I couldn't, and when I tried to break a window, the rock was just . . . absorbed. So I took a chance. I left you there and drove into town and brought back . . ." He gestured toward the ambulance, fire truck, and police car.

He met her eyes. "What happened in there?"

She looked behind him, saw two policemen walking up, shook her head.

He understood. "The cops said the owners may press charges," he said. "Breaking and entering."

"Who are the owners?"

"I don't know," he admitted.

The policemen reached them, asked her what happened, and she concocted an impromptu story about wanting to see the house of her birth parents and passing out inside the kitchen that sounded ludicrously unbelievable to her, but they nodded as she spoke, and one of the policemen suggested that she have one of the paramedics look her over.

"I will," she said. "Just let me . . . collect myself first."

They nodded, and Josh walked with them over to a fireman in a white uniform who appeared to be in charge of the rescue effort.

Laurie looked up at the dark bulk of the House and shivered as she thought of everything that had happened to her since she'd gone in there.

"Miss?" She turned to see an old white-haired man in a police uniform walk up to where she was standing. There was a strange expression on his face, and it made her feel a trifle uneasy. She looked around for Josh, saw him standing by the vehicles, talking.

"I always wondered what happened to you," the white-haired cop said.

She shook her head, not recognizing him. "I'm sorry . . ."

He smiled sadly. "I'm the one who was in charge of your parents' case. The one you talked to when you first came into the station."

She still did not recognize him, but she understood now why his appearance had made her uneasy. She licked her lips, not knowing what to say.

He moved next to her. "What really happened in there?" he asked softly.

"I don't . . . I don't know what you mean."

"I know about that house," he said, looking up at it. "I know what happens there."

Part of her wanted to tell him, wanted to confide in him,

but she resisted the impulse, for his sake as well as her own. She might tell Josh what had occurred, but that would be it. Her lips were sealed. This was not something she wanted to share, not something anyone needed to know.

"I don't remember," she lied.

"But something happened."

"I think so," she told him, feigning confidentiality. "But I've either blocked it out or . . ." She trailed off.

He nodded, satisfied.

"My brother says they're pressing charges against us?"

"Don't worry," he said. "There won't be any charges. I'll make sure of it."

"Thank you," she told him.

Behind him, she saw Josh wave to her, finished with the fireman, and she said, "My brother's calling me." She stepped around the policeman, and her heart was pounding as though she'd done something wrong, as though she was afraid he'd arrest her.

"I would suggest staying away from here," the cop said.

"Don't worry," she told him. "I plan to."

Josh took her arm. "They have our names and everything. I gave them my address and phone number, so they wouldn't bug you." He motioned toward the car. "You want to go? Or is there something else—"

"No," she said quickly. "Let's go. Let's get out of here."

"The paramedics wanted to look at you, but they said they don't have to if you don't want to, and I said you didn't."

She nodded.

They walked to the car in silence, one of the police vehicles already pulling away, the rest of the men packing up their gear.

"An exciting day for Pine Creek," Josh said.

"Yeah." Laurie smiled.

He took out his keys, opened the passenger door for her. "What did happen in there?" he said. "Really?"

She gave him a quick hug and a peck on the cheek. "Get in the car," she said. "I'll explain it all on the way home."

Epilogue

Brian left after dinner, giving her a big hug and shadow-boxing with Tony, and Margot watched his car drive away as Tony went into his bedroom to get his homework.

The house felt lonely, the absence of a man's presence especially noticeable after her brother's departure.

She stared into the night, her eyes focusing on the streetlight across the way, and thought of Daniel.

Daniel.

Burying an empty coffin had been the hardest part. It was difficult enough to accept the death of someone you loved, but when there was no body, the loss was somehow magnified and made even greater.

Even after all these months, it was still a raw wound to her, a bleeding slash across her emotions and her psyche, and though it was even worse at night, alone, in bed, it hurt all the time, and just standing here in the kitchen after dinner, she felt a huge painful emptiness in her gut. She wanted to sob out loud, wanted to cry out her anguish and burst into tears, but she knew that Tony would be back with his homework in a minute, and she didn't want him to see her cry. She needed to be strong for him. She needed to provide him with as stable a home life as she could manage under the circumstances.

She thought of Daniel's "friends." She believed what they'd said, as far as it went, but she thought there was probably more, and while she knew they weren't about to share it with her now, she was willing to wait. She would find out eventually.

A light breeze caressed her cheek, a movement of air

through the torn screen that seemed at once cooler and warmer than the night outside.

She thought she heard her name, whispered.

Margot

Tony walked into the kitchen, put his books out on the table, took out his paper and pencil. She wanted to tell him to be quiet so she could listen, so she could hear the whisper again, but she said nothing, continued to stare.

Margot

She opened the screen door, looked around, but there was nothing. No movement, no sound.

"What is it?" Tony asked, coming up behind her.

She let the screen door fall closed, continued to stare straight ahead, into the night, not wanting him to see her tears.

Margot

"The wind," she said softly. "It's just the wind."